Pen Pals:
A Novella
and
Other Stories

Donna Lawrence

Crescent Hill Press

Published by Crescent Hill Press, LLC
Copyright © 2025 by Donna Lawrence.

Visit the author's website at: donnamarielawrence.com

Cover Art:
Photo of rose and bush courtesy of Annie Spratt/@unsplash. Color Enhancement by author.

Editor(s):
Jenny Quinlan, Copyediting at HistoricalEditorial.com
Proofread by Annie at VictoryEditing.com
Formatting by Tami at VictoryEditing.com

Paperback Print Book ISBN: 979-8-9872168-6-6
Copyright: TXu 2-403-952

TABLE OF CONTENTS

Table of Contents

DEDICATION

To the friends who have listened to my stories
and encouraged me to write... here's to you.
And
To my faithful and loyal friend forever, Bijoux.
Thank you.

PREFACE

The stories you are about to read differ from my usual genre. This is not coming-of-age, historical fiction or poetry. I simply have stories to tell. Lots of them! I decided to take a break from my first novel, *Miss Virginia and the Sweet Sisters: A Novel,* by venturing into publishing a set of poems, *Looking In from Outside: Poetry & Prose.* The possibility of publishing a collection of short stories was also in the offing. I hoped the exercise of writing them would give me a break and time to gather my thoughts for my next coming-of-age or historical fiction novel—it has. However, when I started writing the first story, it became a full-blown, slow-burn romantic work of fiction, a novella. The accompanying short stories diverge slightly from the novella but keep the same theme, which I find interesting.

The novella examines the nature of longing, love, and happenstance, where AI technology helps two people meet on the off chance of finding lifelong fulfillment. The rest is up to fate, technology, and/or the protagonists themselves.

The collection of short stories is about unconditional love, courage, longing, mysterious and spiritual encounters, suspense, human nature with all its failings, and forgiveness. I found it fascinating to intertwine these elements as themes. I was pleased to discover they had circled back to the novella's premise—that of the mysteries of life in all its forms as we journey through an unknowable future.

I hope you enjoy the compatible nature of these stories and the messages they bring, which are sometimes too compelling to ignore.

Happy reading!

The author

Pen Pals: A Novella

— ◦◦◦ —

By

Donna Lawrence

CHAPTER 1

Cassandra

Cassandra hated stumbling into things. As time went on, she felt clumsier with each passing day. Bumping into the mountain bikes alongside Mason's Grocery should not have happened. But it did. One pedal caught her in just the right spot above her left knee, she knew she'd regret her clumsiness later.

Kassie had just turned fifty years old the day before, and even though she looked thirty, some days she felt every bit of sixty-five—or older. Today was one of those days. Ignoring the pain in her knee, she behaved as if clumsiness was no big deal and righted as many bikes as she could, including her own. Then she casually unlocked her Schwinn from the rack and carefully balanced her sack of groceries in the front basket. *It'll be just my luck to spill them in front of everyone too.*

As Kassie pedaled off with Trixie, her border collie, trotting by her side, she was aware of those around her. The smiles and waves she received from others in the small town always made her feel right at home. To her way of thinking, Hadenville should have been named Hiddenville because of its location, which is tucked back into the foothills of Colorado, west of Denver, near Boulder. She loved the town and its winding, tree-lined roads full of sunshine that filtered through the leaves and branches like sparks of light. The air was crisp and clear this time of year. It was late August, and exercising her lungs on a bike ride felt like no effort at all. Despite her earlier misgivings, she thanked God for the ability to maintain a healthy, fit, and strong body.

Born Cassandra LaForte-Hudgens, she had been blessed with the appearance of youth that never seemed to fade with age. She disliked being thought of as younger than her years. Growing up, it was an advantage and a curse, often being asked to prove her age. She smiled at the memory of one occasion when the bouncer at a downtown club in Denver threatened to call the police, thinking she'd forged her ID. However, the joke was on him. Kassie danced the night away, drinking herself silly with enough whiskey sours and strawberry daiquiris to forget the incident had even happened.

Being nicknamed Kassie didn't help anyone think she was older either. *What fifty-year-old still uses their nickname anyway?* This thought ran through her mind whenever she was called Miss Kassie by a young person or clerk in her office. *Jesus!* But she'd dealt with it through the years, embraced it, and accepted the moniker as normal.

However, that was the smaller of the demons Kassie felt she had to slay. Heartache and tribulations from the past had cast a pall over her life. She wished happiness would find her, but that was just a pipe dream. At this point in her life, it was hard to think otherwise.

She had decided to leave the corporate world last year and move to the summer cabin left to her by her father after he passed away a few years before. She couldn't bring herself to visit the cabin since that sad time. It held too many memories of her parents during the long vacations spent in the home they called the Sprawling Villa.

Her Italian mother had died from an insidious form of lung cancer. She had loved her cigarettes, but then so had her father. However, his death came unexpectedly, which was made all the worse because of its suddenness. Kassie had thought she'd have her dad for much longer, but a drunk driver had other ideas. Her dad never stood a chance.

As a successful hedge fund manager, he'd been her best supporter when she entered the marketing world. That night, he'd needed her and wanted to talk, but she couldn't find the time. They were having guests for dinner, and smoking would not do for her obsessive-compulsive boyfriend, so her father was not allowed to attend. The guilt of refusing to spend more time with him was intense. She felt she deserved the worst of whatever came her way. As punishment, Kassie threw herself into her work with abandon, and by doing so, she didn't care whom she had to step over to achieve her ambition—until one day.

⟫⟶◎◎◎⟵⟪

It was like any other day in Denver. Full of sunshine and a promise of things to come. One of her office assistants, whom Kassie considered her favorite and whose infectious smile always radiated even on Kassie's worst days, ran up to Kassie as she strode through the revolving glass door of her firm, Soma Impact Marketing.

"Miss Hudgens, can I have a word with you? Please, you've got to let me talk to you before it's too late," Dorothy begged as she wrung her hands, but Kassie scarcely noticed.

"I don't have a lot of time to waste, as you should know. My meeting starts in an hour. Do you have my reports ready? I should've had them yesterday, but nothing yet."

"That's why I need to speak with you. About the reports—"

"I don't want to hear any more. I don't care about why. I need them now—"

"But Miss Hudgens—"

"Move, Dorothy!" Kassie barked, annoyed by what she considered petty nonsense.

Dorothy's attempt at blocking Kassie from the elevator failed. Her usually perky round face fell into despair as Kassie pushed past her, clearly missing all the signs of someone in desperate need of help and compassion. But Kassie had none and let the elevator door close between herself and Dorothy, who stood quietly on the other side. Kassie knew she was considered "the dragon lady" but didn't care. She had developed a skill for instilling fear in her subordinates. An ability she wasn't sure she liked, but lived with.

Back in her office, Kassie had time to check her numbers, cursing Dorothy's lack of competence because the reports were still not on her desk. *What the hell is wrong with that girl?* Rummaging through her desk drawer for her favorite ink marker, she saw a Post-it note in someone else's handwriting. It read: I NEED HELP. CAN YOU HELP ME PLEASE? DOROTHY JOHNSON.

When had it been written, and when had it been left? Dorothy needed help, obviously more than Kassie had realized. Before she could think of anything else, Kassie heard shouting through the office walls. She felt the vibration of running and stumbling through the floor. Then shots, loud bangs, like fireworks, and wailing screams. Kassie had no idea what to think other than—Dorothy!

In the commotion, Kassie dropped behind her desk for safety. The immediate quiet was deafening. Disconcerted, she tiptoed toward her closed office door. She inched it open only to be met with heat, the smell of fear, and sudden, unmitigated confusion. Office staffers were either crying, stunned into silence, staring at nothing, or milling about, wondering what had happened or what to do next. A high keening wail could be heard coming from farther down the hall. This was where she found Dorothy bent over the figure of a teenage boy.

Ruth Matthews, Kassie's nemesis and office frenemy, stood with one hand over her mouth. Her beady eyes were wide as she exclaimed, "My God, I can't believe that after all the shots he fired, he turned the gun on himself."

"Who is he?" asked Ruth's assistant.

"Dorothy's son! Do you really not know *anything* at all?" Ruth snapped in admonishment. Then, glancing at Kassie, she said loud enough for everyone to hear, "Her boss over there should have known this would happen."

That was when all eyes turned to Kassie, who, for once in her corporate career, was at a loss for words. However, narrowing her eyes, she silently damned Ruth for focusing the attention away from Dorothy and onto her. Ruth whirled away from the scene and strode back to her office, apparently not caring more than necessary about what had just occurred.

In the ensuing chaotic scene, Kassie witnessed Dorothy's intense pain. The outpouring of grief for her dead son was profound. Kassie was deeply moved as she remembered the tragic loss of her own father. Dorothy had come to her for help just a few moments ago but had found none. If Kassie had given Dorothy some of her time, she would have learned more about her situation and ways she might have helped. It might also explain why the reports were late. Kassie should not have been so harsh. She'd let Dorothy down and felt immensely sorry. In an instant, all had changed. Too late, she could only kneel beside Dorothy, offer comfort, and although different, a shared sorrow.

A personal assessment was in order. Kassie had let her grief and ambition consume her to the point where compassion for others had been lost. She had to regain it for herself. Find what she needed out of life. But at her age, she wondered if it was too late.

Kassie decided to resign that day. She left her self-involved, seldom-seen, wealthy, entitled, and controlling "boyfriend," Jerry, who she knew would never marry her. Besides, if Kassie heard Jerry say *again* that she'd never amount to much and needed him now more than ever, it would be too soon. She had packed her belongings into storage, taken what she needed, and moved to the summer cabin in the Colorado mountain town before the month was out.

However, the specter of unforeseen tragedy was never far away, and she feared it was only a matter of time before it would find her again. So here she was, hidden away in Hadenville, where she had pitched her proverbial tent to regroup and find peace with her past.

⇒◦◦◦⇐

Kassie's father had made a nice living for her and her mother; his investments had paid off well, and everything had been left to her as an only child. After leaving corporate life, this allowed Kassie to quickly become a woman of leisure; however, she still needed to be frugal to reach the age of eighty without working. One winter season had already come and gone since she'd been in Hadenville. Now she was looking at another one fast approaching if the air's coolness was any indication. With those thoughts in mind, Kassie parked her teal-colored Schwinn with white-walled fat tires next to the front door. Then she carefully removed her groceries, grappled with opening the heavy wooden door, and stepped inside the cabin's welcoming spaces.

The Sprawling Villa was a two-storied, three-bedroom house, not very woodsy but rustic enough to give the impression of being a modified backwoods cabin. It had all the comforts of home and a fireplace for use only if she needed it, not out of necessity— which was nice. The cabin was designed well, with a main room of vaulted ceilings and floor-to-ceiling windows tempered and strong enough to withstand the worst Colorado could throw at it in the ways of wind and snow or a three-hundred-pound black bear. Then there were the smaller, intimate bedrooms accessed by stairs, which opened to a walkway that looked down onto the living space below. This was home; however, Kassie felt most comforted and warm in the cozy kitchen, especially on cold and frosty mornings.

Most days were spent this way: up at dawn, coffee out on the upstairs balcony overlooking the mountain views, maybe a breakfast of eggs, toast, granola, yogurt, or oatmeal, walking through the woods with Trixie, home by lunch, and some light reading. Then, out with Trixie again before dark, have dinner of green salad, soup, or a sandwich of some kind, and then off to bed. It was the same thing every day, with an occasional bike ride to town to break the monotony. Her Ford Bronco could always be counted on for transportation in the winter. Kassie didn't mind the loneliness. Besides, she had Trixie and her own thoughts to keep her company. What more did she need? But lately, her day-to-day existence was getting her down. She was becoming bored.

Before stopping at the grocery, she had visited the local bookstore. Instead of buying a new book, she had picked up an unlined journal. She was never much for writing—marketing analytics suited her just fine. However, eyeing the journal gave her a wild idea to put her thoughts on paper and see where they took her. Maybe she could recall something pleasant she'd. Writing might bring her more joy than wandering the woods with Trixie and "smelling the roses," as they say.

She took the journal from her bag and studied the black leather cover. There was nothing exceptional about it or the blank pages inside. She felt the smoothness of the sheets and the feel of the vellum, then decided to find a special pen for writing. Who knew what might inspire her?

After putting away the groceries and deciding what to prepare for dinner, she settled into an oversized chair next to the fireplace to find something on television to pass the time. Although satellite reception at this altitude was sketchy, sometimes it worked. Other times, like now, it didn't. After many tries, she gave up and turned her attention to thoughts of writing in her journal. But all she could think of were memories of pain, like the loss of her parents, people she had let down, like Dorothy with her bright eyes and infectious smile, and numerous failed relationships. Particularly her insensitive ex-boyfriend, who had left a hole in her heart. Those memories always seemed to trickle up when she least expected it.

Frustrated, Kassie had second thoughts about the journal and what a waste of time and money it was to try such a thing. She reluctantly got up and sauntered into the kitchen to prepare another everyday dinner—not that Trixie felt this way. Her excitement let Kassie know she was happy to see what could be begged from the dinner table.

Kassie didn't notice her laptop turning on of its own accord, nor did the beep let her know she needed to pay attention to it instead of her journal.

⇒◦◦◦⇐

Kassie was not surprised to wake at 1:30 a.m. to the moonlight streaming into the upstairs bedroom windows. It shone bright and beautiful in the night sky, landing on her face and an outstretched arm. The other she'd tucked under a pillow. Sleep was becoming harder and harder to find. Cursing another late-night vigil of wakefulness, she reasoned it was just too quiet in the hills for sleep to come without background noise. On nights like this, she wished the cicadas were singing, at the very least. *I get enough exercise, Lord knows, so what's the problem?*

Stumbling downstairs in the dark was a stupid move. Kassie nearly tripped over Trixie, whose black-and-white-colored fur camouflaged her being perched at the top of the staircase.

"Damn it, Trixie! What are you doing here? The last thing I need is to break my neck tripping over you."

Trixie looked up at Kassie, tilted her head sideways, seeming to understand what she was going on about, and whined in protest. Kassie bent down and rubbed Trixie behind her ears, settling the issue between them. Once in the kitchen, Kassie decided to raid the fridge; however, nothing enticed her in that early morning hour. She saw the journal and chuckled at the thought of writing down her misadventure about not finding sleep. Kassie sat at the dining table and reached for her laptop instead to surf YouTube for amusement. Like the TV, the connections were always spotty and unreliable—except at night when her laptop performed like a champ. However, for some reason, it never stayed powered down. Kassie dismissed the anomaly, assuming her location was the cause and nothing more. With the laptop already on, she searched for interesting content to watch.

"Let's see what the bushcraft people are up to, shall we?" she said aloud for Trixie's benefit. It was too bad she couldn't convince the municipality to give them better cable service. If so, she could sync the channels to the TV and avoid using her laptop for this kind of thing altogether.

Kassie enjoyed watching the ingenuity of people living off the grid who taught or learned new survival methods. She found herself immersed in watching the skills of men chopping wood, living in frigid temperatures in the Alaskan or Canadian wild, and building simple shelters to ward off the harsh elements when living outside. These men, and surprisingly women, didn't disappoint. She referred to the women affectionately as "cottage fairies." Kassie enjoyed watching the ladies as they cooked, baked bread, gathered herbs from their gardens, and lived simply—alone, like her.

One channel in particular caught her interest. There seemed to be a familiarity about this man. She was intrigued by watching him go about his work silently. He appeared to be about thirty or so and took little effort in chopping wood and lashing poles together to build an outdoor shelter or hammering nails into walls. After a while, she decided to see what else she could find, but she returned to his video as if drawn by an invisible string. She decided his videos would be some of her favorites, so she subscribed.

"Hey, it doesn't hurt to help someone build their channels and make money, right?" she asked of Trixie again, but of the two of them, Trixie was the only one sleeping.

After subscribing, she was surprised to see he had another channel. This one was used for relaxation called ASMR. *Gosh, he looks familiar!* This thought kept nagging at her as she watched.

"I hope this isn't one of those sensory or kinky channels. That might be taking it a bit too far, Kassie. Do you need sleep or sex?" she asked herself.

As it turned out, his was not the run-of-the-mill ASMR, or autonomous sensory meridian response, designed to help insomniacs sleep with sensory or auditory "tingles," *whatever those are*. She discovered most of his videos touched on everyday life events, which suited her disposition quite well. Almost bedtime story-ish. Also, it didn't hurt that he had a sense of humor.

"I'm no insomniac. I just have trouble staying asleep," Kassie said out loud to no one other than Trixie. But snoring loudly, Trixie neither heard nor cared.

She shrugged and watched a set of his videos to see how they affected her. After a few minutes, Kassie thought she'd found a gold mine. His deep, melodic voice was intoxicating and soothing. His British accent made it even more so. She was taken by how sensual the experience was. It was nothing sexual, just a soft-spoken discussion to calm his viewers full of anxiety with affirmations recited for those lacking self-confidence, which she found comforting.

His assurance of safety touched her deeply. He was an expert and wasn't bad to look at. His form of ASMR lulled Kassie into sleep with little effort. Of all the clumsy "stumbles" she'd had recently, this was the best of all. Shortly, Kassie fell into a blissful sleep. It was the best she'd had in a long time. This was when her laptop powered down all by itself.

CHAPTER 2

Davis

Davis needed a diversion. He needed to find peace of mind, escape the stress of his job, and leave the hustle and bustle of downtown Seattle behind for a while. A quick hike in the woods to lessen the stress was just the thing.

He missed his home in London. Northwest America was his home now. His profession, designing building interiors as a mechanical, engineering, and plumbing—or MEP—engineer, was not going well these days. Davis liked designing and building structures. The planning and mechanics of internal operations of pipes and systems didn't take him long to learn. Design programs such as Revit gave him access to abilities and knowledge that 3D AutoCAD could only dream about.

Artificial intelligence was the future. Davis feared this tool would grow into something that would replace him and others very soon. He liked working with his hands, using his brain, and not relying on automation for a design task. If AI evolved as fast as he suspected, or as his boss, Crandall Jamison, kept hammering on about, he hoped to keep up and go with the changes it would bring. At the moment, wanderlust was getting the better of him as he allowed his thoughts to drift back to what had brought him to this state of mind in the first place.

Michael Davis Blakemore, Mike or Mikey as his father liked to call him, but Davis to his friends, was born to better things. Or so his dad had often reminded him. As a young man, his mother supported his career pursuits. However, the haranguing he'd received from his dad was too much for him to take. His father wanted him to become a partner at his iron and steel factories, overseeing the daily running of things. But Davis reminded him, as he had so often said, that he was meant for bigger and better things.

After he graduated from high school, acing all his A-levels, he joined the British Royal Forces. For a time, this stint eased the burden of constant lectures from his dad. After serving only a few years, a shrapnel injury to his head while fighting in Afghanistan shortened his military career, along with his sense of smell. He was told it might return, so he was hopeful. In the meantime, he noticed his other senses had become sharper. His tactile senses seemed more acute, his vision crisper, and his emotional feelings magnified. His sense of caring heightened.

At twenty-one, Davis had seen more than he wanted of man's inhumanity to man. He did not reenlist but returned home from military service and channeled his energy into learning as much about engineering as possible through his studies at the University of Cambridge.

After fighting alongside his army mates and befriending many Yanks, he had been drawn to visit the colonies on America's shores. Once he arrived, Davis couldn't imagine living anywhere else. After obtaining a work visa, he was immediately hired as an MEP systems designer at Stanley, Biddle, and Jamison, an architectural firm in Seattle, Washington. He applied for a green card, and in due time, Davis had gained his dual citizenship.

He'd risen through the ranks quickly, and his reputation as a much-sought-after bachelor also gained popularity. He supposed his ability to care about others made him stand out amid the unfeeling corporate hierarchy. He was empathetic and compassionate, which are rare character traits in corporate America and ones he was unwilling to change.

He was known to be a little clumsy. After his brain injury, this only added to his sense of unease and insecurity. He had many girlfriends who'd helped ease the loneliness and boost his self-confidence; however, they only lasted so long. Ten years later, at thirty-five, he often asked himself, *What am I doing with my life?* Many women wanted more from him, but he didn't feel *it*, that rare, elusive "something" he couldn't quite put a finger on. So, until he did, he would bide his time until the right one came along.

For the past three years, he had discovered trekking through the woods gave him a convenient escape. When not designing MEP systems, he used his hands to build things. The soft soil of Washington's hillsides and the surrounding area gave him plenty of material to use. He didn't even mind the rain, which England had plenty of, so he was used to the outdoor elements. The bushcraft activity was cathartic for him. It was good.

One night, after spilling his secret pastime to a few friends, the idea of capturing the activity on film was suggested. Creating a YouTube channel to showcase his ability to build off-grid shelters might get viewers interested in what he did—maybe even earn a few dollars for the effort, to boot. Before he knew it, one thing had led to another, and now, he was a so-called YouTube star with as many as fifty thousand subscribers.

⟞◦◉◦⟝

The drive on the coastal highway on his way to Bellingham was beautiful. The fog along Chuckanut Drive pulled back enough to allow a view out past the bay to the Pacific Ocean on his left, with an imposing rocky hillside on his right. *Funny,* Davis thought as he drove along, not bothering to take in the beauty as he usually did. *After all this time, I'm still worrying about success in my chosen field.* These, and many thoughts like them, coursed through his mind as he drove the winding roads to escape the feeling of impending doom encroaching from AI technology. *I need to do something different, but what?*

His thoughts raced faster than the speed of his vehicle. He wanted to drive the errant insecurity from his mind. He didn't realize how fast he was traveling as his speedometer inched up the dial. All he could think of was coming up with something to rid himself of doubts about his ability. But it was difficult with so much noise creeping into his head, telling him he *must* do better. He often felt he had to be perfect. He supposed this came from the leftover verbal bashing from his father. He was not prone to paranoia, but still, the specter of his father and the words hurled at him over the years hung over him like a cloud. He had to confront this demon and tame the angst of needing to be perfect. He felt it was eating him alive and chasing him into oblivion.

The deer appeared suddenly. Davis had no time to react. He hit it directly, head-on. The speed of the collision spun his vehicle around in the middle of the roadway. The inertia of the force pushed his car forward and slammed it into the rocky hillside alongside the highway. As luck would have it, his car struck the hill sideways on the driver's side. Airbags were deployed from the driver's side door panel and in front, cushioning the impact, but only just.

⬤⬤⬤

The cool hand of the nurse who felt his forehead and then took his temperature, probably for the umpteenth time, was reassuring.

"You got knocked around pretty good, you know," she said as he slowly regained consciousness.

"Did I?" Davis answered, trying to understand where he was.

"Mm-hmm. Lie still while I change this bag. It won't take long." Then, as an afterthought, she said, "You're in Seattle Memorial." The nurse's tone of voice was matter-of-fact, no-nonsense.

He watched as she moved smoothly through the rhythm of switching out the saline solution to his arm, writing something on a clipboard, shaking a vial, and inserting a needle to withdraw the contents. Then she injected it into the tube that fed his arm. He shook himself from observing her and asked the critical question.

"How long?"

"About two weeks. A lot of work extracting you from your vehicle, which got totaled, by the way. The doctor patched you up well, although you'll need physical therapy to regain the use of those legs at a hundred percent again."

"How many bones did I break?"

"Let's not discuss that, shall we? What's important is you getting some rest. Doctor Emmanuel will be in shortly. Glad to see you've come back to us."

Her voice had changed to a soft whisper and had a calming effect on him. He didn't know if it was that or the injection which caused him to drift off to sleep. But sleep he did.

⬥

The grueling workout with his physical therapist was arduous. Davis's ability to walk again was questionable, which only added to the depression he was already under. Some days, the therapist took pity on him. On other days, Davis could swear he was working with Lucifer himself. However, he progressed nicely and, within a year, much sooner than expected, could walk with only a slightly noticeable limp. Nothing major, but to Davis it wouldn't do. He thought returning to bushcraft as soon as possible would press his body and legs to work better than before, and he couldn't wait.

During his recuperation, Davis had many prospective girlfriends prepare dinner for him once or twice a week, which he took full advantage of. Because of the accident, he was allowed to work from home, which was easy to do in his profession. His bosses at the firm were more than understanding and accommodated him in any way they could. The corporate flexibility also gave Davis the time to work out at home, where he pushed his body beyond its limit to become physically strong again. He forced himself to climb the wooded hills close to his home until his legs ached for relief, and where he silently cried from the pain.

When Davis started a video journal about his experience, using it to chart his recovery, he remembered the voice of the hospital nurse whenever she'd administered to him. It had been peaceful and calming. He didn't speak that way normally, but he thought mimicking her way of speaking, modulating his voice in a soft-spoken or whispered way, would be a nice touch. He'd never spoken on camera when building off-grid structures. That had given him a bit of mystery, but with this new venture, once he started, he couldn't stop; it came naturally.

He later discovered this approach was considered ASMR, meaning something that elicited a sensory response in others. He found this amusing because all he did was talk about the challenges of his recovery. For him, it was like telling a bedtime story using a microphone and a camera. After further research, Davis ditched the idea of how some viewed ASMR as creepy or weird. He forged ahead, honing his craft. His number of subscribers went through the roof.

In his off time, he studied ASMR techniques such as voice modulation, using high-definition microphones with covers to reduce pops and harsh sounds, and how close camera angles affected viewing experiences. Role-play was not his thing, although he liked the idea of using brushes to mimic the sound of ocean waves or hand gestures to stroke the camera as if it were a person's face. However, reciting affirmations, talking about life, or reading prose to soft music suited him best. For now, he concentrated on the compassion in his voice to soothe the anxious, depressed, or sleep-deprived viewer who couldn't relax.

After two years, he returned to the office and took on assignments, traveling to speak with clients or marketing firms to pitch for their services. Sometimes, he'd embarrass himself using his soft-spoken voice, which was unnecessary in most situations. However, according to comments from his viewers, helping others regain their confidence, calm anxiety, and ease their depression or insomnia was something he did well. This knowledge gave him an endless sense of satisfaction.

It was also where Kassie Hudgens found him on a cool fall evening in Colorado.

CHAPTER 3

Cassandra

"What an asshole!" Kassie cursed out loud when she awakened after another night of being lulled by the dulcet tones of Davis's voice. She was getting used to hearing it and couldn't wait to see him on his consistent weekly videos. But a steady dose of this was getting to her; she was becoming dependent.

The curse was not because she disliked him—she didn't know the man—but because she disliked how he was starting to make her feel. Not the initial drowsy, calm, and peaceful feeling he gave when helping his viewers relax. No, no. But the longing and comforting feeling she had pushed aside years ago was rising. And she blamed him. How long had it been since she had been held? *It's been too long, but not long enough to forget how it feels.*

Of course, blaming Davis was unfair. *He's only doing his job. A damn good job, if I might say so myself,* Kassie thought as she shook herself from another night of feeling alone and wishing she hadn't turned down Nick's proposal so many years ago. After him, there had been Alonzo with his neglect and womanizing, then Jerry and his rich-boy entitlements. She'd sworn off men for the past year, no longer trusting her judgment to determine who was right for her. The heartache they brought was brutal, so why bother?

Davis was all good looks and sexy brawn, and if she were twenty years younger, knowing what she knew now—no, thank you. To make things worse, the odd thought of him seeming familiar never wavered. *That*—she couldn't shake.

"Damn it to hell," Kassie said as she stared at herself in her bathroom mirror. She was falling for someone she only knew on YouTube. An ASMR artist. "You've got to get a grip, girl. No more bedtime stories for you, and certainly not with him."

⟶◦◉◦⟵

After her usual morning routine, she decided to take Trixie for a walk and get serious about journaling. She needed to shake the fog of Davis from her mind and focus on the real world. A walk with her dog was a good choice.

The back trails were full of pine, aspen, and elm trees whose branches had already lost most of their leaves. The bright leaves of an aspen grove, just beginning to yellow, caught her attention. The sight of the snow-covered mountain range jutting up against a vibrant blue sky ahead in the distance could not have made for a more perfect spot to think and write.

"Look at this, Trixie," she said as Trixie looked up at her with an expression of understanding. "We are fortunate and very lucky to have this. Don't ever forget that."

Her dad had chosen this location well, and with her trusted bear spray within easy reach, she watched as Trixie frolicked nearby. Even though she knew a bear or cougar could occasionally appear unannounced, she'd never encountered one. There were just too many people whose houses she could see dotted throughout the area to make it a constant concern. However, you could never be too careful. Kassie often ventured out to sit at this spot to daydream, enjoy her favorite soup, or sip coffee brought in a thermos. Today, she would write—and so it began.

As her pen moved across the page, she couldn't help expressing feelings about Davis. Who was he, really? What kind of work did he do? What if he was a psycho? Was *she* crazy for thinking of him? These questions and other thoughts flooded her mind as she wrote. How he made her feel, imagining he was there by her side and wishing someone like him had been in her life all along. She daydreamed about his look, voice, dark hair, beard, and body. His complexion—just the right shade of tan, made the black hair fit his appearance well. His mouth and lips—so sensuous…

"Stop it! Right now, just stop!" She shouted so loudly it startled Trixie, who had been lying beside her, into a sitting position.

"Oh, I can't keep doing this, Trixie. I'm old enough to be his mother, for God's sake! What am I going to do?" Exasperated, she closed her journal and headed back to the house.

Kassie reasoned a year of living alone and away from others was taking a toll on her psyche, causing her to imagine all kinds of things and create psychological mischief not worth pursuing. *That must be it.* Then the phone rang.

"Hello!" she answered, relieved to be taken from her current state of mind.

"Hey, girl, what's up? You lonely yet?" came the question from a familiar voice. Her best friend, Dionne Weems, still worked at her old firm and was always quick to keep her abreast of all the office gossip.

"Hey, Dee, how's it going? No, not lonely yet," Kassie lied. "How about you? What's up?"

"I was wondering if you could use some company this weekend. How about I come up and gossip in front of the fireplace instead of on the phone? How about it? I'd love to escape the city for a few days. I could *really* use the break."

"When can you get here?"

Dionne arrived the next day. Of all Kassie's friends, Dionne was the most fearless. Divorced and loving life, Dionne could be counted on to be the life of the party or to lighten the mood on any given day of the week. With her wild hair and sassy ways, she was just what Kassie needed to get her mind off Davis.

After a spaghetti dinner, Kassie lit the gas fireplace and then enjoyed a glass of wine with her friend. Kassie listened to tales about the machinations of office politics—and who was doing what to whom. After a lull in the conversation, Dionne changed the subject.

"I can't get over how quiet it is up here. Almost creepy, huh? You ever get scared?" Dionne asked, already knowing the answer. "Animals, even the crazy humankind, sneaking up and waiting to attack you?"

"Now don't go thinking stuff up. If I thought like that, I'd never enjoy living like this. Being alone isn't so bad; it's being *lonely* I don't like much."

"Well, I don't know how you'd get a man or beast chasing after you cooped up this way."

"Don't be mean—"

"I mean it! You need to stay active unless you want to dry up and—"

"Like you can talk. What about you?"

"Don't worry about me, okay? I *gets* me mine. *You* know," Dionne said with a sly laugh. "Besides, I'm not the one who moved to the boonies and away from male attention."

"I'm okay, honestly." But then Kassie let her facade slip. She bit the side of her lip and held a throw pillow tighter than she should. Leave it to Dionne to spot a lie when she heard one.

"Hey, it's me, remember?" Dionne asked with concern. "It's a good thing I came when I did. What's really going on with you?"

"I don't know, just stupid stuff. Things I'm too ashamed to tell. I don't know why I'm feeling this way about him and why now—"

"Wait. What? Who him? Him who?" Dionne leaned in close to Kassie with her head cocked to one side.

"It might be better if I just show you," Kassie said, exasperated and defeated by emotions she could barely control. She was caught and thought it must be the wine, and seeing a trusted friend that had let those words slip from her mouth. *Might as well spill the beans. What could it hurt, right?*

Kassie reached for the TV remote and explained while Dionne listened.

"I don't get good cable services up here. What I do have is streaming channels along with YouTube. For some reason, my laptop never seems to turn off. I have to see about getting it fixed, but not today. *Anyway*," Kassie said, drawing the word out for emphasis, "I was able to sync my YouTube subscription to my TV, so it's easier to watch."

"Not to mention a bigger screen," Dionne said as she crossed her legs under her on the couch.

"Yeah, I love YouTube. There is so much to watch, especially since they've expanded their content to include movies, documentaries, and programs about history. What I particularly like is the variety."

"Okay, so…" Dionne let the *so* hang in the air with a shrug and upward turn of her hands.

"So. What I've discovered about myself is that I'm bored, which has led to insomnia—"

"Oh, Kassie. I'm—"

"Wait, it gets worse."

"I'm listening."

"It started off small, at first. Just surfing through the channels on my laptop. Then I found this, and life has *not* been the same since." Kassie finished her sentence by clicking on Davis's channel.

"What the hell!" Dionne exclaimed when she saw Davis's face.

"Exactly. That's what I thought—"

"*That's* not what I mean. Don't you know who he is?"

"Should I? I *thought* he looked familiar, but who is he?"

"Well, you wouldn't remember, would you? You were a rude wreck of a woman after your dad passed away. He's the young man from the architectural firm in Washington state. Don't you remember? God, he was good-looking and still is. He put on a presentation for us, and you shit all over his idea by speaking of how AI technology will replace more of the tools we use today. Remember?"

"Oh my goodness," Kassie said as the recollection slowly dawned on her.

"I remember it well, and although you might have been right—the way you high-handed that man made me wonder if he had wet his pants. I'll never forget his British accent, the way he spoke, and how he looked at you."

"Seriously?" Kassie asked. "Why did I—? Well, he obviously didn't make a great impression—"

"Hey, watch those elevens between your eyebrows. It wasn't that serious, although I think he made some sort of impression, judging by what you've allowed yourself to do lately." They listened silently as he did his vocal magic. Dionne broke the lull, saying, "What a voice!" Then, with concern, asked, "Hey, this isn't that kinky stuff, is it?"

"ASMR does have a certain stigma. Haven't you ever fallen asleep when your mother read you a bedtime story?"

"Yeah, but—"

"Well, it's like that. I suppose some creeps do ASMR, but not him. *Jesus!* Help me out, Dee! I can't sleep without his deep voice whispering in my ear, and lately… I've started to feel more than I should about him."

"What?"

"Yeah! It's insane to think about him the way I have, isn't it? Don't answer, I know. He's got to be at *least* ten or fifteen years my junior; all I want to do is wait for his next video. Oh man!" Kassie lowered her face into one of the throw pillows.

"Whew! Well. He's sexy all right. Look at him! A beast. *Damn,* baby," Dionne said, staring at him in his video. "Just look at those lips. Shit, girl… I don't know."

"I wonder if he still works at that firm in Washington?" Kassie asked wistfully.

"Only one way to find out. I know a little something about this. Let me see your laptop." Dionne reached for it on the couch between them.

"Maybe we should just leave well enough alone," Kassie said as she held it back from Dionne. "I don't want to know any more than I do already."

"It won't hurt to find out. Look! You dragged me into this; now let me have that machine."

Reluctantly, Kassie handed over her laptop, still unsure if it was a good idea. Soon, Dionne motioned Kassie over to sit by her side. She had clicked on his channel tabs and found some additional information Kassie had overlooked.

"Look at that." Dionne dragged out the word *that*, using more syllables than the word called for. "His name is Davis Blakemore. It says he's a native of Sheffield, England, who now lives in Seattle, Washington. No address, of course—smart. He has an email address for business contacts though. He has another channel where he builds off-grid houses, huts, and campsites. What d'ya know?"

"Yeah," Kassie said with a sigh. "Those led me to this one."

"Wow! Lots of videos," Dionne said as she scrolled through the selections.

"How long ago was his presentation?"

"Whew." Dionne blew air from her mouth like a blowfish. "Maybe three years ago?"

"Three years! You remember that far back?"

"Yeah, girl, shit. The man was fine! I never thought about how old he was, geez. He was lovely eye candy, I'll say that! Still is, by the look of it. You should contact him and apologize."

"You're funny. For what?"

"Well, you need to do something. This ain't gonna wait. By the time you get around to doing something, he's off and married with ten kids." Dionne laughed at Kassie's expense.

Kassie play-slapped at Dionne. "Dee, get real. A man like that is *not* about to settle down with anyone, much less have children." Then, under her breath, she added, "Maybe illegitimate ones, but it's none of my business."

"I heard that," Dionne half whispered to herself.

"Well, it's true. Look at him!"

"I have been! Your man. All 180 or 200-pound hunk of burning love is what I see. And you sitting around, just waiting for him to reach through the TV and touch you." Dionne was clearly enjoying getting under Kassie's skin. "Well, keep dreaming. Either that or do *something*."

"What I'm gonna *do* is go to bed. You should too. Get some sleep, crazy woman," Kassie said playfully. "I shouldn't have told *you* anything." Kassie grabbed the laptop and closed the lid, more miffed at herself than necessary. Why she allowed Dionne to egg her on to do something she knew she'd regret later was beyond her reasoning.

"It ain't too late, you know," Dionne yelled after Kassie, who left her alone to go upstairs and prepare for bed. "You're only fifty. He's what, thirty-five, forty? Who knows?"

"Well, I do. Too young for me. Good night, my friend. I'll see you in the morning. We can discuss it more then," Kassie said dismissively as she crossed the open walkway toward her bedroom. "Till the sunrise," she called down to Dionne, who was still on the couch. Kassie hoped to get a good night's sleep despite Davis—and his ASMR ramblings.

CHAPTER 4

Davis

It had been four years since Davis started his ASMR video channel on YouTube, and he was running out of things to say. He had to come up with other ideas, or he'd bore his subscribers to death instead of inducing their sleep. Davis had done several calming videos of affirmations, antianxiety, and de-stressing content to help his viewers relax and nod off. If the sound of ocean waves or rain couldn't ease anxiety or sleeplessness, he was glad he could help by using his voice. Davis had even ventured into lighthearted role-playing, going full tilt into ASMR. Still, ideas were drying up, and even he was becoming bored.

He put feelers out to his viewers. But canvassing them had only returned the idea of continuing with what he'd done already. "No changes at all please, and thank you," were the many comments submitted to him.

After returning home from a taxing day of work, Davis liked to pour himself a glass of red wine and read viewer comments on his uploaded videos. He also liked to check his stats and audience engagement. According to demographics, most of his viewers were women, which was no surprise. Some viewers sounded lonely, seeking to ease their loneliness by watching his videos. As hard as he tried to keep his content clean and platonic, some wouldn't see it that way. However, he was glad most of his viewers found his content helpful.

For a twenty to thirty-minute video, most people watched until the end, so his bounce rates were reasonably good. However, according to another data set, his viewers apparently found what he thought were his most helpful videos—the most boring. That was unexpected. He rubbed his eyes from weariness and peered at the numbers on his laptop screen over the laced fingers of his hands. At a loss on how to proceed or make his content more engaging, meaningful, and relevant, he eventually gave up. Instead, he decided to read through a moderate amount of business emails.

Long ago, he had set up a business link for those who wanted to leave inquiries about sponsorship opportunities or other business-related proposals. While reading through the latest missives, one stood out.

> I found you because I was bored. I'm not an insomniac, but I stumbled on your channel because of the familiarity. I remember you from the architectural firm of Stanley, Biddle, and Jamison. I was one of the female marketing executives at Soma Impact Marketing, to whom you pitched an innovative idea in a presentation. I admit I was extremely rude to you at the time. This is no excuse, but I was going through a tough time in my personal life. It's embarrassing to admit now, but I've wanted to apologize since that incident. Dragging my feet, I felt the time had passed. It wasn't until I saw your video that I felt I could apologize, so I'm sending this email to you. It is my pathetic attempt to say, "I'm so very sorry." You have a gift. I hope you continue to pursue this endeavor. Should you need advice on content reach, please contact me. As an ex-marketing executive, I might be able to help. Until then, take care. K.

Davis had to think for a minute. He had done many presentations at various marketing firms to garner representation for his firm. Still, he had no idea who this might be, nor could he recall the incident this person was referring to.

"Soma Impact Marketing?" he asked out loud. He used his computer to search for the business and found it. A Colorado marketing firm located in Denver. When was he there? Two years or so ago, at least. Who was "K"? It was a cryptic way to end an email, but oh well. Davis's laptop offered little help when searching for an answer to this question. He had looked at Soma's company directory for clues but found nothing. He didn't try to dig *that* hard. However, he was intrigued, so he decided to reply. He could use some marketing help, so what the hell?

After drafting a response and hitting the Send key, Davis left his office and sat to reflect, as he rested his head on his leather couch. His loft apartment was bathed in light from the setting sun. In Seattle, sunshine was rare, and on days like today, it was glorious. Because of this rarity, Davis felt the email was a sign of some kind. *Who is K?* What had this person done to offer an apology to him? What sort of rudeness had Davis suffered from this person? He couldn't remember, and it nagged at him.

In time, he forgot this quest and decided to gather equipment for yet another video, then quickly gave up. *Bollocks!* He could not bring himself to dismiss the thought of who she might be. It was not easy. Maybe stepping away from it for a time might jog his memory.

Ordering Chinese takeout and watching a movie seemed like a good idea. Davis had promised to ring Angela, his current lady friend, or his mate Joe for a guy chat, but *hang it all!* The ache in his shoulders and the open-mouth yawn told him to unwind and forget about the email. To his surprise, it haunted him more than he wanted to admit. But why?

⟫◦◦◦⟪

"Bloody hell!" Davis shouted as he woke with a start. Now he remembered. After eating chicken fried rice and fried cheese wontons, he'd dozed off for what seemed like only a few minutes, but it was actually a few hours. The memory came back like a bolt of lightning.

She was the most beautiful executive he had ever encountered at the time. *Cassandra, something or other.* It had to be her. Cassandra spelled with a "K"? At the time, she seemed self-assured and mysterious but in need of something. He naively thought she needed to hear what he had to say. He was wrong. She was the only one he could remember who had been utterly rude during his presentation. And he didn't understand why.

Jesus, God in Christ, he thought to himself. Like his father, she seemed hell-bent on putting him in his place and keeping him there until he left the building. The nerve of her! The time to apologize would have been then—but after all these years, oh no! Now she, of all people, sends an email and offers help *if he needs it*! It was too much. This whole business of YouTube and ASMR, with lonely, stressed-out people with anxiety issues or who just couldn't sleep, needed more than him as an answer to their problems. His anger was getting the better of him. *This whole thing is nonsense on stilts, and I'll be damned if it's gonna bring me down with it.*

Davis bolted from the couch to get a drink of cold water from the tap and, while doing so, splashed some on his face. The icy water cleared his head for a moment. On the way to the bathroom, he passed the studio where he recorded his videos. His temper began to flare again, which was unusual.

As he walked into the studio and scanned his equipment, he picked up the new gimbal he'd just purchased to hold his camera. He had the strong urge to chuck it across the room into the wall out of frustration. He sat down and toyed with it instead. He fingered the camera and felt the hard edges. *It's just a camera.* No more than a piece of plastic designed to capture moments and create content for viewers to enjoy. *What do they want from me?*

He was no psychologist, far from it. Neither was he a magician nor a soothsayer bringing sleep under a hypnotic trance. He was an average guy with a gift. He used brushes and other tools to mimic the sound of ocean waves and his voice to touch and soothe. It was all pretense, but his *intent* was no joking matter. The only thing real about what he did was his willingness to help those in need. He actually felt their suffering and empathized. And, as the saying went—therein lay the joke.

The laughter started as a chuckle, then a full-on guffaw. It came from somewhere deep inside. Crazy as it might seem, Davis finally got it. He had to show he was in on the pretense. Then, Davis got an idea without input from an *ex*-marketing executive. With regret, he could kick himself for responding quickly to K's email.

And so, in the pre-dawn hours, before his next working day, he set up his system and began recording.

⟫◦◦◦⟪

"Hey, man, what the hell was that video last night?" Joe asked when he saw Davis settling in at his drafting table the following day.

"You watched it? Early for you?" Davis said, half ignoring his friend.

"Yeah, well, I did. You know I can't let a day go by without some inspiration to get me through the week. So what gives?"

"What do you mean, mate?"

"That whole act of knowing what the viewer wants from you and smirking on the other side of the camera. Aren't you supposed to be cool? White boy cool is back, and you, my man, are the embodiment, but last night? Whew! That was a whole new vibe. Not saying I'm digging it," Joe said with a shake of his head.

"Who asked you?" Davis said, giving Joe a look to cut through bricks.

"Hey, yo! My bad, but give me something to hang my hat on, huh?"

"Sorry, just working through some things." The dismissive look now turned into a frown. "I don't know. Burnout maybe?"

"Last night didn't look like burnout to me. You on something, man—"

"Hey!" Davis let this comment hang in the air between them with a knowing look. He'd known Joseph Randall since their days in Afghanistan. It was he who had persuaded Davis to come to Seattle after his studies ended in Cambridge. Joe was a good man and his best friend. He didn't deserve Davis's misdirected anger.

Davis relaxed his shoulders, sighed, and ran his hand over his dark mustache and beard. "I'm such an arsehole." He cupped his hands in front of his mouth. "I should've called last night, Joe, but figured I'd work it out alone. Don't mean to whinge, but I've been feeling… I don't know, lacking new ideas. Then I got this email from someone from a few years back. Reading what she had to say sparked something, and I got *angry*. I haven't been that *barking mad* in a long while. Bugger!"

"She? Who's she?" Joe asked, unfazed by the avalanche of British expressions.

"I think she's someone who attended a presentation I gave in Colorado. A real bitch at the time, but there was *something*."

"Yeah? I'm intrigued." Joe leaned across the drafting table to listen.

"Reading the email sparked it all. It got me thinking about what I was doing and why. Really *thinking* about it, you know what I mean? Then I got it. I'm pretending. I wondered if most viewers think it's real. I know it sounds bonkers, but I had to *jolt* them somehow. Bring them back to the fact that it's all make-believe noises. It's as if I'm there beside them through electronics, but I'm not. *That's* the joke—don't you see? A fabulous *fake* that got to me somehow, and I lashed out. Eventually, I brought it back to being a safe haven for viewers."

"Thank God, but—Jesus! You gotta tell me about this chick, man."

"Yeah, a real head twister. Let's have a chinwag over lunch, okay? You free?"

"Sure. Can't wait to hear more, so yeah."

"Cool. Thanks, mate, and look… sorry about being such a wanker. Can't help it, you understand?"

"When it comes to women, yeah, man. I understand."

CHAPTER 5

Cassandra

"*What?* Tell me I'm dreaming, or better yet, slap me to wake me from this *nightmare!*"

"I tell you, I didn't do it! I don't think." Dionne said the last comment under her breath while scratching her head with a confused look. "Last night is all kind of fuzzy...."

"Oh, Dee! You had to have. Who else, if not you?"

"Well, even if I did, you were all wound up and uptight. If you ask me, you were subliminally telling me to do it."

"Dee! That wasn't your place—"

"Well, who left the laptop with me? I'm telling you, all I did was email my staff last night. You saw me do it before dinner, remember? I checked this morning for delivery. I might add that it was still powered on, which was strange, and there it was—staring me in the face."

"Oh God! It's *always* on. I told you. Why would you do that? How could you?"

"Maybe it was the wine?" Dionne asked, ignoring Kassie's complaining as she pursed her lips, furrowed her brow, and looked down at the unwashed wineglass from the night before. "So maybe I took the liberty of sending an email without knowing what I was doing. Big whoop!" Dionne continued.

"Oh, *give* me that thing," Kassie said as she snatched the laptop from Dionne. "Jesus, Dionne, what a mess!"

"He might not even respond. What are the odds, huh?"

"That's *not* the point. Will you listen to yourself?" Kassie asked in frustration. "You shouldn't have done it without my permission. I don't care what you think is good for me, but this is my life. God, I'm so embarrassed."

"Embarrassed by what? It isn't signed, just your initial, 'K.'"

"What did you write anyway? I'm afraid to look."

"Be my guest. Read. It's all right there, but I'm telling you, hand before God, and on a Bible, *I* don't remember doing this." Dionne seemed pensive as she hugged her knees and waited for Kassie to finish reading what she already had. "I need to lay off the sauce," Dionne said under her breath.

"You told him I was an ex-marketing executive from Soma Impact Marketing? Might as well put a big sign on my forehead. Oh yeah, *he* won't know who I am, right? *Idiot!*"

The admonishment had no effect on Dionne, who only giggled at Kassie's embarrassment. Then Dionne flopped her head back on the couch with a sigh of resignation. "Whatever! My head hurts," she said, holding her hands to her head. "Now, don't go acting like you're really pissed. *You* know you wanted this to happen. I don't know *how*, but I'm tired of trying to convince you I didn't write nor send that message."

"Shit, shit, *shit!*" Kassie said, then puffed her cheeks out and ran her hands through her hair. As she reached for her coffee mug, Dionne sat up and looked at her directly.

"You're curious about what he'll do next, aren't you?" Dionne asked.

"Not one little bit." Kassie smiled at Dionne over the top of her mug.

"Yeah, you are. Mm-hmm. Let's see how he responds. Watch his next video and see if it had some effect on him. Then you'll know."

"I'm going up to shower while you wallow in glee over your misdeeds, *Miss Thing*." Kassie grabbed the laptop from the table, pointed her finger at Dionne with an admonishing look to indicate, "I'm watching you," and headed to the stairway and the open walkway that looked down over the living area.

Dionne held a throw pillow to her face to stifle a scream as best she could. Kassie tried not to laugh but, after taking only a few steps, was surprised to hear the TV and the laptop in her arms turn on and off simultaneously—all by themselves.

"See!" Dionne, wide-eyed, said through her hangover fog as she pointed both index fingers to the TV and the laptop.

Kassie only shook her head at Dionne and looked suspiciously at the laptop, then quickly dismissed it as a coincidence. She wouldn't let Dionne off the hook easily. How dare she take the liberty of speaking for her—and to a stranger no less? She knew Dionne had the best intentions but doing something at her expense had taken things a little too far. She couldn't figure out why Dionne hid what she'd so obviously done. Blaming the laptop for sending emails on its own was hard to swallow. However, she knew her friend well, and it wasn't like her to lie.

As Kassie listened to the water spray from the shower, she took a cursory glance at the laptop and wondered if it was waterproof. She quickly dismissed the idea, thinking that, between her and Dionne, one of them had to act rationally and like a mature adult. They had been friends for a long time, and the adage of opposites attracting was true. Kassie knew she couldn't stay angry for long, and a good hot shower might help her put things into better perspective. After all, what was done couldn't be undone at this stage. *What are the odds he'll respond to some crackpot desperate woman out of a million anyway?* Kassie let it go and began her morning routine while listening to Dionne prepare breakfast for them downstairs.

⸻◈◈◈⸻

All seemed forgiven as Dionne and Kassie moved through the rest of the weekend. Since the day after the email incident, neither one had looked at the laptop nor watched YouTube on TV. For

Kassie, it was a means to apply discipline she otherwise didn't have. She had to return to her normal sleep patterns and stop fantasizing about someone she could never have. Dionne was convinced the electronics were haunted by "ghosts in the machine." So, going without watching a movie or two was fine by her.

Dionne was due to leave the following day. Kassie would miss her friend, so they spoke of ways for her to engage in other activities and put the whole business of Davis and his YouTube videos behind her.

Surrounded by the beauty of her location, giving Kassie an endless supply of inspiration to draw upon, Dionne encouraged her to paint. While that was true, secretly, Kassie was afraid her "inspiration" might lead her back to Davis. Writing had already proved she'd fail. She had to engage in activities that wouldn't require her to think much.

Over a plate of lamb chops, roasted asparagus, and simple green spinach salad with mushrooms, Dionne spoke of something Kassie thought she'd never contemplate again.

"You need to get back in the game."

"What are you talking about?" Even though Kassie asked, she knew precisely what Dionne meant. "We agreed not to bring up Davis again, so what do you mean?"

"What I mean is asking what you're doing two months from now? I'd like to invite you to our promotion *soiree* for our engineering partners in November. Our marketing team has developed a pitch we think most engineering firms, including architects, will jump to accept. I am so excited."

"All this time, you never mentioned this to me. What kind of pitch?"

"You'll just have to see for yourself. For firms in the States, it's an opportunity for representation if they want to expand into the international arena."

Kassie was reluctant to respond, so Dionne hurried to add more encouragement.

"Come on, Kassie, it'll be fun. I promise."

"I'm not so sure anyone will welcome me after how I behaved before my resignation. I don't know."

"I'll say it again: you're being too hard on yourself. You took the blame for something you had no control over. I understand how you felt, but what could you have done that would've changed the outcome at the time?"

"Listen. Dorothy needed me, and I wasn't there for her. That's what got me—in the end. I don't know what I could've done to change anything. But one thing I do know is I at least should've been there for her. To help somehow."

"There you go, coulda, woulda, shoulda!"

"Well, it's true! I couldn't live with myself after. I was callous and cold to her. I had lost myself. They say grief will do that, but it's no excuse. Retiring and living here helped get me through the episode and put it in perspective, but I don't know."

"Well, I do. Just say yes. I'll be there to hold your hand, literally. It'll do you good. *Leave* this place for a while. Get out with others. Take a deep breath and live again. As your friend, I want that for you."

How could Kassie ignore Dionne's plea? Her friend was sincere, and the ask was heartfelt.

"Okay. Give me the details, and I'll see. No promises, mind."

Dionne reached across the table, took her friend's hand, and gave it a good squeeze.

⋙◦◦◦⋘

The morning of Dionne's departure came bright and early. It seemed Trixie sensed Dionne's visit had ended and lay relaxing at Kassie's feet whenever she sat down from tidying up, begging for attention.

Autumn in the elevated hills during late August was in full swing. The air had turned cooler, and Kassie felt snow would start to fall sooner rather than later. Last year, the snowfall in September had been light, but that didn't mean it would be the same this year. She would need to trek into town to stock up on supplies. She prayed the snow would not come before Soma's event in Denver toward the end of November. Otherwise, it would be hard to get there and back to Trixie, so in preparation, she needed to find a boarding kennel just in case. What had she agreed to? Better yet, why would she consider seeing her old work associates after all this time?

Taking a moment to reflect, Kassie gave Trixie a loving scratch and belly rub, then walked over to face her dreaded laptop. To her, it had become a Pandora's box. She had to unplug the machine to power it off and now pondered if she should recharge it to learn more about Soma's gala in three months. Kassie didn't allow herself to acknowledge that what she actually wanted to do was check her emails.

During the rest of Dionne's stay, she managed to contain her curiosity about Davis's response. Still, now that Dionne had gone, the temptation was too great for Kassie to abstain for long. The draw to partake was overwhelming, like a piece of dark chocolate she craved to devour. Kassie plugged it in quickly, then busied herself with other things. She tried not to calculate the time before the charging was complete.

⊰●●●⊱

Kassie needed to feel space around her as she attempted to check her emails. She brought a large mug of coffee to the upstairs balcony outside her bedroom and sat in one of the brown wicker chairs. The off-white cushion was comfy as she settled in. The view from this vantage point was even more spectacular than the one near the aspen grove. However, staring at her laptop on the table gave her a feeling of dread. She didn't expect to receive a response from Davis. Not really. She had only anticipated watching his latest video to see what she had missed; at least, that's what she told herself. But the anxiety building over his possible reply was almost too much to take.

To her surprise, fully unexpected though it was—a response. *Why?* She stared at the unopened email for a long time. Her hands were shaking. In trepidation, she opened the email. The response was short and concise. Very businesslike, which she could appreciate.

> Thank you, K, for reaching out. I am in a spot where I could probably use some marketing advice and/or content ideas. I look forward to hearing your thoughts soon.
>
> Yours, Davis.

Based on his response, she was more than willing to forward it to Dionne. *Damn it, Dionne! You should be here to answer this.* It would serve her right. But did Kassie really want Dionne to respond? Did she really want to compete with her friend? Of course not. After all, Kassie and her big mouth had brought Dionne into this. As misguided as Dionne had been to send an email *if* that were the case, it was Kassie's task to set things right. So no. This was her issue, and she would handle it as best she could.

What to say in response? She reread his email and tried to figure out what he might need. She had no idea what he meant about being in a "spot" or what content advice would suit his needs. Maybe that's what she should say in response. Or better yet, watch his latest video, as she had intended in the first place, to get a clue.

However, she was not prepared to see what he had recorded. He seemed angry. His contempt for his viewers and his dismay with their reviews and comments showed. He was patronizing and insincere. This was a departure from his regular ASMR videos. *What's happened?*

Then he softened and told his viewers he imagined this was how they'd feel from others who wanted to hurt or belittle them. How this could result in all manner of anxiety and stress, leading to a lack of sleep. Well his video was the answer. His viewers could always count on his video to provide reassurance; it was a safe place for them. Always platonic, always professional, and above board. Then, he provided the soft-spoken and whispered content video he was known for. *Whew! I don't think he needs me, after all!* But despite herself, she responded anyway:

> Hello, Davis. I'm so glad you responded to my email. But I have to say, based on your latest video, I'm not sure you need any marketing or content advice. I might be wrong, but I think you did just fine on your own. I admit I was shocked at the approach, but how you brought it back to your usual content was nothing short of brilliant. Seeing the honesty come through, pure and authentic, was not only a shock but also an eye-opener. I loved it! It would be interesting to see what your stats reveal. If you'd like, I would love to know them.
>
> All the best. K.

She thought to polish it to read better, but how she portrayed her feelings should be enough. Kassie pressed the Send key before she could overthink it. Better to let the chips fall where they may, which should be the end of it.

CHAPTER 6

Davis

Davis barely tasted the club sandwich and chips he had ordered for lunch. He was pouring his heart out to Joe, which was unusual for him. However, Joe could scarcely commiserate and had no idea what to say in return as Davis fumbled over his words.

"I don't know what to say, dude. It seems like you were able to circle back on the content, and I applaud you for that. Where to go from here is anyone's guess."

"At least I got some things off my chest." He added almost solemnly, "Too bad I took it out on my viewers. If I only hadn't responded to that email."

"Give it time. She might not take you up on your offer. Who knows? If she's a real ballbuster like you remember, the most she'll do is apologize and move on."

"I hope you're right."

"I *know* I'm right."

Davis was quiet. He wanted to choose his next words carefully.

"Since I'm crying in my beer, as Americans say, let me share something more." Joe didn't comment but looked on as Davis continued. "Maybe it has to do with this feeling of something missing in my life or work. I'm getting on in age, mate. It's been four years since I started ASMR videos. I'm thirty-nine now. Time to settle down and all *that* business. Goodness knows I've heard enough from my mom on the subject. My dad has given up on me returning to England, so it's in America I need to find someone special." Davis softly chuckled to himself.

"Life can be that way, dude. Hell, I think about it myself. The damnedest things can happen, and as mysterious as this all sounds, that email and shit… *maybe* the something you seek just might show up around the corner."

They went on to speak about this and other things, but in the back of Davis's mind, he felt the "email shit" would not be the end of it. He wasn't sure what to think about the direction he was prepared to move. Still, one thing was certain—Davis secretly hoped to hear back from the mysterious "K." He felt he could use her feedback. If not, he would analyze his feelings and see where tomorrow led him.

⟫⟨⟩⟪

Kassie's response invigorated Davis. Reading what she had written was very intriguing. He was about to break a golden rule. *Never respond to viewers in a personal way. Ever!* But this was different, wasn't it? She wasn't just a viewer; she was a marketing expert who knew a thing or two about branding and how to promote without shooting yourself in the foot. He had advisers, of course, but nothing to guide him in a direction that made sense. Aside from all that, he strongly desired to test the waters and respond back—just to see what transpired.

> Hello, K. I appreciate your response, and yes, thank you for the support. I am happy to know the impact my latest video had on you. As to stats, the numbers are phenomenal, and the comments are encouraging. I might be on to something. I understand we've met before, and I thank you for your apology. After so much time, it really was unnecessary. That aside, I wonder if you watch often. If so, I'm interested in knowing what brought you to seek relaxation and de-stress in this manner.

> It might help me with a broader audience going forward. Please let me know. Btw, what is your name—it can't be just K? If you're who I think you are, is it short for Cassandra? Confirm, please.
>
> Yours, Davis.

Now, all he had to do was wait. He didn't know how long the wait would be, but he hoped she would respond soon.

And thus, it began. Kassie responded right away.

> Hello, Davis. So nice to hear back. First, my name is Kassie, and you're correct. It's short for Cassandra; thus, the K. I'm so glad what I said gave you encouragement, and your stats show promising success in your new approach. Second, in answer to your question, we don't have very good reception here in the mountains of Colorado. However, we have streaming services, and one evening, I started to surf channels and found your bushcraft adventures. I liked watching you work. One thing led to another, and on one odd sleepless night, I tuned in to discover you had moved to soft-spoken ASMR. Your voice eased me right into sleep. It was magic. I'm afraid I've become addicted (LOL). It wasn't until a friend recognized you that I realized who you were. Then, through circumstances beyond my control, here we are. I hope this helps put some pieces together for you. I would like it very much if you reached out again.
>
> All the best. K.

Davis waited a few days before responding. Every cell in his brain told him to give this up and not answer. However, every sense in his body told him otherwise. He didn't know it yet, but Kassie was becoming a bother he liked very much.

> Hello again, K. I hope you don't mind that I call you "K" instead of Cassandra. Seems too formal. Well, I think we should settle a few things before continuing. I don't understand the circumstance you refer to as your reason for reaching out to apologise.

Again, I'm glad you did. I recall a beautiful female marketing executive at Soma who seemed to need something more from life. Now it's my turn to apologise for being forward, but that was my sense of things. I'm unsure what it was to bring me to that supposition, but there you have it. Maybe your exquisite rudeness made me think there was more going on beneath the surface if you know what I mean. I use the word *exquisite* because the words were so well placed, and you were brilliant in delivery. I, however, was in awe.

A few years back, I needed something in my life, a release of sorts, so I started the bushcraft videos. It was gratifying. When an auto accident laid me up for a few months, I got interested in reaching out to others who suffered from anxiety and needed to relax. This is where I am now. I was in a bad way a few weeks ago and wondered how useful my content was to others. I was losing ideas and felt stuck. Your email sparked something in me. I went bonkers and let my viewers know how I felt. I was able to rechannel myself, and here we are today. Sorry for the length of this email. I must be off to do another video. If you have any suggestions, I honestly would love to hear them.

Yours, Davis.

Her rapid response the next day did not disappoint. He could get used to this.

Davis. It's good to have you open up about your life to me. Thank you. I have been on quite a journey myself. I suppose living alone in the foothills of Colorado will prompt bouts of loneliness and boredom. I love it here, so don't get me wrong. Yes, I was that horrible person three years ago who behaved so badly at your expense. I was in an awful place that reached a crescendo a year ago. I had to step away and reassess my life and how I chose to live the rest of it. If I had to do it all over again, your impression of me would have been far more pleasing. I'd like to think we can move past that and on to more pleasant things. As for suggestions on your videos, I really like the idea of the platonic stance you've taken with your viewers. I see you've amassed 150K subscribers. Bravo! You seem to have the most views (135,000) on one role-play video, a little more than three-fourths of your subscribers! I liked this video quite a lot, but you haven't done it again, and I wonder why. I would suggest sticking to what works. Change it up a time or two or vary your approach, but don't mess with a good thing. Let it become your brand. I hope that makes sense. Anyway, that's my two cents for what it's worth. Let me know what you think.

All the best. K.

His response:

K. Thank you for your suggestion. I like what you have to say and understand precisely the video you reference. I did only one because I didn't want my viewers to think I was sexualising the platonic nature of my content and message. Anything, in particular, you liked about it? It would help me immensely to understand how I could vary it and keep it clean and fresh. My goal is to help others. I don't want to bring dissatisfaction or lead my viewers to think anything other than what I want to convey. Thank you for the insight. Please let me know so I can start work on it straightaway.

Yours, Davis

D. Well, I liked the sensual nature of it, but that can get away from you quickly. I liked the fantasy of being alone with a man who cared deeply about me. An intimate setting kept purely platonic is the key, and you manage this aspect well. I'm glad you enjoyed filming it. It shows. I hope what I said gave you more insight for improvement purposes. Although, I can't imagine you need much. Can't wait to see what you come up with next. I don't want to sound impertinent, but surely your wife or girlfriend can also help. I'd hate to cut myself out of the creative process by suggesting this, but there it is. I really hope you continue to reach out. I love to hear from you. It breaks the monotony of talking to my dog, Trixie, all the time.

All the best. K.

K. I've never had anyone come off as clever as you to inquire about my love life. HA! HA! I had to laugh. I would never label you as "slick," but I give it to you for the sake of cleverness. So, to answer your question, I'm not married and don't have a steady girlfriend. I don't know what I'm waiting for, but I guess the right one hasn't shown herself to me yet. So until then... how about you?

Yours, Davis.

D. In my infinite wisdom, I turned down a marriage proposal years ago. Unfortunately, it was a springboard to worse relationships. After my mother's death, I found myself in an abusive one that should have ended long before it did. Then I found myself married to my job for a long time. When my father passed away, I lost all interest in establishing *any* romantic relationships. This became apparent in more ways than one, which you can personally attest to—hence the apology. Since then, nothing. Your videos continue to intrigue and lull me to sleep. How's the newest video developing? Can't wait to see it.

All the best. K.

K. What are your thoughts on love? Don't need to answer if this is uncomfortable for you. I'm merely interested in your thoughts.

Yours, Davis.

D. Oh wow! Well, let me give that one a try. Without getting too personal, I'll try to answer it this way: The attraction between a man and a woman is a... thing. A chemical animal attraction... like a human magnet that pulls somewhere in the primordial consciousness of the mind and body. But it's more than cerebral. A feeling deep inside stirs you and spins you around to where you must, no, you *need* that connection. It's a constant—always. Without it, you feel you might die... or some such nonsense like that. It's more than limerence or lust—that's fleeting and too much work to maintain. Love is an all-encompassing feeling. It's comfortable as it attaches itself to you and comes as easily as breathing. That's what I think anyway. Why do you ask?

All the best. K.

K. That's beautiful. Thank you. There is a boundary that shouldn't be crossed when making videos, and I don't want to run into risks, although I've come close. There are very lonely people out there. I can't be that *one* person for everyone, so I ask myself where love, desire, or loving others fit. We're told to make love to the camera. Well, I don't want to intentionally generate a "desire" response from my viewers—so I ask. ASMR is a minefield full of slippery slopes, which can easily lead to lascivious behavior. It does have a stigma of creepiness I want to avoid. Well, I'm not *that* guy. It's been good communicating with you, Kassie.

Yours, Davis.

D. I understand. I feel the same way about our communications. I only know what you look like on YouTube. I don't think I want to know the rest. The mystery is enough. But of loneliness, yes, be careful. You walk a thin line when treading on emotions through the kind of content you create. I used to have a select number of friends whom I held close. Then, one day, it hits you.

You're alone. It kind of sneaks up on you. If other people say they'll call or come by, you think, okay, I have a social network of friends who care. But then you realize that they never call. They only talk to you because *you* call *them*. They never come by, and you are always by yourself. Alone. Maybe you tell yourself this was how it was meant to be. You tell yourself that we are all alone, so it's time to get used to it—but how can we? Especially when we see others who don't *look* alone. They seem fine and don't look lonely. They're with others, for God's sake, so they can't be. But you are.

A long time ago, being a so-called "loner," I wondered why God made it this way for me, constantly alone. They say God has a plan for you—maybe this was His for me. To prepare me for the many days of being by myself. It never gets easy, especially when sociologists and psychologists say man was not meant to be solitary. "No man is an island" and all that. Man is a social animal, so being alone and wanting to be alone makes you weird. Right? It's unnatural. Well, I don't like it. Never have. I like my alone *time*, but I don't want to be lonely. I don't like *feeling* that way. Maybe that's why I was drawn to your videos and bushcraft. Alone, living quietly. I like that. But loneliness is scary.

Oh well, I've gone on far too long rambling nonsense. It's time for bed. I have to turn it in now. Good night, my friend.

All the best. K.

Kassie, you are not alone. Rambling? Not at all. Thank you for your honesty and openness. I understand. I'm here for you always. I hope you'll start to share your day with me. I'd like to hear what you do each day, even your daily walks with Trixie. Tell me. One day I hope to share myself with you. Until next time. Sleep soundly and be safe.

Yours, Davis.

Davis, thank you. Life for me is pretty mundane, I have to say. Until now, Trixie and the walks through mountain trails and rides into town on my old Schwinn bike sometimes make the days go by faster than others. I find myself stymied at times when the days move like molasses. I want more. I often tell myself there has to be more to life than this. But it's what I've chosen—so there! Lately, I've started to draw. I love nature, and drawing has brought a certain peace of mind that I like. I challenge myself to do better each day. Not bad. How about you? Tell me about Davis.

All the best. K.

Kassie, I love it! Like you, I'm a loner. I enjoy the outdoors and building things. Much like a person's self-esteem, I enjoy uplifting others. It seems we have a lot in common, but instead of creating and depicting life in drawings, I build things. MEP engineering is my so-called claim to fame. I guess you know I'm from across the pond, England, born in Sheffield and educated in Cambridge. My dad wanted me to follow in his footsteps, but I couldn't see myself in management. I've tried to move out of his shadow, so making a living in America, far on the other side of the continent, is where I ended up.

I can also be very clumsy, constantly stumbling into things, but that's since improved. I served in combat with the British Royal Forces in Afghanistan, where I lost my sense of smell due to a shrapnel injury. Whilst I was told it would return, no promises were made. (But happy day, it is slowly returning.) Because of the temporary loss, my senses were sharpened. During that time, it seemed I developed a heightened sense of everything: feelings, touch, vision, you name it. It's as if I could sense what others were feeling. Still do. I suppose that may be the reason we've connected. I don't know. All I do know is I enjoy our communications. What do you think? Shall we continue?

Yours, Davis.

It was sealed. They continued communicating in this manner almost every day for the next few months or whenever Davis's schedule would permit. However, they never allowed much time to transpire between their communications. Each time, they came closer and closer to knowing more about one another. Before long, Davis couldn't wait to see what she had written so he could respond.

He had found an old executive photo of Kassie from Soma's website, so it wasn't difficult to envision her when communicating. For reasons they couldn't explain fully, writing seemed to be a more intimate and personal form of contact and connection. Because of this, they agreed not to exchange phone numbers and let the mystery of their friendship continue to build using the lost art form of written communication. Davis liked it that way.

Before long, keeping Kassie out of his mind was becoming harder to do. Through their communication, he could almost hear her laughter, see her smile or the tilt of her head in understanding. The desire to hold her close was ever-increasing. She had become part of his life whether he liked it or not. Davis was treading on dangerous ground, and he knew it. He couldn't help himself. In each video, he could see her in the camera. He was losing himself to her.

However, her rapid response to his latest video left him stunned. He wasn't sure what to make of it.

> Hello, Davis. I watched your latest video, which was much more intense than before. The attention to detail and content was more erotic than expected. It seemed you were speaking directly to someone, but of course, I couldn't be sure. Was that your intent? I understand you need to keep the videos platonic in nature, but I wonder if you risk stepping over the line. As a reminder, we discussed this possibility a while back. I admit I was moved beyond relaxing, which can be dangerous for some women who need companionship from the opposite sex. Unless you want to go in another direction from soft-spoken ASMR, I suggest you share your life experiences with stories or continue with affirmations. Remember your intent, and back away from such intimacy. Sexy

though you are, it is hard to say "keep it clean," which you do for the most part, but I must caution you on this one. Is there something more you're looking for that you don't have right now? I might be overstepping my bounds. I apologize in advance if I'm coming off like the old "dragon lady," but I'm concerned.

All the best. K.

He had done the unthinkable. He had let his innermost feelings come through the camera. It wasn't professional, and it showed. Because of his correspondence with Kassie, he was beginning to relate to her on a personal level through the camera and, thus, his viewers. He was emoting to her on the other side of the lens, which wasn't good.

But why Kassie instead of someone he already knew? Maybe it was because she was elusive and utterly unavailable to him. Had she become his muse? How could he allow himself to get attached to someone so soon? He'd even found himself imagining holding her after his video session. Each time, he told himself to *get it together, man.* However, exposing himself in this manner, he felt he had let her down. He had to step back. He had to get grounded somehow. If he was going to use this technique, he had to remove himself emotionally from her.

The whole point of relaxation and helping someone sleep was to get somewhat personal. But Davis had let his emotions get the better of him. He had to regain control.

Hello, Kassie. So what to say in response to your latest email? Let me start by saying, "You're right." Yes, I suppose I was talking to someone special and letting my feelings show more than I should. I need to get back to basics if I'm to continue this hobby of mine with any degree of success. I'm not an actor, so I don't do role-play very well. I'm just me. Thank you for pointing out the obvious and putting me in check.

Yours, Davis.

Davis waited for a response that never came. To say he was disappointed was an understatement. He didn't think what he'd done was enough to have Kassie distance herself this way. Without a phone number, the only way of reaching her was through email. He had sent another asking if all was okay, but still no response. Being busy was certainly possible, but it didn't seem to fit the pattern they had developed in communicating.

Out of frustration, he went on the attack. He had other matters to contend with in his personal and work life, the least of which was Kassie being miffed over his latest video. *Damn it to hell. Let her wallow in pettiness if she wants. I have better things to do.* As much as he tried to convince himself that was true, it was hard to forget her and the friendship they had established together. He only wished he could have developed something more before she'd brushed him off.

CHAPTER 7

Cassandra

Kassie closed the cover of her laptop more violently than was necessary. She couldn't believe what she was allowing herself to feel and actually write to Davis. Was it her imagination, or were they moving much too fast?

Who did she think she was to say those things to him? Offering advice? Didn't he already have a publicist who knew what to do? How pretentious to assume she could be that for him? *Problem is he's allowing it. Don't forget*, she admonished. He was younger than her, so he had an excuse to be reckless with this endeavor. She, on the other hand, had no excuses. She was losing herself to him, and *that* she could not allow.

It was bad enough to feel him throughout the day, which was odd. Was it her imagination, or could she really feel his touch? His voice, lips, and caress were all too real at times. Sometimes, when watching his videos, when she smiled, he smiled. When he made a joke, she understood immediately where it came from, and she got it. *Is he speaking directly to me?* She found herself asking. *He's a sorcerer. That's who he is. A devil in disguise who manages to touch me whenever he wants. Moving in and out of my mind willy-nilly just isn't fair.* This thought, though mildly amusing, was disturbingly real.

Of course, Davis wasn't talking directly to her, but he made it *feel* like he was. That was the genius in his gift. She'd bet anything that she wasn't the only person who felt this way. *I'm just a lonely old woman.* Yet, at fifty she didn't feel old.

Kassie told herself to stop this nonsense of communicating with someone she could never have. But how? Their communication had taken a turn Kassie was not fully prepared to make. In his previous email, Davis seemed keen on keeping things at a distance. Now, he wondered why she hadn't responded to his email. Ghosting Davis didn't seem fair, but what other choice did she have? What else could she say without showing her true feelings for him? *Damn, just when I was starting to feel desire again, I ruined it by getting involved too quickly and letting my feelings rise to the surface—unchecked. This madness has to come to an end.* Her emotions were getting the better of her. She had to take control. So, she decided not to respond and hoped she could go on without reconnecting. She'd let fate take charge instead.

How long had it been since she had a man look at her with affection and desire, and she'd returned the feeling? How long had it been since she had a man in her bed and felt the passion of a lover's embrace? How long had it been since she wanted to please a man and share her life and love with him? She did crave it, but not with this *younger* man. More gray in his beard would be more to her liking, or it should be. *It's been too long; that's the problem, Kassie. You need to get laid, woman.* She wasn't a prude. She loved men and wasn't too old to enjoy a down-and-dirty, hair-pulling, bodice-ripping kind of make-out session. A good roll in the hay would do her a world of good. However, these thoughts only led her back to Davis.

As strange as their communication had come about, she was glad of it. Feeling unsettled, she rose and paced the room. Each time she passed the laptop, she felt tempted to throw caution to the wind and respond to Davis. Within a few minutes, she felt the familiar ache of longing, and that just would not do. After all, she had no concrete indication that Davis felt a desire for her—a connection, yes, but that was all. The rest was only supposition on her part. *Foolish, old woman,* she admonished. A distraction was necessary; finding someone to squelch the desire she felt rising in her body was in order.

"Right," Kassie said aloud to Trixie. "Time to get a grip and get on with life. A good getaway to Soma's event in Denver is just the ticket."

She left the unopened laptop where it was and busied herself with other things, like washing the dishes by hand or sweeping the floors with a broom instead of using the vacuum.

The event in Denver was less than a week away. She had scheduled Trixie's boarding in a kennel and stocked up on supplies. However, she hadn't thought of what to wear, and if the snow held off, she wondered what would be appropriate. Thinking about her mission to get out, socialize, and maybe get involved with a lonely bachelor, she had just the dress in mind for the occasion.

Without Kassie being aware, the TV and laptop worked in concert with each other, as if speaking in code, arranging airline ticket boarding passes for a certain someone in Seattle, Washington. When all was done, they both powered off with a discerning "whoop" sound that caused Kassie to wonder if a power outage had occurred in the surrounding hills. It hadn't.

⸺◦◦◦⸺

The room was large, made even more so by the tall white Doric-capped columns spaced around the room in a circle with a walkway behind. Kassie noted each column was made of white granite and marbled in ribbons of black and gold. Wearing a bare-shoulder chiffon dress of yellow and white with ruching that hugged her bust and waist but fell into loose folds as it cascaded around her hips, stopping just above her calves, Kassie felt underdressed for this kind of event. She should have brought a wrap for her bare shoulders—her self-consciousness was starting to raise its ugly head. *Stop it, Kassie. Be confident. Be brave.* She was late, but Dionne should be happy she showed up after what she pulled with the email to Davis. She had forgiven Dionne and her denial, of course, but allowed herself this little bit of peevishness just for show.

When she arrived, the event was well underway. The live music was played by a set of musicians just a few seats shy of a complete ensemble. What was more pleasant to the ear was the type of music played. It was not ethereal or orchestral but more upbeat and contemporary, with just the right amount of jazzy saxophone mixed with sultry guitar strings, chimes, and synthesized piano.

"Well, it's about time you showed up. Wow! You look great, in a 1950s kind of way, but wow!" Dionne said in greeting.

"Not as good as you, my goodness," Kassie sincerely returned the compliment. "You're not leaving much to the imagination, I see. Thanks for inviting me. I'm so sorry I'm late. My nerves got the better of me at one point. I almost didn't make it, but here I am! You didn't tell me how lavish this whole affair would be. Look at this place! There're so many faces I don't recognize; where are the ones from the old days?"

"What are you talking about? Some old faces are still around, like Mark Bennett over there," Dionne said, pointing in his direction, then turned to point in another direction. "And the wicked witch of the west herself, Ruth Matthews, looking amazing as ever. The bitch!"

"My nemesis. Both of them. Looks like Mark'll need an Uber to take him home before long."

"You might be right about that. I admit there are quite a few new faces, but not many. The company went all out to invite from far and wide, thus the swanky setup."

Just then, a waiter came by with a tray of champagne, and right behind him came another waiter with a tray of canapés. Kassie took one glass of the bubbly but passed on the hors d'oeuvres. She knew she should have something to eat along with the champagne, but she had time with the night still youngish. As she stood alongside Dionne, Kassie's nerves were starting to subside. She could have moved away to mingle, but for now, she wanted to enjoy the sights and be in the moment.

"It feels good to get away from my home in the hills. I booked a room at the Westin, not too far from here. I hope we don't get an early snow, tonight of all nights."

"Judging by how you look, no snow would *dare* fall!"

"God! Here come the jokes. You're funny, Dee." Kassie laughed with Dionne while raising her glass of champagne for a sip.

Then she saw him. She felt blood rush from her head to her feet, grounding her in place. Davis was there. How? Why? He stood beside one of the tall granite columns, leaning against it with his right shoulder, legs crossed casually at the ankles, as if keeping the column from falling over, and talking with a group of other men gathered around, champagne glass in hand.

My God, he's more handsome in person. Tall, tan, and broad-shouldered, with black curly hair, just long enough to cover his neck, brushed back from his face. His white shirt made his hair stand out starkly and complemented his complexion well. His black trousers seemed to fit nicely as they fell from the waist. Kassie felt the blood rush back into her face and turned away in case he looked her way.

"Why didn't you tell me he was here?" Kassie hissed at Dionne.

"Who?"

"*Davis.* You know who," she said through clenched teeth.

"Oh damn!" Dionne exclaimed after she saw him. "His firm was invited, but I couldn't have known he would be the one to represent them. Oh no. Kassie, I'm so sorry. I didn't know. What are you going to do?"

"What am *I* going to do? What are *you* going to do?"

"Me!" Dionne was incredulous, then rose to her full height and squared her shoulders toward Kassie. "You'll just have to face him—"

"What?"

"You have to! What else is there—?"

"Leave!"

"You will not!"

"Yes! I will! Watch me."

Kassie turned on her heel and promptly walked directly into Mark Bennett, who was coming up behind her, almost spilling her champagne.

"Well, look at Miss… What's her name? Nice to see you again. Cassandra, is it?"

"Hello, Mark. It's so nice to see you." Kassie's annoyance was beginning to show because not only was the presence of Davis unnerving, but Mark, of all people, was more than a little tipsy, making it more awkward for her. "I was on my way out."

"Why? The party's just getting started," he said, but his jovial nature was misleading.

"I see, but if you'll excuse me, please."

"What's the hurry?" Mark asked, then became insistent, rough handling her. "Here, let me steer you toward meeting some folks from our prospective clients, abroad and otherwise. You've been away so long. I want to know what you've been up to—try to persuade you to come out of retirement and help us out."

Dionne tried to intercede. "Kassie and I were just on our way—"

"Now, now, now, Dionne. You can't help her out of this," Mark said as he handed Kassie's glass of champagne to Dionne. "I have her now, so away we go…." Kassie was being whisked away despite her protest.

Kassie looked back helplessly toward Dionne, who only shrugged her shoulders, obviously confounded on how to gracefully get Kassie out of her situation. As she was being steered toward the very group of men she wanted to avoid, Davis and his companions, the music mimicked the panic Kassie felt rising in her body. As the dance floor began to swell with people, an idea came to her.

"Oh my goodness, these shoes!" she said, bending down to fiddle with the strap on one of her heels. "I need to adjust the straps if I'm going to be comfortable."

"Well, I'll just wait—Hey, Jack Wilford!" Mark exclaimed as another partner approached him.

Just as Kassie rose from the floor, she was relieved to see the party of men were no longer around the granite column. They were nowhere in sight. Even Mark Bennett had disappeared. She scanned the room to find Dionne, but she was nowhere to be seen.

Many people jostled for a position to dance or mingle for conversation. Knowing very few people, Kassie found herself alone. With her plans for making a hasty exit thwarted, Kassie headed for the spot she had tried to avoid just minutes before. Kassie imagined Davis holding "court" from this vantage point. She looked over to where she had come from and was surprised. He'd have had a clear view of her if he'd looked in her direction. Kassie's saving grace and hope was he wouldn't recognize her even if he'd found an old Soma Marketing photo of her online.

When Kassie leaned against the column, the music switched to a sultry tune, which was pleasant to her ears. As the lights dimmed, a waiter came by with a tray of champagne, and she took another glass. She wasn't much of a social drinker; in fact, she didn't drink at all. But the chilled champagne was tasty and eased the heat building in her body over the thought of running into Davis. She welcomed the coolness as it slid down her throat and felt the almost immediate effects the bubbling beverage was having in her head. Kassie moved away from the column just enough to touch the dance floor's edge. She watched others move closely together and felt herself sway to the sultry notes of a familiar tune she hadn't heard in years, "The Dream" by David Sanborn. Seeing Dionne dancing closely with a handsome man, she smiled and thought, *Good for her!*

Just as Kassie started to return to the column, she felt the body of someone standing directly behind her. His left arm moved deftly around her waist as he said softly, "Don't leave."

She knew the deep voice. The soft and familiar accent. It was Davis.

"Move with me. Sway with me."

She could feel his breath as he softly whispered these words in her ears. She could sense his strength as he pressed into her from behind. "Don't turn around. Close your eyes. Just feel me. Focus on us and the music."

Kassie did exactly as told. All inner thoughts, such as *Suppress your desires, Kassie. Don't let them rise, Kassie. He's too young for you, Kassie,* vanished in the blink of an eye. It was just her and Davis swaying to the jazzy saxophone as it mixed sultry, sexy notes filled with longing and passion. There were no words. Kassie let the moment take her with Davis guiding her to a place she hadn't been in a long time.

CHAPTER 8

Davis

———◦◦◦———

Davis had been persuaded to attend the event by sheer threat if not coercion. Having Joe around had eased the tension of returning to Soma. Secretly, he thought it would be nice to have a go at the company again. Test his chops at the art of schmooze and do some coercion of his own. Because of this, the decision to make an appearance had been reluctantly accepted. These were his thoughts as he listened to his colleagues who slugged down glasses of champagne at Soma's gala. He recalled the conversation with his boss and cringed at the remembrance.

Crandall Jamison would not take no for an answer. Davis knew this instinctively as they stared each other down. *How ironic*, Davis thought while resisting the request to attend the event in Denver hosted by Soma Impact Marketing. Since Kassie's last email and brush-off, he hadn't had enough time to process his feelings toward her dismissiveness. Now, he was being asked to represent the firm at an event hosted by the company Kassie used to work for, and what's worse, where he had been so soundly humiliated by her just a few years ago. He did have *some* pride.

"You'll do this, Davis, whether you like it or not. I know it's last minute, and things didn't go as smoothly last time we made a bid for their help, but times change. Make an appearance at Soma as our representative," Crandall said bluntly, squinting his eyes at Davis.

Davis knew he was beaten. His argument had fallen on deaf ears. He said no more as he listened to Crandall continue. "Look, I like you. Hell! We all do, which is why you're the best person for this assignment. Make the most of your time, schmooze, and do what you can to win this firm over. We need the marketing clout in Europe, and you're just the man to get Soma to do this for us."

"Not that my connections in Britain have anything to do with it," Davis said smugly, not caring what Crandall thought of the sarcasm. He hated being used.

"We need to expand internationally." Crandall was stern. "Our presence is well established here in America, but now it's time to move our efforts to international markets abroad. Britain is our springboard. This will happen, Davis. You will do this, or we'll get someone else to do it for us."

"I see—"

"No need to say more." Crandall gave him a wry smile. "We have the tickets already, although I don't have the vaguest idea how we got them so soon. Anyway, we'll get your buddy Joe to go with you. How's that for sweetening the pot? He's always good for a laugh and keeps you honest—if you know what I mean."

Davis wasn't sure what Jamison had meant by that comment, but by that point, he didn't really give a damn. That had been a few weeks ago. Now in Denver and surrounded by his workmates as they schmoozed, drank, and rubbed elbows, he was astounded to see the very last person he had expected to see. Kassie.

<hr/>

He knew it was her from the photograph in Soma's old directory listing. It had to be. At the time of searching, it was as if the computer had known what he was looking for. She was beautiful then and even more so now. She never told him, but the gray streaks in her hair confirmed what her bio had reported. He didn't know what to think about the ten-year age difference—but it was of no consequence when he saw her.

Standing with his colleagues and business partners, he tried not to stare. As discreetly as he could, he stole glances in her direction as she laughed and looked furtively around. Her girlishness showed, and the softness it brought to her face indicated a confidence he understood. The curve of her neck was inviting. The lines of her dress as it caressed her body and how the skirt swayed when she moved were mesmerizing. Her hair, dark wavy chestnut with glints of highlights, gave the gray enough coverage so it wasn't as noticeable, but he noticed. He watched and studied everything about her.

When she was grabbed by Mark Bennett, a man he had met earlier and didn't like much, who then moved in his direction, Davis became concerned about how she was being manhandled. His companions didn't see this blatant display of chauvinism, but it disgusted him. Then Kassie made a move as if she'd stumbled. *Brilliant!* When Davis's buddy, Joe, tapped him on the shoulder to join them outside, he declined. He wanted to step back against the wall, behind the column, to observe more of the scene—and Kassie.

She seemed to glide in his direction, no doubt without noticing him in the shadows behind the column. Her movements were fluid, like a gazelle. The animal nature of her drew him. When the music started and the lights dimmed, he felt pulled to her. He couldn't help himself.

Standing behind her, he could smell the fragrance of her perfume. Amazing! The recent return of his sense of smell told him it was light and soft, like freshly scented flowers mixed with an ocean breeze. He couldn't get enough of it. She was earth, and he was fire. The feel of the moment was like magic. It felt right to do what he did. Feel her up like he did and say what he had to say.

Kassie responded to his touch without reproach. She fell into his embrace naturally. Her movement had no clumsiness as she matched her hips to his. She was slightly shorter than him in heels, but they seemed perfectly matched.

Davis reached with his right hand to take the champagne glass from Kassie and bent to set it gently on the floor away from them. She didn't stop or turn to look at him. He instinctively knew she was anticipating the next move.

As Davis rose, he positioned his right arm around her waist to join his left one. She placed her hands on his, allowing him to guide their movements of slow dips and sways. They moved together in that way, just him and her. She matched him move for move, and each time she tried to face him, he refused to let her do so with subtle gestures.

From behind, he kissed her neck. That felt right as well. She leaned her head back to rest on his chest, and for a second it was as if no one else was around. He could see the side of her face and noted her eyes were closed, feeling the moment, taking it all in. *Good!* He danced her back slowly and placed the granite column at his back, which gave him leverage to hold her close.

"Kassie," he whispered into her ear.

"Davis," was her response.

"Keep your eyes closed," he softly commanded.

The saxophone was nearing a crescendo of notes. As it did so, Davis increased his embrace and held her tightly. He kissed her neck again, passionately this time, then lifted her left arm from her side to above her head. He felt her caress his head with her raised left hand and the coolness of her fingertips as it ran through his hair.

Slowly, he stepped to her left, leaned her against the column, let his fingers caress her uplifted hand, and then slid them down her arm. His fingers glided down her left side, grazing her breasts, waist, and hips.

That was where he left her.

CHAPTER 9

Cassandra

Kassie felt dizzy, dreamy, and lightheaded. *What just happened?* She felt a bit silly looking around for a ghost. Had that been the case? All she knew was that the champagne had gone to her head, and what had just occurred only happened in movies. Right?

Her left side still tingled as she reached with her right hand to feel the back of her neck where the kisses had been placed. The feel of Davis was delicious. His voice was intensely masculine, deep and hoarse with passion; his touch soft and sublime.

The band began to play an upbeat tune. The dance floor still contained people who milled about or chatted with colleagues, making promises she knew few would keep. Judging from where she stood, no one seemed to look in her direction. That might be due to being shrouded in the shadow of the dim lights next to the granite column.

Then she got angry. *It's not fair!* First, it was Mark Bennett, then Davis Blakemore, who treated her like an object and not a person to be respected. Mark had taken advantage of her vulnerability, thinking he could order her around and have her do his bidding. *So had Davis, damn it! Who does he think he is, and how dare he seduce me on the dance floor and then leave!* She didn't like the ideas forming in her head. Angrily, she pushed herself away from the granite column and toward the venue's entrance. She needed air and time to think.

On her way out, she passed Dionne but was not in the mood. "Not now, Dionne."

Dionne persisted and followed Kassie to the coat-check area. "What a jackass Mark can be. I'm so sorry. You know how he is most of the time."

"To hell with that! *He*, I can handle, but Davis? Oh!"

"What are you talking about?"

"Well, I guess you didn't see, did you? What with you cozying up with your latest boy toy, you couldn't bother to look for me, huh? Well, *I* don't *need* a boy toy, *thank* you very much! Here I was, minding my own business after narrowly escaping—what's his face. Then I'm grabbed from behind… by Davis! Who does he think he is with his smooth talk, ridiculous touch… and the feel of him, oh God!" Kassie could not contain her tears. Feeling she had control over nothing. "Damn it!" Embarrassed, she gave her ticket to the coat-check attendant and continued. "Oh, Dee, he felt so good. Then he left me—just standing there looking ridiculous! God, I hate I got into this mess. I don't know him, and he damn sure doesn't know me *that* well. What am I doing?" Kassie asked, choking on her tears. Her coat was handed to her, and she jerked it away from the clerk with unintentional rudeness.

"Sit down over there with me for a second," Dionne said. But the look Kassie gave her caused her to plead. "Please. It's quiet over there, and no one can see us. You're in no shape to leave right now, so take some time to calm down. Besides, snow is starting to fall."

"Oh great! This is just turning out to be a *fabulous* evening, huh?"

"Listen to me. I know you're angry, hurt, and embarrassed. But you're my best friend, and as a friend, I must tell you that you're being too hard on yourself—again. I don't know what to make of what happened or what Davis's intentions were, but you've got to let the past go and live for today. For all I know, he's probably as big a jerk as Mark. I wish I could've done more to protect you. I'm so sorry, Kas."

"He's so young, and I'm so old," Kassie lamented.

"That's what you're worried about? You're a beautiful fifty-year-old who looks thirty-five—"

"It'll matter a lot when I'm eighty and he's sixty-five or seventy. Holy hell!" Kassie began to cry in earnest. "Life's a bitch, ain't it?"

"Yes, it is. So, while we have the *time*," Dionne let the word "time" linger in the air until she continued, "live it. You've gone through so much, but don't let the passing of your parents or idiot ex-boyfriends keep you from living life! There's so much you can give and offer to the world, so let whatever happens—happen. Okay? Will you live as long as eighty? Will he? Will I? Who cares? What matters is what's happening right now."

"It was heaven, Dee. To be held like that… touched like that. How could he seduce me and then disappear just like that?" Kassie snapped her fingers.

"I don't know, but listen," Dionne said as she took a furtive look around, "go to your hotel and chill out if you must leave. Think about what happened, and maybe decide how to feel about it all tomorrow. Remember the feel of Davis and this night. Something will shake loose soon."

"Will do, boss," Kassie gave a sigh of resignation. Then she hugged her friend and blew her nose in a tissue Dionne handed her.

"I need to get back, but I'm glad you got to see Davis at least. Who knows what he might be thinking or what he'll do next? However it turns out, it was exciting, don't you think?"

Kassie said nothing; just kissed Dionne on the cheek and left.

CHAPTER 10

Davis & Cassandra

D avis hated leaving Kassie the way he did. Still, he hoped it was with a memorable impression. He would be back, guaranteed. The feel of Kassie was too much to ignore. She had awakened a desire in him on a level not on par with any other woman he had known. He doubted if he would ever have another like that one moment of swaying with her.

But first, he needed to have a word with Mark Bennett. He had to put his firm on sound footing in the international market without having that jackass of a man be part of it.

Coming upon the person in question, Davis stood aside and listened to Mark's meanderings. The man was clearly drunk and, by Davis's guess, would not remember what he had said to him tomorrow. Instead, Davis gambled on Mark's colleague's ability to enlighten him upon sobering up.

"Here's the young man I've heard so much about," Mark said louder than the situation called for. "I wanted to introduce you to one of our former colleagues, but she seems to have disappeared for the time being. Yes, sir, she was a crackerjack when she was with us! She could surely get some marketing work done for you, create a proposal, and seal the deal with less overhead than you can shake a stick at. She could buy and sell you to any international company, yes, sir."

"That's a shame. Sorry I missed her," Davis said.

"Too bad about her clerk though," Mark continued. "She could've helped avoid the disaster of her clerk's son killing himself in front of her very office. Yes, sir! She lost her cool and *quit*! Damn it! Nice piece of ass too! I never had her. Too much of a ballbuster, if you ask me! But the work was good. I heard one lay on the boardroom table, and that was all it took for some to get back in her good graces, eh?" Mark winked and nodded at Jack Wilford, who seemed to object but then hung his head in embarrassment at the mention of inside office gossip.

"Maybe she didn't want to be pushed around assholes or tight deadlines. Maybe it hurt too much to stay," Davis said, unfazed by what he'd heard.

"Huh?" Mark seemed confused.

"Maybe she wanted to be her own boss. Maybe she didn't want to be anyone's lap dog. Do her own thing; what d'ya think?" Davis's ruse of fishing for answers was lost on Mark. No matter. Davis intuitively knew the answer anyway.

"You British boys with your fancy *accents* think you can say and do anything, and no one'd notice. Well, I do!" Mark tried to sound offended and imperious at the same time.

"Do you now? Tell you what I think." Once Davis had their attention, including a lady previously introduced to him as Ruth Matthews, he continued, "Our company can do business with just about any marketing firm. This one is as good as the next. You've been after Stanley, Biddle, and Jamison's business for a while now. I say," here Davis paused for effect, "unless you lose that attitude about your best employees, former or otherwise, we'll continue to look elsewhere. However, if we decide to sign with you, I'll recommend we do it with someone with a bit more tact than what you've displayed tonight."

Davis got close to Mark, whose alcohol breath anyone could smell a mile away. He continued, "I don't like bullies or ignorant pigs. I would like to work with a firm that respects its employees. Cassandra Hudgens, I believe her name to be, has my respect over any others as a marketing agent. If she's no longer with you, give us an alternative. Oh, by the way, although my nationality is

British, I'm English actually. Not Welsh, Scottish, or Northern Irish. Just so we're clear. Now if you'll excuse me. Good night."

Davis left them alone to watch after him as he grabbed a glass of champagne and downed it in one gulp. He then proceeded to locate Kassie, but she was nowhere to be found. Davis almost gave up until he saw the person Kassie seemed to know well. Going up to her, he introduced himself.

"Hello. I'm Michael Davis Blakemore from Stanley, Biddle, and Jamison in Washington State. How do you do?"

"I'm fine, thank you," she answered, eyeing him up and down with a smirk.

"I saw you chatting with Cassandra tonight, and I'm trying to find her. Can you tell me where she might be?"

"I know who you are, Mister-got-a-lot-of-names. How do you do? I'm Dionne, her better than good friend, but most people call me Dee—so can you," she said, full of innuendo, while Davis chuckled. "You just missed her. She's headed to her hotel. Says she was left high and dry, or hot and bothered, depending on your perspective, by a man she hardly knows. But I think she'd like to get to know him better   if you know what I mean. What do you think?"

Ignoring her playful dig, he asked, "Hotel, you say? Which one might that be?"

"Now hold on a minute! I ain't about to give information to someone who *might* do Kassie harm," Dionne answered, full of playful indignation. "Do you plan on doing her any harm?"

"In the best possible way."

With that answer, Dionne wasted no time telling Davis how to find Kassie's hotel.

CHAPTER 11

The Hotel

All Kassie could think about as she rode in the back of the courtesy limousine was Davis. The seductive dance had been surreal, even though it seemed spontaneous and natural. She tried to push the thought of Davis out of her mind, but it was useless. Back in her hotel room, she could still feel Davis's arms around her. The sensation of his hands on her lingered, torturing her mind and body. She didn't want to change out of her dress and, at that moment, wanted nothing more than to imagine seeing the sunrise with him. If only she could.

However, the snow was coming down heavier than the weather experts had predicted, obstructing the view of the city from her room. She felt agitated and paced. *I need a stiff drink of the worst-tasting alcohol I can find. Nothing sweet or pacifying but with a bite to make me feel like I'm doing something.* Drinking alone in her room wouldn't do, and Kassie didn't like the feeling of being hemmed. She decided to go to the lobby's hotel bar. From what she could remember, they had a lovely view of the city from there. She hoped it would provide better visibility despite the snow.

Davis was full of thoughts for only one person as he rode in the limousine alone. Kassie. He thought to himself how, just a few months ago, he had no idea what path his life would take. Then Kassie appeared out of nowhere. Who would've thought this hobby of his, this ASMR video, would lead him to chase after one of his viewers, a special someone, the way he was now?

Davis had left the event, telling Joe he had an emergency. He didn't think Joe would mind because Dionne had his full attention. She was funny. Davis liked her immediately.

In hindsight, he felt lucky that his firm had sent him to this gala. *God bless fate for bringing me close to Kassie.* He silently prayed he would be granted the opportunity to see her again, if not tonight, then one day soon. He at least wanted the chance to explain why he'd left suddenly in hopes of easing the embarrassment she must have felt.

He still felt the heat from her body, her curves, the feel of her skin, her amazing smell—hell, everything about her set him on edge. He had to resolve this torment of passion if he wanted to continue his channel without emoting to her each time in his videos. Letting this continue without resolution would be unfair to his viewers. His ability to help them was hampered by this unrequited yearning.

Those were his thoughts as the limousine pulled up to the Westin Hotel. It was situated on a hill high above the city with the lights on full display. It took on a romantic quality in the falling snow, which he thought fitting given the night's events. He noted a bar with windows that stretched from floor to ceiling and thought this would be the perfect place for a proper face-to-face introduction and to clear the air between him and Kassie.

He took the steps two at a time and moved swiftly to the registration desk. He asked the clerk if he could call Cassandra Hudgens to the lobby because she had a visitor. After a short wait, the answer was disappointing.

"I'm sorry, sir, but there's no answer. Would you care to leave a message?" asked the clerk.

Crestfallen, he answered, "No." Then he reconsidered. "Yes, tell her Davis sends his regards and wants—" But he stopped as he watched Kassie exit from the elevator doors and walk gracefully toward the hotel bar. "Never mind. Thank you."

"Sure thing, sir. Anything else?" the clerk asked.

Davis didn't answer as he hurried to find Kassie in the bar. But much to his surprise, he ended up behind her as she waited to be seated. The bar was not crowded, so the table wait must have frustrated her. However, he didn't know exactly what approach to use. This time was different; there was no music to pull him forward, no shared moment of passionate, sultry notes to engage them both. He stood there looking at the small of her back, struck dumb as to what to do. But when he finally decided on his move, Kassie took him by surprise. She turned to face him.

<hr>

Kassie could feel him behind her. She knew by instinct he was there. At first, she thought it was her imagination, but no. He was there; she just knew it. *He's a sorcerer, all right. Conspiring to overtake my mind and bend me to his will. He's winning.* She was confused as to why he wasn't moving or announcing his presence. Maybe he wasn't there, but the tingling sensation down her spine told her otherwise.

She turned. His expression was not one of surprise but expectance. When the waiter said, "This way, please," she reached out her right hand for Davis, then walked backward a few steps to follow the waiter and said, "Come talk to me. Sit with me."

CHAPTER 12

Face-to-Face

Davis smiled and followed willingly. He never took his gaze off her. He only spoke to thank the waiter as he sat them at a table that gave a spectacular view of the city stretched out below them.

They didn't speak. Occasionally, Kassie turned her head to look out the window at the falling snow or lowered her gaze to the linen napkins on the table. Davis did the same. After a short time, Davis ordered drinks for them both. When the waiter brought their order, they were left completely alone to contemplate what would happen next.

Davis didn't reach for her hand. He simply laid his hand on the table, palm side up, expectant. Kassie didn't disappoint. It wasn't immediate, but the feel of her hand, finally in his palm, felt right. Her hand was smaller and delicate. The skin was smooth. The feeling—tender and intense.

As for Kassie, she was transfixed by the sight of his strong hand caressing hers. She stared at it for longer than she should have to take in the sight and feel of her hand in his. This was real. This was happening. All thoughts of him abandoning her earlier faded like the melting snowflakes on the windows.

There was a sadness on his face. Surely, there was no need to feel this way with her, so she tried to reassure him.

"You don't have to fear me. I'm not the dragon lady of long ago. Not really. Why the sadness on your face? It comes through on-screen sometimes, and I wonder about it. Are you okay? You can tell me, you know."

"I know," Davis said softly. "But I've upset you twice now if you count tonight, and I don't know how to fix it. You never responded to my email when I tried to reach out. Why?"

The sound of his voice, soft and whispered, sent shivers down her spine. It was hard to ignore.

"I had my reasons," Kassie said. "They seem silly to me now, but they were real all the same. I'm sorry if I hurt you. It wasn't my intent."

The feel of him stroking her hand was unmistakably sensual. She was finding it hard to concentrate, but she managed.

"I know that too." Davis frowned as if trying to find the right words to say. "You asked if I was sad. I'm not. Just concerned about following my feelings appropriately. I wanted to step back from you, too, which is why I wrote what I did in my last email. I lied—sort of. The truth is, I *was* speaking to you in that video. You caught me. I didn't know what to do, but trying to sort it out in my head did no good. Until I saw you, felt you, even smelled you." Davis smiled, then turned serious again. "Until then, I questioned if I was doing this correctly. Making some wrong move. Ultimately, I wonder if you feel about me as I do about you." There was an uncomfortable pause between them until Kassie broke the silence.

Speaking softly, she said, "I feel you; you know. Through the camera, I mean. I didn't want to say this before because it sounds crazy, but when you look at the camera and ask questions, it's as though you're speaking directly to me." Kassie chuckled. "Then when I answer, it's as if you hear it and smile or respond appropriately. For some reason, I can anticipate what you will say or do next. When I smile, you smile. When you stop doing something, I knew that would happen. It's as if you know what I'm thinking and doing and vice versa. I refer to you as a sorcerer, and why not?

"For me, it's a term I use when a man travels inside my head, leaves again, and returns, upending all my thoughts for the time being. I'm bewitched, completely lost in my thoughts about you. On the screen, you seem open and vulnerable—purposeful and intense. I feel I can trust you implicitly. I think that's what makes me feel the way I do. It's as if we've known each other for a long time, and I don't mind it."

Davis said nothing in response. The conversation became intimate as he reached out his other hand to cover both of theirs. They were speaking without words, and they let the moment take them.

"I'm sorry I left you suddenly at the column," Davis said. "I had to take care of some immediate business. It couldn't wait. I didn't want you to forget the feel of my body on yours while I stepped away. I was sure I'd find you shortly after, but you were gone. Your friend, Dionne, filled me in on the rest. I don't blame you for feeling embarrassed, hurt, and betrayed. Can you forgive me?" Davis said with hope in his voice.

Kassie said nothing but hung her head, feeling the heat rise to her face at the remembrance of that dance. However, there was an elephant in the room, which nagged at the back of her mind. The age difference. She had to touch on this at some point, especially if the night turned out as she hoped. Kassie looked up from the table and turned her head to look out the window and then back again.

"I'm older than you." There, she'd said it. Let the chips fall where they may.

"I'll be forty next month," Davis said, seemingly unconcerned with the age difference.

"Forty! I thought you were thirty or, at most, thirty-five."

"Does it matter? Really?" Davis asked as he looked directly into Kassie's eyes. He seemed nonplussed. "Your eyes are beautiful. That's all I want to think about now."

Kassie was left speechless. Then, stating the obvious, she said, "You're not drinking."

"Neither are you."

"Yes, I am."

She let the innuendo hang in the air as she felt the heat of blood rising to her face. Davis needed no invitation. He took it. The ice had watered their drinks by now anyway, so what good would it do to engage in unnecessary conversation? The snow falling outside only added to the ambiance they had created between them.

"Let's go," Davis said as he smiled at Kassie.

�⟶◎◎◎⟵శ⟶

"I can't wait to have you," Davis said as he kissed her neck.

"Maybe we should wait. I don't want to move too fast. Do you think we're moving too fast?" Kassie asked, beginning to get nervous.

"We aren't. This is supposed to happen. Don't worry. It's been long enough," Davis said as he slowly unzipped her dress.

Kassie knew he was right. It seemed they had known each other for longer than a few months. It felt right, and she let it happen. She felt her dress slip from her hips and fall around her ankles in a pool of chiffon and slippery goodness.

Davis's shoes and socks had already been discarded. He allowed Kassie to take his shirt off while he peppered her with small kisses on the neck, face, and shoulders.

"Stay still for a moment. I want to look at you," he said with a husky voice, full of desire and need, taking in the whole of her nakedness. "You're exquisite."

She thought Davis was perfection. As manly as a man could be. When Kassie felt his lips on her breasts, she shuddered. She thought she would melt when he kissed her mouth for the first time. The softness of his lips was like pillows on her mouth. The sweet taste of his tongue was delicious, like nectar to her soul. He undid his trousers and deftly stepped out of them, then slowly lowered her onto the downturned bed.

Nothing about this coupling was clumsy. Nothing about this union was second-rate. It was magic, and they both felt it.

"I said I hoped to share myself with you one day. Do you remember? Will you allow me now?" Davis asked.

"Please" was the only response Kassie could give him.

<hr>

For Davis, everything about Kassie was captivating. The light from the open drapes where they could see the falling snow gave her deep brown eyes and the waves of her brown chestnut hair a glint of perfection. Davis felt her smooth skin and breathed the sweet smell of her breath and hair. Lying together, they stayed this way, breathing each other in, nose to nose. He wanted to experience being with her fully before taking her body to him.

When they kissed again, it was deep and heartfelt. He heard Kassie moan at the sensation. Davis cried out under his breath at the feeling. He could not deny the electric sensation that seemed to course through their bodies. Kassie lifted her thigh and caressed his back and waist with her leg to signify she was ready.

Davis looked down at her and ran his hand over her breast that perfectly fit in his palm. He kissed her once more as he entered her gently. He felt her tightness and grew concerned.

"Are you okay? You feel so warm, Kassie."

"Don't worry. I'm fine."

Their movements were as perfect as those on the dance floor. Kassie matched him thrust for thrust until he could stand no more. Like a need to quench a thirst held at bay for ages, the release was impossible to describe. The primal coupling peaked in a gush of orgasmic splendor, and the pulsating rhythm they felt deep inside was so intense that they held each other tightly until it passed.

Breathless, Davis looked down at her as if for the first time. Kassie was a glorious vision of female to his maleness. Until that moment, he had never known what it was to appreciate the female form and its power over him. The feel of her lips, the way she kissed him, urging him on. He wanted more than this one time. He was hers for the taking, and he felt she was his.

For Kassie, the sensation was unbearably wonderful. She felt him fully and was taken by his strength and gentleness. She was sharing herself with him in ways she had only dreamed about. She wanted to give of herself again and fully appreciate what he could make her body do and feel. How he said her name, the caresses he gave her, and how he brought her so quickly to release was incredible. She was in awe, and she allowed him to take her over and over again until sunrise.

⊰◈◈◈⊱

The sun shone brightly in a crystal-blue sky, with snow blanketing the landscape visible from their hotel room. Kassie sat alone in a chair and watched Davis as he slept. She took in the shape of his face and remembered the weight of his body on hers. The curve of his lips and how they parted to allow his voice to speak words that soothed and caressed. His kisses—sweet and tender. The shape of his fingers and the size of his hands looked strong yet gentle in their touch. The darkness of his beard and how it shaped his face so well; she was surprised at its softness and how it didn't chafe her face. She loved how the loose black curls of his hair looked wet and his trim physique—all male. His brows shielded deep-set brown eyes that seemed to look straight into her heart and knitted together when he was serious, contemplative, or aroused, especially inside her.

But he wasn't hers. Kassie knew it couldn't continue and wondered how it would end. She knew men usually hated being asked what they were thinking, so she didn't dare ask that of him. Was she strong enough to face the rejection that was sure to come?

She watched the sun etch traces of her reflection on the hotel windowpane and wondered about herself. Yes, she took care of herself and looked younger than her years. What did she want from him? What direction did she want this to take, exactly? She didn't know. She'd thought he was much younger, but was a ten-year difference that bad? Could she trust him with more than what she had given the night before? *Remember to guard your heart,* she told herself. What if tragedy struck again to rock her world, as before, concerning him? Heartache, death, the loss of something was sure to come—that was her fate. These thoughts overwhelmed her as she sat looking at her lover for the past twelve hours. She didn't know if she had the strength to withstand the loss of him, which was the heartbreak of it all.

Kassie watched Davis turn and stretch, then reach out to her side of the bed, finding no one. He slowly opened his eyes and searched the room for her. She smiled at his handsome face.

"Come here," Davis said in his dreamy, sleepy voice.

"No," Kassie said with a definitive shake of her head.

"I need you," he playfully replied.

"No, you don't. You want me. You don't need me."

"What is this? Why so coy?"

"I don't know. I like your night sounds. I like hearing you breathe and how you snore when sleeping. I like that maleness about you. When you hold me in your arms, I practically melt. It feels so good." Then she paused as Davis waited to hear more. "I've been thinking. What are we doing? You'll return to Seattle, and I'll be here waiting for your next video. Watching you. Alone. Remembering our time together and what we have left to us in these last few hours. I don't know how I'll not regret—"

"I'm surprised at you," Davis said. "I've spent the best night of my life and can't wait to have more of you. You, as smart as you are, can feel that from me, can't you? Yet here you are talking nonsense as if we'll never see each other again."

"I don't know what I'm feeling—"

"Yes, you do. Come here, darling Kassie," Davis said with eyes that seemed to pierce her very soul.

Well, when he says it like that, what other choice do I have? Kassie did as requested, and he nestled her in his arms for reassurance.

"I don't know what the future holds for us. But I do know last night was transformative. You are amazing and gave everything of yourself. I never felt so loved, and I mean it. You spoke of bewitchment last night, but it's you who's enchanted me. You've bewitched me, surely." Davis chuckled. "The way you walk and move causes me to want to watch you all the time. You're beautiful to me. We're a match, you and I. Getting to know you has changed me. And you as well, I suspect. You retired from your firm for reasons I can only guess at. I'm so very sorry for your pain. It lives within your heart, and you must release that, darling.

"I think I fell for you the moment you dared to reach out to me," he continued. "You have a self-assurance that's magnetic. Maybe you used to be a dragon lady, but I haven't seen her yet. Not really. How could I possibly think of you as older when you bring out the best in me the way you do? I like it. You help me be a better person, especially when making videos to help others. You can be a part of that as well if you want—"

"But I—"

"Shhhh. I'm not done, sweetheart," Davis said as he kissed her on the top of her head. "We'll work it out as time moves on, but soon, very soon, we'll be together. I'd like to be in your life and play an active part in it, Kassie. Can you accept that?"

"Yes, but it sounds too good to be true. In what way will you be part of my life? We live miles away from each other. We're not children, and I can't give a child to you at this age. You were a surprise. You can have any woman in the world. What do you want from me?"

"Your love. If you allow yourself. I want to be there for you in any way I can. What I'm trying to say is…I don't want to let go. Ever. I want this with you. Do you understand?"

"Do you mean that, Davis? I mean, *really* mean that?"

"Yes, my darling Kassie. Yes. You matter to me. I need you to know that. We have a cognitive connection, remember? I'll always be with you, sorcerer or not. You'll always feel me," Davis said as he turned her face to his and kissed her deeply. Kassie returned his kiss with as much desire, if not more, than she had the night before. For one last time, they resumed their passion for each other.

It was urgent and full of need that exploded into lightning flashes of ecstasy. For one glorious moment, Kassie thought this must be what being loved felt like, and she trusted it. She hoped it wasn't a dream she'd wake from full of disappointment and unfulfilled hope. But Davis's response squelched any doubt.

Still pulsating inside her, he held her close and whispered, "My love, my darling babe, be with me always. Don't ever leave me."

At that moment, Kassie knew she never would.

CHAPTER 13

Together

In the ensuing months, Davis and Kassie visited each other often. Davis had kept his word to Kassie, allowing her as much access to his life as possible. She quickly became more than a casual girlfriend to Davis, and he let it show, not only to her but to his friends. She was a constant fixture in his life. She liked his best friend, Joe, and his friendly flirtations with her never ceased. His recognition at the firm steadily climbed, as did his video viewership of more than 190,000 subscribers.

Kassie was blissfully happy. She had fallen in love with Davis so quickly that she often wondered if she should trust the feeling. Was it the first time she'd seen him or how they'd danced together that fate-filled evening that caused her to fall so hard for the man? She didn't know and thought it better not to dwell on it for long and let the mystery remain. *Crazy how events have a way of turning out and coming together in the best possible way.*

Dionne couldn't help but let her jealousy show in friendly banter. She complained any time they spoke with each other. On one of Kassie's particular visits to Denver, at a restaurant on Larimer Square for lunch, they had a long discussion about her future with Davis.

"I can't believe you! Snatching him up so fast and all because of a computer glitch," Dionne said with a wink.

"Well, I still believe it was you, no matter what you say."

"I keep saying it wasn't me. You'll never let it go, will you?"

"Nope," Kassie said, teasing back. Then she turned somber. "I don't know, Dee. Sometimes, it feels like something bad will happen. I just know I'll wake up and it'll all be a dream."

"Nonsense. You won the lottery, baby. I can't say that about many people, so be grateful and thank the Lord."

"Did I really win the lottery? He *is* wonderful. We tried to slow it down, but nope. I couldn't hold him back! Christmas and New Year's were magically fantastic."

"Magically fantastic? Look at you using fanciful words! Is he really that good?"

"He's amazing! Just so you know." They giggled like schoolchildren. "Geez. I feel like a young girl when I'm with him, you know? At first I thought he was like a puppy, but no. *I* was the puppy, lapping up anything he threw my way and begging for more."

"It looks good on you; I'll tell you that much. It's as if the hands of time have reversed, I swear. A shame you can't bottle it." Dionne laughed. "If you ever get tired of him, send him my way, won't you?"

"Oh, not on your life!" Kassie exclaimed. Then, she took on a different tone and spoke earnestly with her friend. "I think he's getting serious on me. I mean *really* serious. He doesn't make as many videos these days and constantly works on engineering projects. The company loves him, especially since he grabbed the contract with Soma. He's so good at what he does. Dee, what do I do now?"

"Do what comes naturally. Take it a day at a time and go with it."

"It's been about seven months, and it feels like I just met him."

"You love him then?"

"It is love. Yeah, with all my heart. I think he's the best thing to happen to me." Then she sighed and ran her hands through her hair. "I'm doomed!"

"What is it with you?" The worrisome frown on Dionne's face was deliberate. Frustrated, she asked pointedly, "Why do you keep saying that? Like the world is going to end or something. Are you afraid of being happy? I can't believe you still doubt his intentions or your future together." Dionne sat back, looked at Kassie with as much seriousness as she could manage, and then said, "Insecurity is what it is!"

"Of course I'm *insecure*!" Kassie was emphatic, with arms opened wide. "Davis is forty and will be forty-five in a few years! We never discuss children or anything, but I suppose he wants them. He can't have them with me. What if he decides that's his desire and dumps me for a younger woman?"

"A younger version of you, you mean? Jesus Christ!" Dionne set her glass of wine on the table with a loud thump, but it was not hard enough to break it. She was clearly exasperated. Then she leaned in and said, "If he wanted that, don't you think he would've *spilled* those beans to you a while back? From what I hear, he isn't shy about sharing his feelings with you or anyone. He's as honest as the day is long." Dionne seemed to contemplate more as Kassie sat and listened.

"I don't know. He doesn't seem to be the type to lead you on, Kas. I'd give anything, you hear me? *Anything* to have a man like him show up in my life. Count your blessings, and don't just live life—let life live." Dionne let her words sink in for a second, then said, "Speaking of which, I need to say something that might jar you a little. Sorry. You've had your share of trauma, for sure. But let's face it… I've never, *ever* seen you cry over it—not once. Maybe privately, but you can't fool me. Yes, I was there when you lost it over a perceived humiliation from Davis. Still, I think it was over something much more significant. I love you, and I have to say I think it eats you up inside to be left alone. Forgive me, but I don't think it's the age thing for you with Davis. You're more afraid he'll leave you like your parents did. Or like Dorothy's son left her."

Kassie's eyes widened with shock, which must have shown because Dionne quickly rushed in.

"Honey, it happens," Dionne soothed. "It's okay to feel some kind of abandonment because of what you've lost but look at what you've *gained*. Tragedy can strike any one of us at any time, but don't let it hold you back from happiness. I don't understand what forces brought Davis into your life; I really don't. But don't fear it. Embrace it! It's God's gift to you."

"I never thought of it like that before," Kassie said, stunned at the revelation. "I was hung up on being older and not enough for him when he is more than enough for me. I thought I was fated to be alone." Then Kassie let her true feelings show, and it overwhelmed her. "Oh, Dee, I don't know what I'd do if he was taken from my life. He's been through so much already. Bad luck comes in threes, right? Afghanistan, the car accident, what's the third one, huh? I'm not superstitious, but this scares me. I just know I'm going to lose him. Dee, I'm so afraid to love him completely for that very reason."

Dionne reached out to hug her friend tightly. At that moment, on Larimer Street, in front of many onlookers, Kassie let the tears of grief consume her in the quiet corner of their favorite restaurant in downtown Denver.

<hr>

Kassie's fear of something dreadful happening to Davis while he was away from her eased with time. It was now ten months into their relationship. Kassie never thought it would last this long. However, try as she might, she couldn't keep the worst thoughts at bay, even with Dionne's assurances. She tried to steel herself against the eventuality of Davis ditching her for someone younger or tragedy striking. Still, the doubts remained. In the meantime, she vowed to make each time they were together the best moment to remember.

As usual, she could feel his presence when they were apart. She wondered if she had the same effect on him and smiled at the possibility. The tingle and manifestation she felt during his absences were palpable. This uncanny feeling seemed to come out of nowhere, day or night; she imagined his caresses, kisses, and presence.

Kassie had learned a great deal about Davis. She enjoyed their conversations and his insight. During one of their late-night talks, he told of his insecurities, the trauma of combat and losing his sense of smell, the miraculous day it started to return, his concerns about living up to his dad's expectations—everything.

"I know I can never live up to his standards," Davis confessed. "My dad has a way of making me feel inadequate because of it. I've moved on from his criticisms, but it still rankles."

Davis even shared his love conquests before her. He wasn't shy about letting her know the quandary of figuring out what made Kassie different from the rest.

"I don't know exactly, but you have something I can't quite grasp. I don't think I want to know, really. I'm just thankful for the mystery of it all."

"I think you know. It's my *animal* magnetism," Kassie said.

"It's more than that," Davis said, pulling her close. "I'm not stupid. I don't want to look a gift horse in the mouth, so I'll let the mystery remain." Kassie could only hope it would linger until their dying days.

Davis liked Hadenville and Trixie, or was it the other way around? He enjoyed going into town, especially in the early morning when the smell of freshly roasted coffee was in the air. With Trixie by his side, he was instantly recognized by the locals who loved to have, as Davis said, a good "chinwag" with him. He would stop at the local bookstore with coffee in hand to sample the latest releases. He couldn't wait to tell Kassie about his literary finds.

Her collection of books had grown, thanks to Davis. Discussing his love of engineering principles showed his brilliance. Yet his cautious nature let her know he could be stubborn regarding risks and some marketing tactics she had suggested. He challenged her on many concepts, from politics to religion. They agreed on most things, and those they didn't—well, that was easily solved through a very special method of compromise. He was easy to love.

Together, they discussed her newfound love of drawing and watercolor paintings and how well they sold on her Etsy shop. She also picked up her pen again and tried her hand at writing. Although it wasn't her main passion, most of what she wrote were random thoughts about nature, some of which Davis thought he would use as an idea for his videos. But only if he decided to revive his channel, which was all but defunct at this juncture in his life.

For Kassie, buying a new laptop didn't seem to matter much now that Davis was in her life. Besides, her old one had decided to behave and operate as most laptops did. It no longer stayed on all night. The same was true for the TV, which used to turn on without warning.

As often happened, her thoughts took her back to Davis. She relied increasingly on his presence, but lately, he'd been away more than she liked. The specter of dread was rising in her more frequently as his absences increased. In hindsight, as much as she wanted Davis to know how much he meant to her without smothering or overdoing the affection, it was probably good to have some time apart. Until she saw him again, her projects kept her busy and her mind off any catastrophe that would permanently separate them. So, she distanced herself from thoughts of tragedy by busying herself with artistic projects.

And so it was this day. Kassie stretched her shoulders and put down her watercolor brush to study the trees in her drawing. She didn't know if the raised nap of the new watercolor paper would be adequate for the effect she wanted to achieve, but it looked fine for now. She hoped Davis would be pleased with the results as much as she was. *Damn it to hell, there I go with thoughts of him again!*

Months had passed without any word from him until recently. Davis was still in England and due back that night. His firm was expanding its market internationally and had recently acquired a failing architectural firm there. She only knew he planned to live permanently in England once he finalized his business dealings and established himself in the new corporation in London. What it meant for them was still up in the air. Despite her efforts, dread was building within herself, and she couldn't shake the feeling of impending doom.

⋯◇◇◇⋯

The plane ride was a rough one. The nine-hour flight from London was a misery Davis could do without. However, considering the stakes for Stanley, Biddle, and Jamison, it was necessary. The merger was going well. He has been recently named Chief MEP Designer for the latest project. He was thrilled beyond measure, making his parents proud, especially his dad. He couldn't wait to share the news with Kassie.

Kassie. What a pleasant surprise his affair with her had turned out to be. The life he had led before meeting her seemed like a blur. His only thoughts these days were of Kassie and the life he wanted to have with her by his side. Had the fates aligned at the right moment to make it all possible? Maybe. But whatever it was, he was thankful for it.

Joe had his bachelor days numbered for sure with a cute little hottie he'd met a few months ago. He often made jabs at Davis about his relationship with Kassie. Davis knew Joe might be a little envious, and that was okay. It made him more aware that what he and Kassie had was special and something Joe could only dream about.

Joe was his best mate, who just happened to sit beside him on this trip, snoring away. *Anyone who could sleep through this turbulence must have superhuman powers.* The plane ride was unnerving. Davis understood that cool air made for a smoother plane ride, while hot air, rising from the earth's surface, was choppier. Nearing the Rocky Mountain range was very often turbulent, which was why he chose to fly in the cooler months. But this chop was ridiculous.

Davis put his headset on and listened to calming music to take his mind off the roller-coaster plane ride. However, this took his thoughts back to Kassie again. Her laughter was contagious, her smile brilliant, and her heart immense. She was honest. Her sense of humor was dry and always cut to the truth of any matter, and he loved it. Her cooking wasn't bad either. Kassie was older, yes, but so was he. Davis had grown in maturity since their time together, which had helped him reach his full potential before he realized it. Because of his YouTube channel, he'd started practicing what he preached in his videos. He applied his knowledge and shook off his insecurities. He was a good negotiator and listener, an asset in his work.

Kassie wasn't perfect, thank God. She had her faults, sure, but he didn't dwell on them. Her cold nature of a few years ago had dissipated. She had learned from her experiences and had become a better person because of them. He'd had his share of bad relationships, but Kassie was not one of them, thank God.

On the contrary, Kassie's feelings and needs mattered more to him than any woman he'd ever dated. He desperately wanted Kassie to know this. He missed her very much.

He let his mind wander to imagine what she might be doing at that moment. He imagined her walking with Trixie or on a bike ride into town for supplies. He imagined the wind in her hair as she rode, smiling or laughing as if she hadn't a care in the world. He thought of her skin and wondered if she'd picked up any color from the sun to match her dark auburn-chestnut hair. He loved looking at her. Kassie had no wrinkles to speak of, and he wondered how much more beautiful she would be once they arrived. He hoped to see them around the edges of her eyes, like his, to indicate how much he had made her smile through the years.

His plan was simple. After dropping off Joe at his hotel in Denver, he would surprise Kassie by proposing marriage to her as soon as he got to her home in Hadenville, to use Kassie's description, *west of Denver, near Boulder.* The notion of marriage had nagged at him for some time, and why not? He couldn't imagine living without her, especially if he moved to London. He loved her more than life and wanted to share the rest of it with her.

Davis knew Kassie was concerned about his desire to have children, as he thought most women would be. Davis loved her dog, but to Kassie, Trixie was not a substitute for someone who looked like them and had his last name. However, he'd never considered children as a future for him, which was okay in retrospect. But adoption was always an option he would gladly support or whatever he thought Kassie would want. As long as they loved each other, any child brought into their lives would be loved just as much—if not more.

Joe shifted in his seat as the plane made a sudden lurch. They were nearing Denver International Airport, and the pilot had turned on the FASTEN SEAT BELT sign. The airline stewards walked the aisle to ensure this was done while the captain announced their arrival.

The flight had smoothed out some, which was nice. As Davis looked out the window next to Joe at the city of Denver in the distance, thoughts of his impending proposal came to his mind again. He amused himself, thinking of the surprised look on Kassie's face.

"Well, that was nice," Joe said as he woke, then stretched his arms before him.

"You snore."

"Tell it to those who already know, mate," Joe said jokingly. "See, I've been in Britain so long *I'm* even starting to sound like you."

Davis chuckled, then said, "We'll be landing—"

Just then, the plane shot upward at a high rate of speed. It felt like they were in a rocket pointing straight up to Davis. Then the plane leveled out and banked to the right, almost too sharply in Davis's opinion. Then it seemed to turn and banked left. As it did, it hit an air pocket, making the plane fall several hundred feet, far more than was conceivably possible. Screams were loud, and panic filled the cabin as lights from the ground rose closer than was comfortable. Davis turned to Joe, whose eyes were tightly closed, as the oxygen masks dropped. Davis sprang into action and applied the masks to Joe and then himself. His mind hit overdrive as he thought about the choppy atmosphere, which was unusual in September. Something was wrong.

He panicked, thinking the worst. He thought of his mother and how much he loved his father. He couldn't help but ask himself when he'd last told Kassie he loved her. When was the last time he'd held her close? His absences away from her were many and far too much. He had to get back to her. *This can't end now!* His thoughts raced as the screams within the cabin increased.

When the overhead bins popped open and luggage fell on some unfortunate passengers, he braced himself.

It was clear to Davis the pilots struggled to control the plane, and after what seemed like an eternity of free fall, the plane finally leveled out. The passengers were silent for the most part, waiting for the next event, daring to breathe. The pilot's voice of reassurance crackled over the loudspeaker. This startled some nerve-racked passengers, such as Joe, who screamed.

"Ladies and gentlemen, this is your captain speaking. Some ride, huh? Sorry for the poor attempt at a joke, but we just avoided a plane on the runway as we came in for our landing. Unfortunately, the air was more unstable than we suspected during the climb, and we ran into some turbulence and an air pocket. We're flying fine now, but please remain seated, seat belt fastened until we land safely."

The very matter-of-fact announcement ended with heavy sighs from passengers and some concern from others. Joe released his tight hold on his armrest and blew air through pursed lips.

It was still tense as the plane touched the tarmac for a safe landing with much applause from thankful passengers. It wasn't until the captain announced, "On behalf of the staff and crew, I want to thank you for flying with us today," that they said anything.

"*Fuck*, man!" Joe spoke for both of them.

"I have to get home to Kas," was Davis's only reply.

Chapter 14

Something Must Be Wrong

Kassie had just settled down with a cup of tea and a good book. The light from the flames in the fireplace soothed her in the quiet of the cabin. The sudden static noise from her TV and laptop jolted Kassie out of her seat. The hissing sound was so loud that it threw her into a panic. Despite her efforts to turn them off—she couldn't.

As it continued, the sounds grew louder and closer together. It was as if the TV and laptop had minds of their own. Both started turning on and off simultaneously as if talking to each other, reminding her of the movie *Close Encounters of the Third Kind* when the giant computer spoke to the mother ship on top of Devil's Tower in Wyoming. The noise they made vibrated through the wall and reverberated around her.

Dionne's words echoed as Kassie recalled her swearing that the TV and laptop were turning on and off by themselves. Now, *she* was experiencing the same phenomenon Dionne had warned her about. *What the hell?* she thought while observing Trixie run from room to room, trying to find a safe hiding place.

Kassie instinctively knew something terrible was happening, and it had to do with Davis. She didn't know how she knew this, but Kassie fell to her knees, cupped her hands to her ears against the noise, and prayed for Davis's soul. "O, sweet Jesus, keep him safe; if not, take him quickly."

Then, as suddenly as it came, the static noise was gone with a resounding *zip* sound after their electronic tantrum. Kassie slowly stood, alone in the stillness of her cabin with the unmistakable, though faint, acrid smell of burnt electronic chemicals in the air.

Hours later, a still-shaken Kassie waited for Davis, who hadn't arrived from the airport. She couldn't get him on the phone and started to panic again. She was about to make another call when she heard a car come up the driveway. It was Davis.

At once, he spotted the concern on her face. "Hey, babe!" He hugged her tightly and held the embrace longer than usual. His kiss—tender.

"Where have you been?" Kassie asked, noticing a slight tremble in his body as he held her. "I was starting to freak out. Davis, there's something wrong with the laptop and TV. They went crazy, turning on and off at the same time. Like they were warning me of something. I just knew something was wrong; what is it?" she asked as Trixie jumped and clamored for equal attention from Davis, who reached down to scratch behind her ears.

"Shhh. I just want to look at you," Davis said as he held her face between the palms of his hands and slowly smiled. The rise of his cheeks crinkled his eyes, full of admiration and pure love. He shushed her when she tried to ask again, saying, "Let's go inside and get warm."

The acrid smell lingered in the cabin as Davis tried to explain what he'd just gone through in the skies above Colorado.

"I've been through and seen a lot in my life. Afghanistan was no picnic. But never in my life was I more afraid… than today in that airplane. I'm not afraid of dying… or death. No. It was not getting to see you—at least one more time—that scared the shit out of me."

"My God! The electronics are connected somehow," Kassie said in wonderment. "I just know it. Something is horribly wrong.

Aside from the plane ride, you have more bad news?" Kassie asked as Davis pulled her down gently beside him.

"There's more. Just as the plane banked again and dropped, I felt my whole world spin, and instantly," Davis snapped his fingers, "I knew what I had to do. As you know, I've been setting things up for the firm in London. AI technology isn't developing as quickly as we thought. I'm feeling more secure in my knowledge of the interface—it's not the boogeyman I thought it was." Davis gave a nervous chuckle. "They've offered me a partnership, Kassie. I'll return to London in three months as their chief designer. What do you think?"

He smiled expectantly at Kassie, who looked heartsick. Instinctively, Davis knew she misunderstood his intentions and the implication this would have on their relationship. He reached for her hands, held them tightly, sighed, and continued, "I know how it sounds, but this is not bad news. I want to share my life with you. Only you."

Kassie didn't seem to comprehend his words. She broke her composure and attacked. The dragon lady had finally shown up.

"Couldn't you have told me this over the phone?" Kassie asked. "Prepared me somehow for the inevitable? I've been expecting and dreading this day for so long. I just knew when I gave my whole heart again, the bomb would drop!" Then she started to cry.

"You don't understand," Davis said. "Hear me out." He reached for her, but she swatted his hand away. "Please," he begged.

"No. I won't hear you out!" Trixie ran from the room, whimpering, as Kassie continued, "*Each* and *every* time you're away, I feel you hold and touch me, and I can't wait for your return to make that real. But I also know each day might be our last. You say you had the shit scared out of you, well, guess what? *I* had the shit scared out of me. Pissing my pants over what my electronics were doing or trying to tell me *in my own home*. Over you!"

Davis could see her anger building. Her emotions spilled out as if from every pore of her body. He was gobsmacked! He didn't know what to say in response or if he should say anything. He was astonished at her anger, irrational thoughts, and anxiety. When Kassie shook her head from side to side and pointed her finger for emphasis—he knew to ride the dragon and tame it by letting her rip while he listened. All this time, the one person he needed to reach out to comfort and assure was the person he loved dearly, and she was standing before him. He opened then shut his mouth, entirely at a loss for words as Kassie continued.

"Now, I have to contend with fearing each time you fly that you'll die and leave me too—alone, just like my parents. Or you'll find someone else to love in my place. How long do you think I can take this, huh?

"If you think, in your infinite wisdom, you can just *waltz in and out* of my life, and I'm supposed to just *wait* for you to toss me out like *dirty dishwater, then think again.* It just won't do, *Davis!* I won't have it! I can't keep anticipating your death or the death of our relationship. It's too much! I can't!

"Am I supposed to be happy for you and your promotion? I am, believe me, *God,* I am! But I'm not *about* to *stand* here and listen to *one… more… word*—still care about you and dream of how *wonderful* our life will be while you go off roaming," Kassie spread her arms wide, "all over Europe and leave me one day!

"I'm *not* the only woman you've treated this way. I just *know* I'm not. *God, I hate you,*" Kassie lied.

She rushed out of the room and ran upstairs to her bedroom with a stunned Davis close behind. He had let her rail at him without saying a word, almost feeling bad for her and her misguided way of thinking of him. She should know better, and that made him angry. Before she could slam the bedroom door, he blocked it with his foot.

"Bloody hell, woman!"

He threw his weight into the door, knocking it open farther to face an angry, righteously indignant Kassie. She stood her ground with flared nostrils and then pointed at him in demand.

"*Get out!* Leave now before you make it worse. Just *go!*"

"This is what you think of *me?* After all this *time?* For your information, I don't roam, trek, traipse, galavant, or whatever word you want to use for crip's sake!" Davis struggled to keep his anger in check and apply perspective. "I'm trying to make a life for *us*. My place is here—*with you*. I've said this before, but you *matter to me!* That hasn't changed. I won't leave you, Kassie. God *help* me... I can't," Davis said, breathing heavily.

"Why not?" she asked, mocking him in a singsong voice. "Why'd you come here to tell me this if you didn't want to leave? Aren't you doing the British *gentlemanly* thing by telling me goodbye this... way?" Kassie choked and tried to hold back her tears. "Don't prolong it... please. It hurts too much... to think you'll..."

"*God* in Christ! I didn't think you'd react this way. I really didn't." Davis tried to gather himself and ran his hands through his hair as he watched Kassie with arms crossed at her chest. "God will have to take me *against my will* before I *ever* leave you, and that day is *not* now."

Davis was incredulous. He took a deep breath, slowly stepped forward, and put his arms around her as she cried heartbroken tears.

"My darling Kassie," he whispered. "I had no idea how scared you've been all this time. Forgive me if you left clues I failed to pick up on." He was relieved to feel her arms encircle him for added comfort. "You know I love you. I wanted to share this news *and* ask you to be my wife. Share my life with me until we are no more. Marry me, my darling girl."

He pulled a box from his jacket pocket and slowly knelt before her.

"Will you marry me, my love? Come. Live with me in England. Please say yes to me, Kassie, because I couldn't live the rest of my life—do what I do without you. We found each other through incredible circumstances. I don't know how fate moves the universe; all I know is that I found you and don't want to let you go. Don't be angry. Don't be sad. Love me always, as I'll always love you."

He held his breath and waited for her reply. Trembling, Kassie touched the perfectly round-cut diamond ring, then caressed his face.

"I'm so embarrassed." Kassie hitched back her tears.

"I know, sweetheart." Davis smiled and waited.

"I was afraid, *so* scared. I thought something else entirely and—"

"Don't, darling. Just answer me. Tell me something… please."

"Yes, Davis. Yes," Kassie said. Then she smiled through happy tears.

While Davis tenderly kissed her wet face and lips, he swore he could hear the laptop and TV turn on briefly and simultaneously shut down. As if in a sigh.

CHAPTER 15

Hudgens-Blakemore

——————

It was Davis's forty-fifth birthday, and Kassie could not have been happier. Dionne had arrived, and preparations were underway for an affair commemorating his big day. Kassie had planned a surprise gathering of close family and friends. Joe was busy ensuring the turkey was not burning, and, of all things, she could hear Dionne arguing with him over stuffing. For Dionne, it seemed essential to answer whether it should be stuffed inside the Christmas turkey or served on the side.

In England, Christmas traditions were different than in America, but not by much. She was determined to have as American a Christmas as she could manage. For Kassie, to forgo the American tradition of Christmas ham for turkey was no colossal compromise. Kassie was stressed but in the good sense of the word.

Davis was out with his father, who kept him busy and away for the day. They were to pick up various supplies while his mother played host to many other friends gathered around to discuss multiple topics, from the weather to the royal family. Kassie had excused herself for a few minutes to reflect on the past five years.

Alone in their bedroom, she reminisced and fingered the dried flower bouquet of her wedding day. It had been a quiet affair in the Episcopal Church in Hadenville. They honeymooned in a village in Tuscany and then settled in a small town just north of Windsor, England, in Berkshire. That put Davis close to his office in London and just far enough away so he could come home and relax at the end of the day.

Davis's family was welcoming of Kassie for the most part. It had been touch and go in the beginning. His mother was skeptical and cautious, not because of the age difference but of his union with a foreigner. As fate would have it, Davis was born late in life, and Kassie's charm slowly won her over as the daughter she never had. Their age difference was never discussed, especially after Davis told them the issue was "dead on arrival" as soon as he'd seen Kassie.

Kassie adapted to life in England a lot easier than she'd imagined. Driving on the left side of the road took some getting used to. Still, the nearby village allowed her to ride her bike whenever she needed to go anywhere, so getting used to navigating traffic differently than in the States, or Colonies as the British termed it, became second nature to her.

In the past five years, except for a few more gray hairs, she hadn't changed in appearance. Davis had become more handsome with age. He had grown into his looks, and the gray hairs that sprouted in his dark hair, especially around the temples, gave him an air of sophistication most men craved, and women swooned over.

Electronics issues were a thing of the past. Kassie's laptop, which had been replaced long ago by a new one, didn't seem to have a mind of its own. Because they were outdoor people, and the now-defunct YouTube channel had served its purpose, the need for television wasn't necessary. The mystery of what occurred with her electronic devices was never discussed much. They adopted the term "ghost in the machines" for the nuisance it had caused. But Kassie secretly felt what occurred was far more special than she could comprehend. Could it be that her parents had intervened through the electronic instruments, using AI technology, to direct her to the place of peace she had found with Davis? It was too much to dwell on for long, and as far-fetched as that notion might be, she liked to think—maybe.

The only sad spot to all this was the loss of Trixie. Kassie was heartbroken and still grieved at the thought of her. The idea of getting another dog was put off for months on end. Kassie wasn't ready. It would betray Trixie's memory to her, and Kassie just couldn't do that. So, it was just she and Davis for the next few years. Today, Kassie wanted to give him as much joy as he had given her. The more she thought of him, the more she was glad to have accepted him into her life.

The subject of children had been brought up a time or two, but in the end, they settled on remaining childless. The only stipulation was he would move heaven and earth to make that happen if she wanted them badly enough. For now, she was content. Her husband and the life they had built together made her very happy.

⚬⚬⚬

It was almost time for the festivities to begin. Kassie didn't dress for the occasion. It wouldn't do to doll up for her husband. The Blakemores were of landed gentry whose family estate and farms had been divvied up long ago, but their name and crest remained. They lived simply, and that was how they wanted to be viewed. Kassie had accepted this way of life. It felt natural and right.

Kassie was jolted out of her reverie by shouts from Davis's mother, Cora. "Here they are, everybody! Kassie, remember to act normal when he arrives," she reminded her.

Kassie ran down from upstairs, smiled, then winked in Cora's direction and opened the door to greet Davis. He stood just outside the car with his dad, Jonathan, close behind. Standing in the cold, misty afternoon, Davis gave her a wicked smile. *God, my husband is simply incredible.*

"There's my girl. Wait right there a minute," Davis said as Jonathan went to the back passenger-side door and opened it to the delight of a border collie puppy, who yipped and ran straight to Kassie.

"Oh my God, Davis!" Kassie exclaimed.
"Do you like her? Find her a name then," Davis said as he moved closer.

By this time, Kassie had picked up the puppy, who wiggled and licked her face with kisses from a wet tongue.

"Hang on a minute. I haven't had my turn yet," Davis said playfully to the dog. He warmly kissed Kassie, which embarrassed his father, who excused himself to go inside the house full of guests secretly waiting.

"I love her, my goodness, what a wag!" Kassie laughed as they held the dog together and scratched her behind her ears. "It's your birthday today, not mine. What gives?"

"I know, but I wanted to give you something special to make you happy."

"You make me happy, honey. I don't need anything else. We talked about this."

"Yes, we did, but here she is. I know she'll make a grand addition to our home." Davis put his arm around Kassie with the puppy between them, who seemed to settle down a bit as he kissed Kassie again. She returned it as best she could, but it was a bit clumsy, with the puppy wanting to get in on the action.

"Oh my Lord!" Kassie said as she held the puppy out for a full view. "I might need to call you Kitt. How about that? You like that name? Play on the word *kiss*?"

"Kitt it is! I like it. Let's go inside, darling. It's cold."

"I love you, Davis."

"I love you more, sweetheart."

As the afternoon slowly turned into twilight, in the December of their fifth year of marriage, Davis walked Kassie into their home to the sudden shout of "Surprise!"

Kassie then whispered, "Surprise" in Davis's ear. The day was as much of a surprise to her as it was to him because she realized she had slowly let unconditional happiness and love into her life. No self-imposed restrictions, regretted pasts, or what-if futures— just the here and now with Davis, family, and friends.

Davis looked into her eyes and with telepathic comprehension, interlocked his fingers with hers, and said, "It will always be—you and me."

The End

OTHER STORIES

———◦◦◦———

BY

DONNA LAWRENCE

THE CRUSH

I was seven years old when I saw Marcie for the first time in 1975. As I clambered out of my uncle Tony's car, three matchbox muscle cars in hand—there she stood. I'd heard a lot about her because my parents often spoke about things as if I wasn't there. But nothing could prepare me for my preadolescent reaction when faced with the real thing. In my mind, she was perfect. She was my first crush.

With her wide-toothed grin and wavy black hair cut below her ears that shone in the sun, light golden-brown skin, and deep, expressive brown eyes, it was love at first sight. I trembled and shied away when she reached out to shake my hand. I continued to stare but didn't dare for long. Eventually, I closed my mouth for fear of blurting out something weird.

"Vincent, say something. What's wrong with you?" my uncle Tony asked.

"I think he's shy or scared of me," Marcie said.

"Are you kidding? He was talking a blue streak before I pulled up—"

"Hi, Vincent, or is it Vinny?" she said. "I'm Marsha, but you can call me Marcie if you'd like. All my friends do. Glad to meet you."

Her soothing voice took me by surprise, and I almost fainted. A light breeze floated by us and brought with it a fresh and powdery scent that was all her. Her laughter was utterly infectious. Marcie's café au lait complexion told me she was not like us. I didn't care. Whatever she was, it added to her beauty and complemented Uncle Tony's dark good looks.

From that day on, I had to be around her whenever possible. She was generous, kind, and funny. Because she spoke her mind, I knew not to lie to her or try to get away with anything. She could see through the nonsense. Not only was she pretty, she was smart. As a teacher, she was curious about… well… everything. She understood my struggle with math and history and helped channel my imagination and focus without much effort.

My dad's medical practice kept him away most days, and because I was an only child, I was often lonely. One day, Marcie brought over a rubber ball, and we played catch with my uncle— almost all afternoon. It was the best day ever! She was a girl, all right, who loved my uncle very much. I was jealous, and it showed—a lot.

To my childhood mind, Marcie was magnificent! After a few visits, I found all I wanted to do was either run and hide or climb onto her lap and smother her with puppy dog kisses. That was if she'd let me, which she didn't. I often squeezed between her and Uncle Tony just to be near her. When Marcie wasn't around, I wanted to know why or where she was. I just *had* to talk to her, and when I did, I blathered on without anyone else getting a word in edgewise. Within the year, I'd call her on the phone and beg her to come over and go on outings with us.

She also had a knack for disengaging from a situation without hurting anyone's feelings. Being a good listener didn't hurt either. She was really good at that too. My uncle and mom teased me about my crush, but I didn't care. It must have embarrassed Marcie; God only knew how she stood it with such grace. It felt like she was already a part of my Sicilian American family, and I couldn't brag enough about her to my friends. Yep, I had a crush of the worst kind.

I was sure I would marry her one day, but Uncle Tony was in the way. I was a brat and a nuisance at times, but you see—I wanted Marcie all to myself. However, that was unlikely. After a while, I decided Uncle Tony and I could love Marcie together, and I'd be just fine. Or so I thought until the month before I turned eight. My loyalty, love of family, and values at that tender age were about to be tested.

⟿⊙⊙⊙⟾

My grandma's brother, Great-Uncle Leo from New York, had come to visit during the Easter holiday. After my parents and I had attended Easter morning Mass, we met Grandma, Uncle Tony, and Great-Uncle Leo for breakfast at a local neighborhood restaurant. I hardly ate anything because I was excited about the afternoon Easter egg hunt and Marcie coming for dinner. I even thought I might share the solid chocolate bunny with her if she wanted. What a day it would be! But a strange thing happened when I expressed that feeling to my family over bacon and eggs.

"I can't wait for Marcie to come eat with us. Won't that be great!"

I can't recall the feeling exactly. It was a shift, like a subtle change in electrical current as it moved through the air. I instinctively knew I was about to encounter something that would test my belief in my universe and of others in it. The event is forever etched in my mind because it was not so much what was said—but what was not.

In his thick New York accent, Great-Uncle Leo said, "We don't break bread wid dem—moulinyans. Lauwn jockeys belong on the lauwn, not in our houses wid us." He never looked up from shoveling food in his mouth as he said this.

At the round table, Uncle Leo sat between my grandmother and me; I was on his left. I looked back and forth between the faces at the table, but no one said anything. And, except for Uncle Tony, who stared out the window, they all continued to eat. I didn't know what a *moulinyan* or lauwn jockey was; however, my grandmother, who looked sickened, sensed my confusion and explained.

"Vinny, a *moulinyan* is Italian for the eggplants we eat occasionally. But my brother also uses that word to refer to Black people. We have to respect Leo's wishes on this visit and not allow Marcie to come for dinner." Then Grandma shrugged.

"I still don't understand." I looked up at Uncle Leo and asked, "Why can't Marcie come over for dinner? She ain't done nothing to you."

"Youse too young to understand. Shat up and eat you eggs," Uncle Leo responded.

"But—"

"Look youse!" Uncle Leo pointed his fork toward me and continued, "Let me explain the finer points o' life wid youse."

As he talked, I looked around the table. My grandmother gave up trying to eat while listening to Uncle Leo's explanation. My mother stared down at her plate. My father looked on, a little concerned about the fork in my face. But Uncle Tony looked worse. He looked unhappy, uncomfortable, and powerless. Uncle Tony wouldn't look at anyone. I instantly felt sad and protective of him.

I disliked Uncle Leo intensely at that moment. Never in my short life had the issue of race been explained to me. Not like this! Oh yeah, I knew there were "them" and "us." I knew we all looked different and some dramatically so. I also knew there were various kinds of people in other parts of the world and even in my school. There were Black, White, Asian, Hispanic, and Native American kids. There were also Italian, Jewish, and German people. But I was never told what I was being told then. The ugly truth of separate but equal that still existed in some parts of our modern world made no sense to me. To be told they couldn't eat with us at our homes, let alone marry outside their *kind*, I didn't like. No, sir! I didn't like it one little bit.

I hit Uncle Leo. I struck him with my fist. Hard. I hated him for trying to make me dislike Marcie, the love of my life. I hit him for saying nasty things about her in front of my family and Uncle Tony. I hit him because he hurt my feelings, and what he had to say was *just* not true! He hurt Marcie's feelings; even though she wasn't there, I knew she hurt just the same. I socked him so hard his nose bled. I kicked him and kept on kicking and punching him. The restaurant was in an uproar as I kept yelling at Uncle Leo, saying, "I *hate* you! Take it *back*! *Take it back!*"

All that anger spilled out from a boy of seven and a half. The rage was directed at my family, a great-uncle I barely knew, and Uncle Tony, who didn't have the courage or nerve to strike out at him for Marcie's sake. I fought for Marcie, and I fought for Uncle Tony. Then I cried. I cried for myself and my innocent world, which had been shattered. I loved Marcie. Unconditionally, I loved her. Now I was told I could not.

I can't imagine what Uncle Tony went through that day or what he must have thought of me. The conflict of emotion and frustration must have been overwhelming. I suppose he thought the wisdom he had accumulated over the years had led him astray. I don't know. All I knew then was that he looked defeated before I struck out against ignorance.

The rest of the day was confusing and annoying. The remainder of my great-uncle's stay was a time of making up and coming to grips with my new understanding of the world. It wasn't until Uncle Leo's visit had ended that I saw Marcie again.

They lied to her. I watched my family fabricate an elaborate tale of how busy they had been and "had no time to entertain others with the house already overrun with visitors." But she was no fool. As I said, Marcie could see through the nonsense. The fact that she was gracious in accepting what she was told endeared her to me more than ever.

However, I drifted away from her, not because I wanted to but out of embarrassment and need for perspective. I tried to put it all together to have it make sense. The *why* of it, the unfairness of it. I didn't want to lie to her or blurt out the truth. Her eyes would force that out of me, so I avoided her at all costs. I wonder if she thought my crush had faded. Maybe it had.

◦◦◦

Through the years, I watched Uncle Tony wrestle with many issues; however, his love for Marcie was never one of them. My family grew in wisdom and changed after that day. They were good people and had learned a great lesson. I never heard anyone speak of Great-Uncle Leo again. In time, I grew up and, as young kids do, came to my own understanding of the way of things.

I reminisce over that experience now because I'm about to marry. I stand here waiting for a wonderful girl to come down the aisle to meet me and take my last name. I've grown into a successful young man who didn't follow in his father's footsteps but went his own way into the business of law. My parents, grandmother, and uncle are happy for me. I am reminded of many things as I look out at them all in Saint Paul's Cathedral, even of old Great-Uncle Leo. He sits among them, much older and, I think, wiser. I see the faces of those who love me, but there is one whose gaze I lock onto for a long time. That of Marcie.

She sits there next to my uncle Antonio Gianni, the man I used to refer to as Uncle Tony. They've been married for twenty years, and she looks happy; I know he is because he told me. I smile to myself, remembering the conversation. I wonder if she knows how much she is loved by Uncle Tony and everyone who knows her. I wonder if she knows she was fought over and won by a determined little boy who, at seven and a half, would let nothing stand in the way of his beliefs. Of course she does, is my revelation as she nods and winks at me.

That determination has held me in good stead in my chosen profession. I often reflect on those times and that day's events, though I've never discussed it. The episode shed light on what could be done and accomplished. It gave voice to a coward and raised the bar for all in my family to follow and emulate. I don't say these things to be grandiose. I say them because they are true.

I say these things and think about those days because loving Marcie unconditionally gave me the model to live by today as I watch my bride walk down the aisle to meet me. I hope we have half the love that Uncle Tony and Marcie share. God, hear my prayer.

The End

MISS AMERICA IS NO MORE

I was twelve, almost thirteen, the day it happened in the hot summer of 1973. My sister, Anne, was six, and Francine was my best friend. My name is Shirley. When I was a little girl, I thought my name was Shirley Ann because whenever my mother called us, she said, "Shirley Ann, come here." I didn't know she was actually saying, "Shirley, Anne, come here." I was always referred to by other names, like Sheila, Shar, and Lee Lee, to name a few. I didn't mind those names so much. But Francine's mother never called me anything but "Miss America," which was annoying.

Don't she know there ain't no Black Miss America? In the early '70s, it wasn't allowed and never would be. That was what I thought anyway. It was embarrassing to hear her say, "Well, look at Miss America," or "Well if it ain't Miss America." I suppose she meant well, but I never understood why she called me that. The moniker should have been given to her daughter, Francine. She was beautiful!

Francine didn't seem to mind her mother giving me this kind of compliment, which made her all the more beautiful in my eyes. She had a delightful spirit and cared about everything and everyone. As an only child, she had nothing else to occupy her time but to hang out at our house. Francine was a caring soul; if not for her, I wouldn't care as much about others as I did, least of all my troublesome baby sister.

My parents ran a boarding house with many guests from all over the country. Francine never complained about helping out with chores at our house. Like a family member, she was always around, willing to do whatever was required, often without being asked. Francine and I were considered the "responsible ones." We were the ones who made sure the work my parents did during the summer months was smooth and without much bother. We were polite and quiet. That is if Anne wasn't around.

Our house seemed enormous to me. As kids, we had many rooms to get lost in and play. Whenever Francine and I were together, my little sister always wanted to play along or go places with us. Because I was older, it was my job to look after her, which was easier said than done with her mischievous ways. She constantly got into trouble with the pranks she'd pull. Usually, I could stop her antics before they got out of hand, like when she chewed a wad of candy and then placed the sticky mess under the doorknob of a dining room used by dinner guests. I found the gooey mound and dislodged it before anyone found out. Or that time I saw her hiding to watch a sleepy guest stumble out of bed to the bathroom without realizing she had placed thumbtacks on the floor for them to step on. Quick thinking got us out of that mess! The guest was none the wiser.

At those times, I wished I could lock her in a closet for a while, long enough for her to realize what a pain she was. But what good would it do? It would only make her behave worse, or she'd resent me in the end. Aside from Francine, it was just the two of us, and we had to look after each other, especially when boredom was a constant companion. Anne seemed to be bored all the time.

In our small town, many people traveled through on their way to vacation spots such as Mammoth Cave, horse farms in Lexington or Louisville, or southeast to the Cumberland Gap. When allowed, which was seldom, I got a chance to sit on the steps of our front porch and listen to visitors talk about their travels, where they came from, where they were going, and what they'd like to see. Mostly, they wanted to talk about themselves. I suppose having a listening ear allowed them to explore the hidden meaning behind the need to travel to places far from their homes. When they spoke, I could tell by their expressions and the light shining from within them how excited they were to travel to another place and explore. The anticipation of traveling was infectious, and I couldn't wait to grow up and travel to faraway places from home. But not too far.

When the conversation turned to comments on my appearance and how wonderful it would be if I grew up to be a movie star or someone famous, my mother would interrupt. Thankfully, she'd change the discussion to other topics. She was very skillful. I would slip away during those times, recognizing it was my time to check on Anne again.

My parents were always gracious, accommodating, and considerate of their guests' needs. Mom seemed to know what they needed before they knew or asked for anything, which was nice. She always ensured they had a pleasant stay and were well-fed and rested. Mom always said my father was a "man's man." She said it was because he provided directions and made sure their cars were what he termed *road-ready*, checking their tires and such. That was his way of ensuring their vehicles had no unforeseen mechanical problems before they went on their way. He was always there with a smile and handshake when each guest departed to points unknown.

On this particular Saturday, my father was busy attending to things other than watching out for us and Anne's shenanigans. We had only one guest who had already taken off early. It was a slow day, freeing my parents to do other domestic chores they wouldn't have had a chance to do otherwise. While I helped Mom clean and change the bedding, Anne only watched or got in the way of progress. It was exhausting work, but the payoff was well worth it. The next day, Sunday, meant a lazy day of doing nothing.

The afternoon sun shone bright as Francine and I sat on the front porch swing. Francine's mother worked part-time at the rail station. Her father was a railroad porter who was hardly ever home. Her parents were seldom around, and because of this, she was free to come to visit with us often.

It was Francine's thirteenth birthday, and she wanted to show off a locket she'd received from her parents. It was beautifully etched on one side and perfectly caught the sun's light. The inside contained a photo of her mother on one side and her dad on the other. I secretly wanted a bracelet and was envious of her locket.

"Gosh, I wish I had something like that. It's *so* pretty. Maybe I'll get a charm bracelet for my birthday. I keep hinting at it, but no one ever says anything."

"Typical," Francine said, then sighed. "I was surprised to get this. I never said anything at all, and then there it was."

"Dang!"

"It's not as pretty as you, though," Francine said with a genuine smile, trying to change the subject. "You'll get the bracelet. I just know."

"You think so?" I asked expectantly.

"I *know* so," was her definitive answer.

"How?"

"As pretty as you are, I'm sure of it."

"Well, I'm not gonna get my hopes up. I wish all that 'pretty' talk would go away."

"Why? Ain't you glad people think of you that way?"

"No!" My annoyance was hard to hide. "It's like that's *all* there is to me. You're pretty too! But people see you for more than that—like I do. Me? All they seem to see is a *pretty* girl. It ain't fair."

"What ain't fair is you not appreciating what God gave you— or what your parents gave you through Him. Lighten up, okay? One day, you'll wish for it more than ever."

We went on talking in this way as the afternoon wore on, discussing everything from the best way to catch lightning bugs at dusk and how to avoid chigger bites to stupid boys at school. We never gave Anne a second thought. If I had known then what I know now, things would have turned out differently than they had. Francine and I were nearby but not close enough to see what Anne was getting into. But apparently, the smell of kerosene was too much for Anne to ignore.

<hr>

The sides of our house sloped to the backyard, giving the underside of the house a higher profile than was seen from the front. The unfinished basement was poorly insulated, and the foundation was made of exposed wooden beams and vinyl flooring. An outside door was the only access to that part of the house, which held boxes, books, dollhouses, old furniture, unused and forgotten toys, and paint. My father used it as a place to hide things away. He promised to convert it into a workshop one day, but a few years later, it still held old and used stuff, musty-smelling with age. It was considered "under the house." I never liked going down there. I don't think my dad did either.

Far under the house and away from view, Anne sat with a large can of kerosene and began investigating its contents. Troublesome as she was, she wasn't aware of the dangers it could cause if not handled carefully. The grunts she'd made trying to open the can of the stuff with her tiny hands should have been heard by all of us, especially above her in the kitchen. Still, with the clanging of pots and pans overhead, they were not. With a heavy sigh from exhaustion, Anne decided to get something to help leverage the strength she did not have.

As she ran from under the house, she was unaware her efforts had paid off. The can fell over and knocked into a container of turpentine with a much looser lid than the kerosene she had been fiddling with. The mixture flowed freely and pooled around the base of the beams holding the floors above in place. The sour smell of the contents filled the space as the liquid found its way close to the boiler and furnace next to the pipes that fed gas to the kitchen stove above.

<hr>

My mother opened the screen door and yelled, "Shirley, Anne, come on in now! It's time for supper." Surprised I was within earshot on the front porch, she said, "Oh, honey, I didn't know you were so close. Francine, you're welcome to stay if you'd like."

"Yes, ma'am, that'd be fine. Mom has to work tonight, so I don't think she'll mind, plus it's my birthday!" Francine replied, trying to sound happy. I knew all too well how sad not being with her mother made her, especially that day. But you would never know by looking at her.

"Well, happy birthday, sweetheart! Why didn't you say so earlier? I could have baked something special for you." Mom walked over to us with her hands on her hips and asked, "Where is your sister, Shirley?" She looked around, concerned. "Where's Anne?"

"I don't know." I shrugged. "She was around here a minute ago. Maybe she's inside playing hide-and-seek by herself." I wasn't sure if that was true, but I didn't care. I thought I'd seen her flit inside right before Mom called to us—but I couldn't be certain.

"Anne?" Mom called out again. "Where'd she get off to now?" Mom asked no one in particular.

"I'm here, Mama." Anne appeared in time to answer my mother's concern. "I came to get something." I wasn't sure why Anne said the rest of what she had, but Mom was perplexed.

"Get what?" Mom asked.

"Just something I needed."

"And what would that be, Anne Marie?"

"This!" Anne answered, pulling from behind her back a big pair of pliers.

"Give me that," my mother said, taking the pliers from Anne's tiny hands. "What *in the world* are you doing with these? Girl, let me put them back before your daddy finds out you were rooting around in his toolbox. I swear!" Mom said in exasperation, then turned to me. "Shirley, keep a better eye on your sister, please." Then Mom left us on the front porch, looking at each other.

"What are you up to?" I asked Anne.

"Nothing. I just needed some help."

"Help with what?" I demanded to know.

"I can't *tell* you," Anne answered. "It's nothing anyway." She demurred while looking down at her shoes.

I meant to ask more, but Mom's admonishment silenced me. "Y'all get in here now before this food gets cold."

"Yes, ma'am," we said in unison. The incident was quickly forgotten.

The day had been a hot one. After a dinner of pork chops, mashed potatoes, and green beans, it was time to get ready for bed. There was no further need to light the gas stove, but the furnace was constantly used to heat the water in the tank below the house.

"What *is* that smell?" my mother asked of my dad while taking our plates away.

"I don't smell anything. You and your nose, Dorothy. I keep saying you smell stuff most folks pay no mind to."

"Well, I smell something just the same, Jerry. I get a whiff of it every now and then. You sure there's nothing under the house done spilled or spoiled in this heat?"

"I was down there earlier, and all seemed fine. That downstairs door stays shut, good and tight, but sometimes the lock doesn't work to well." Then, scratching his head, he said as an afterthought, "Hmm, I think I shut the door. It could be a skunk got in, maybe." He sighed. "I'll check before we go to bed tonight."

"You do that, thank you. Let me get these children up to bed before closing up. I need to get things ready for guests coming in tomorrow. Gonna be a full house. I thought about putting coffee on, but it's too hot. Iced tea?"

"Yes, ma'am, I'll take some!" Dad stood and stretched. "I'll be out on the porch before long. I need to wrap up a few things; check downstairs, like I said, then get me some of that tea before bed."

"Thank you, sugar. Shirley, Anne, come on. Francine, you get on now before it gets too dark and your mama starts worrying."

"Yes, Miss Dorothy. Thank you for dinner," Francine replied.

"Good dinner, darlin'," my dad said as he kissed Mom on the cheek.

I wasn't quite ready for bed and waited until Anne bathed before I took my turn. Francine lived just around the corner, so it wasn't unusual for us to linger after dinner. As I sat on the front porch with Francine, listening to the sounds of the katydids and occasional car traffic, I saw my father saunter down the hill toward the basement under the house.

Then I smelled what Mom had mentioned and thought more about what it might be.

"Do you smell that?" Francine asked, sniffing the air.

"Yeah. Wonder why it's stronger out here than inside."

"Smells like turpentine my daddy uses sometimes when he has to paint our house."

"Really?" I asked, screwing up my nose at the acrid odor.

"Yeah." Then she sighed. "I wish he was home more. I miss him. Well, I should get going," Francine said quickly before I could comment. Then she exclaimed, "Oh wait. I forgot my locket! It's inside. I'll be right back."

She had taken her locket off to show my parents during dinner. I was disappointed she was leaving so soon. But maybe she wanted to leave because of the smell or to avoid saying more about her home situation with her parents being gone so much. Either way, I didn't want her to leave just then.

One fault my dad had was saying he would do one thing but then get sidetracked and start doing something else. That day was no different. While I waited outside for Francine to return, he came up the hill and asked,

"Do you know what I did with those oil pans?"

"No, sir. How should I know?" I shrugged.

"No need for sass, young lady. Are you okay? You're mighty quiet this evening."

"I'm fine. Sorry, Daddy. I'm just feeling… I don't know. Just thinking about Francine's birthday gift is all. It's so pretty."

"You got your own birthday coming up soon, don't you?"

"Yes, sir!" After saying this more enthusiastically than necessary, I put on my best smile. Daddy chuckled and changed the subject.

"I wonder where those pans got off to. Damn if I can find them out here, excuse my language, sweetie." He stooped to look under the lattice skirt of the front porch. "I think I know what's smelling to high heaven, and I need to dispose of it properly. Course, I can't be sure, but I don't think it's a dead animal. Anything's possible."

"You didn't go see?"

"No, not yet. I have a suspicion, but I need those pans first." He seemed more preoccupied with moving stuff around under the porch than answering more questions.

"I'll go see if Mom knows." I was tired of waiting for Francine anyway and used this as an excuse to find out what was taking her so long.

"Good. I'll keep looking around to see if I can find 'em before it gets too dark to see," Dad said.

Mom was admiring Francine's locket and holding it in her hands when I found them. By the embarrassed look on Francine's face, I could tell she had spilled the beans about me wanting something just as lovely. It would be just like her, but I was annoyed all the same.

"Well, I do declare. I just can't stop looking at it," Mom said as I got closer.

I didn't say anything in reply. I stood there waiting to be rescued from blurting out my heart's desire for a bracelet. That's when Francine came to my rescue.

"I-I-I was just saying how nice it might be for you to get one or something like it," Francine stuttered.

Amid the discussion of the locket, we could hear Anne splashing, blubbering, and chatting away to her rubber duckie in the tub upstairs.

"Hmm, I don't know," Mom said to Francine. "We'll see what comes after this summer season is over." Then she winked and asked me, "How come you never told me about this new crush of yours? Francine had a lot to share on that score—and you?"

"Francine! I can't tell you *anything* anymore—"

"Don't go getting all upset," Mom said. "It was a harmless piece of information—"

The discussion was shattered by horrific screams from upstairs.

⚬⚬⚬

We ran up the stairs, me taking them two at a time, to the bathroom. Flames traveled up the exposed water pipes behind the toilet and spread across the linoleum floor. It was curling back the charred remains of the flooring while Anne stood in the tub, screaming at the top of her lungs, clutching her duckie. I stared at the blue-and-white tentacles of flame as they licked the air.

My mother reached for Anne and pulled her out of the tub. I heard "Run!" just before the explosion rocked the house. The concussion knocked us back and out of the bathroom. Flames were everywhere, as was the sheeting from the house and fallen beams. The whole side of the house and ceiling was either gone or caved in on top of us. Francine was on the floor, not moving. My mother and sister were struggling to get up. I thought of getting out. Fast.

Smoke filled the air and our lungs. Mom pushed me ahead as I navigated what remained of the stairs. Once down, I could not reach the door fast enough, then my thoughts returned to

Francine. She was left on the floor upstairs. I quickly turned to go back for her. I knew it was no use, but I had to try.

My mother instinctively knew my intentions and tried to prevent me from returning. I pulled away from my mother's grasp, knowing she was screaming for me to not go up, but I couldn't hear her—the explosion had caused temporary deafness. Daddy was pushing Mom away to safety outside, but even his grappling attempt to grab me was ineffective. Mom was safe enough with Anne in her arms, but Francine was not.

The smoke was thick, and the stair treads were few but sufficient for me to reach the top. Francine was groaning on the floor and too hurt to stand. The flames were close, burning near her back and across her flank. I reached for her with my right hand. The searing pain where the flames grabbed at my hand and arm was excruciating. But after a while, I felt nothing. Francine grabbed my upper right arm and hoisted herself up. With my left arm, I encircled her, and we moved as best we could down the now barely there staircase. The flames surrounded us, and smoke, black as night, filled the space at the bottom of the stairs. Then, I felt a strong push from behind.

The falling beam missed my back, but just barely. It hit Francine hard. I tried with all my might to lift the shaft that fell on her, but it wouldn't budge. Then smoke flashed over, and that's when the flames were on me, my body, back, and head. I ran screaming, leaving Francine alone. All alone. I was in pain, too much pain, flaming red and hot.

⟴

I remember a locket shining bright in the sun. It was years ago, but I remember her smile, laughter, and girlie giggle. A life snuffed out in an instant. We were young. I have no regrets. My parents are still with me and were unharmed on that horrible day. It was the Lord's will. Dad had waited for my return at the front of the house when the explosion occurred. It was he who tackled me to the ground the day I ran from the burning house, on fire and terrified of dying. My recovery had been painful and slow.

My sister was irresponsible and paid a heavy price for her actions. After a thorough investigation, my parents suffered greatly for their supposed "lack of guidance" according to child welfare. It was my parents whom the law had looked unfavorably upon. Anne was taken from us until my parents could prove fit to continue to have her under their care. Like all of us, Anne had been traumatized by the event, and rightly so. All she could comprehend was that the house had exploded without explanation, and she had been ripped from her parents' home for no good reason. It took a while for her to understand how her actions had contributed to an explosion that took the life of Francine.

Forgiveness has been difficult, but I've learned to let go over the years. Miss America would have forgiven Anne readily, but Miss America died that day. My sister and I communicate now only on an occasional basis. Through years of therapy and careful counseling, Anne has grown into a lovely young woman, more responsible and compassionate. Her curious mind has led her to study medicine, specializing in treating burn patients. I suppose that's only fitting.

I've learned to write left-handed. A white glove always covers my right hand. Always a white glove. My husband is not allowed to look at my back, and the wig I wear hides the scars on my head. I was lucky he came into my life, and the two children I bore him tell me I am blessed. One we call Frannie, short for Francine, and the other Marie.

The flames missed the front of me, so my face was spared. The tremendous push from behind me that day has remained a mystery, somewhat. All I know is that Francine was with me, by my side, as we came down the barely there stairs. In the shock of events, had I *actually* reached her in time? I'm haunted by the memory. I suppose I've always known the truth behind the push that saved me. But I hold that secret close to my heart and will until my dying day.

Even though she's lost so much, Francine's mother still calls me Miss America. Now I don't mind it so much. I wonder if she continues to do so in memory of Francine or to bolster my spirit.

I visit her often and know she relies on me for comfort. I will always be there for her. She still thinks I'm beautiful. I have no comment on that.

I was twelve, almost thirteen, the day it happened. My sister, Anne, was six, and Francine was my best friend. My parents did right by others. My sister was mischievous as a child. It was my job to look after her. It was long ago. All I know is I had a wonderful friend with a beautiful soul. And that memory has to be enough for me.

The End

MILLIE & THE STRANGER

Surprise!

Cheryl hyperventilated whenever she rode in a car that moved more than twenty miles per hour. Beginning in childhood, she suffered through this until her grandmother came up with the idea of having her sit in the passenger seat instead of the back whenever they traveled anywhere. She reasoned Cheryl would feel more comfortable if she could see the roadway. It worked.

In high school, Cheryl took a class in driver education and excelled. The instruction was helpful because she learned a lot about road safety; besides, there was no one else to teach her. Cheryl's father died when she was young, and her mother's work schedule didn't allow much time to teach her how to drive. Cheryl was a cautious driver and observed the rules of the road well. She watched the speed limits and followed them religiously. But at night, she secretly dreaded having to drive the next day, which caused her palms to sweat at the thought. Once behind the wheel, her heart pounded wildly against her chest and wouldn't stop until she pressed her foot on the accelerator.

These were the times she'd talk to herself. *Don't grip the wheel too tightly. Don't brake too hard, and watch out for others. Remember to look frequently into the rear and side view mirrors.* Only after this self-talk had calmed her nerves did Cheryl feel relatively in control. Her fear eased up a bit, but only just a bit.

She obtained her driving license at seventeen and bravely practiced driving around town with her terrified boyfriend in tow. When she graduated from high school in 1975, she received a surprise scholarship to attend college in a small town in Kentucky. Her grandmother had already given her a bracelet of exquisite beauty to remind her of who she was and where she came from.

Cheryl would never expect anything from her mother because she knew they couldn't afford much. So, a special gift from her was more than she had bargained for. What she had received was enough, so what else could there be?

"Close your eyes, or you'll ruin the surprise," her mother said, steering Cheryl in the direction she needed to go. She was prepared to accept whatever gift her mother had to give with grace and humility. Cheryl took no chances at peeking.

"Now stand still. Keep your eyes closed until I say when. Okay?"

Cheryl nodded but heard distinct nervousness in her mother's voice. *Why are we outside, of all places? Why is Mom nervous?* She dutifully kept her eyes tightly shut until given the word.

"Open your eyes!"

Then she heard a loud swooshing sound as a covering was removed. Cheryl opened her eyes to other family friends' shouts of, "Surprise!" Before her, near the curb of the house, was parked a 1966 Ford Mustang, black with red leather seats and chrome details and wheel rims. Many oohs and aahs emanated from the group of onlookers.

"Oh my gosh!" Cheryl was stunned.

"What do you think, honey?" her mother asked.

"It's a car. Why a car, Mom?"

"Well, I thought you'd love it."

"I… do… but you know how it is with me and vehicles—"

"But you've done so well over the years. I thought you were over all that foolishness."

"I suppose so, but oh my goodness!"

Just then, her mother's friend Ace, who happened to be the local small-town mechanic, spoke up.

"I drove it over for the surprise, so let me show you what she's made of, huh?" he asked.

"All right," Cheryl answered, still in awe. Was it her, or did she really sense the car was pleased she was its owner? Cheryl had never felt this from an inanimate object, let alone one she was terrified to drive.

"Now, she needs a little work, just so you know," Ace said in his high-pitched gravelly voice. "I have an engine ready to install to make it run better than it does now. It has a few scratches on the outside; see 'em here? And look!" Ace said as he opened the trunk with a flourish to show the interior and what was hidden inside. "It has a trunk to store all your gear. It's not a fastback model, so no one can see what's inside. Here's where the spare tire goes. It's just a spare in case you get a flat, but you know that already. Just so… there it is. And over *here* is the jack to hike up the car and jumper cables just in case the battery dies."

"Wow! Ace, you thought of everything," Cheryl said. "But why do I need a new engine?"

"To give it more speed!" Ace said with a lot of enthusiasm.

"Do… I need it?" Cheryl asked with skepticism and hesitation.

"You getting one whether you like it or not," her mother added so that Cheryl knew it was a done deal.

"Go on, sit inside. See how she feels," Ace encouraged. Cheryl got in and immediately smelled a moldy, wet odor.

"Ewww, stinky!" Cheryl held her nose in disgust.

"Here's the thing," her mother said. "It has some flood damage, which is how I got it so cheap."

"That's the other reason for getting a new engine—I don't trust this one," Ace said, chiming in. "Once we clean it up, it should be just fine."

Cheryl heard the nervous chuckle in her mother's voice and felt embarrassed for her. So Cheryl focused on the shiny chrome surrounding the dashboard and automatic gearbox instead of the usual four-on-the-floor shifter. *Nice!* The red leather front bucket seats seemed to hug Cheryl like an old friend. Cheryl sat high and close enough to the steering wheel to see the road at the right height. Then Ace suggested she give it a spin.

"What? Now?" Cheryl asked.

"Yeah, *now*. I'll get in with you." Ace seemed eager to help her navigate the road in her new Mustang.

"I wanna go. I wanna go too," said a chorus of others gathered around.

"No, now, just me and her mom… if she wants," Ace admonished them as he motioned to Cheryl's mom.

Ace pulled the front passenger seat forward to allow her mother access to the back seat before he sat in the front and closed the door. With trembling hands, Cheryl put the key in the ignition and started the engine. It was a rough start, but after a while, she pulled slowly away and drove around the corner and down the street. However, the car's engine died when Cheryl returned to the house. Her disappointment was acute, but Ace said it was just as well.

"Good to get the kinks out and see how she runs," he said, then left to call for a tow.

Cheryl was relieved she wouldn't have to drive it for a while. She didn't feel she could trust herself behind the wheel alone. She didn't feel comfortable—at least not yet.

There were more discussions about the car and its safety. It occurred to Cheryl that she hadn't shown her gratitude in the initial excitement. So, taking the opportunity, she hugged her mother warmly as they waited for the truck to tow her "new" car away for repairs.

Millie

After a few weeks, Cheryl's car looked and smelled like new. The exterior was buffed and waxed; all signs of scratches and the moldy smell of wet, dirty socks were gone. The red leather seats and chrome trim had a high sheen, gleaming and bright. Cheryl could not be more pleased.

"I can't believe it's the same car!" Cheryl said, amazed at the transformation.

"Ain't she a beaut? Take a look at the power under this hood," Ace boasted. "Now, that's what I call a souped-up engine!" Ace stood back with a sideways grin and allowed Cheryl to peer inside. "Don't go doing 'Joe 50' in it until you get used to the feel and sensation of moving faster. That there's a new battery! It won't die on you again, so don't you worry."

"You do good work for very little money," Cheryl's mom said to Ace.

"Happy to do it. Not every day we have one of our own attend college. I'm just glad I can contribute in some way. It's my gift to you, young lady. Enjoy!"

"She looks like a million bucks! I think I'll call her Millie," Cheryl said, still amazed at the transformation.

"Well get in! Take me back to the shop, and then take Millie for a spin. Break her in, as they say! If anything goes wrong—I guarantee it won't—you know how to reach me," Ace said confidently while getting into the car.

After waving goodbye to Ace at the mechanic's shop, Cheryl put Millie in gear and pulled away. Alone with her fears and insecurities behind the wheel of her car, she could move at her own pace and then test the power under the hood. As Cheryl felt the pull of the car moving her forward, her anxiety began to seep away. She and her car became one. Cheryl felt in control and was determined to beat the demon back from her conscious mind and slay the dragon of fear, as it were.

The ride was exhilarating! Driving along the winding roads of Kentucky was indescribable. The previous anxiety, which had plagued her for so long, slowly dissipated. She thought how silly she had been to be so fearful all those years before. She thought maybe being alone and in complete control made her feel unafraid. Perhaps the feeling of freedom, driving to "who knew where," made the demons of fear fade. Whatever it was, she was glad of it. Whatever this newfound freedom was, she accepted it gladly. As the wind rushed through her hair and the car sped forward, she and Millie were one. Cheryl could only hope she would be a faithful steward to the care of the newly formed friendship she found in Millie.

<hr>

As summer gave way to autumn, Cheryl slowly realized her beautiful car was a clunker. Something always went wrong. Either the alternator or the drive chain, whatever that was, would go out or would have to be replaced. The oil filter was a used one, and who knew how long *that* would last? Her tires were retreads. She couldn't afford new spark plugs. The old ones had to be cleaned regularly so the connections to the distributor were kept tight— but the battery was still good. Driving home from Lexington one day, a tire blew out. Thank God she was able to maneuver to safety in time. She had to buy a new one, which set her mother back something awful. In Cheryl's mind, Ace was *not* the best mechanic, and in her opinion, shady dealing with false promises became his claim to fame.

Cheryl's summer job, retailing at JC Penney, was ending. As she prepared for college, Cheryl realized she had nothing to show for the long hours of work because it had all gone toward car repairs. Even though her fear of driving had gradually dissipated, it had been replaced with the frustration of constant maintenance and lack of money. Cheryl no longer referred to her car as Millie. She was just a car with a lot of problems.

Cheryl looked forward to attending college. Of course, she didn't want to leave her mother; however, facing a new world of learning, being away from home, living in a dorm, and making new friends was exciting. She'd need to find a job to put what her mother called "spending money" in her pocket. Nice thought but only if her car held up. Barring that, she feared all her money would be spent on car repairs.

Cheryl couldn't help being tearful the week before leaving for school. She cried at the least little thing. She was terrified her car would let her down, and the anxiety it brought was overwhelming. Her car had become costly and lost much of its luster and panache. To her dismay, this was her reality until her grandmother put things in perspective one day.

"I thought I'd find you here," Cheryl's grandmother said, joining her on the front porch swing.

"Hi, Grandma," Cheryl said while holding back tears threatening to fall from her eyes.

"Why so gloomy? You sad to be leaving tomorrow?" her grandmother asked. "Now don't you worry. With your personality, you'll make new friends in no time at that college. After a while, you'll forget all about us!"

"Oh, Grandma—" Cheryl's solemn sigh was a dead giveaway of her unhappiness.

"Don't tell me you're still afraid of driving after all this time. Your mother plans on following behind you, so there's no need to be afraid. Is that it?"

"No'am." Cheryl hitched, trying to prevent the tears from rising, but it was a losing battle. She sobbed, saying, "I just don't want to show up at a new school in a hooptie. It's embarrassing."

"Well, I'll be! A hooptie, you say? That car? I don't think so." Cheryl's grandmother reached out to hold her hand, then continued, "It may not be the shiny new toy you hoped for, but it's far from a hooptie. She's yours."

"But Millie breaks down all the time!" Cheryl said, wiping away her tears. "Ace had us fooled into thinking she was good as new.

He *lied*. I spend so much on repairs that I have nothing left, and Mom's broke."

"Shush now, young lady. You know what I think?" Cheryl shook her head, and then her grandmother continued, "That hunk of metal needs a lot of love. Nothing in this life comes easy. Didn't Ace say Millie needed some work? So he didn't *let on* about the maintenance issues you might face. Ever ask yourself why?"

"No, ma'am. But he shouldn't have lied."

"I think he wanted you to feel good about what your mother could afford. He has a big heart. He *and* your mom knew you must face your fear of driving *someday*. I think having your car has helped you do that, don't you think?"

"I don't think Millie will ever be whole again. I'll have to change her name. I call her Millie because she looked like a million dollars after Ace returned her the first time. Now, it'll *take* a million dollars to get her up to speed! I'm even starting to be afraid to drive again—"

"*You're* the one in control. If you're afraid, it's because—"

"But what if she *blows up* while I'm driving?" Cheryl jumped in, waving her arms to mimic an explosion.

"Blows up! From driving?" Her grandmother broke out in laughter. "Good Lord, I never heard of such a thing. Honey, I don't mean to laugh, but you have to admit the thought is ridiculous. I'm so sorry," her grandmother said through uncontrolled laughter, which she tried to suppress but snorted instead.

Cheryl joined in the laughing fit despite herself. "Okay. I see where you're going with this. I can see me now, driving and *kaboom*! It's not funny… but it is." The giggles soon subsided. With a sigh, Cheryl asked, "Grandma, what am I gonna do?"

"Take care of your car. It *is* yours. Or, if worse comes to worst, leave it here until we can ensure it's right as rain. Right now, it runs fairly well, doesn't it?"

"Yeah, but what about tomorrow?"

"Worry about that when it comes. Until then, love your car. Embrace your car. You'll be okay."

Then she placed an arm around Cheryl's shoulder, hugged her, and patted her arm as they gazed at the black Mustang near the curb.

New Beginnings

Cheryl had the sensation of flying as she drove along the Kentucky highway to college amid the beautiful and serene rolling hills. She was surprised at how easy it was to let go. Grandma was right. She loved driving her beloved Mustang. Her car had become a friend she didn't want to let go of or let down. She silently vowed to never allow her fear or embarrassment to overtake her again.

It was an hour's drive, and before Cheryl knew it, she'd arrived at her destination. Milford State University was sprawling for a small college with many buildings of various architectural styles and compositions. However, the layout was orderly and easy to navigate, so finding her dormitory didn't take long. While Cheryl sat in her car thinking about the drive she'd just had, she couldn't help but look up at the tall dormitory where she would live. Sandstone in color, the tower of rooms was arranged in a circular configuration and rose high overhead. Many students filed in and out of this building, which was a little intimidating.

"How was it?" Cheryl's mother asked, coming from her car in the next row alongside Millie. "Slow down next time. It was hard keeping up with you driving so fast."

"Was I?" Cheryl responded absentmindedly. "Will you look at this place?"

It was like stepping into an uncharted land full of wonders for Cheryl. Some students and their parents wandered around; others greeted old friends and welcomed new ones.

"It is beautiful. I like how the campus is laid out, but you didn't answer my question. How was the drive?"

"It was fine… just fine." Cheryl wanted to take it all in and felt the answer should satisfy her mother's curiosity about her well-being, at least for a while.

"Well, let's get you checked in, okay?"

"Yes, ma'am," Cheryl answered, looking around wide-eyed, mesmerized.

Cheryl's mother inspected the accommodations after checking in at the front office and finding her room. Cheryl was thrilled and satisfied with her room but sad at the same time as trepidation of being alone started to set in.

While they shared a tearful goodbye, her mother knitted her brow, showing mild concern. "I know you'll be fine, but I can't imagine being home without you. Be a good girl, study hard, and remember where you come from, okay?"

These words stayed with Cheryl long after her mother drove away. Embarrassed by her tears, Cheryl quickly wiped her face and headed inside to unpack. However, her sadness soon vanished when her assigned roommate, Evelyn, showed up. Cheryl was delighted with the match-up.

Susan and Jasmine seemed to be a perfect fit as suitemates. The four shared a bathroom, or suite, between the two rooms, which Cheryl thought was cool. They even helped each other unload their cars. Many were impressed with Millie. Cheryl's embarrassment melted when one guy was so taken with her car that he called it a classic and much better than a Volkswagen.

Cheryl made friends quickly. Her roommates seemed to like her as much as she did them. She was eager to transport her friends wherever they wanted to go: to the grocery, around town for shopping, or to impress a boy or two. She felt her first semester was off to a good start.

Her roommates were the best. They shared a lot: clothing, dating stories, cleaning duties, and grocery expenses. As an only child, Cheryl enjoyed the camaraderie and lighthearted teasing. Becoming a member of their sorority, Alpha Kappa Alpha, didn't hurt either. Her work at the downtown boutique provided spending money to buy new clothes and other items. Cheryl's scholarship covered extra expenses, such as books and meals in the cafeteria. Millie was holding up just fine, making Cheryl the envy of the campus. For now, she had no reason to spend more on car repairs. In the meantime, she had more important things to consider, like her studies, boys, clothes, and sorority events.

During the spring of her first year, Cheryl, her roommates, and Susan's friend Bette, who had a refined Southern drawl, were shopping at the local A&P. After placing the groceries in Millie's trunk, they talked about grabbing a bite at the local Kentucky Fried Chicken or K-Fried, as they called it. The parking lot was crowded as the five girls piled into Millie, talking over each other as usual. As Cheryl started the engine, smoke wafted up from under the hood.

Screaming, they all got out faster than they had gone in and watched as Cheryl popped the hood, thinking the worst. It was! Flames shot out from under and around the engine, distributor, and air filter.

"Oh my God!" Cheryl yelled.

"What's happening?" Bette asked.

"Jesus, Jesus," Susan prayed.

"*Find* some *water*, somebody!" Evelyn shouted.

"What do I do? What do I do?" Cheryl danced around, waving her hands in front of her chest. Panic overtook her as she tried to reason what was happening to Millie, unsure how to put out the flames.

The chorus continued. "God, this is so dangerous!"

"I can't believe we were *just* in *that* car," Jasmine said.

"We could've burned alive," Evelyn said while Bette stood in shock.

"Somebody call the fire department! Hurry!" said a bystander.

"Oh *no*!" Cheryl cried helplessly as she watched the flames grow higher, imagining that Millie would soon be a burned-out hunk of charred metal.

From the corner of her eye, Cheryl saw a guy casually walk up and shake a can in his hand. *Why is he smiling? He probably thinks this is funny: "Look at those clueless girls, haha! Don't they look silly?"* To her amazement, he walked to the front of her burning Mustang, popped the cap on the can, and sprayed. The fire was extinguished immediately.

Mouth agape, Cheryl could only look at him and then at her car. She watched him walk away without looking in her direction as if what he'd done was nothing unusual.

"Thank you!" Cheryl yelled after him. That was all Cheryl could manage once she'd found her voice. She was astonished. They all were.

Who was that guy, and why does he look familiar? The most important thing to Cheryl was what to do now. Many people were standing around as lookie-loos, but without much else to see and providing nothing in the way of any additional help, they gradually moved on. The girls had different thoughts on what had caused the flame-out of Cheryl's car engine: gas leak from a hose, faulty wiring, bad carburetor, anything. However, Cheryl could only think, *What was in that spray?* It was all bizarre. Cheryl was not alone in her thinking.

"They actually *make* stuff like that today, in 1976?" Evelyn asked someone, and then another asked, "Who would have a spray like that on hand?" Still, another asked the obvious, "Who was he?"

"I have no idea," Cheryl answered. She wished she could find him to thank him properly. In a state of acute embarrassment and sudden clarity, Cheryl blurted out, "This is all my fault! I should have at least changed the oil and filter, but I forgot."

Cheryl had been negligent in caring for her car, and it showed.

⟫⟪◦◦◦⟫⟪

Only when they returned to the dorm did Cheryl break down in tears. Evelyn called Cheryl's mother, who said she'd call Ace as soon as possible. Within two hours, Ace arrived. After he hitched Millie to his tow truck, Cheryl realized her classic cool car was again in the hands of getting further repairs.

The girl with the cool car. Is this what I am to my friends, a convenient chauffeur to carry them around? A sorority sister they can depend on to make them look cool. Who would I be to them if I had no car at all?

But these proved to be false thoughts. Cheryl's roommates came through as they tried everything to get her to cheer up. Even Bette had come to their room with candles in chocolate Hostess Cup Cakes to help lift her spirits. Her friends stayed by her side, not caring if she had a car or not.

Cheryl spent a miserable few weeks waiting to hear word on the progress of the repairs to her car. She was told a faulty spark plug had ignited the fuel inside the distributor, which caused the engine to flame. It all sounded like gibberish to her. The repairs were costly, and her mother simply didn't have the funds to pay for a new engine. So until they could afford it, Millie would have to sit for a while.

One day, Cheryl's friends took her shopping to cheer her up, but without extra cash, she was strapped to purchase anything except a pair of lace-up leather boots that zipped down the side. She accepted the good-hearted teasing for the boots' half-plastic, half-leather, or "pleather" look. Considering they were tight around the ankles, she could walk in them just fine.

All went well until she was on her way to an art class. Cheryl realized she could not bend them significantly enough to walk down a set of concrete steps that ended at the sidewalk below, crowded with students on their way to their classes. To avoid another embarrassment, she walked on as if all was well—until it was not. Then the worst happened, and it was quick. Unable to bend one ankle significantly, she stumbled and fell forward headfirst toward the crowded sidewalk below. In the seconds it took to plunge, her thoughts were, *Oh, God! I'm going to break every bone in my face and body in front of everyone!*

As fate would have it, a guy stepped forward and caught her in midair. "Whew, that was close! A near miss on the face-plant. You okay?" he asked as other students looked on and made comments of astonishment such as "Wow!" or "Whoa!"

"Geez! Thanks for catching me!" Cheryl was dumbfounded about what had just happened but glad for his quick thinking. She was almost too embarrassed to look him in the eye. She blinked to see him more clearly but couldn't because the morning sun was in her eyes, which caused a shadow to cross his face.

"Ah, that's all right," he said softly. "Here, let me get your books."

"I shouldn't have worn these boots—still new." She looked at the scuff marks on them from the stumble as he bent down.

"Nah, they look good… So do you." He handed her books to her. "Take care now." And he was gone, disappearing in the crowd of students who had moved away from them.

It all happened so fast Cheryl forgot to get his name. At the same time, she couldn't help but think this was twice she'd been saved by someone, a man, whom she thought looked or sounded familiar. Coincidence? Probably. Cheryl shook her head, passed this thought off, and continued to her class.

When Millie was finally repaired that summer, Cheryl was beside herself with delight. She didn't know where the money had come from, but in her heart, she knew her mother and the church must have been behind it. Because of this generosity, Cheryl vowed never to neglect Millie again, no matter what. She had her car again, and all was right with the world.

However, promises made weren't always kept as her second year at college began, and mysterious events were just around the corner.

The Stranger

A new school year had begun, and the excitement of seeing her roommates was overwhelming. Cheryl had grown more confident, assertive, self-assured, and no longer afraid of driving. She also hoped she'd get lucky and run into the guy who caught her last semester when she clumsily fell down the steps.

Before the homecoming football game, Cheryl was invited to spend a weekend with her roommates in Louisville. She was the only one of her friends who didn't live there, so she looked forward to getting away to spend time in the big city. They all pitched in with expenses and calculated how to get there and back before the big game on Saturday. They ditched their last classes midweek, after which they crammed into Cheryl's Mustang and headed out.

Cheryl had the time of her life. She enjoyed visiting the many sites of Louisville, like touring the *Belle of Louisville*. Eating out at the restaurant near the river on the wharf at Waterford Park was the best! She tasted her first Hot Brown at the Brown Hotel and chauffeured her schoolmates wherever they decided to go. After an exhausting few days, she was eager to return to school.

Driving eastbound from Louisville, Cheryl felt a hitch under the accelerator travel through the touch of her hands on the steering wheel. *Oh no!* She quickly ran through the list of maintenance she'd done to keep her car from failing her again. Oil change, check. New air filter, check. Gasoline filled, check. Radiator coolant, check. Brake fluid? Did she forget to check it? She wondered if this minor neglect would bite while she sped along the highway toward school. Cheryl started to feel the car pull to the right. However, she kept the car on the road and prayed they would make it back in one piece. She bit down on her lip to hide her concern from others. To her relief, they chatted away, unaware.

"Come on, girl, come on," she said under her breath, reassuring Millie that she could make it all the way. Just as she reached the last leg of their journey on the other side of Lexington, the engine and oil lights came on simultaneously. Then she heard a pop in the right front tire. She could no longer hide her fear. The others screamed as she swerved and gripped the wheel tightly. Cheryl remained calm as she controlled the car's movement and slowed to a safer speed.

She had already moved into the slow lane when she'd first felt the wheel shimmy and the car pull to the right, which was good. Just as she pulled over and onto the rise in the shoulder of the highway, she noted her braking power was little to none, and then the car died. Cheryl tried unsuccessfully to restart her car before lowering her forehead on the steering wheel. It also occurred to her that the front right tire was probably flat, so an attempt to fix it seemed silly if the car wouldn't start. *How could I be so stupid?*

"Y'all, it's dead as a doornail, and the tire's flat," Cheryl admitted. "I need to get out and look at it. You guys can stay inside if you want." Just as at the grocery store last spring, the chorus of complaints began.

"What the hell?" Evelyn cried.

"We'll never get to the game now," Susan said

"A flat tire? Really?" Jasmine's sarcasm was not lost on Cheryl.

"I'm sorry, y'all!" Cheryl said.

"Yeah, like last time?" Jasmine complained. "I should've known we couldn't trust this car."

"Why now? Of all times, why now?" Susan asked, lying her head back.

"Well, at least it's not on fire!" Bette's sarcastic remark was a direct hit.

Cheryl was devastated. As the sun set low on the horizon, cars and trucks sped by on the highway without stopping to help. It was early October, and the waning twilight was starting to put a chill in the air. The speeding vehicles didn't help matters, especially when the wake of their speed as they passed caused the girls' clothing to whip about, chilling them even more.

Cheryl was at a loss and silently prayed for an answer to what she should do. They were stranded in the worst possible way. She looked around at the defeated, disgusted faces of her friends. She saw no compassion, only frustration and anger. She glanced at Millie, who seemed to look just as apologetic as she felt. It seemed Millie was trying to say she'd done her best but could do no more.

She thought of the only thing she could do: raise the hood to signal for help and hold out her thumb. In the twilight of evening, she hoped she could flag someone down. She'd had just about enough of this self-pity and everyone blaming her. It was time to take control.

"What are you doing?" Evelyn asked as she walked over to stand by Cheryl's side.

"The only thing left *to* do," Cheryl shouted loudly enough to be heard above the sound of passing vehicles. "I just hope we can get a tow back to town. We'll figure out something later." She paused before continuing, "You have any money left? I have twenty, and that's all."

"Just a few bucks. I spent most of my wad in Louisville," Evelyn answered, then turned to the others and yelled over the sound of highway noise, "Hey, y'all have any cash?"

They all shook their heads. "We had just enough money for gas. Looks like it's on you, kid," Evelyn said and sighed in resignation. She leaned back against the Mustang and crossed her arms for warmth.

Cheryl continued to hold out her thumb and then felt hot tears slide down her air-cooled face. *I put my selfishness ahead of responsibility and my friend's safety, let alone my own. Now I've jeopardized my friends. We're not safe out here in the middle of nowhere.* She bit her lip again and steeled herself against further self-pity. *God, please help us.*

Somehow, she had to get out of this, come hell or high water. They needed help. Wiping away tears, she bravely stepped out farther into the coming traffic. She thrust her right arm straight out with her thumb held high and defiant. *One of two things is bound to happen. Either someone will stop or hit me.*

"Cheryl! What are you doing?" Evelyn cried out.

As soon as she'd made this risky move, a red pickup truck pulled to their side of the road. Cheryl couldn't believe her eyes. The others stood back hesitantly and watched as Cheryl approached the stranger.

⟫◦◦◦⟪

"Looks like you girls need help," the man said as he walked toward them.

"My car's died, and we have no way to get back to Milford University."

"Good thing I came along," the stranger said matter-of-factly as he looked over her car. "You got a flat tire, too? Any lights come on when you turn the key?"

"No, sir." Cheryl couldn't look him in the eyes. She only looked down at the ground as she continued, "The engine and oil lights came on at the same time. It was pulling to the right before I pulled over. I think it needs brake fluid, but I can't be sure. I just had a new engine and *everything* put in last spring." The frustration building in her voice was unmistakable and difficult to hide. "I don't know what's wrong. It's all my fault," Cheryl said, trying to conceal the catch in her voice, indicating more tears to come.

"You don't say," the stranger said, almost mocking, but the look in his eyes told Cheryl he was showing compassion rather than making fun of what she had to say. Then she swallowed the lump in her throat, stuck her chin out, and looked him in the eyes without wavering.

"My friends and I ain't safe out here, and we have little money. I don't know what to do. Can you help us?"

The stranger had a kind face. He looked at Cheryl with soft eyes and, after a moment, said, "You hang tight here. I'll be right back. Don't go nowhere." Then he left.

"Where does he think we're gonna go? 'Don't go nowhere,' my foot," Evelyn said as they watched him get into his truck and pull away from the shoulder.

"Girl, he ain't coming back. You just wait and see," Jasmine said.

"Yes, he will. I have a feeling," Cheryl said with confidence.

"Yeah, like *feeling* this car would make it to Louisville and back." Jasmine was not giving up on her disappointment.

"Stop it, Jaz," Evelyn said in Cheryl's defense. "Cheryl's doing what she can to get us out of this. I don't see you offering any solutions."

"Like you are?" Jasmine's sarcasm solved nothing as she stared Evelyn down.

"Come on, y'all," Cheryl said, trying to ease the building tension. "Let's give him twenty minutes, at least. If he doesn't come back, we can take turns putting our thumbs out. Until then, let's try to stay calm, all right?"

"I'm waiting in the car," Bette said. "Y'all should get out of this cold before a psycho pervert comes along and kidnaps one of us."

Susan agreed and followed, leaving Evelyn, Cheryl, and Jasmine alone to wait for the stranger's return.

⟣⟐⟢

It didn't take twenty minutes. It took less than ten. Cheryl watched as a tow truck pulled up in front of the stricken Mustang. The man introduced himself.

"Evening, ladies. I'm the mechanic down the road. I hear you gals need a tow?"

"Yes, sir. We do; it's my Mustang," Cheryl said.

"Well, I'm here to help. Stand aside and let me do what I came to do."

Just then, the red pickup truck pulled in behind the Mustang. The stranger got out and offered to take them to the garage where Millie was being towed.

"Come on, now," the stranger insisted with his down-home no-nonsense demeanor. "Climb in as best you can. No use waiting around while he gets the car hooked up."

"Mister, we don't know you," Jasmine countered, looking him up and down as he stood in the headlights of his Ford F-150.

"I mean no harm; really, I don't," said the stranger apologetically. "You can trust me, okay? I'm only here to help."

"You can trust him, ma'am," yelled the tow truck driver as he pulled the chain to wrench Millie to the truck's bed as it lowered. "I can vouch for him. He's a good dude."

"You could be a pervert or a psycho for all we know," Jasmine persisted.

"Look. I can't convince you one way or the other. Make up your minds because it's cold out here, and I ain't got all night." The stranger rubbed his hands together and blew on them for emphasis.

Cheryl took the lead. She was grateful for the help and climbed inside the truck's passenger side with Evelyn close behind. However, the others took the offer with trepidation and wariness. The stranger got in beside Cheryl and Evelyn while the rest piled into the truck bed.

"I'm sorry, but this is all I have at the moment," the stranger said about his truck. "How's about I get y'all warmed up and out of this chill? I'll drive slow so the chill won't be so bad for them in the back."

Cheryl didn't know why, but she trusted this man more than anyone else who might offer help to them and Millie. For her, there was no fear, no second-guessing his intentions. The more he talked, the more she felt comfortable in his presence. She felt safe and that Millie was in good hands.

It wasn't a long drive to the garage. In fact, it only took a few minutes. The mechanic's shop was right off the highway and not far from a set of condominiums.

"This is where the car'll be towed, which is convenient because my condo is up the street. Y'all hungry?"

"Sure," Evelyn said before Cheryl could answer.

"Evelyn, I only have twenty bucks, remember?" Cheryl reminded, then to the stranger, she asked, "Maybe if you take us to a White Castle for a burger?"

The stranger chuckled. "I have food at the condo. Let me take y'all there, get warm, and relax for a bit. You can make a few phone calls too. Then we'll take it from there, okay? Believe me, I promise I won't bite. It's a crazy world out there. All I want is for y'all to be safe."

Maybe it was the tone of his voice. Maybe it was the gentleness of his mannerisms or the look in his eyes. It could have been a lot of things, but whatever it was, it felt right that they should take him up on his offer. There were five of them, after all, Cheryl reasoned. *Strong, healthy young ladies. If he tries anything, at least one or two of us will survive to tell the tale. Right?* They had nowhere else to go. Millie was being towed to the shop; they had no choice but to walk by faith and trust him.

⚬⚬⚬

The condo was beautiful! *Is this his home?* The girls gathered around each other and looked at the vastness of the space with high ceilings. The stranger showed them around. First, the kitchen to the left of the front door looked out into a living space with gold-colored hardwood floors running throughout the home. The Plexiglas dining room table with fake flowers in a black bowl as a centerpiece was surrounded by chrome and honey-colored wicker chairs. This faced a balcony, which was too dark to see in the gloom of night. The pink-and-green floral brocade couch and love seat faced a large black television console. These sat on a short pile shag area rug. Wooden stairs, the same color as the floor, led to three bedrooms upstairs. To their amazement, one room even had a waterbed!

"Now y'all make yourselves at home. Don't you worry none," the stranger said in his folksy way. "I'll be back in a little while, and if you get sleepy, well, there are beds ready for company."

"You're not staying with us?" Susan asked.

"Hush! Let him go," Jasmine whispered as she nudged Susan in the arm.

"You'll be safe here." The stranger chuckled as he headed toward the door. "The fridge is stocked. Or, if you want, there's a Pizza Hut just down the street. Do what you want. I won't be long." Then he was gone, closing the door softly behind him.

They stood around for a minute, taking it all in. Then Bette asked something incredible. "Any of y'all get his name?"

Cheryl and Evelyn decided to pool their money together to buy a pizza instead of raiding the stranger's fridge, which they never bothered to investigate. Besides, he had been too kind to them, and dirtying his kitchen and nosing around seemed disrespectful.

Long before the pizza's arrival, the stranger returned with their luggage while Cheryl was on the phone with her mother. Again, they were thankful. Then, he was gone before they knew it, and still, they forgot to ask his name.

Cheryl ate until she was stuffed. They all did. After discussing the stranger's kindness and this rescue miracle, they watched TV until they became drowsy. Finally realizing he would not return, they flipped a coin for the "waterbed experience." None of them had ever slept on one, which would be a treat. Jasmine won the toss. Evelyn and Cheryl shared one room, while Susan and Bette shared the other.

The morning was bright and sunny when Cheryl rose the next day. She fully expected the stranger to be downstairs on the couch, but to her surprise, Jasmine was there.

"I couldn't sleep on that thing, girl; it moved so much I felt seasick," Jasmine lamented as she moved over to allow Cheryl to sit beside her. "I don't know how people do it. I almost climbed into bed with you and Evelyn." Groggy from lack of sleep, she feigned disgust with the waterbed.

Cheryl laughed at Jasmine's idea of a crowded bed answering her sleeping woes, especially when sleepiness still hung over her.

However, she was grateful for the bright sunshine streaming through the balcony's sliding glass doors. It was refreshing.

"I take it you didn't sleep well then," Cheryl said, stifling a yawn as she stretched. Then something caught her eye. "Hey, who brought the roses?"

"I know, huh?" Jasmine said. "You know I didn't trust that man. After all that pizza and tossing on those waves of water, I got up and came down here to sleep and keep watch. There they were, as pretty as you please."

"Weird."

"Ain't it though? What's even more strange is I didn't hear a thing. Not a squeak on the floor, nothing. I tell you, I was sure surprised. I slept most of the night on this couch, waiting for him to return. I tried to sleep with one eye open and saw nothing more."

"No kidding? Maybe Evelyn went out last night or something and got them before you came down."

"Evelyn did what?" Evelyn asked as she walked down the stairs, scratching her head and yawning.

"The roses. Did you leave last night and bring them here?" asked Cheryl.

"Girl, I told you I don't have no money. Spent my last dime on pizza," Evelyn said, bending down to smell their fragrance. "They're beautiful, six of them. Well, I'll be."

"Where'd the roses come from?" Susan asked as she and Bette joined the rest downstairs.

"We don't know," they said in unison as Evelyn sat on the arm of the couch next to Jasmine.

"Probably from that weirdo," Jasmine said.

"Don't be such a bitch," Evelyn said as she playfully flicked Jasmine's hair with her hand. "He's nice, sweet, and kind—I like him. Not every day you run into generous people."

"Yeah." Again, they said this in unison, then went quiet in reflection. Thinking.

"It *was* strange how he went about helping us, huh?" asked Cheryl. "He didn't know us. Just took care of everything. Letting us stay here and all, he must trust us a lot, which makes me trust him."

"Let's keep beating that dead horse, shall we?" Jasmine's sarcasm was not lost on them.

Evelyn stretched and yawned again, ignoring Jasmine's caustic remark. "I'm hungry. Who wants eggs? Might as well take advantage of the time. He said, 'Make yourselves at home,'" Evelyn concluded in a low-pitched voice, trying to mimic the stranger's own.

As they tried to shake off the morning grogginess, all five got up and walked toward the kitchen. However, food was the last thing on Cheryl's mind. She was eager to learn the progress of Millie's repair, how to pay for it, and then get back on the road toward school.

When Evelyn opened the refrigerator door, they were stunned. One entire shelf contained a beautiful platter filled with scones and muffins. There was also freshly squeezed orange juice in a glass pitcher and sliced fruit in a bowl.

"Who *is* this guy?" Bette asked again.

"I wish I knew," Cheryl answered.

⸺◈◈◈⸺

After gorging on muffins and scones, they cleaned up as best they could and began packing their luggage. A knock came at the door, where a mechanic from the shop told Cheryl that her Mustang was parked downstairs for her.

"It's repaired and ready to go!" he said while dangling the keys in front of Cheryl. "New engine replaced the refurbished one, top-notch too, new alternator. Oh yeah, and the fluids are filled too. You know the brake fluid was almost gone, and the brake shoes were about worn down to almost nothing? Now it's refilled, and new brake shoes put on. You're lucky. Gotta tell ya that. A-frame's just a little crooked, but she'll ride just fine. New tires all around *and* balanced. Y'all have a good morning."

"Wait! What? I don't understand," Cheryl said.

"No charge." The mechanic held up his hands, thinking Cheryl was about to pay. "It's all taken care of. Have a good day!" And then he was gone.

No one said a word. After he left, the group went about the morning as if in a daze. It was as if a veil had come over them, and like robots, they gathered their things, cleaned up after themselves, and prepared to leave.

Each took one red rose for themselves. Cheryl made sure to leave one rose for the stranger. She left a note of thanks to the man who had come to their rescue. A stranger more like a loving father than any she knew. Another thought that came to mind was that of an angel sent from heaven.

Cheryl was the last to leave, and as she turned the lock mechanism inside so the door would lock when closed, she saw a note taped to the door. It looked like no one else had seen it, so she read its contents.

> You are blessed. We have been with you when you felt alone, afraid, stumbled, and fell. We have been there when you felt unloved and those you cared for had failed you. Even when you were scared to venture out on your own, We were there to ease your fear. Your Father loves you. His passing wasn't your fault. Never fear. When you call out. When you least expect Us. We will always be with you. Have faith.

Cheryl could not believe what she had read. She had come so far in facing her fears. She fell against the door and slid to the floor as the memory, so long hidden away, flooded back in a rush:

Her dad took her. She screamed and cried while reaching out for her mother after their horrific fight. She was just three years old when her dad, angry with her mom, lost control of his car. She was the only one who survived. The trauma had been too great to carry, so she'd blocked the memory. Only anxiety and the fear of speeding cars remained. No one ever discussed the death of her father, and she wondered why but didn't dwell on the reason for it. It wasn't her fault her parents had fought that day. It wasn't her fault her dad had died. It wasn't her fault she had survived.

Cheryl had never given miracles much thought. However, the note and recent events were proof of them. They culminated in bringing back a memory that had crippled her for so long. She had come so far in facing her fears. In retrospect, she questioned the many coincidences she had experienced up to that moment. She wondered if they were, indeed, miracles.

Was the gift of the car to a girl paralyzed with fear her mother's way of having Cheryl face her demons without bringing up the past to hinder her progress? Now, she saw the wisdom in that. Was it providence when the guy put out the flames of her car or when the guy caught her when she stumbled and fell? Did divine intervention save them from death due to faulty brakes by causing the tire to go flat? Was it by chance that compassion was placed in a stranger's heart so he would open his home to them? Was it a gift of love that allowed the car to be repaired without cost? Were these all just a matter of coincidence? Knowing her dad loved her without question brought joy to her heart. He and God's angels were always with her, watching over her. She was loved with all the love a father could bestow. These thoughts ran through her mind as she slowly walked to her car and wiped away silent tears.

Her friends were busy placing their bags in the trunk of her Mustang. Cheryl looked at her car with a new appreciation, making her keenly aware of many things. She was grateful not only for the return of her lost memory and who she had become because of it but also for having her beautiful, faithful car returned to her. Millie.

⚯

As she drove away in a car that felt like new, it seemed as if Millie wore a new dress and welcomed her friend's return. But the silence remained. After driving some distance, Evelyn finally broke the peace.

"What did we just go through?" she whispered, staring out at the passing scenery.

"Did you notice the color of the couch and love seat? Pink and green. Our sorority colors," Susan said, almost wistfully.

"The flowers. The breakfast. No footsteps heard—only ours. Why us?" Jasmine asked softer than usual for her.

"Yeah, it was *really* strange," Susan said, obviously lost in thought.

"We never got his name," Bette said, not giving up on the issue.

"I know His name, and They are many." After saying this, Cheryl said nothing more.

No one asked her to explain.

⟞◈◈◈⟝

Millie drove like a champ from that day on. Of course, Cheryl hoped she could raise enough money to donate to the mechanic shop and give something to the stranger for his generosity. However, they were never able to find him again. It was as if he, the tow truck driver, and the mechanic never existed. The repair shop had no knowledge of ever repairing her car. In fact, Cheryl was practically laughed out of the shop by the workers there. Her friends could make no sense of it, but deep inside, Cheryl was not surprised. Consequently, the money raised by Cheryl's fundraising efforts was used to repair the church roof instead. It was her way of giving back, especially after the money they raised to get her car repaired many times before.

Her friends agreed not to ever speak of the experience again. But that was a lie. Occasionally, in the quiet evening, after much girl talk, someone would ask, "Remember the stranger, or was he an angel?"

No one ever answered.

The End

A Dog's Life

There isn't much for me to do except wait for her to come home. After my morning walk and treats, I don't see her again until she returns. She leaves every morning, and I can't wait to see her face again. During the day, I sleep mostly, and each time I wake, I hope she's there. But she isn't. I can tell precisely when she'll come back by the light outside, the smell in the air, and the amount of sleep I've had. This is when I sit at the big glass and wait until I see her in the rolling box.

There she is! *Oh boy, oh boy, oh boy, yes, yes, yes, please come see me, please, please, please!* I've managed to hold it all day, but I'm so excited. I really *must* pee now. *Please hurry, hurry, hurry. I don't want to wet the floor.* Here she is! Now she's making those happy sounds with her voice, and I can't help but lean my head into her hand when she bends down to scratch behind my ears and give me smooches. This makes it even harder to hold my water, but I manage. *Can we go out now, please, please, please?* Yes! She says something. I don't know what she's saying, but I think her words mean to wait while she clips the long strap to my collar.

I don't know why she makes these sounds, but I understand the tone. I lick her face in gratitude and joy because I know we are about to go for a walk whenever she does this.

Outside, I squat in my marked space to pee and feel relief. Then I sniff and smell around. *Oh joy, oh joy, oh joy, this smell is my mark.* Good. I move on. *Uh-oh, this one isn't mine. I'll have to rewet the spot to claim it again. Now, that's done.* Off we go for a good long walk. I hope.

She's my tall one, and I like walking next to her. We pass other tall ones like her. She greets them by stretching her mouth and showing her teeth. She makes a funny sound to them. This tells me all is well. She waits while I take my time to explore. I see other doggies, and we greet each other in the usual way, nose to butt. Smells are important; some are better than most.

The light has faded from the sky, and I see a strange white object in the gloom. It is large, and it scares me. It might be something that will hurt me, and I whimper. I hide behind her legs, but she doesn't understand. She tugs the long strap at my neck as if to tell me it's all right.

But I can't move. I look at the object, sticking my head forward for a better look without moving. Because I'm small, she picks me up. As I quiver in her arms, she takes me closer to the huge solid object on the ground and touches it just like she does when she moves her hand over my head and back.

She takes me closer to inspect it for myself. Her soothing tone further tells me it's nothing to fear. I lean in to sniff and smell only dirt and wet moss. It doesn't smell like other dogs at all, so I relax. I lick her face in gratitude and bark at it, but not too loudly. I feel safe and can't wait to explore more.

⟞⟞⟞●⊙●⟝⟝⟝

Sometimes, we go to places in her rolling box. When I stare hard at the glass inside the rolling box, it rolls down for me. Neat trick! My big eyes squint against the wind. With the long fur on my ears and my short, stubby nose, I put my face through the opening of the rolling box. I lick the wind blowing in my face, making my nose cold and wet. I can't do this if it blows too hard, so my tongue hangs out instead.

Other times, like now, we go for walks just to be out. I don't know why she likes to do this, but I'm glad she takes me along. I love it! Walking in the daytime, I can see other doggies with their tall ones chasing things. I often see a tall one throw a round, twirly thing in the air. Their doggies chase it. But when they wave their arms in the air as if they threw the twirly thing but didn't, their doggies run to retrieve nothing at all. I don't understand why they do this, but their doggies don't seem to mind. They just like being outside with their tall ones—like me.

I don't care for that kind of play. I like to lay my front paws down in front of another doggy, and before I know it, we're off chasing each other. Sometimes, my tall one will play this game with me. I like to hear the squealy noises she makes as we run around together. It makes me happy when I catch her or she catches me. But when I see the *furry thing* with the long tail that lives in the trees and makes chirping noises as it scurries near me—I want it. She tries hard to hold me back, and I do, but *boy, oh boy*, it would be nice to get one, just to see why it chirps and chatters the way it does. But right now, it's time to head home.

<hr>

Now we're back inside, and I watch as she removes the fur she wears when it's cold outside. Except for when she puts water on her body, she always wears different fur when we are inside. I wait until she fills my bowl with food. It's been a long time since I last ate. She makes sure I have enough water, and then I dig in. She leans against the place where she makes food and drinks water from a different kind of bowl. After a while, she takes something out of the cold box and makes food for herself. She peels back the wrapping on a tray and places it in another box that hums after she closes the door. While she waits to hear the beeping sound it makes before opening the door, she gives me a yummy treat. It tastes so good!

I watch as she takes her tray and sits in the big room to watch others move inside a big, noisy box on the wall. They make the same funny sounds she makes when she moves and stretches her mouth. But for some reason, she says nothing back to them. I watch back and forth, cocking my head from side to side to understand why she does this or watches them. I give up after a while. Her food smells good, but I know begging her to share is useless. I cock my head to one side when she looks at me and makes those funny sounds with her mouth, gesturing with her hands. It sounds as if she's sad because she can't share with me. I accept her sadness and lie down at her feet while she eats. I'm just happy to be next to her.

⋙⊶◎◎⊷⋘

Where she goes, I go. Where she is, I want to be. She sits on the floor and pats my head, and I lick her face again. She makes another funny sound, which tells me she likes it, so I keep it up. Her teeth show, and the sound she makes causes me to feel good too. I want to make her as happy as I am. She puts her arms around me and squeezes tight, then gives me a fuzzy thing to play with. It doesn't move like that small furry thing outside or the big flying things with wings that quack, but I don't care. Maybe one day, I'll be able to catch one. Until then, I'll play with this funny, fuzzy thing instead.

The sound of running water causes me to hide under her big doggy bed. But the water is for her—not me. She stands in the water box and makes a melodic sound with her voice. I like to hear this sound when she's in there. I wait patiently for her to come out, almost falling asleep at the sound of her voice. Unlike me, she has no fur on while doing this, so it doesn't take long to dry herself and put on softer fur. I think this fur is meant to keep her warm.

Now I have to pee again. I've learned to stand by the back door to let her know this. She seems to understand because when I do, she opens the door, and I quickly dash out, smell around for my spot, and having found it, squat. She watches out for me. I know because I always look back to check.

We're in her big doggy bed now. I'm glad she allows me to lie next to her here. I look down at my doggy bed in the cold, dark corner. I don't like it down there. She watches a smaller noise box on the wall in front of her big doggy bed. The light from this box is the only one shining in the whole place. I snuggle under her arm, resting my head on her soft, warm belly. She strokes my head and slides her hand down the fur on my back. She makes soothing noises that tell me how much she loves me. I love her too.

As she drifts off to sleep, I close my eyes to join her in dreams, only to wake to another day waiting for her to come home. I wonder if she knows that I live just for her. It's a dog's life, and I wouldn't have it any other way.

The End

GHOST DANCER

The Spirit Seeker

There was nothing unusual about the day. It was the same as the day before. He felt the sun's warmth as it bathed his dark black fur. He could lie there forever, languishing in this warmth, except his belly told him it was time to feed. Ghost Dancer opened one of his yellow eyes to view the tiny blades of green grass closest to his line of sight. No, nothing unusual at all about the day.

He raised himself and stood on his four legs, then shook himself from nose to tail, loosening ground debris collected in his thick, shiny coat. He moved his head right, then left, and lifted his snout to sniff the air. The faint smell of smoke, moss on the north side of trees, wet grass, dirt surrounding mushrooms, and more assaulted his nostrils. He stretched his forelegs before him, bent his head down, and yawned long and wide. His thick tongue licked his nose as he lifted his head high. He was ready to begin.

He was not the alpha. He was not the beta. He was just another member of his pack of seven. Humans would consider him a lone wolf within his pack, unsociable, unpredictable, yet content. He liked the sound of his name when he heard it move through the wind. He understood this sound and answered when the keepers of the preserve called. He understood all the name sounds, such as Lilly Bell, Mister Hanks, Lovely Stella, Koco, Angry Bear, and Cochise.

Cochise was their leader. They looked to him for guidance; if left to the wild, it would always be that way. Koco and Lilly Bell were the pups of Cochise and Lovely Stella. Angry Bear challenged Cochise on occasion but never won. Angry Bear wanted pups of his own. Mister Hanks was the oldest of their pack and was revered for his length of years. Ghost Dancer could be found near him, some distance away but always nearby.

Ghost Dancer longed to be free. To roam the hills and valleys bigger than the preserve provided. The occasional shanks of venison their keepers gave were enough for a time. Still, there was nothing like hunting down prey, capturing the kill, and eating meat fresh off the bone. He wanted to feel the wind rush through his fur as he ran for miles and miles over unfamiliar terrain claimed as his own. He wanted to touch with his paws and scratch his pads on rough ground in anticipation of what might come. He wanted to feel the mist of water as it fell from waterfalls or smell fresh water pooling in ponds or lakes full of fish or other game. To forge ahead into the unknown of what tomorrow might bring instead of the humdrum day-to-day-ness of the preserve. Yes, Ghost Dancer wanted more.

As a pup, he could do most of those things. Long ago, he had been left to fend for himself after losing his mother. All he knew, he had learned by himself. Struggling, frightened, and alone, he'd survived as best he could until he was caught trying to snatch a clucking bird from within an enclosed pen. After he was brought to this place, it took time for him to feel comfortable. He was fed daily and initially welcomed by the enclosed pack. But he grew bigger than his pack members, and because of this and more, they regarded him cautiously.

His memory of exploring and his sense of freedom had never left him. It was these memories that fed his desire to run free again. He wanted to explore and learn more than Mister Hanks could show him. He wanted to bring knowledge back to his pack and share the many surprises and wonders he had found. But he was limited in his quest. His deep desire to hunt, build a den of his own making, and raise his young was causing impatience to rush in. The pull was undeniable as he lived day-to-day within the confines of the enclosure.

His was a lonely parcel of land that stretched only so far. The chain-link fencing was a prison he could only dream of breaching. But one day, he knew his time would come. One day, his longing would be realized.

⊰◈◈⊱

Roslyn was bored but happy to be out on this beautiful spring day. Her friends had convinced her to come along on this adventure. She was far from home in the hills of southern Colorado, and the switchbacks were making her dizzy. Whenever she asked where they were going, the answer was the same, "Wait and see. You're gonna love it!"

They were longtime friends, and she trusted them, but this was ridiculous. They had been driving for over an hour and a half, and her patience was running thin. There were four of them. The driver, Kenny Frost, was a financial executive engaged to her best friend, Kari Asher, who sat next to him in the passenger seat. Roslyn was saddled with Jeremy Ketchum, who fawned over her whenever possible, which was cute but annoying. Jeremy had just become a partner at the law firm of Childers and Soames, where she worked as a paralegal, and was surprisingly humbled by his success. An endearing quality, she had to admit.

"Roslyn, you need to loosen up," Kari said.

"But it's been *hours*. I'm gonna throw up if we round one more switchback."

"Lean over on Jeremy if you do. You won't mind, huh, Jer?" Kenny said, joking.

Roslyn rolled her eyes at Kenny's attempt to be funny. Jeremy looked out the car window on his side, behind Kari, and suppressed a smile with his hand to his mouth. Kari looked back at Roslyn from the car's passenger side, tilted her head down, and, with raised eyebrows, smiled just for fun. So many times, Kari had tried to get them together as a couple. But, as tenacious as he could be in the courtroom, he lacked the finesse to sway her to accept him completely. She didn't know why. He was attractive and aloof, but something was missing. Something she couldn't put her finger on held her back.

Roslyn "Roz" Soames was a daddy's girl. Her father ran a tight ship at the firm, where Jeremy made quite an impression. She was cautious with him and watched to see if his fawning was an attempt to obtain favor with her dad or if he was genuinely interested in her for herself. Not who she was. Now, he was a partner at newly named Childers, Soames, *and* Ketchum. Somehow, she was neither thrilled nor impressed.

Kari was her best friend from high school. When Kari met Kenny, there were many jokes about their name combination. Kenny had come up with a few of his own, like Kenkari Ken Ross or Karikens; Roslyn instantly liked him for Kari. She was the only bridesmaid at their wedding, and Jeremy was Kenny's best man, which is how they had met. Kenny and Kari, Roz and Jer. From then on, they were inseparable, but too much closeness was wearying. The pressure to open her heart to Jeremy was almost too much.

These days, Roslyn longed to be herself, her own person—freedom. Being the boss's daughter had its perks, but it also came with slog and confinement. She was uptight, and the case laws given to her to research kept her busy most nights. She wanted quiet days and the peace of simple tasks instead of the grueling and relentless pursuit of finding precedents for up-and-coming attorneys jockeying to make a name for themselves or a political office appointment.

She was expected to follow in Daddy's footsteps, especially after her brother, James, turned down the opportunity. But paralegal work was the most she could manage. Like her brother, her heart just wasn't in it. It was a drudge, and she was bored. Maybe that was why she found Jeremy annoying. Roslyn supposed she didn't want to support his success at the firm because it would bind her tighter to the one profession she wanted to escape. She felt trapped in a thankless job of clerking, never achieving anything of her own or branching out to explore who or what she could be. To her, Jeremy represented everything that would suffocate her in life.

She was lost in these thoughts as they came to a rise in the landscape, and then there it was. The name COLORADO WOLF RESCUE AND PRESERVE had been burned into a long, wide, rustic plank of wood supported by enormous log posts on either side. The building looked like a cabin made of rough, hewed wood. Roslyn could see chain-link fencing surrounding the hills behind.

"Here we are," Kari said, almost chirping as she exited the SUV.

"Why are we here? What is this?" Roslyn asked as she carefully left the seat she had occupied behind the driver for almost two hours.

"A preserve for wolves. My parents helped sponsor this place. The donations come from many different agencies, which I think is cool. Isn't it great! Come on, let's go see them." Kari grabbed Roslyn by the arm, but Roslyn's feet didn't want to cooperate.

"Who? Do you mean wolves? Are you crazy?" Roslyn asked incredulously.

"I don't know about this," Jeremy said, hesitating.

"You wimping out on me, Jer?" Kenny needled. "Come on, it's fine. Let's meet the people who run this place." It was Kenny's turn to grab someone by the arm, and Jeremy reluctantly complied.

Kari came from a wealthy family who, through their generosity, willingly gave to good causes. Their philanthropy was legendary, always a topic of discussion at the law firm, but this venture surprised her. Kari had never said anything about it, so Roslyn was naturally curious about why. She was suspicious and cautious of wild animals, especially wolves. She needed to understand why she'd been asked to come along on a trip like this.

"Why'd you bring me here? I don't get it. What do they do here? Are there really wolves inside the enclosure? Can they break loose?" Roslyn asked as she pulled Kari aside.

"Don't be silly. It's perfectly safe. You need to loosen up and experience something different. I thought this adventure would do you good. Wolves have to be reintroduced into the wild. Ranchers have hunted them for so long, and their numbers are dwindling. My parents wanted to do something, so they helped start this small rescue where wolves are caught and brought here for safety, observation, and possible rehabilitation."

"Safety and to observe what? They kill people."

"That's not entirely correct, Roz," Kari said with her hands on her hips. "Do some research on things other than the law, and you'll know. They attack if threatened, their territory has been encroached upon, or there's a lack of food. They're skittish around humans, which is a good thing. What I find interesting is they have a social hierarchy much like ours. They're very intelligent. Come on." Kari softened and pleaded, "Take a chance. Learn something new for a change." Kari had piqued Roslyn's curiosity, but only just. She was still uncertain.

"All right," Roslyn conceded. "But only if it's safe."

"Come on, silly. You've come this far. Why not see for yourself?" Kari cajoled.

"Well, not by my own choice, but okay." *This'll be different.* Roslyn's thoughts and nerves were in overdrive.

Together, they walked a path with a gradual rise to the cabin office, where the men talked to the caretakers, the Logans—Lars and Emily. They were younger than Roslyn expected and wore the wrinkled, tanned lines of outdoor adventurers who loved nature. Despite the chill at this altitude, they were dressed in faded jeans and thin T-shirts embossed with the rescue's name across the front.

On the other hand, Roslyn was reasonably dressed in all black, from a pullover sweater to black hiking boots. To keep her fingers warm, she absentmindedly placed them through her shiny, thick, wavy black hair, which was loose around her. Jeremy put his arm around Roslyn's shoulders when she shivered slightly, but she moved away out of nervousness. She wanted to be alone with her thoughts while listening to the Logans as they explained the preserve's purpose, maintenance, and, most interestingly, the history of the wolf.

From Roslyn's vantage point, she could see out the back windows of the large cabin and was drawn to this side of the room to observe. On closer inspection, she could see the wolves roaming back and forth along the fence line, some too close for comfort. They were huge! Larger than any breed of dog except for Great Danes. Their legs, not as spindly as the coyote's, didn't seem to support the weight of their heft. Lars explained their gait was like that of walking, but he liked to think of it as a lope, and, like dogs, their pointy ears turned independently of the head when alerted to any sound. Still, unlike dogs, it was hard to tell what they thought because they didn't have eyebrows. Roslyn found herself fascinated by these ancient beings, ancestors of the dog.

To roam free, hunt in packs, and behave with humanlike social skills was amazing to see up close. Roslyn could only imagine the interaction these large carnivores had with each other and wondered about the majesty of their kind. Wolves, Wolfen, Lycus, Canis lupus, whatever the word, to her mind, were a fierce force of nature that needed to be respected.

She heard the conversation behind her and listened to the questions and answers Lars supplied. The enclosure was about five acres, which equated to about four football fields, with chain-link fencing all around. He talked about the size of the barbed overhangs and deep skirts, but Roslyn was too lost in her imagination to care about these facts. Curious about how they lived and socialized, she didn't hear when her name was called.

"Roz… Roz! You still with us?" Kari asked.

"Yes. Yes, I am. I couldn't help but observe them out there. What magnificent animals. So huge!"

"You ready to meet a few?" Lars asked with a grin.

"Excuse me, what? Aren't we good at observing from here?" Roslyn asked as her comfort level began to slip.

"Sure you are, but that's part of what we do," Lars explained. "We conduct visitors to meet wolves all the time. If they want. The less human contact, the better, I know. But it's a way of introducing us to them before reintroducing them to the wild. You see, it's their world. We are the encroachers, not the other way around. It's good to keep them wild, but we don't need to be afraid of them as we were before. It's good for us to know them and give them a better understanding of us. So what d'you say? Y'all ready to go out and meet a few?"

"Ah—" Roslyn hesitated.

"It's fine, really," Emily Logan chuckled. "My husband does this all the time. Come on, be brave!"

As Roslyn followed the group outside, she listened as Lars told them what to do *and* what to expect once they were inside the gated enclosure.

"The size of your group is fine." Lars cautioned, "Wolves get agitated when they see larger numbers, but don't worry. We'll move a select group of 'em from the big fenced enclosure you see all around to a smaller enclosure adjacent to where you'll enter and sit. It's a double-gate system. I'll walk you in. There'll be five of 'em. There *is* one larger than the rest. He reminds me of the ancient dire wolf. We call him Ghost Dancer."

He paused while lifting the gated enclosure's lock, then continued, "Now. When you go in, crouch down and duck-walk over to that bench. Never stand. Take your seat and wait. Don't smile or show your teeth; that's a sign of aggression to a wolf, and we don't want that, now, do we? Stay quiet and let the wolf come to you. If you want to stroke 'em, you can. But not from the front of the face, mind, only under the chin. And dig deep. They need to feel your hand. Remember, they're watching you. *They* are in control and will lead you. When they come, and they will, it'll be one at a time."

"I don't know about this. It sounds dangerous," Jeremy said.

"Not if you remain calm. Remember, this pack has just eaten, so they're not interested in you for dinner. They're just curious.

The first thing they'll do, now this is important, is come up to you and nip at your lip."

"You mean bite my lip? That's *not* okay, man." Jeremy was emphatic.

"No. Nip, like this." He demonstrated this by pinching his lower lip between his thumb and index finger. "It doesn't hurt. They're pretty adept at not intentionally hurting us. Otherwise, I wouldn't take you in. And, no matter what they do, don't show fear! They can smell it a mile away."

"Why do they nip?" Kenny asked.

"We think they do this to gauge who you are. It's kind of a test to see if you're afraid of 'em… or can trust 'em or they you. So far, that's what we've decided anyway."

"I don't think I can do this. It's too risky," Jeremy said, looking green about the face.

"Ah, come on, guys!" Count on plucky Kari to convince them to try.

"Hey, I'm game." Kenny wasn't as fearless but usually followed Kari's lead.

"I'm ready." Roslyn's tone of voice was matter-of-fact. She was first to walk up to the interior gate of the enclosure. Jeremy looked at her in amazement; they all did.

"Well, all right!" Lars said. He followed after Roslyn, and so did the rest except Jeremy, who elected to observe from inside the cabin.

Roslyn wasn't sure what drove her. The change in her attitude was no more apparent to her than to the others. She felt a pull inside her like no other at the sight of the wolves. Her knees barely shook, but enough to know she had to calm herself. Her fear was no longer paralyzing but exploratory. Besides, Jeremy's protest and sissy attitude got under her skin, which only served to bolster her courage. She wanted to experience the rush, the exhilaration of facing danger. Metaphorically speaking, she wanted the triumph of overcoming fear, real or imagined. She was ready to do something daring. To touch and experience firsthand the unknown was a step in the right direction. She was being given a chance to embrace something new, a chance to let go, and for her, this was a test to see if the spirit of freedom lived in her heart and courage lived in her soul.

As Lars opened the enclosure, she slowly stepped inside.

His pack was chosen to meet the long-legged humans. Ghost Dancer's yellow eyes watched closely as four entered the enclosure dedicated to human interactions with them. Cochise and Lovely Stella, Angry Bear, and Mister Hanks were curious. Too young to explore, Koco and Lilly Bell lay in the adjacent enclosure to watch their parents. Ghost Dancer waited.

One of the keepers came over to them. His voice was familiar, and so was his smell. He was welcomed in the pack; he was trusted. He spoke the sound of Ghost Dancer's name, but there was caution in it. Ghost Dancer was momentarily confused, and then he saw her. The human with thick black hair. Her coat was dark like his. He lowered his head slightly and looked at her with a steady gaze.

Slowly, they walked out to greet the humans. Ghost Dancer watched as Cochise placed his two forepaws on the shoulders of a female and then nipped her mouth as she stroked his chin. Cochise loped away after the encounter. Ghost Dancer watched as Mister Hanks and Lovely Stella did the same to others. No one touched the black-haired human. This was his moment, his turn. He slowly walked toward her with the black hair and lowered his head again. He smelled no fear. His yellow eyes never wavered from her eyes as he stepped closer. He lunged quickly, placed his forepaws on her shoulders, and nipped her lower lip. His head went back as he watched her. He stayed this way, watching her. She didn't move. Then he slowly moved in closer to her face and licked.

He was enormous in size. Heavier than Roslyn could have ever imagined. She wasn't afraid. He stood taller than the rest and was beautifully majestic. He smelled of earth, grass, and pine. He was primal and intense. His black fur glinted in the light. His eyes were as yellow as the sun. They watched each other. She never moved. She didn't smile or show her teeth. She was guarded but relaxed. Thank God Jeremy had decided to watch from inside the cabin with Emily. She didn't think Jeremy could sit still during this inspection.

His paws were so large they covered her entire shoulder space. His nip was gentle; she hardly felt it at all. She marveled at the adeptness of this maneuver; it was stunning. The intelligence in his eyes, size, and weight told her this must be Ghost Dancer, the progeny of the ancient dire wolf. She felt honored to be chosen by him. As Roslyn reached out to stroke under his chin, he moved in again, but this time he licked her face instead. He kept on licking and then moved his licks to her mouth. She started to panic, not being told about this or what to do. The force of his tongue was so strong she thought he would force her teeth to show.

She remembered to relax and show no fear. No one could help her if Ghost Dancer decided to bite her face off anyway. She held her lips tightly shut, but this was no match for Ghost Dancer. His forceful tongue forced her lips and teeth apart. She felt his tongue enter and probe her mouth. The shock of realizing she was being deeply kissed by a wild animal was overwhelming.

It was brief and quick. Ghost Dancer got down then and turned to face the pack.

⟫◦◉◉◦⟪

This human was different. Ghost Dancer could feel it in his bones. Her scent was good. Her eyes were kind. He sensed her spirit was exactly like his. He wanted to know her. He wanted her to know he trusted her and she could trust him. His lick became urgent as he felt a need to find her spirit. He had to know where it was and needed to determine if it was inside. He wanted to explore that place humans kept locked away, that shiny white place on the face, under the eyes, which they hid so well. He had to seek it out. He pried it open, felt the softness inside, and sensed the strength held within. Then he tasted her spirit, and the welcome it gave back was what he wanted and found.

Ghost Dancer sensed she was unafraid. The trust was immediate. This was what he wanted. In her, he felt a passion for freedom. His wolf sense told him the need to run free was in her veins, just as the need was in his. Like the sound of the wind, he understood she would accept this knowledge and hopefully lead him away from the prison he found himself in.

He was emboldened and, for the first time, clearly embraced how different he was from the rest. He was the lone wolf within. He was bigger. He was stronger and knew with certainty that her spirit could walk with him. Ghost Dancer had felt, sought, and found something he didn't want to lose. He sensed she had as well. She was his to protect, and he wanted his pack to know and understand this.

Just then, Angry Bear approached to nip at her, to test her. But Ghost Dancer knew her spirit, and this Angry Bear could not have. He had never challenged any of them. In that instant, he knew he would never back down. He stood his ground facing Angry Bear and growled. Angry Bear paced in front of Ghost Dancer and the black-haired human, who wore a dark coat. Ghost Dancer bent low and matched the pacing movement of Angry Bear.

<hr>

Roslyn was stunned as she realized it wasn't every day you got French-kissed by a wolf. But she had, and the experience was amazing. She sensed he wanted something from her that only she could give. But what it was confounded her. Then she knew. A freedom she had longed for. A space and courage to be who she was and wanted to be. The same as Ghost Dancer. To be set free.

But her amazement turned to bewilderment when she realized Ghost Dancer had claimed her as his. Instinctively, she knew he would protect her if the other wolves approached or tried to harm her. She was not afraid of Ghost Dancer, but this other wolf was another matter. The whole encounter left her transfixed and scared shitless.

Yet there she sat, watching a drama of animal possession play out before her. She watched as another gray wolf paced in front of Ghost Dancer. She watched as the growls and snarls became more menacing. She realized the danger she was in but was too terrified to move. This was primal. This was spiritual. She *had* to be part of it.

Lars motioned the others to tiptoe out of the enclosure, and they did. But Roslyn remained. Like a stone, she was frozen to the spot. She wanted to watch the match unfold as she was fought over and protected. She couldn't help but think this must be how most female animals felt when they knew they were the prize. Roslyn was flattered beyond what made sense.

As the wolves paced each other, Roslyn was surprised by the sudden jerk of her arm. It was Jeremy who had bravely entered to pull her from the ensuing drama.

⇒◈◈◈⇐

She was gone. Ghost Dancer could feel the emptiness of her presence. The fight was over almost before it began. His hackles relaxed, but he remained guarded as he faced Angry Bear. Cochise came to stand between them, looking from one to the other. The meaning was clear.

The long-legged man was back, and he ushered the pack into the large enclosure. Ghost Dancer looked around for black hair, but she was no longer in sight. He walked over to Mister Hanks and whined. Mister Hanks licked him to cheer his sadness. Ghost Dancer didn't know if she would come again, but if she did, he wanted more than ever to lick her face and feel her spirit until he could find absolute freedom from that place.

⇒◈◈◈⇐

Jeremy moved slowly and guided Roslyn out of the enclosure, putting himself between the wolves and Roslyn. He was careful to close the gate behind him. Roslyn was in a daze and couldn't comprehend what had happened or why. Lars tried his best to explain, but it made no sense to her. The feeling was overwhelming.

"I'll be damned. Ghost Dancer really likes and trusts you. Usually, wolf kisses are that and nothing more. I admit the meaning can be complex, but *I* think he needed to feel your spirit. I should've told you to expect it, but it didn't register to tell, what with you all's apprehension about the visit."

"I wasn't apprehensive. I felt drawn to do it," Roslyn said.

"Well, you were kissed, that's for sure. French-kissed, and by a wolf no less," Kari said, teasing her.

"Knock it off, Kari." Jeremy was clearly annoyed. "It could've been worse."

"I'm just bewildered by the whole encounter. Why would Ghost Dancer do that but then turn to guard me from other pack members?" Roslyn asked Lars.

"It's a wolf thing, the kiss, I mean," Lars responded. "It's complex and can take on different meanings. Usually, if they trust you or want your trust, they'll plant a good kiss and protect you. It's a way of accepting you to his pack."

"They do that?" Kari was incredulous.

"No!" Roslyn was emphatic, then turned to Lars. "That experience felt like something... more...," Roslyn said, lost in thought. "It was as if he was looking for something within me. It was as if he was searching, and once he found it... I was his."

"I'm still shaken by the whole ordeal," Kari said as she took Roslyn by the hand to soothe her.

"There's a need, a drive in the wolf to be free, roam, and claim," Lars explained. "I've heard some Indian legends speak about the spirit animal that lives deep inside the wolf. It exists in all of us, but for some reason, wolves tend to pick up on it more than other animals. Once the wolf feels it within another person or animal, they lay claim, so to speak, to that which is then bound to him. They feel protective."

"Sounds perverted to me," Jeremy said.

"It's not a sex thing; don't get me wrong here," Lars said, sounding offended as he defended the spirit of the wolf. "Deep connections don't happen often. But his need to run free is sparked when it does if it wasn't there already. The spirit gets easily confined in these places. That's one of the reasons why we'd like to release 'em. To reintroduce them to the wild so the spirit's need to run free is set loose.

"Like I said earlier, Ghost Dancer is unusual. His coloring, size, and demeanor are like the ancient dire wolves. They were mystical animals, and stories passed down through the ages speak of their loyalty and a fierce need to protect. He found you, miss, and you're his forever."

They listened, enthralled by the story of mystic legend, loyalty, protective bonding, and freedom. What Lars said was interesting, but Ghost Dancer had awakened a human need to break the bonds that had tied her down for too long. A need to belong, be loved, and be loved in return. To be accepted for who she was, not by who her father was or his last name. Roslyn wanted to be seen as her own person, free, fierce, and loyal.

"Is it strange to feel an urgent need to discover something deep inside yourself after an encounter like that?" Roslyn asked wistfully.

"I only know what we've heard of the wolf. I have to say, what I saw today was unusual, to say the least," Lars said, scratching his head.

"I think we've heard and seen enough for one day," Kenny said. "How about it, folks? Let's get going. We have a long drive ahead." Kenny looked at his watch and then at the rest of the group as he headed toward the door.

"We've got to do something to release him *and* the rest," Roslyn said. Turning to Kenny and Kari, she continued, "Can't your parents do something to make this happen any faster? Can we find the funds to get the government to push this effort?" Then, to Jeremy, she asked, "What about the legal system?"

"Now hold on there, Roz," Jeremy said with raised eyebrows and wide eyes. "I don't know anything about the laws regarding animal husbandry or reintroducing wolves to the wild, for that matter."

"Oh hush, Jer!" Kari admonished. "Roz, I'll talk to my parents. Well, me *and* Kenny will. We'll see what we can do. I thought I'd seen everything, but this is something I'll never forget. Right, hon?"

"I guess. Yeah, I'll see what I can do." Kenny was reluctant, then quickly acquiesced. "I think Ghost Dancer and others like him deserve it. What about it, Jer? Care to give it a look-see, at least?"

"I'll do what I can." Jeremy shrugged in response. "I thought my heart was gonna jump out of my chest when Ghost Dancer was on Roz. I'm feeling a little stupid right now. Sure, I'll take a swing at it." Then he turned to Roslyn and asked, "Forgive me?"

"Of course, you big weenie," Roslyn said, smiling at him for the first time that day. "You were brave today. Thanks for agreeing to look into this for me. It's important."

They said goodbye to the Logans, and while walking to the car, a single howl, long and deep, forced Roslyn to turn around. There, high on a cliff, was Ghost Dancer. He howled again, and Roslyn knew this was his way of bidding farewell. She vowed to see him again. She had to.

The Mission

Jeremy rose to the occasion and found legal assistance for the wolf rescue, which was untrue to form for him. With this news, he rushed in to tell Roslyn.

"You won't believe what I have in my hands," he said casually.

"If it's another precedent you need researching, I'm not interested. I'm up to my neck in cases as it is. You know that, right?"

"That I do, but this isn't one of those requests."

"Now you have my attention," Roslyn said as she looked over her reading glasses at him.

"Good. Look at this." Jeremy slid a document across her desk.

In front of her was a document from the Colorado State Government, signed by the United States Secretary of the Interior and Land Management. It was a record of decision (ROD) giving the Wolf Rescue and Preserve of Colorado the right to reintroduce any and all wolves in their protected preserve into Yellowstone National Park and Idaho when necessary.

Roslyn was elated. With a whoop and a squeal, Roslyn jumped up and embraced Jeremy. He was delighted to receive this unsolicited affection from the woman who had stolen his heart. Roslyn's response seemed natural, which caused him to want to hold on to her longer than was necessary. However, the glass enclosure of their offices didn't allow for public displays of affection without starting the tongues of office gossipers to wag. Knowing this, they awkwardly separated themselves, with Jeremy looking sheepishly down at his shoes.

"I'm sorry, really. But this is great news!" Roslyn said, trying to contain her excitement.

"I thought you might think so—"

"How did you ever—?" Roslyn rushed in before he could explain.

"As you know, it took a while. Like Sisyphus, the struggle of rolling that stone up the hill was tremendous."

"But unlike Sisyphus, you didn't fail. You continued in your quest and won!"

"Well, when you put it like that… I suppose. But it was hard-won. I didn't do it alone, you know. Without help from Kari, her parents' influence, and Kenny's savvy understanding of finance, I don't think we could've gone past go."

"Stop being modest, will ya?" Roslyn said jokingly. "You didn't become a partner of this firm because you're not tenacious. I've heard Dad talk of your prowess in the courtroom, and I'm sure you applied yourself with the same kind of tenacity. I watch, you know, and *I've* come to learn what you're capable of."

"Well, if you say so, ma'am," Jeremy said without averting his gaze from Roslyn. Then he cleared his throat, embarrassed, and asked, "You want to deliver the news personally? I have to get the proper signatures ready for submission. Other than that, it's a done deal."

"Road trip?" she asked.

"You got it," Jeremy replied.

⋙◦◦◦⋘

Something didn't seem right. Ghost Dancer felt panic and fear race through him as the night lit up like day. He raised himself from slumber and looked over at Mister Hanks, who was also on the alert. Cochise and Angry Bear gathered in front of them, with Lovely Stella hanging behind with her three-month-old pups, Koco and Lilly Bell. The night was for rest, and they took advantage of it, while the daytime was for eating and playing. His senses told him the noise meant danger. Then, there was a scurry as many keepers entered the enclosure.

Mister Hanks moved to protect Ghost Dancer and the rest. In this, he knew best. Cochise followed his lead and moved his pack to the back of the enclosure. Far away from the long-legged humans carrying large shiny cages and sticks with long barrels pointed at them.

When the first shots rang out, there was panic. The tranquilizers worked quickly, one shot and down. To Ghost Dancer, the keepers were hurting them, and there was no other reason behind what they were doing. Ghost Dancer thought the keepers must be hungry and wanted to eat them instead of providing for them. As the noise increased, the clumsy attempt by the keepers to tranquilize and round them up became apparent.

After a few minutes of chaos, most of the other wolves had been rounded up when the keepers came for his pack. Ghost Dancer could smell the sweat and fear from the long-legged human keepers. He could hear their hearts beating in their chests. Ghost Dancer knew nothing of round-up processes. He only knew that they were the hunted animals, caged inside an enclosure, who needed to find an escape.

Many keepers approached his pack, who snarled and gnashed their teeth. Just as Mister Hanks was shot, Angry Bear pounced on one of the keepers. Cochise, in an effort to pull Angry Bear away, was knocked back against the fence. He was hurt and lay still where he fell. Angry Bear tore at the arm of the keeper, who screamed and yelled for help. In the melee, Ghost Dancer thought only of Lovely Stella and her pups, Koco and Lilly Bell. He sensed all this was a mistake, but how could it be when he saw a keeper hit Angry Bear in the head with a club?

But wait, was that an opening in the fence? In the chaos and out of confusion, and just before Angry Bear was hit, Ghost Dancer wasn't sure it was there, but now he knew. He had to take a chance and act quickly. He was right!

Lovely Stella was scared but knew to follow Ghost Dancer, who tried to motion her and her pups through the opening with his head. As one of her pups scrambled through, the keepers saw them and took aim. The tranquilizer hit Lovely Stella just as the last pup made his way through the other side of the opening.

To Ghost Dancer, they were being killed. He had to fight back—the need for freedom burned in his heart and could be seen in his eyes. The pups cried for Lovely Stella, but Ghost Dancer used his growl to tell the pups to hide far away from the keepers on the other side of the enclosure, beyond the fence. The timbre of his growl was more than enough for them to understand. Ghost Dancer was angry. He was bigger and braver than most. He was not alpha. He was not beta. He was just one of the pack. This was when Ghost Dancer stood his ground to face his human foe.

He pulled his hackles up and planted his four huge paws firmly on the ground in a wide stance. He sensed the humans' fear, as they seemed to understand and feel his rage. As Ghost Dancer bent his head low for the attack, one of the keepers pointed his gun. It didn't fire. The horrified look on the faces of the humans was satisfying to Ghost Dancer. He approached them in a stealth-like manner, slowly and methodically. The long-legged humans backed away, almost tripping over each other as Ghost Dancer advanced. Then he lunged.

However, the human keepers were fortunate to be closer to the enclosure's gate than they thought. Ghost Dancer had backed them up that far. The gate closed just in time to keep them safe on the other side of Ghost Dancer. He loomed large over those who fell on the ground beyond the gate. Then they ran, yelling and screaming at each other and him. It was an ugly sound.

Ghost Dancer stood alone for a long time before deciding what to do next. He looked over at Cochise, who lay beside the fence, still alive but barely breathing. Ghost Dancer knew Angry Bear had breathed his last. Lovely Stella, surrounded by Koco and Lilly Bell, breathed as shallowly as Cochise. This brought painful memories to Ghost Dancer of the mother he'd lost. He knew what he must do.

⟤⟤◈◈◈⟤⟤

The trip to the wolf preserve was different than before. For Roslyn, the drive didn't seem to take as long, and this time, Jeremy's lame jokes were actually funny. It had been months since her encounter with the wolf pack. Since her last visit, Roslyn had been determined to pursue the wanderlust Ghost Dancer had sparked within her. Since then, there had been much to be thankful for, and because of these changes, she was secretly grateful to Ghost Dancer.

While waiting for the wolf reserve paperwork to clear, she'd convinced her father to allow her to pursue other interests. No longer chained to her desk, she had been given an assistant for the clerical grunt work. At the same time, she was freed to attend more important court cases, brush up on her studies, and engage in debate with Jeremy and "co" during afternoon lunch or cocktail dinner parties.

She blossomed under this newfound freedom to speak her mind and was appreciated for her intellect. Now, she had time on the weekends to dabble in painting abstract art pieces, which she enjoyed immensely. Jeremy even joined in on her semi-bohemian lifestyle, loosening up and becoming less anal. To her mind's eye, he had become more attractive than she'd ever thought possible. This was evident when Jeremy told her the news to reintroduce the wolves. Roslyn had surprised herself with the affection she had developed for Jeremy. On this weekend drive to the preserve, Roslyn had decided not to push him away if he was so inclined to show his affection toward her again.

Jeremy's tone turned serious after an hour of discussion and singing along to their favorite songs on the trip.

"So I talked to Lars. He received a notice in the mail about the state's decision."

"Was he thrilled?" Roslyn asked as she readjusted herself in the passenger seat to look at Jeremy's handsome profile.

"I'm not sure," Jeremy said with a worried tone. "He sounded strange. I couldn't figure it out, so I decided to make this drive to see for myself what was what."

"Really? You didn't tell me."

"I didn't want to alarm you. I wanted to tell you when we got closer to the preserve. After what you went through last time, I didn't want to get you worked up about your *favorite wolf's* predicament. Better to see for ourselves, don't you think?"

"I suppose that makes sense. What do you think's going on?"

"I don't know. We're almost there, so we'll see." This was Jeremy's only reply.

As they drove up the drive, the place looked like nothing had changed. But as Roslyn got out of Jeremy's Jeep, she knew something was wrong. It was quiet. Almost too quiet.

"Do you hear that?" she asked.

"Yeah. Nothing."

She wished they had brought a rifle, but the thought seemed silly. Even though the silence in the air was unsettling and gave off an ominous feeling, Roslyn was unafraid. They stood close to the Jeep, cautiously looking around. Then Jeremy put his pinkie fingers in each corner of his mouth and whistled. The shrill sound cut through the air and echoed off the surrounding hills—still nothing.

A faint sound came from the side of the cabin. Against the chain-link fence encased in chicken wire at its base, a wolf pup was trying to bite through or dig under the fencing on the other side. The soft mewling sound was offset by another, which was much the same.

"What the hell?" Jeremy asked as he walked closer to the pups. To Roslyn, he said, "Go to the door and see if it's open. We have to figure out what's going on."

Roslyn ran to the cabin door and was surprised it opened easily and was empty inside. Horrible thoughts of abandonment ran through her mind as she thought, *Lars, how could you? Son of a bitch!* She rummaged through papers in drawers, trying to find contact information or anything to tell her what had happened to the wolves under the Logans' protection and care. To her relief, she found a few phone numbers written on the notepaper in the ledger.

"Those pups sure grow fast, but I think they seem okay; just scared," Jeremy said, walking in shortly after. "It's been what, three months since we were here last? Is that phone working?"

"I didn't try. Here are a few numbers I found to call."

They were in luck. Jeremy had Lars on the phone, who told him about the round-up catastrophe. However, Jeremy's patience ran thin after only a few minutes of listening.

"That makes no sense," Jeremy said, trying to remain calm. "We *just* talked a few days ago. … You're damn right you screwed up! … Why didn't you tell me all this then?"

Roslyn tried to get a word in edgewise. "Ask Lars if we can bring the pups to him. With any luck, we might—"

Then she stopped. Staring at her were the menacing yellow eyes of Ghost Dancer.

The Last Goodbye

A week had passed since the day the long-legged humans had come to take them. Ghost Dancer and the pups stayed hidden in the hills, far away from the keepers looking for them. He heard humans at night and hid as best he could during the day. They couldn't travel far because of the preserve fencing. Water was scarce but could be found in puddles left by occasional rain or under the shade of a cactus or pine tree.

Without the keepers to rely on for food, Ghost Dancer's intuitive skills for hunting came in handy. He found mice and a rabbit or two for the pups to eat, but the larger game was not in the offing—at least to satisfy his appetite. When the main keepers left, Ghost Dancer sensed their absence. This was the only time he ventured to the cabin. He was hungry.

As he got closer, he sensed her. The black hair was back. He didn't know what to make of this or what he would do. Was she alone? He had to be careful and not get caught again. His instinct to protect the pups was high.

He could see the rolling vehicle come over the rise and smell her scent as it wafted into the open air. He had to try to get to her. He needed her help. Just then, the pups raced by him and scampered up to the fencing. Despite his warning, they ignored him, probably thinking these keepers wouldn't hurt them. They missed their mother, and Ghost Dancer understood the pull of this loss.

He watched as black hair got out of the rolling vehicle. There were only two of them. He heard the human make a shrill sound with his mouth. He saw him kneel at the fence to touch the pups. He watched black hair run to the cabin and saw the other human follow shortly after.

Ghost Dancer was cautious as he crept to the side door of the cabin. The open door allowed him to listen to the strange human talk. By their sound, Ghost Dancer could sense they meant no harm. However, he knew instinctively that she, and only she, could be trusted. He stood his ground at the door as black hair turned to face him.

<hr>

"Lars, we'll talk later, but *get here now!*" Jeremy said with urgency in his voice. "We have company." He gingerly put the phone receiver down on the cradle. His gaze never left the wolf, who watched them menacingly with a low growl.

"Don't move, Jer," Roslyn said. "Whatever you do, don't smile. You're going to be just fine. We just need to figure out what he wants."

"Easy for you to say—"

"Shhh!" Roslyn admonished softly. "Follow his lead. His name is Ghost Dancer."

At the sound of his name, Ghost Dancer crept in closer to Roslyn, who knelt at his level, ready to receive him if he wanted to nip her.

He sensed caution. He smelled no fear. He knew black hair's spirit was with him. Ghost Dancer walked around the room, circling her, then paced as if deciding what to do. Ghost Dancer's uncertainty was causing unnecessary fear. He sensed this by observing the man's dry mouth and the glisten of sweat on his brow. However, black hair didn't seem afraid. No. She wouldn't be. She trusted him. Because of this, Ghost Dancer trusted her. Then he made his move. He pushed his hunger aside and greeted her in his usual manner. He sensed he might be rewarded with kindness if he did this.

<hr>

Roslyn fell back onto the floor when Ghost Dancer put his paws on her shoulders. His weight was almost too much to take. She was utterly powerless. She managed to rise on her elbows and welcomed his nips of affection and licks with his thick tongue. She returned it with scratches under his chin.

She looked up at Jeremy, who seemed unable to figure out what to do. She knew he'd remain where he was and intervene if necessary. But there was no need. After a few seconds, Ghost Dancer leaned back on his haunches and stared at Roslyn. His yellow eyes bore into her so intently that she actually thought she understood what he was trying to convey.

"You okay?" Jeremy whispered.

"I'm fine. Do you have any jerky on you?"

"What?"

"Give me some of that jerky you brought and put it on the floor near my hand. Slowly."

Jeremy reached into his coat pocket and did as instructed. He was amazed at how gingerly Ghost Dancer took it from Roslyn's fingers.

When the pups, Koco and Lilly Bell, entered the cabin, Ghost Dancer stepped back to allow them time to enjoy the scratches, pats, and more jerky from Jeremy and Roslyn. During this time, Jeremy explained what Lars had said about the round-up and the mess the authorities had made of it.

"Apparently, the state notified Lars and Emily long before we did, so the Logans decided to move on the transfer and reintroduction without waiting. They never let on—go figure."

"After that fiasco, they were probably embarrassed to say anything," Roslyn said in controlled anger. "They didn't expect us to come out here, did they? Good thing we did. Great call, Jer," Roslyn said, careful not to smile up at Jeremy. Ghost Dancer was still watching.

"Running out of tranquilizers saved those guys in what must have been a hell of a scrap, which is how these guys were able to escape. Lars and the rest looked all over for these three, but they were able to elude capture. It was too bad for one named Angry Bear, but the pup's mom and her mate survived. According to the authorities, a few deputies had to change their underwear after facing Ghost Dancer. Probably one hell of a showdown. Damn government pukes!"

"Ghost Dancer. My hero," Roslyn said softly as she mystically stared into Ghost Dancer's eyes from across the room.

After more discussion, they walked outside in search of water. Jeremy grabbed a steel tub and turned it over next to a water spigot. The wolves' lapping sound in the water gave them an idea of how close to dehydration they were. After what they'd been through, it amazed Roslyn how docile they seemed, not aggressive at all. But she remained respectful and cautious of the wild wolf inside. She couldn't imagine what that terrifying round-up must have been like for them. The confusion and misunderstanding stood out larger than Ghost Dancer could stand tall. They didn't deserve what they'd gone through. They deserved to run free without any more government intervention. Then she had an idea.

"What do you say we take off with them?" Roslyn asked.

"Huh?"

"Yeah, just ride outside the reserve and set 'em loose."

"I'm not sure that's legal."

"Are they tagged? Are they chipped? I don't know, but look, Jeremy, you've seen them cooped up in that enclosure. After all these years, don't you think Ghost Dancer should finally have the freedom to roam as far and wide as he can? Look at him."

"I know, and I understand," Jeremy said, seemingly weighing the thought and options as he leaned back against his Jeep. "I'm just not sure it's the right thing to do. I've already told Lars that Ghost Dancer is here. He's probably on his way now."

"Based on what you told me, I wouldn't be surprised if they consider Ghost Dancer a renegade or rogue lone wolf." Roslyn tried to keep her voice calm in case Ghost Dancer got any ideas. "He's got a target on his backside, and I don't trust he'll be taken care of—if you know what I mean. And the pups? Who knows if they'll see their mother again, so what will happen to them?

They'll stand a better chance with Ghost Dancer than anywhere else."

"They're being released in Yellowstone, Montana, and Idaho. *Not* Colorado."

"Yellowstone Park isn't that far away once you get into Wyoming. If you don't tell, I won't," Roslyn said, smiling mischievously.

Looking up at Jeremy with the sun streaming in his wind-blown hair, Roslyn thought Jeremy was the most beautiful soul she'd ever seen. Of course he would do as she asked.

⟞⟶◈◈◈⟵⟝

After securing the wolves in the enclosure again, Roslyn and Jeremy stayed at the preserve to ensure they were safe. Jeremy went into action and took care of everything. He asked Kenny to rent an open-sided trailer so the wolves could sit comfortably on the ride to Wyoming. Jeremy had to have Kenny and Kari be part of the reintroduction and told them all they knew so far. Kari was eager and took only a day to prepare for readiness. She was instrumental in handling the small details of the transfer without anyone being the wiser. Thanks to Lars's contrived story to the authorities, it seemed the lone dire wolf would never be caught, now lost in the wilds of Colorado. But Roslyn and her friends knew better.

The ride to Wyoming was uneventful. Roslyn was amazed at the calmness of Ghost Dancer. It was as if he knew what was happening and allowed her to sit with him anytime she wished. At one point, on the drive up, she even sat in the trailer with the wolves to ensure their comfort. That was what she told Jeremy anyway. In truth, she wanted to be near Ghost Dancer. He welcomed her presence and seemed content when she was around. She sensed that he felt safe with her. They trusted each other. After inching closer to her, he would look into her eyes, lower his head on his huge paws, and sleep.

Letting go was bittersweet. The winds of Wyoming could be tremendous, and Roslyn always thought this made sounds carry for quite a distance into Montana. It made sense with its wide-open spaces and skies, however fanciful she thought the idea. They left the highway a mile behind them and traveled on a dirt road, then settled onto a flat piece of land whose sky was as big as the hole in Roslyn's heart. They had taken a risk and didn't want to travel farther into the state's interior than necessary.

"Do you think they'll find Yellowstone and the others on their own?" Roslyn asked.

"I don't doubt it. Not with Ghost Dancer leading the way," Kenny said in reply.

Roslyn watched Jeremy walk forward to unlatch the trailer's back gate as she stood with Kari. At three months, the pups were *almost* as big as adult wolves, but not quite. However, they would never be as large as Ghost Dancer, and maybe that was a good thing.

⸺◈◈◈⸺

Ghost Dancer stood close to Roslyn but never turned to look up at her. The dire wolf in him commanded that he breathe in this freedom and embrace what was to come. He stared into the vastness of the land, wondering what awaited him once they ventured forward. Black hair was exactly as he had suspected. She had the spirit of the wolf within her, and they were forever bound. For him, this wasn't goodbye. For him, this was necessary. He knew not all long-legged humans were like her, but her pack of humans came close.

He felt her as she knelt by his side, and he turned slightly to acknowledge her presence. He then looked at Koco and Lilly Bell, who waited patiently for his lead. He allowed black hair to rub his chin and whined in acceptance. He stepped in front of her and sat on his haunches, head high and proud, towering over her as she knelt. He stood and moved slowly forward and nipped at her lip, then forcefully licked her with his tongue, kissing her as he had the first time they met. As before, the wolf kiss was a brief encounter. When Ghost Dancer moved back from her, he saw her face wet from her eyes water. Then he bowed his head, thankful for her spirit, friendship, and acceptance of his pack.

Like a shot, he turned and raced away with the pups following after him.

The return trip was a quiet one. Except for clearing a few throats, no one said a word, not even when they closed the gate of the trailer and rode back to the highway on their way to Colorado. Roslyn's tears fell silently while Jeremy held her close. She allowed this, thinking only of the spirit of the wolf, its pull, and the freedom Ghost Dancer had finally received.

As serendipitous as it was, she would never forget her encounter with Ghost Dancer. She knew not to worry about him. He and she both would find their way. In fact, she already had. As she nestled into Jeremy's arms, she wondered if Ghost Dancer would find his mate. Just to see that would make Roslyn very happy. *She'd be a lucky wolf, indeed.* These daydream images and her own future occupied her thoughts as they moved along a distant stretch of highway on their way home.

It was windy in Wyoming, but somewhere during the long, quiet ride home, Roslyn swore she could hear the howl of one lone wolf. Roslyn knew she'd always hear it, and when she did, she'd tell herself it was Ghost Dancer calling to her in thanks.

The End

MYSTERY AT THE STANLEY

The helmet I wore bothered me. It was hot and made my head sweat, especially when we weren't moving and were caught by every traffic light in town. Feeling the wind in my hair was my favorite way to ride; however, helmets were necessary for safety and protection. Especially when riding a motorcycle through the foothills of Colorado.

This was a day trip, or so my boyfriend, Sean, told me. He was an adventurer. Me? Not so much. I loved his energy, though. His ability to always try something new never failed to impress. His encouragement was infectious, and more times than not, I found myself going along with his crazy wanders and outdoor adventures. This day was no different.

"Let's take the bike and go up to Estes Park."

"I love Estes, but isn't it going to rain?"

"Who cares? It's Colorado, and as they say, don't like the weather, wait fifteen minutes—it'll change."

"Easy for you to say," I said doubtfully. "I don't know. We just came out of the July monsoon, and I'm not so sure the rain gods are done with us yet. It's supposed to be hot today. I don't like riding in wet, muggy weather, and it's only the first week in August."

"Stop it, my fair lady." Sean chuckled and playfully pinched my cheek. "You worry too much."

"Maybe, but… well, promise we won't stay long if it looks like the clouds are rolling in?"

"By that time, it'll be too late anyway. We'll stop somewhere safe and wait out the weather. Okay?"

This was how I found myself, Amanda Adams, on the back of a motorcycle, holding tightly to the love of my life, Sean Evans.

<hr>

On that day in 1998, Estes Park was as beautiful and touristy as ever. Visitors crowding the street and an elk or two walking casually by were typical to see. The elk were famous. Seeing the long antlers of bucks almost guaranteed a photo op for many, which subsequently snarled traffic worse than it would have been otherwise. But on a motorcycle, it was easy to traverse traffic and weave between cars. It gave me the feeling of being "cool" and "above it all" to skirt convention by traveling easily wherever and whenever we wanted.

Self-assured and fun, Sean could always be counted on to make any trip memorable. With his dark-haired good looks, he was approachable, friendly, and not bad to look at. He made it look easy to initiate conversation and engage with others. On the other hand, I was more reserved and hesitated to venture forth anything other than my first name. He was encouraging, protective, and loving—I trusted him implicitly.

After Sean parked the bike, to my relief, I instantly took my helmet off and shook out my hair. The cool air helped ease the tension from the ride and my thoughts of impending nasty weather. Despite my trepidation, I enjoyed being outside and feeling the warm sun on my face. We strolled around the streets of Estes Park and looked at the curio displays in the many novelty shop windows, which was always fun. We tried on cowboy hats, laughed at ourselves in buckskin vests, and talked with other tourists, quickly making time pass. Sean surprised me with a charm bracelet made by a local artisan. It was absolutely stunning.

"I saw you eyeing the turquoise jewelry, and when I saw this bracelet with touches of jade and turquoise, I thought, yeah. That'll do." What a guy, huh?

For my part, I bought a silver-plated flask with a buffalo head etched on the front. Knowing Sean, he'd show it off as a sign of how "cool" he was to his friends—if not use it outright full of his favorite brand of whiskey. He loved it. We made it a special day, just the two of us.

As the afternoon wore on, I was surprised when Sean suggested we ride to the famous Stanley Hotel.

"Really? Why?" I asked, not because I didn't want to go but because I never knew he was interested in the infamous haunted hotel of Stephen King's book *The Shining*.

"It's early and doesn't look like it'll rain. We can come out of these mountains on the other side of Estes if we go that way, so why not?"

"Okay then, let's go," I said, just as excited to visit the hotel as he was.

⋘⊶⊷⊶⊷⋙

That day was scorching hot in the mountains of Colorado, which surprised me because of the elevation. It was usually cooler than in the city. *Maybe it's just me, but it didn't seem this hot in Estes. This heat is almost unbearable!*

This thought came to mind as the Stanley Hotel loomed into view, looking as it always had from the many photos I'd seen. It stood on a hill, white and imposing. The hotel lobby didn't look at all like I had imagined. The stairway in the middle of the lobby was grand but not nearly as steep or wide as the movie version. Apparently, by the sound of hammering, construction was underway in the rooms to the left and right of the reception area at the bottom of the stairway.

The lobby was absent of tourists compared to what, I suppose, it would have been but for the construction. While Sean chatted with the receptionist about the activities and obvious renovations within the lobby, I left him to inspect the commotion myself.

The room to my right of the front entryway, which was being renovated, had a piano pushed into the back corner. Some workers with hammers were pounding on planks in this darkly paneled room. Dust lay everywhere. Just a few tourists with their children were roaming around the room; some were playing despite admonishments from the workers to be careful and watch their step. This instantly deflated their sense of fun, it seemed. The room wasn't very inviting, so I returned to the desk to meet Sean. He and I went on to explore the room on the other side of the reception desk, and I listened as he filled me in on his conversation with the receptionist.

"The remodeling and renovations should be completed within a few weeks for ski season *and* when guests arrive in the fall," Sean said. "This is the hotel's quiet season, so they're taking advantage of the downtime."

"Oh! Okay then. Can we go upstairs to look around if no one's here?"

"Nope. We are not allowed to visit any rooms upstairs unless we have a reservation, my dear Amanda."

"Fair enough, I guess. What a bummer though."

This other room was a complete contrast to the piano room. It was light and airy; pale colors decorated the walls and vaulted ceiling.

"Wow!" was the only word I could express at the sight of this room.

"Yeah," Sean said as he gazed up at the ceiling. "Too bad we can't see more of the other rooms."

"Yeah, too bad, but *look* at this place."

The renovations to this room could only improve the elegance it already possessed. It was clearly a ballroom, and I imagined the many events held here in the past and more to come in the future.

Scaffolding had been erected, but no workers were there. Maybe it was due to an afternoon break or something, and I thought no more of it. We wandered around in this room a bit longer before leaving its faded and pre-renovated splendor.

We made our way to the other side of the reception desk, with the stairway between us, where Sean stopped to read a plaque telling the hotel's history. Just then, other guests came to the reception desk to ask questions. With the clerk's attention diverted away from us, Sean seized an opportunity.

Taking advantage of the clerk's preoccupation with this latest set of guests, Sean grabbed my hand and motioned for me to follow. He held his index finger to his mouth, and we tiptoed up the stairs out of sight of the receptionist's desk. The construction noise helped muffle what could be heard of our steps as he pulled me behind him. We made a quick but quiet dash up the stairs to the top landing area that led to rooms on either side.

⟫⟩◈◈◈⟨⟪

I was terrified of being caught, but not Sean. He continued to the left of the landing where another set of stairs led to other floors. We took the stairs two at a time, with weird jogs left and right to either side of the hotel hallways, like a labyrinth. When we reached the top floor landing, Sean let go of my hand.

"Where are we? What if we get caught?" I asked.

"We won't. There's no one here except us."

"That's not entirely true, you know. There *have* to be guests."

"Look down," Sean insisted. From this vantage point, I could look down onto all the other landings and stairwells that led to hallways of rooms within the bowels of the hotel.

"My God. This is beautiful." The hotel's beauty, if not its outdated decor, astonished me. Here, I could envision the hotel's old-world charm bringing visitors in droves each season.

"Let's look around at the rooms," Sean suggested, and I followed.

"Do you think any are open?" I asked.

"I don't know. Let's find out."

It was typical of Sean to have a devil-may-care attitude about life when he was mischievous. However, to my amazement, the first room I came to had an old-fashioned doorknob for turning and opened to a small room. The decor was puzzling because it wasn't modern at all. It was decorated in a calico motif, orange and brown, with an Old Western theme—even a spittoon. *They have themed rooms? Now this is interesting.* I walked around the room for a minute but soon felt out of sorts and dizzy. It didn't feel right. *It's so hot up here!* What's more, I didn't know where Sean had gone.

When I came out of the room, I was relieved to see Sean exiting another farther down the hall.

"Hey, what did you find? Any more rooms open?" Sean asked.

"Yeah… I don't like this. I just left one decorated in an Old West kind of way. I wonder why they haven't updated these rooms. Are they all themed like that?"

"Mine wasn't. It looked fine. Maybe some people request to stay in older rooms, so they leave a few done up old-timey. Who knows," Sean answered in an offhanded way.

"That makes no sense. People can rent a room in Golden if they want. I was creeped out. I got dizzy in there too. It's way too quiet up here and hot. Can we go now?" I pleaded.

"Amanda, you scared? You all right?" Sean asked with a laugh in his voice, slightly teasing. Then he looked at me closely, seeming to sense my concern.

"Well, yeah. I don't know, there's something… I don't like it. Let's get going. My shirt's sticking to my backbone up here," I said, wiping the sweat beginning to bead on my forehead.

"Okay, just as well. All these rooms are probably the same anyway." Sean grabbed my hand and led me back to the staircase landing.

⟞⊙⊙⊙⟝

Where he came from, I'll never know. Now, we were caught and in trouble. We looked at him with that deer-in-headlights look. He stood at the top of the landing dressed in formal evening wear, a black tie and tails, a white shirt, and a cummerbund around his waist. He stood there, studying us without expression in black patent leather shoes, blocking our way down.

It was a hot August afternoon. We were sweating. He was not. It was very strange. *Why is he dressed like that? Is there a wedding or something we weren't told about?* Clasping the front lapels of his dinner jacket in white-gloved hands, he was the first of us to speak.

"May I be of help? Is there something I can assist you with?" As a language major, I noticed his speech was perfect. It was not Midwestern but more mid-Atlantic, almost British, but not quite. I almost laughed as visions of the movie *Titanic* drifted into my mind. Sean's grip tightened on my hand, quickly reminding me this was no laughing matter. At our silence, he repeated himself.

"Is there anything I can assist you with, sir?" he asked again, speaking directly to Sean.

"No, not at all," Sean said, finding his tongue. "We were just looking around and kind of got lost." He lied.

That seemed like a lame excuse, and I thought this guy would see right through the fib. But, again, he said nothing more. He just studied us as if waiting for something more to be said.

"It's so quiet up here you startled us. We were just leaving. I think we'll be fine," I said, hoping the guy would accept that and leave us alone in our embarrassment at being caught there without permission.

"If you say so, miss. Have a good afternoon," was his only reply.

At that, we walked to the other side of the landing, which led to a hallway on the opposite side of the floor. I had only taken a few steps when I thought of thanking the man for his concern and offer of assistance. But, when I turned, he was gone. No sound announced his leaving; no footsteps could be heard on the tread of the stairs. Nothing.

"Where'd he go?" I asked.

"What the hell!" Sean said, astonished.

"He was just here. What…?" I was stunned into silence and felt the cold hand of fear as it slid down my hot and sweaty back.

Sean and I looked down the stairwell and saw nothing. No shadow of him descending the stairs, no sound at all. Vanished as if into thin air.

"Maybe he's down this hall," Sean said as he walked to the opposite side of the landing where I had been in that weirdly decorated room. But again, there was no sign of him. We raced farther down the hallway to see if he might have entered another unlocked room. But no luck; all the rooms were locked.

"He *was* there, right?" Sean asked incredulously. I'd never seen him so perplexed.

I said nothing in response; I just nodded my head in agreement.

"Holy shit!" Sean said. I think he knew I was thinking the same. The realization of where we were hit us at the same time—the Stanley Hotel.

⟁⟁⟁

We ran as if the hounds of hell were chasing us. We ran down the hallway as fast as we could, not caring about the noise we made; that is if there was anyone to hear the commotion of our footfalls. We didn't scream or yell. Pure panic and adrenaline propelled us on in the hot and clammy air. We had no idea where the hallway would lead or where we would end up. We were desperate to get far away—and out of that hotel quickly.

At the end of the hall was a set of stairs. They went down, down, down and ended at a back door. We burst through, like bats out of hell, thankful for the sunshine and warm summer air.

We ran until we hit the retaining wall made of stone at the back of the hotel. It was full of stinking trash bins and construction debris. I had no idea the back of the place was like that, but I assumed it was only temporary until the remodel was done. However, it was real, and I was thankful.

Breathing hard, we tried to collect ourselves; Sean bent with his hands on his knees, me facing the stone wall sucking in air, smelling the dirt, and feeling the roughness of the blessed uneven stones. Then we burst out laughing at the ridiculous nature of our escape. We started talking over each other all at once, and with no one there but us to hear our conversation, we let our nervous fear and laughter overtake us.

"What was that?" I asked, trying to catch my breath. "Did you see how he was dressed?"

"The black tie and tails—" Sean said, still breathless.

"It was hot as hell up there. What was he—?"

"I don't know, but—"

"A ghost! Do you think he was a ghost? He was as solid as you and me—"

"Disappeared right in front of us—"

"I know! The way he spoke, who talks like that these days? We should tell somebody—"

"Like *hell*, we will! To hell with that!" Sean said, making it emphatically clear.

"But *that* was crazy!"

"Yes, and we shouldn't have been there. At all!"

We paused to consider what we had just gone through. Finally, I spoke again.

"You're right," I said, giving in to Sean's logic. "We can't say anything—"

"To *anybody*. It'll be our secret. Don't tell anyone—"

"What? That you almost shit your pants?" I laughed almost too loudly in a feigned attempt to admit I was scared shitless too.

"No, that we're crazy as hell. Shit!" Sean reached out and hugged me then.

We held each other briefly, rocking back and forth in comfort. As I felt Sean's sweaty arm around my neck and tasted his salty cheek when I kissed him, I knew I was safe. It was too hot to hold each other long, so we made our way around the hotel and exited from the back, acting as if it was normal for us to come from that part of the hotel.

We didn't need to worry. There were few people around even then. We casually walked to the adjacent building to peek inside and to further settle our nerves. The sign outside told us it was a theater. Judging by how it was boarded up and with nothing but theater props inside, maybe it was also waiting for renovations. Just then, a man came into view. Sean couldn't help himself. He had to ask the unanswerable.

"Hey," Sean called to him as he walked past us with a tool belt around his waist. "I'm curious about something. You work here, right?"

"Yeah," the man answered.

"Is there a formal function going on today, I mean tonight… or something?"

The man stood back and looked at Sean with one of those looks that said, "He must be on something." Then he said, "Are you kidding? With all the dust we're creating? Not tonight." Then he excused himself with a perfunctory "have a good day" wave of his hand.

With nothing more to see or say, we headed to the waiting motorcycle, which would take us from the hotel with our secret ghostly encounter intact.

⟞⟶◦◦◦⟵⟝

I often think back to that day, especially since I've been married to Sean all these years. We never went back. It was even suggested we honeymoon there, but that suggestion was met with a resounding "No!"

It was a lovely hotel then and still is now, don't get me wrong. But there is something. A mysterious *something* that might have been either friend or foe, who knows? Maybe our imaginations went wild on that hot August afternoon in 1998. But as we rode away, I, holding tight to Sean's waist on the back of the bike, looked back and up at the hotel windows.

I swear the ghostly figure was there… looking down at us as we rode away.

The End

Forgotten Memory

I've known her for a long time. She seemed so polished and put together. Never a hair out of place. So, imagine my surprise when she began this incredible story over a glass of wine. To this day, I don't know how true it is. But the shocking events she told with such eloquence and, at the same time, with pain tell me it must have been. I will not write her name or indicate who she is because of the investigators among us. Suffice it to say this incident is probably not uncommon. I share it, hoping others might know that life is complicated for the young. How we treat others is important, if not for our soul's salvation, but for understanding our penchant for compassion when we learn of someone else's pain. It is here she begins her story.

It is all so vivid to me. Even now, it feels like yesterday. We were young. I was six, my sister was five, and my baby brother was four. We were happy that late Sunday afternoon in the autumn of 1961 as we walked in our small town to the Dairy Queen for ice cream. Mommy was so pretty in a white blouse and blue skirt with many slips or crinolines underneath. The poodle on the skirt was white and fluffy with a red collar around its neck. Grandmamma wore her best suit, a jacket buttoned down the front, and a full pencil skirt that hugged snugly around her calves. Mommy wore heels, and Grandmamma wore stilettos, black with red trim. I remember singing and skipping alongside as we came over the hill across from the high school. At the same time, Mommy and Grandmamma strolled slowly behind us down the sidewalk. The leaves were just turning into rich, vibrant colors—and it was all good.

The car came over the top of the hill as we walked along. It screeched to a halt on our side of the walk. It was Daddy. He smelled funny, like the drink he used to swallow after a long day at work. He started yelling and screaming at my mother about things I didn't understand. We were in front of a house that sat on a rise. Loose bricks were on the front stoop of the steps leading up to it. Daddy picked one up and started hitting Mommy with it. Blood spurted everywhere, on us and her blue poodle skirt. I watched as the white poodle turned red from her blood. My grandmother removed one of her stiletto heels and began hitting Daddy with it in the head. Red blood was now running down his face. They were all screaming, except me.

I looked up at the house and saw two people looking down at us from their front porch. They were White. One was an older lady sitting in a white wicker rocking chair. The other was a man dressed in overalls with only one side buckled to the front bib, both hands in his pockets. I screamed and pleaded with them for help. They did nothing. The man only leaned against one of the pillars on the porch, watching, while the lady continued to rock with interest. I felt helpless.

I turned to try to help my mom, but I had never seen blood before. And there was so much of it. To a six-year-old child, it was horrifying. I didn't know what to do except watch as Daddy dragged my sister and brother to his car by their hands, holding one pair in each of his huge ones. Mommy leaned against the brick wall, bleeding and holding her hands to her face, crying. Everyone was still screaming and yelling; my brother and sister were the loudest. I thought I could get them away from Daddy, so I ran to pry his fingers loose. But I couldn't get them loose or him to let go. I looked up at the house and, once again, called for the people to help us.

The lady got up from her chair and said, "I can't take this anymore." She went inside while the young, big-bellied White man stood there watching us.

Daddy opened his car's back door and forced my sister and brother into the back seat. Then he reached down to grab me; I realized I was caught and couldn't escape.

I kicked and screamed at him, "No, no, no, no! No! Let go, Daddy! Let me go! Please help, please help us!" I cried and yelled at the people of that house again, begging for help, but still, no help came. Daddy pushed me in to sit beside him in the front seat, locked the doors, and then drove off at an amazing speed.

⟶◎◎◎⟵

The car was an old model with bench seats, front and back. There were no seat belts. The windows at the back were small, and I couldn't see over them; neither could my sister and brother sitting in the back. I could barely see out the front windows, but I knew Daddy was driving too fast. Every hill or bump in the road made the car fly and hit hard on the roadway with a loud *whoomph* sound when it landed. Our small bodies rose and slammed into the seats after each *whoomph*. The car careened around corners, making horrible screeching noises, and he didn't seem to care. I begged Daddy to slow down because he was hurting us.

My sister held tight to the seat's cushion and screamed constantly. But, being so small and not knowing how to hold tight, my brother's little body bounced everywhere. Only a thin covering concealed the steel rods that ran across the chassis of the car's roof, so he'd hit his head on the ceiling and cry out each time because of fear and pain. I begged them to be quiet, but it was no use. If they would just *stop* crying, I thought it would be okay. *Their crying must be making Daddy do this.* I wanted them to stop so that Daddy would leave us alone, so I stayed quiet. They always did what I did. They always followed my lead. But not that day.

Daddy drove this way for what seemed a long time. Before I knew it, the afternoon sun had gone down, and it was getting dark. When I spoke again, I begged him to stop or slow down. But he'd only look at me with a sideways glance.

I didn't think I would ever see my mother again. I had to try to get away and see if she was all right, but I didn't want to leave my brother and sister. The thought of my mother being dead was terrifying, but then again, so was Daddy. I was helpless and couldn't do anything but be a good girl and do what Daddy said. If I did, maybe he wouldn't hurt us more than he had already. But how could I when Mommy might be dead, and we could be next? I didn't know what it would be like to die, but the thought horrified me.

Then Daddy drove down a street that, from the top, seemed like a dark hole. It was black and dark—a dead end. It had only one light pole, with a bare bulb for illumination, creating a bright circle on the asphalt, but no more. One or two houses sat in the recesses of darkness on either side of the alley street. The trees all around seemed to hover over the area, waiting to swallow it whole. This is when Daddy finally stopped the car.

My father had become the boogeyman we were always told about. A mean, scary monster who would harm us or eat us whenever he wanted and in the worst possible way. I didn't like him anymore.

"Daddy, please let us go. I want to see my mommy. Let us go. Please," I pleaded.

But Daddy only rolled his eyes at me, got out of the car, and opened the back seat to grab my little brother. He was wounded and held his head with his tiny little hands.

To my horror, with one of his hands, Daddy lifted my baby brother into the air by one ankle. With the other, he undid his belt and drew it out of the loops at the waist of his pants. He began beating my brother with the buckle end of the belt. *How can he hit him like that? Why?* My sister, who had stopped screaming when the car came to a stop, began to scream again. I thought this was why Daddy beat my brother, so I begged her to be quiet. But my sister wouldn't stop screaming and crying no matter what I said to hush her. I don't remember crying at all; I just observed what was happening.

When Daddy was done beating my brother, he put him down. He made him stand in the circle of light illuminated by the single bulb of the utility pole. He then came to my side of the car, and instead of opening the door to grab my sister—he came for me.

I remember wondering why Daddy came for me. I never cried or screamed until that moment. I was being a good girl—the best girl. I didn't want him to beat me like my brother. I couldn't see my brother from my side of the car, but I could hear him crying. I knew he must be hurt. I didn't want to be hit like him by Daddy. So, with all my might, I held on to the inside door handle with my left hand as he pulled on my right one. He pulled so hard.

"No, Daddy, stop! I didn't do *anything*, Daddy. I didn't *do anything*! I promise to be good. I *promise* to be good." I yelled and screamed as loudly as I could. I held tight to the door handle.

He finally pried my hand loose. I remember accidentally scratching myself as I clawed at him, trying again to get loose from his grip. But that only made him grab both my hands in his huge one. I dug my heels into the dirt to prevent him from pulling me forward, but he dragged me to the other side of the car despite my attempts. I failed miserably.

My sister was no longer screaming but crying and looking out at us. Her face was as white as a ghost looking out from behind the glass pane of the car window. I could finally see my brother standing in his Sunday shorts, whimpering under the light; his legs were wet from peeing his pants. I wanted to go to him. I pulled myself in his direction, but Daddy held me tight, shaking me. He wanted me to listen to him, but I couldn't. I was so scared. The thought of being lifted upside down by the ankle and beat like my brother had been was terrifying. I didn't want to have blood on me like Mommy.

I didn't know what to do. I realized that I couldn't help them or myself. I just knew Daddy was going to hurt me. I couldn't think clearly. Why didn't he grab my sister instead of me? Was it because he loved her more but hated my brother and me? He didn't look or even smell like the Daddy I knew. What was wrong? Why did he hate us? I didn't want to see any more blood. My brother was hurt. I wanted my brother to be okay. I wanted *everything* to be like it was before Daddy came for us. But it wasn't. I couldn't understand what was happening. I wanted to be somewhere else.

Daddy kept talking to me, but I didn't hear anything he said until he said, "I love you, honey. I love you so much."

But that couldn't be true. Loving and hating us at the same time didn't make much sense. It was just silly. How could Daddy hurt us if he loved us? I tried to reason. I was confused, hurt, and scared. He became the bad daddy to me then—the awful daddy.

That's when I started to laugh. It was all I could do. I couldn't help it and couldn't stop once I started. I laughed. Not a loud chuckle or even a guffaw, but a constant hysterical laugh. Daddy looked down at me. I thought he was going to hit me, but all I could do was laugh with my eyes wide so I could see clearly. Warm tears ran down my face. Maybe I thought I could laugh the pain away. Laugh the nightmare away. I don't know.

"Baby, you have to stop laughing. Stop laughing. I love you so much, honey," Daddy said, trying to get me to stop. But I couldn't.

Then Daddy knelt down and hugged me. Still, I kept laughing. His words "I love you" were constantly repeated. No matter how often he said it, I couldn't get them to make sense. I didn't want him to touch me. I tried to wiggle out of his grasp but couldn't get free because of the laughter.

Other cars came then with bright red lights and sirens. Daddy let go of me and raised his arm into the air. The men in the cars came over and grabbed my daddy. They put his hands behind his back and placed shiny things on his wrists. The men took my sister out of Daddy's car. She had stopped screaming when they arrived. I saw another one go to my brother.

A man with a shiny star on his shirt led me by one of the cars with shining lights. I was still laughing. The man knelt down to my level.

"It's okay. Y'all okay now, but you have to stop laughing so you can tell me what happened." But I couldn't stop, and he continued, "You know it's not nice to laugh at a time like this." I knew he was right, but I couldn't stop long enough to tell him I *couldn't* stop. He said, "Calm down now and breathe. Take a deep breath and breathe. Breathe with me now, in… out, in… out."

I tried to do what he said and breathe with him, but I would start laughing again every time I tried. I tried really hard to stop so I could breathe and speak to him. The laughing frightened me. It was getting hard for me to breathe. I had to tell him what happened because he was a grown-up with a shiny badge and lots of stuff on his black belt.

If I didn't stop laughing, I was also afraid something terrible would finally happen to me, and I'd never see my family again, especially my mommy. I tried hard to do as the man said, but the laughing got worse. I wanted to say, "I'm trying to stop! I've been a bad girl because I couldn't protect my brother and sister from the bad daddy. I tried to be a good girl." But I couldn't because of all the laughing.

"What's wrong with her? Why is she laughing? None of this is funny," another man with a shiny badge asked. I know he tried to be kind. But he didn't understand either. When he reached out to me, I leaned over and threw up on his shiny black shoes, the ground, and his long, dark-sleeved shirt.

⋯⊰⊙⊙⊙⊱⋯

I didn't know what to do or how to make it right. I was so young, yet I was the oldest, and I should have known better than to throw up on that man. Good girls didn't throw up on people, especially those with shiny badges. He tried to reassure me it was all right and got some cloth to wipe my face and his sleeve. He was so kind to me, which I think was what helped the laughing fit subside. I was so sorry, and that's when tears came. The torrent of tears wet his sleeve again as he held me close.

"Okay, little lady. You'll be all right now," he said as he rubbed my back.

I was not behaving as I should. The way he held me, I could see my daddy in the back seat of one of their cars. Daddy looked out at me with a sad look on his face, then hung his head. I think he was crying.

I didn't want to get into the other car with the shiny light on top. No more cars. But my brother and sister were there in the back seat. They needed me, so I guessed it was all right. The man with the shiny badge helped me get in, and when he shut the door, it was quiet. I didn't speak, just stared straight ahead without saying a word, no crying, and no laughing. I stared out at nothing.

"Are you wokay?" my sister asked. I didn't answer; I just stared and stared and stared. She stuttered, asking, "Pa-pa-pa-pa… please say somefing, come on. Sa-sa-sa… say somefing." I didn't. It was strange to hear her speak that way. She never stuttered or lisped before. My brother began to cry again and reached out for me. I said nothing but pulled them to me and hugged them tight.

I don't remember much of the ride home. However, when we got there, Mommy was with Grandmamma and others. Mommy hugged my sister and brother as they ran to her, but there wasn't enough room for me. All I did was stare at her in disbelief. Stunned. Mommy wasn't dead, and I didn't know what to make of that. I stared at her shirt, which was now dirty and torn. The poodle on her skirt had been torn halfway off. It was not stained red with blood but still white. Mommy's swollen face was bandaged and bruised. She looked like a scary monster as she talked to the men with shiny badges. I felt ashamed because I couldn't find help for her. I hadn't kept her safe from the bad daddy.

The men left us soon after. I didn't want my sister and brother to hurt Mommy's face, so I tried to pull them away. That was when Mommy struck me with the back of her hand. The blow sent me flying across the room. I landed on something hard, hitting my head. It hurt so bad. The loud noise, like a high-pitched shriek, rang in my head. I couldn't hear anything. Not even Mommy, who was screaming at me. Neither could I hear anything my Grandmamma or what my mommy's friends said when they grabbed at her. Mommy was coming for me, and I didn't know why, except I was a bad girl. Now, she was the monster trying to hurt me. Just like the bad daddy.

"It's all her fault, damn it!" I could faintly hear her say. "She looks too much like him not to be! Why was she ever born?"

The shock of Mommy hating me, too, started the laughing to begin all over again. I tried hard to keep it from returning. I thought I could swallow the sound, but it was useless. Like before, they tried to help me make it stop, but I couldn't. My stomach hurt from the laughing. I hurt all over, inside and out. I thought the nightmare of that day would never end.

⚬⚬⚬

In those days, my life changed dramatically. During those times, the spankings got worse and became more like beatings. Whenever my sister and brother did something naughty, Mommy always blamed me. She punished me for not keeping them safe, and instead of disciplining them, I got their spankings instead. She told me I should know how to keep my brother and sister from getting into trouble when she was at work or dancing and drinking at the local club all night. I believed her when she told me, "You're the oldest and should know better." I was only a year older than my sister. But it didn't seem to matter to Mommy that I was a child also. I came to feel they were more important to her than me—I didn't matter.

When she got home from work, I would get a spanking if she couldn't find them. I would get a spanking if they did something that caused them to get a cut or scrape. I would get a spanking if I was not at home when she got home from work. On the rare occasions when my brother and sisters *did* get a spanking, I would laugh. You see, it was my fault they were spanked because I didn't keep them safe. I was a bad girl for laughing, so I also deserved the spankings I got for doing that. For years after, I would laugh inappropriately.

<hr>

Outward appearances were everything to my mother. No one knew the horror I suffered at this woman's hands. My mother's arms never held me. I had difficulty saying *arms* and especially *hands* for a long time because they scared me. My mother's hands were weapons used to hurt me, so psychologically, I suppose that was why those words were hard to say.

I grew up thinking her treatment of me was normal. I tried hard to be perfect, to be a good girl. I tried to stay quiet, observant, and watchful, careful not to make a wrong move. I was considered stupid and slow because I only stared around at people, barely saying a word. To her, the attempted kidnapping by my dad was one thing, but to have a daughter afflicted with a strange malady of staring at people all the time without speaking was another thing altogether. That only made her despise me more.

<hr>

I was twelve when we were sent to visit my dad. It was summer, and he had remarried. It was touch and go with us for a while. It took years before he and I managed to reconcile.

"I can't re-raise you," he said to me. "I've made some horrible mistakes, honey, but I never want you to hate me. I want to take you out of the home environment you're growing up in. I don't like what I've been hearing."

I hadn't quite understood his meaning; as I said, I thought how I had been treated was normal. It wasn't. It's hard to recognize child abuse when you're the victim of it. But his words helped me realize my misfortune didn't lie with knowing and loving him. It was from a different source. From that day on, I never again saw the evil side of the "daddy" I encountered years ago. This father was kind, tender, loving, and caring.

I had to find a way to forgive the then-handsome young man driven to take such action without fully understanding its effect on us. My dad must have realized, through my hysterical laughter and the disassociation that came after, what he had done. Although he never said it, I could tell he hated himself for doing such a thing.

He could never undo the psychological damage, but he must have lived with the shame of his actions until the day he died. He atoned for his behavior by trying to get me to understand how a father's love could strip a man bare to the bone when hurt the way my mother had hurt him. I loved my dad; like him, I wanted Mommy to love me too.

⚬⚬⚬

It wasn't always bad between my mother and me. Some days were very good. Like the time I asked about the incident. She couldn't believe I remembered it at all. She told me it was the White lady who actually called the police. She was the one who finally came to our aid, applying cotton kitchen towels to my mother's wounds. It was her son who looked on but then ended up taking them to the hospital. My mother tells how the mother "chewed him out something awful" for being a lay-about, lazy, good-for-nothing son.

The memories of that horrible day in the autumn of long ago began to return, but only in bits and pieces. Many years later, I finally remembered everything, which came to me in a flood of connected memories. I recalled the horror and the people who did nothing but look on as my mother almost lost her life and of those who saved us. I never told anyone what had happened because I repressed it from my memory. It stayed hidden—until now.

I grieve for the young girl who fought to do the right thing, consciously thinking she had failed. I cried for the young man my father had been, lost in his grief over losing his wife and wanting her back so badly he thought taking her children away was the answer.

We have all paid the price. The headaches I suffered through the years were a latent result of a brain injury I suffered at my mother's hands that horrible day. However, my brother and sister thrived through the love and support of our family.

It wasn't right. It never would be, but forgiveness starts in the heart and reaches the soul. I will always love my father. Growing older, I could fully understand his pain and forgive him. I also know who the *real* boogeyman was.

My mother did the best she could. She made plenty of mistakes over the years, but in *trying* to love me—she did her best. I need to find comfort in that.

⸺◎◎◎⸺

It's here she ends her story. As I said, I don't know if it is true. All I know is I was struck by the trauma and willingness to forgive. Love your children. Hold their feelings close to your heart. They are little people who hurt more than you realize. Let them know they are safe—and always will be with you.

The End

THE UFO

Every day was the same. It never seemed to get any easier to go to work, do a good job, and then feel good about myself at the end of the day. The same old grind was getting tiresome. Every day when I woke, I thought this would be the day I'd make a difference. *This* was the day I would be heard. *This* was the day I'd impress the boss. But that day never seemed to come. It still hadn't until one day in November.

For the sake of argument, I'll just refer to myself as Jane. No need to know my real name; it doesn't matter anyway. I'm just an ordinary person trying to get by. I'm a regular gal, not trying to "stick it to the man" but to feel good about my contribution to this life. To find validation for the reason for my existence. Corny, I know. But bear with me.

I have lived alone in a two-bedroom bungalow in Denver, Colorado, for a while now. I don't reside in the city per se, but on the outskirts of South Parkhill. My neighborhood, which is full of diversity, small mom-and-pop shops, and restaurants where a sampling of ethnic food can be had at reasonable prices, is the best around. Local church bells chime the hour. Neighbors are tolerable, some even friendly. A polite wave of the hand, "Hello, nice day today," or a simple greeting of "Good morning" reminds me of how lucky I am to reside here. Thank goodness petty crime is down, so evening walks and late-night strolls still occur without concern. Lawn mowing, backyard barbeques, vegetable gardens, and an occasional chicken crowing in the early morning are typical in summer. At Halloween, children in hobgoblin costumes playfully scare their neighbors into giving them treats. I usually play along, dressed as a witch, with my dog, Lucky, barking at my side. I always look forward to the merriment the upcoming holidays bring and the promise of a prosperous or better year than the last one.

My parents left this earthly plane years ago. I've built a somewhat solitary life here in the city of Denver to escape the pain of their loss. My friends are few. Most live in the western foothills of Boulder, which is farther away than I'd like to think. Although I've kept myself relatively busy, nothing much changes from day to day. My typical routine has been to work out, eat healthy meals, watch my favorite television shows, and read voraciously. Most mornings and afternoons, I'll take a long, leisurely walk with my Shih-Tzu companion, Lucky, in the park located diagonally from my house. As much as I love my little doggy, it amuses me to think I might have gone mad from loneliness if it weren't for her. But that's baloney! I do like my solitude. Lucky is just along for the ride; bless her.

I like my job, "like" being the operative word. Each day is a torment from when I get there until I leave. It's hell. I'm usually questioned about everything. My Bachelor of Science degree in data management, a master's from MIT, and many certificates obviously mean nothing to my boss or cohorts. *"If I verify my data as correct, why isn't my word and expertise good enough? What does it matter if office gossip says I'm better at analysis than my colleagues? If my coworkers are jealous and resentful of me, that's their problem, not mine. It's all so petty."* These affirmations help, but because of these issues, I'd find myself analyzing everything until my head hurt long before I had to turn in my weekly reports.

Most days I feel exhausted when I get home, and some days, taking Lucky for her evening walk is all I can manage. Afterward, I collapsed on the couch, then slowly pull myself to the kitchen. Preparing dinner is starting to be a real drag. As the night wears on, the doubts of my workday actions eventually creep into my thoughts. I silently kick myself for an incident or talk aloud to no one other than Lucky, reliving what I *could* have said or *should* have said during an offending confrontation. The torture is relentless.

I need to improve at corporate politics or face the fact that I would never be good at political maneuvering. I feel stuck in a thankless job. Nothing I ever do or present seems good enough, especially when coworkers question my ability. It seems Jane-bashing is the name of the game. This internal torment keeps me awake at night and on my toes every working day.

As the days move closer to the Thanksgiving holiday, my workdays become longer. The one thing I never dreamed of in a million years was to encounter something unusual. I have become too rational and too analytical. The anxiety of hearing, "Jane, I need to see you in my office," paled to what I was about to experience. I was not prepared when it happened.

⋙ ⦿⦿⦿ ⋘

I had always felt spirits around me. Protecting like guardian angels. I welcomed the feeling even more after my parents' tragic death in an auto accident. They were driving home from my college graduation when a freakish spring snowstorm moved in. Slick roads were to blame when the car skidded off the road and into a tree. Death was instantaneous, or so I was told. I'd like to think that was true. However, strange occurrences only increased as the years progressed, regardless of how analytically I could reason them away. I guess these instances caused me to rationalize the irrational. Analyzing a situation, like data, seemed the logical way to deal with the unknown. Thus, my work life and chosen profession.

Before buying my current home, I had lived in an apartment close to Cheesman Park, which had once been a vast graveyard. I felt I was being watched all the time. Dishes fell from counters without explanation. The cabinets opened and closed on their own, and light bulbs flickered during the day. Faulty wiring, misaligned cabinetry, clumsy when handling dishes? Who knows? Without explanations, I chalked these occurrences up to my parents looking down on me, letting me know they were around.

It wasn't until I heard an occasional whisper and deep sighs from the other side of an open window facing the outside stairwell that I knew something different than the normal realm of the natural was occurring. It always seemed to happen at night. No one was ever there. This was supernatural. I decided to find another place to live and quickly. So yeah, I have been faced with ghosts or spirits, if you will.

The house was a lucky find. That was when my dog came into my life, so I named her Lucky. Odd bumps and noises are commonplace in older houses; mine was no exception. I'd even seen Lucky look up a time or two with perked ears, having detected something I couldn't see or hear. She was my tiny protector and alarm sounder if anything was amiss. She usually barked when she needed my urgent attention on something or in play; otherwise, she was very docile and friendly. Lately, however, there seemed to be an uptick in the unexplained, far from the mundane, and her frequent alerting behavior put me on notice that something mysterious was afoot.

My house sat two blocks from the main thoroughfare to the neighborhood. This location was excellent, so late-night road noise was minimal, and it gave me easy access to the freeway two miles away. From the outside, my bedroom, on the right, had one window exposed to the side garage and street corner. Spying on any mischief around the garage was easy from this vantage point. Next to that window were two other windows facing the front yard. My only privacy was a pine tree to the left of the front porch and living room windows. Juniper bushes—spider hotels, I called them—situated under the windows on either side of the porch were a nuisance that needed constant spraying and trimming.

There was always work around the house, especially in the backyard, which was long and narrow and needed a lot of care. A chain-link gate sat low on either side of the house, which served as an entrance to the yard. These were attached to the wooden fence of my neighbors on either side. When the branches and leaves from the elm trees started to fall, I had to rake and bag them. It was backbreaking work but, along with my aerobic workouts, kept me in shape.

To prevent Lucky from running through the mounds of fallen leaves was a challenge. However, sometimes, I'd join in the fun and play with her, much to her delight. One afternoon, a few weeks before Halloween, I bent to pick up an armful of leaves. And just as I turned to carry them to the trash bin, I caught something out of the corner of my eye. I saw a tall figure with white and translucent skin. It was standing against the side of my house, peering at me from behind a lilac bush. It was somewhat human in shape—but not really human. I dropped the leaves and clasped my hands to my mouth in surprise. I froze in place. Lucky stopped romping in the leaves to look in the figure's direction. Then, the figure eased itself back around the corner of the house. Lucky began to bark and quickly ran over to me, whining.

Because of Lucky's reaction, I knew I had seen something. Shaken and recovering my wits, I gingerly tiptoed to where I'd seen the figure but found nothing. No disturbance was evident as I inspected the site. No footprints in the soft dirt. Nothing.

"What *was* that, girl?" I whispered to Lucky, who only looked up at me and began to sniff around the area.

My rational mind said *there has to be an explanation for what I saw, right?* I suspected it was an early Halloween prank done in broad daylight, but that was unlikely. I eventually shrugged off the incident and got on with the task of gathering fallen leaves. However, I constantly looked back toward the house throughout the day of bagging leaves because I half hoped the figure would reappear. If nothing else, to confirm that what I saw was not my imagination.

<hr>

Halloween had come and gone, and the memory of the "visitor" had faded. Now, Thanksgiving was staring me in the face. I had put off accepting an invitation to observe the holiday with one of my girlfriends and her family. After days of equivocating, I couldn't bring myself to say yes or no. I was mentally drained from yet another day of self-deprecation at work. Instead of whining to my friends about a work situation I could do nothing about, a quiet evening with Lucky and a microwaved frozen dinner sounded great.

One evening, after coming in from walking Lucky and setting out preparations for dinner, I decided a hot shower sounded good. The water felt soothing as it moved over my body to warm me. The feel of the wet mesh loofah and suds washed away the day's weariness, and I started to feel better. As I stepped out, Lucky was in her usual spot, waiting by the bathroom door.

"Ah, what's the matter, girly? Lonely?" I said, bending down to scratch behind her ears.

Her tail wagged to the right of her body. This let me know she liked my scratches, which was always a good sign. *At least I'm doing something right.* Once again, my boss's words, "Are you sure these numbers are correct? I can't believe them," and his constant mantra of "trust but verify" echoed in my ears. So Lucky's small reassurance helped validate my ability to get something right for once without question.

I never understood why my boss bothered me with what I considered unnecessary nonsense. Each day, when I developed analyses to determine waste and inefficiencies in processes, he and other colleagues challenged me, especially one woman who seemed to have the boss's ear. His constant second-guessing always forced me to provide justification to support the position of my analyses. Invariably, I would prove myself correct in my data assessments. His practice of sniping at me was bordering on harassment, and the constant stress was becoming more than annoying.

"You'd think he'd give up already," I said aloud for only Lucky's benefit—not that she cared.

With my wet hair in a towel, I walked directly across from the bathroom into my bedroom, where I disrobed and put on comfy sweats. Just then, Lucky turned and barked into the darkened spare bedroom, which was used as a study and situated to the left of the bathroom. The outside wall of this room was where I'd seen the translucent figure a few weeks before.

"What is it, girl?" I asked when she backed away and whimpered.

Slowly, I walked over to Lucky, whose gaze didn't waver from the dim light emanating from the room. When I got to where she stood, a burst of bright light illuminated the study. A roundish-shaped orb lit the entire space with beams of white light pointing in all directions as it slowly turned to span the room. Faster than I could blink, it flew through the closed window into the darkened backyard and was gone. There was no sound. But if anyone were to ask me at the time, I would swear there was a loud boom.

I was on the floor with Lucky. She shivered in my arms, just as frightened as I was. *What just happened?* My immediate thought was to call the police, someone! *Who'd believe me?* I desperately tried to reason it out. *I must be hallucinating. Stress will do that to the rational mind, right?* But were they *all* hallucinations? If it weren't for Lucky and her reaction, I would've convinced myself of just that. She was my only witness.

"Holy cow! What do we do, Lucky?" I asked of an animal who could only cower at my feet as I stood up.

My thoughts were all over the place. What if it wasn't a UFO? What I saw didn't behave like those in movies like *Close Encounters of the Third Kind*. No electrical surges or any appliances were dancing on the countertops. No radio or TV turned off and then on by themselves, either. My hair, wrapped in a towel that was now on the floor, hadn't stood on end. To borrow a line from that movie, "This is nuts!" And it was.

"That was no poltergeist or ghost, Lucky; that was the real deal… I think."

I thought twice about calling my girlfriend for fear of being judged over what I would tell. However, her husband was an engineer. He might be able to shed *some* light on what had just happened. So, I took the plunge and called. After I explained the event, she put the cell phone on speaker so her husband, I'll call him Jack, could share his expertise with me.

"You sure it wasn't a blown bulb or something?" Jack asked.

"I'm telling you—it was a *white orb*. A bright white light came from that thing, and then it flew straight out a *closed* window!"

"I've never heard of UFOs traveling through walls or windows—"

"This one did! I'd have thought I was losing my mind if it wasn't for Lucky's reaction."

"You say it didn't trigger any surges or anything."

"It's not like *Close Encounters*. My face isn't scorched on one side—"

"That's not what I mean." His chuckle calmed me somewhat. "You checked your circuit box, right? Did anything trip?"

"I looked before I called to make sure." I sighed at that moment in exasperation. "All seems okay, except for Lucky and me."

"You call Xcel Energy to see if anyone else reported something?"

"Not yet." I realized that Jack had no more answers or explanations than I did.

"Try calling them, just to see. That's all I have. Otherwise... I got nothing."

"Okay, I will. Thanks, Jack." Then he put my friend back on.

"I don't know what to tell you, Jane. Be careful and call me tomorrow. Things always look better in the morning. You've been under a lot of stress lately, so..."

She let that comment trail off; I knew what she meant. "You're right. About Thanksgiving, would it be okay to bring Lucky? Considering what we just experienced, I don't want to leave her alone."

"Sure you can! Of course. I'm glad you finally decided to come. You can stay over if you'd like. I'll have the guest bedroom ready for you. Think about it, okay? I'll check on you tomorrow."

I knew calling the energy company wouldn't give me the answers I needed. I was glad I hadn't shared seeing translucent figures in my backyard. I didn't think that would go over well. But, coupled with what I had just experienced, it told me what I saw wasn't a hallucination from stress. It was a UFO.

My friend was wrong. The following morning had not erased what happened the night before, sorry to say. Going through my day, I worried about the smallest of things. I checked and rechecked the windows to ensure they were locked. I checked my kitchen drawers to see if a sharp knife was handy or if I had enough batteries in case the power went out without explanation in the middle of the night. I jumped at the slightest sound. I couldn't concentrate, let alone make heads or tails of what had occurred the previous night. It was surprising to think it even happened at all. After the night of the sighting, the memory of that evening stayed with me even as the days moved on to other days that settled into the mundane.

The routine of walking my dog, watching TV or reading, working out, and going to bed, only to begin a night of uneasy sleep and waking to another day of dread at the thought of what the workday had in store for me, continued.

I was on edge the final week leading up to Thanksgiving. I was being watched. By what or whom was the question. *The translucent figure I saw appeared in broad daylight, for heaven's sake!* Each hour at work, I worried about Lucky being at home alone. To my relief, each day I returned home, she was there to greet me, full of excitement and love, vigorously wagging her tail.

⟫⟪◉◉◉⟫⟪

It was the day before Thanksgiving. I don't know whether my courage came from an overload of stress or unanswered questions about the UFO incident. But to my mind, the event of that day was epic.

"Jane, you got a minute?" the boss asked.

"Sure," I said unenthusiastically. I had a feeling this would not be good.

In his office sat the very person, my nemesis, whose professional petty jealousy had driven me to this point in my career. The sneer on her face told me unmistakably that she had no goodwill toward me. Her legs crossed at the knee made her look smug and sure of herself.

"Where'd you get the data for these graphs? What source did you use?" she demanded.

"You my boss now?" I was not in the mood. "Last I checked, I answer to this man here, not you."

"Answer the question, Jane," said the boss, who sounded exasperated. "It seems your graphs fly in the face of what your colleague has reported."

"They always do. I'm starting to wonder why, which should be your question of her, not of me. Each time you question my numbers, I confirm my data as correct. I always check and verify before submission. My bar charts are above par and clearly tell the monthly and quarterly business story per the data model, unlike the useless spaghetti or bubble charts *some* of us like to submit to leadership. In a concise summary, I might add. I don't like to be baffled with BS. But I guess that's not good enough."

"The data program has scalable issues, which you are aware of," she started again. "We can't track any manipulations you've—"

"I disagree," I said, ignoring the accusation sure to come. "The BI program we use accounts for anomalies. Sure, scalability can cause easy manipulation of data scorecards to fit the metrics. *You* should know that." To my boss, I said, "Scalability deficiencies are built into my analysis. This is why I closely check the numbers before submitting my scorecard reports. The margin of error is very slight, as reflected in the graph. May I suggest that if there are any other questions about my data, please recheck *her* data sources and the software program she uses? Otherwise, the next time you drag me in with questions like this, I'll consider it harassment. I promise you. We don't want HR involved, do we?" Turning to her, I quickly added, "If you need help with your data and ways to manage scale, let me know. I'll be happy to help. Now, please excuse me."

Fed up, I walked out without shutting the door behind me. Saying all I had physically drained me. But I felt mentally strong, and that was a good sign. I knew what I had to do. It was nearing the end of the day, and as far as I was concerned, it was time to grab my purse and leave.

Arriving home an hour early surprised Lucky, judging by how she greeted me. I welcomed all her doggy love. As we settled into our routine, my thoughts raced about what I had said to my boss. I didn't regret a word, although I wondered about my continued employment afterward. *Well, it's high time I found a job that will appreciate the talent I bring to the table anyway.* This thought gave me a drive I never knew I had before. I felt very good about myself for the first time in a long time.

⚬⚬⚬

After dinner, while watching TV and slowly stroking Lucky, who sat on my lap, drowsiness overcame me. The next day was Thanksgiving and a welcome relief from work for a few days. I didn't prepare for bed with my usual routine. Instead, I crawled into bed, fully clothed in my comfy sweats, and fell into a deep sleep. Lucky joined me on the bed, and I didn't mind at all.

The sound outside was annoying. I'd heard a dragging car muffler before, but this was as if it was being dragged a long way. I barely woke, groggy, thinking, *God, I wish that sound would fade away already. Why's a tractor-trailer dragging a rusty muffler on this street anyway? It's taking forever.*

I was facing the window overlooking the garage and corner of the street when the small orb came in through that very window. It was oblong and multicolored—pink, blue, white, and orange. The light was soft and not bright at all. *I guess there really are UFOs.* I was unusually sleepy. This was my only thought as I turned over and away from the orb, unconcerned. I noted the time on my alarm clock as 11:15 p.m. Lucky did not stir. I fell into a deep sleep as the room grew dark again.

Am I dreaming? What is that? A UFO! This larger oblong orb took up the entire bedroom space. I was still facing my alarm clock, which now read 3:15 a.m. This orb also had a soft glow of pink, blue, white, and orange lights that shone down on me and spanned the room as it slowly turned, deathly quiet. I couldn't move. I tried. I willed myself to squirm, but my limbs wouldn't cooperate. Lucky slept quietly. *Is Lucky dead? I have to move, scream, do something! Why can't I move?*

It was less than a minute, but it seemed like a lifetime. *What does it want?* As shaken as I was, I felt a sudden sense of peace come over me. For reasons I couldn't understand, I knew they meant no harm. I also knew this would be the last time they would visit. I looked up at the massive thing and tried rationalizing how it got inside my house. *How are they getting in? Did I leave a door open or something? This is just like last time.* The screeching sound of the dragging muffler came again. It seemed too loud for the room to hold, yet somehow, only I was awake to hear this.

Suddenly, the craft flew through the walls of my bedroom and the adjacent walls of my study. It was gone. In its wake, I heard a few things topple over and some pictures fall off the walls. It was then that I was able to move. Sitting straight up, I shouted, "What the *hell* is going on!" Lucky moved, too, and barked. I bounded out of bed to inspect the rooms while Lucky kept up her noisy barking.

I was shaking badly. I panicked. I turned on every lamp and ceiling light and inspected what had just fallen. I noted the directional path the craft had taken as it flew through the house. Figurines on a side table in the study were on the floor. As I suspected, some family photos had fallen from the walls. Loose papers had also been blown around and scattered on the desk and floor; otherwise, all seemed fine. The miniblinds on the closed window were moving slightly. I stood in amazement and tried to understand or rationalize what happened.

Did an earthquake or slight tremor cause the pictures to fall? But that was a silly thought because the house hadn't shaken at all. It was also foolish to think the craft got in through the front door, which was still locked. Besides, it wasn't wide enough to accommodate a giant UFO. So how did it get in? How could it be? Was I so dead tired that I dreamed the whole thing? How could I account for the paralysis and that rusty, dragging sound? I briefly inspected Lucky, who seemed to be just fine. Why didn't she wake when the orbs or space crafts were in the room?

Were we paralyzed? I could not move, and Lucky wouldn't or couldn't wake. It was like a kind of sleep paralysis. Four hours had passed from when the first craft entered the room until the last. Had I been asleep the entire time, or was I made motionless while they observed or examined me? Panicked, I stood in front of my mirror to check my body. Every inch.

Of course, I had heard of alien abduction. The strange things done to the bodies of those who had the misfortune of such incidences came to mind. There were no markings I could find on my body or Lucky. *That sound!* A dragging sound—no, it was a rusty *turning* sound! It was as if an old, rusted-out lid or covering was turning around and around on a dusty jar.

My head started to hurt from the stress of the experience as I tried to rationalize the irrational. I grabbed a few Tylenols and hoped for the best. I sat with a cup of coffee, watched the sunrise, and listened to the meanderings of the newscasters on TV. After a while, I took Lucky out for an early morning walk. The briskness of the air cleared my head. It was comforting to smell the impending snow in the air. I was starting to feel better.

"We're going to have early snow, I think," I said to Lucky, who ignored me completely while sniffing at the ground. I wondered how much accumulation we would get in Denver compared to the foothills where my friends lived.

Later, I watched the Thanksgiving Day parade and called my friend to thank her for the dinner invitation. Still, I decided to stay home with Lucky. It was full-on snowing by then. Besides, the drive from Denver to her home in Boulder was long, so it was just as well.

I told my friend about my outburst at work and how it had ended, but nothing else. She applauded my courage and supported my decision to find other employment. She'd mentioned her husband's engineering firm was looking for a good data scientist. That was encouraging.

⟳⟳⟳

I've moved on now. I've never told my friend about my UFO encounter. I just couldn't. The incident has remained a mystery and unspoken of until now. The alien's visit was one I will never forget nor have again. Whatever they want or are seeking, I hope it is for the good. I recount it here because I remember the overwhelming feeling of peace washing over me when I was most afraid. My courage to speak up to my former employer began my awakening. I was once too scared to speak out and take on those who meant to do me harm. I'm different now.

I wish I could tell you a profound mystery had been uncovered in this experience. It wasn't. This story is not an allegory. No life-changing event occurred afterward other than telling my boss where to go. I hope you get my meaning.

I still walk my dog, my circle of friends has grown a bit, and I love my new job. I now have a meaningful relationship with a guy I've always considered a longtime friend. I think it's getting serious.

I must add that none of this has diminished my belief in God or an omniscient being greater than myself. I know there is more to life than believing we are alone. We are not. Never have been and never will be.

The End

Crystal Palace & Ivory Towers

⋯✦⋯

Shaken and scared, Laramie sat in a cozy corner of her office, waiting for the phone to ring. It wouldn't be a welcome call—not at all. The anticipation of the next shoe falling was excruciating. At that moment, the love seat in her office seemed too big for comfort; however, her oversized chair held her just fine. The long shadows of the late evening streaked across the floor of her comfortable yet moderately large office. She looked up at the floor-to-ceiling windows, which afforded a view of the Cash Register Building of downtown Denver. She knew an attorney who worked at the top of that building. He might be useful as she considered her options if worse came to worst.

Denver's version of New York's World Trade Center, now called Denver Energy Center, loomed large across the street from her office at Republic Plaza. Clustered together, these crystal palaces, as she called them, were full of empty office spaces, a metaphor for the empty-headed people she'd encountered in her career. She amused herself by thinking it would serve her boss right if she obtained another position in one of the other buildings. She took special pleasure in the thought of kicking him in the crotch before announcing she quit.

Laramie Ellis was just twenty-six years old, and her star had been rising at the Stanford & Greene Advertising Agency. She was the advertising project manager, and her new boss, Simon Lathan, was a first-class sleazeball and smarmy at best. He was not liked much. She tolerated his behavior and, until now, managed to avoid the pitfall of being near him for any length of time. He always said the right thing. He always anticipated what you were about to say. Out of nowhere, he'd appear as if sneaking up on the unsuspecting. His eyes darted about, looking for approval anytime he spoke. Even though he was just above average-looking, with a fit body that looked good in a suit, he was creepy nonetheless.

"What an asshole!" she said out loud to her empty office.

Her fear had now turned to anger. She had done her best to thwart her boss's advances and failed. She knew better than to meet him alone in his office, but what choice did she have when summoned at the last minute on an urgent matter? That was a lie, of course. After her last encounter with him and the warning she'd given under her breath to "keep your hands off me," she thought he'd get the message—well, the joke was on her. She saw the ambush coming before it had begun, and still, she'd ignored the signs. This time, when he grabbed her as she'd tried to leave— she lost it.

The slap she'd given him didn't deter his advances. It only spurred him on. His groping and awkward attempt to kiss her were too much to take. He had overpowered her and, against her will, had forced himself and pushed her against his ornate desk. They were alone. There was no one to hear his hands grappling as she tried to remove herself from his grasp. No one could hear the shuffling of positions as she tried to fight him off. He had placed his hands over her mouth to stifle her scream, but it was a lost cause. She only hoped he would feel the bite of her teeth for a long time. Her workouts at the gym had given her some leverage and thank God. Otherwise, the hideous figurine on his desk, a gift from his wife, would have been smashed over his head.

As he held her from behind, she swung her right elbow back and into his side. It was a surprise move he obviously had not expected. His ardor was too high to anticipate. In the instant he let go, she had fled.

That was just ten minutes ago, and here she sat, waiting for the inevitable. In retrospect, she didn't know what to expect, really. At that hour, the Human Resources office was closed. Tomorrow would be too late to file a complaint. It had to be done as soon as possible to lend any credibility to the charge of assault. The security officers would only make matters worse if she called for help; they had no real power to do anything except call the police. She doubted if they'd believe her anyway. In fact, the whole affair would be her word against her boss's unless… the bite on his hand and the bruise on his face from her slap, if visible, could be used as evidence. *Why am I waiting? Damn it!* She should do something fast.

<hr>

"It was just a misunderstanding, officers, really," Simon Lathan said sheepishly to the two police officers who answered her 911 call. "I don't know how Ms. Ellis thought otherwise. Care for some coffee, gentlemen? I just put a new brew on for another late night of paperwork." The officers shook their heads in polite decline as he continued, "I fell; she heard the noise and came running. Next thing I knew, she was at me like a hellcat! Scratching and clawing at me. See, she even bit me when I tried to restrain her—"

"My God!" Laramie exclaimed in disbelief. "That's not true at all—"

"Let him finish!" one police officer said in admonishment.

"You know how women are sometimes." Simon casually poured himself a cup of coffee and slowly stirred in creamer as he spoke. "I don't know why my colleague would react as she did. She's been on edge lately for reasons I can't make out." He shrugged.

"I'm not your colleague. I'm your employee," Laramie said, then turned to the officer closest to her and pointed her finger in Simon's direction, "He's my boss! He tried to *rape* me *right here* in *this* office. It's *not* the first time."

"Oh really? Care to enlighten us on when the "first time" might have been, exactly?" the lead officer said with a sideways glance in Laramie's direction.

Laramie could not believe the smugness of this jerk of a boss. He had the *nerve* to sit down and cross his legs as if this were a casual meeting, entirely at ease. She was not, and it showed. She was the one on the verge of hysterics and uncontrolled emotions.

"Well, miss?" the officer asked her again. "You want to elaborate on any other assaults? This is a serious matter, and I'm afraid we can't just let that comment go."

Holy shit! she thought. *What do I do now?* "Well, I-I-I can't tell you *exactly* when it was, but just, what, twenty-five minutes ago, *he* forced himself on *me*! *Not* the other way around. What do I need to do to get you to believe me?"

"Shut your mouth!" the lead officer yelled. "That's what got you into this in the first place—"

"What?" Laramie put her hands on her hips, incredulous.

"You heard me!" the lead officer said with a stern face.

Laramie had the presence of mind to tell herself to close her "*said*" mouth, which was agape as he spoke those outrageous words. There was no need to say more. The fact that *she* called to report an attack on *her* would have been lost on them anyway. They probably would never think to ask themselves why she'd do so if it didn't have merit. It was clear they didn't couldn't, or worse yet, wouldn't believe her.

The other police officer, who was leaning against the doorjamb of Simon's office, decided to speak.

"I think we have all the information we need. Ma'am, if you care to file a report, we can take you downtown to do so. Otherwise, I suggest you take a break and leave well enough alone—if you know what I mean. Filing a false claim is against the law. Have you been under a lot of stress lately? Office pressure can get to you, have you do things you wouldn't ordinarily do or say."

Simon had been convincing. By his demeanor, it was evident that he had been attacked by her unprovoked. An outrageous lie, to be sure, but there it was all the same. She squinted and squared her shoulders, then stood tall as she faced the officers, the two security guards assigned to her building, who hung around just outside the door, and her boss.

"That'll be all right," she said, composing herself. "Maybe it was a misunderstanding after all. I need a moment to convince myself that I'm delusional and that this didn't happen in any way. I suppose I just dreamed it up, huh, Officers? However, I'd appreciate your escorting me to my car. For some *odd* reason, I don't feel safe."

She heard one security guard stifle a giggle, then clear his throat when the other officers looked at him.

⊰◦◦◦⊱

The officers waited outside her office door with Simon as she packed her briefcase to leave for the evening. She overheard them say something about his ability to file a complaint on her, but he declined. *This is beyond ridiculous!* Her disappointment in the way she was treated was profound. Laramie could hear the men laughing and joking with each other as she gathered her things. One said he had a wife who was just like her, unpredictable and hormonal. *What the hell! The nerve of that guy! Why is he in the police force?*

She didn't want to hear anymore. She was disgusted and felt like an idiot, thinking that calling the police was a good idea instead of handling the situation within the confines of the corporate offices. But what Simon had done to her was alarming, and she'd thought reporting the incident was the right thing to do at the time. Now she felt foolish. She should have done a better job reporting the incident the second after it had occurred rather than doing what she did by waiting minutes after the fact. Self-recrimination was not her strong suit, but this time, she wallowed deeply.

In this day and age, she didn't think sexual harassment or sexual assault in the office was still an issue women had to face. She thought things had changed with the #MeToo movement, but no. Apparently, it was alive and well within the walls of Stanford & Greene Advertising. And those who sat in ivory towers among these crystal palaces were immune to justice—protected. Women would lie; of course, they did. All women who brought assault charges against their bosses should be weighed and measured carefully. She didn't want to be one of those who waited years to file a complaint because of fear and retribution. In her mind, if she was being subjected to sexual assault or harassment, it needed to be reported immediately. She thought she had done the right thing, but apparently not.

It didn't take long for the police to leave, and now she was left with only the security detail to escort her. She steeled herself for the walk to the parking garage below. She hoped the security guards would be more considerate of her plight and not laugh at her along the way.

To her surprise, only one security guard remained. He seemed pleasant enough, if not downright shy, the same height as she in heels. He appeared to be a few years older but said little, which was just fine by Laramie.

"Long day, huh?" he asked.

After an uncomfortable pause, she responded. "You could say that."

"Hey, listen. It's probably not my place, but I want to apologize for how everything went down and was handled." Laramie let his unexpected apology settle on her like a warm blanket. "He's a real jerk, you know… if you don't mind me saying."

"I… don't mind, and… thank you," she said as they walked to the first bank of elevators. It was silent as they waited for the elevator car to arrive.

"What floor?" he asked when they got inside.

"Garage, parking level one."

"P1 it is."

"I'm sorry," she said after a moment. "Do you mind if we stop at forty-two?" she asked. "I need to retrieve something before I leave tonight."

"Sure thing." Again, they were silent as the elevator traveled from the 44th floor to the 42nd.

Stanford & Greene occupied three of the fifty-six-story Republic Plaza building. The 42nd floor was where the analytics for the agency were done. Laramie decided to retrieve a report on sales projections and didn't want to call for it the next day. She suspected the gossip of what had happened that day would be rife with speculation by then. It would be hard enough to face without something to focus on to occupy her mind. Laramie wasn't exactly sure where Bonnie, her analyst, kept the reports but found them after a few fumbles. It took time to scan the massive report to ensure she had all the information she needed, which was just as well. Besides, Laramie felt more at ease away from the creep upstairs. Doing this allowed her to breathe and relax while the guard waited patiently. Laramie saw him look over occasionally and smile in her direction. He seemed nice.

They walked at a leisurely pace back to the bank of elevators. Silence filled the space in the elevator again, and then he spoke, seemingly unable to help himself.

"Something about him gives me the creeps," he said, shaking his head. "I mean, we fellas… well, we talk, and that guy up there… ain't right."

Laramie looked at the guard this time, intent on his demeanor. He seemed honest, and she found herself warming to him.

"What's your name, Simpson, is it?" she asked, looking at his badge.

"Yeah. Name's Charlie, ma'am. Been at this building for a while now. Kinda like home, if you know what I mean. There's just two of us, me and James, my brother. He went to grab us both something to eat. I'm not hungry now, but later—oh yeah."

Laramie smiled. The first smile she'd had in a while. She appreciated his down-home way of speaking. It grounded her, and she liked him for it.

"Thanks for your observation and for sharing your thoughts on my boss. It's not every day you hear that kind of honesty, and I appreciate it."

"Ah, it's no big thing," he said, looking down at his shoes. When the doors opened and they walked out, he asked, "What happens now? You gonna be all right?"

Laramie sighed and then shrugged. "I think so. I'll take it one day at a time, which is all I can do right now." Charlie Simpson nodded and said nothing more.

When they got to her car, she said, "This is me."

Charlie let out a low whistle. "They sure pay well. Wow!"

"Just a little something I gave myself," Laramie said with a chuckle.

"You got taste, I can tell you that." He smiled, admiring the 1960 Studebaker. Then his demeanor turned serious. "Look, you be careful, and just between you and me, you watch your twelve—I got your six."

"Huh? Oh right. Thank you… for everything."

❧

There was more to Charlie Simpson and his brother James than met the eye. They were a year apart in age but looked nothing like each other—no resemblance whatsoever. James stood taller at six feet three inches. He was huge and could bench press three hundred pounds easily. He ate all the time. Charlie was younger and smaller. At five feet eleven inches, he was agile and strong. He was also watchful, while much to his consternation, James tended to trust far more than he.

Charlie had a keen sense for people. To his mind, Laramie Ellis seemed to be a lovely person. He could only imagine the shitstorm she would face the next day at the hands of that CEO creep. He didn't buy one single bit of the song and dance Simon Lathan told the police about *her* attacking *him*. *What a load!* He was glad that phrase hadn't slipped from his mouth earlier. It was all he could do to hold it in.

Watching Laramie drive away, he wondered if that creep was still in his office upstairs. For grins, he decided to check it out and, if he saw him, act like he cared about the bastard as an excuse for doing so.

Except for the chatter of the cleaning crew, the hum of vacuum cleaners, or the swish of a rotary brush on a floor polisher, office buildings at night were very quiet affairs. This was when Charlie liked his job best. The quiet gave him time to relax and reflect on his life.

His stint in Afghanistan had taken a toll on him. The training he'd received as an engineer was great. He'd served four tours and got his engineering degree afterward. He could have had any job he wanted, but a slight case of PTSD was tough to shake, so he never lasted very long in his profession. It was one thing to focus on his God-given understanding of mathematics but another thing to control himself under the bullshit a boss tended to bring. He was a terrible employee in the corporate world. However, his brief run had given a unique insight into the machinations of corporate politics. He'd observed the seedy side of those who wanted nothing more than to climb the ladder of success and would, without thinking twice, about who was hurt along the way. The arrogance of corporate bigwigs was astounding and something he couldn't stomach for long.

The first time he'd seen Simon Lathan, his internal antenna went on high alert. He had "that look." That look that said he could do or take anything he wanted, and no one could do a damn thing about it, regardless of how vile the act of getting it would be. Blink, and you'd miss him looking down on people as if they were dirt. His way of kissing up to, well… everyone was a huge red flag. And there was something else. A meanness and craftiness beyond anything Charlie had experienced before made him wary. Tonight, his suspicions were realized when he listened to him weasel his way out of an assault charge.

The police were useless. That bunch had seen too much street time and needed reassignment as far as Charlie was concerned. Thank God there were more good cops than bad. Laramie had the misfortune of running into the worst DPD had to offer. Because of that and his need to see a wrong made right, Charlie felt compelled to step in with his "awe, shucks" mannerisms. Yes, Charlie Simpson was more than met the eye.

⟿⟾⟿

"I got your six." That phrase, uttered by Charlie, stayed with Laramie as she drove the darkened streets home. It wasn't late, but not early either. She had half a mind to stop in LoDo for a drink but thought better of it. Lower Downtown, or LoDo, was a haven for young adults looking to hang out with friends after work or to start a long weekend. She didn't live far and thank God she didn't have a long drive to challenge an already horrible day.

Who was security guard Charlie Simpson? She wanted to learn more about him, if nothing else, to better understand those who worked in the building. She had needed a friend, and it seemed she had one in him. Her 1960 Studebaker Lark VI convertible, a compact classic she had coveted after watching an old black-and-white movie, purred as it weaved through the Denver suburban streets of the Sloan Lake neighborhood. A shiny black convertible with red leather seats and a three-on-the-tree manual column shifter was her one vice, and she loved it. Apparently, so had Simpson. She smiled, recalling the look on his face when he'd seen it. The memory helped fade the awful assault she had experienced at the hands of her boss. As she pulled into the driveway of her Sloan Lake bungalow, she never considered her nightmare of nightmares was just beginning.

Her home had none of the sterile or austere look anyone might associate with Laramie. Unlike her office, it had a comfortable, lived-in quality that was welcoming. Her Craftsman-style bungalow was typical architecture for Denver. Unlike the Denver Foursquare, it was just the right size and cozy enough for her. Her furnishings mimicked the home's straight lines, nothing frilly or girlie, just lean with clean lines of sight to offset the structured rooms defining each area.

Turning on the TV was a habit. She didn't need the noise, but the sound of other voices in her home was strangely comforting. Miss Purdy, the cat, hissed out of protest at seeing Laramie, who had been away for so long. As typical, when Laramie ignored her and began the business of putting her favorite brand of cat food—in this case, a can of tuna—in a bowl, Miss Purdy meowed lovingly. She was out of chicken-and-liver pâté, so this would have to do.

"Silly cat. How you been today?" Laramie asked, stroking Miss Purdy's head as she ate her tuna cake. "Well, it's been a hell of a day for me, but little you care, huh?"

Laramie left her cat in peace and took off her jacket and shoes. She was careful with her possessions, never tossing them around carelessly. She was fastidious that way. Neat and clean, orderly and exact in her person and surroundings; that was Laramie.

In her upstairs bedroom, she quickly changed into comfy duds. They were nothing fancy, just light cotton yoga pants and an oversized T-shirt. She then busied herself in the kitchen, brushing her blunt-cut auburn hair behind her ears. It hung at an angle to her face as she chopped carrots for the night's dinner. As she turned to grab an onion from the pantry, she froze.

Standing in front of her was Simon Lathan, her boss. Then everything went black.

⇒◎◎◎⇐

Charlie Simpson shouldn't have been surprised to find the upper floors of Stanford & Greene Advertising dark when he returned, but he was. The large oak doors were not locked, which was odd. Either someone left in a hurry or was careless. He cautiously stepped inside with his flashlight illuminating the interiors of the space. All seemed in order as he walked past the front reception area into the side aisles of the floor and then past the many offices comprising the place.

It was as spooky and quiet as a morgue, but that never bothered Charlie. He had grown used to the disquieted edginess dark spaces could do to one's psyche. When he came to Ms. Ellis's office, it was also open. Papers were scattered about haphazardly. He knew this was not how she'd left the office when he escorted her to her car on request. It had been vandalized and not in a good way. If he wasn't mistaken, her photo had been violated with a substance he didn't want to speculate long on.

Disgusted, he hurried out of her office and did a quick step run to Mr. Lathan's back corner office. When he arrived, he was shocked. It was as if a bomb had gone off. The blinds were bent and torn, and the office desk and chairs were overturned. Pencils, pens, and papers were strewn across the room as if thrown. The place smelled of fury and sweat. The hackles on the back of Charlie's neck rose when he saw the photos of Simon Lathan's family torn to pieces. This was rage. Unmitigated rage from someone out of control. He thought he had Simon pegged, but he'd missed the mark. The quiet demeanor of the man he saw being questioned by the police earlier hid a dangerous maniac drunk on power and control. Charlie guessed that Simon wanted something he couldn't have, which must have mightily *pissed* him off.

Laramie was smart and brave, which made her dangerous to him. How Simon had controlled himself when being questioned was anyone's guess. Charlie was no psychiatrist, but he'd seen this kind of uncontrolled rage before in combat and knew one thing. Laramie was in trouble. This thought became an overwhelming hunch he couldn't shake if his life depended on it.

He acted quickly. Leaving the offices of the advertising agency, he got on his two-way radio. The radio's static sounded as he spoke.

"Charlie One to James One, you copy?" The static stopped as he eased off the button, waiting for a response.

"Affirmative. What's up?"

"I'm up here on forty-four. How long you been back from Grub-In?"

"Been a while. Why?"

"Stay there. Coming down to you."

"Copy that."

To hear James say he'd been there a while was reassuring. He might have seen Simon leave the building. Or worse, Simon might be lurking around somewhere. Charlie had to make sure before calling the authorities. The urgency he felt was overpowering. He had a terrible feeling Laramie was in danger, but his suspicions could be wrong. Charlie couldn't shake the feeling that something very terrible was about to occur or had already happened.

He could see his brother munching on something from a long way off. When he got close, his brother put the sandwich down and rubbed his hands together.

"Sorry, bro. I couldn't help but eat your sandwich. I'll get you another if you want," James hurried with a backhanded apology. But Charlie waved it off.

"You know the dude accused of assaulting that lady today?"

"Yeah."

"You see him this evening?"

"Sure! Came down the back stairs while I was coming up from Grub-In. Why?"

"Anything seem odd to you?"

"Stairs are kinda narrow, so I could feel heat coming off him when he passed. He seemed in a hurry, so maybe that's why. You think the cooling system is out up there or something? Or was it just hot in the stairwell?"

"Why'd he take the stairs, not the elevator? He say anything?"

"Huh?" James asked, clearly confused. "What's this about, man? What you getting at?"

Charlie ignored his brother and went to the console on the desk. It held information on everything about the building, from company names, names of occupants, room numbers, phone numbers, and parking spaces. It also had a bank of monitors where CCTV cameras could be viewed. The cameras were scattered throughout the building, inside and outside. They were of beneficial use for viewing the parking areas for security. Each space on parking levels P1 and P2 was allocated as assigned parking to upper-level employees. The basement level was for everyone else. Charlie quickly found Simon Lathan's designated parking spot.

"Simon Lathan, Level P1, space forty-six," Charlie said aloud as his brother looked over his shoulder. Then he looked at the CCTV camera that scanned this set of spaces.

"Car's still there," James said, then sat beside his brother to man the CCTV camera angles. This was his specialty.

"I wonder where he was going when you saw him. Let's see the camera footage. Roll the time stamp to 6:40 p.m., when the police left. I want to see what happened from then to 8:00 p.m."

They watched the camera footage of the halls and elevators. At 6:55 p.m., they saw Charlie and Laramie enter one elevator and exit on the 42nd floor. Then, at 7:18 p.m., they watched Simon enter an elevator on the 44th floor. After a few minutes, he exited on the 10th floor and took the stairwell.

"What the fuck?" Charlie said to himself.

Then they watched as Charlie and Laramie entered the elevator again at 7:23 p.m. on the 42nd floor. Looking at the parking lot footage, they could see many employees leaving the area. They thinned down to a trickle just as James was seen coming back from Grub-In. At the 7:25 p.m. mark, to their astonishment, Simon Lathan was seen walking *past* his vehicle.

"Damn! We just missed him!" Charlie exclaimed. "Pan out. I want to see where he's headed."

"Can't, man. This camera only scans so far."

"Isn't there another camera at the back of the garage?"

"I've asked to have one put in a lot of times, but no one listens to me."

"You telling me there're no cameras to scan even the *back* set of elevators? The ones Laramie and I exited from?" James shrugged in answer. "I can*not* believe this." Charlie was unaware he was holding his breath until he saw Laramie drive by in her car at 7:35 p.m. The convertible top had already been rolled back.

"There!" Charlie exclaimed when he saw an odd movement on the back seat floor as she drove out of the camera's view.

⋘⟨⊙⊙⊙⟩⋙

Laramie woke in her bedroom. Pain throbbed in her head from the blow she'd received. She realized she couldn't move very well. She was restrained with ties on her legs and arms, lying spread-eagle on her queen-sized bed, naked. Simon was there. She could see him stroking Miss Purdy while sitting in an antique vanity chair in her room. He kept his head low and caressed her cat; he smiled at her from under heavy brows.

"Such a pretty little pussy. Oh, was that offensive? Maybe I should say *cat*."

"How—?"

"—did I get here without notice? Yes, about that." Simon slowly set Miss Purdy on the floor and steepled his fingers in front of his face. "You see, I laid low on the floor of your marvelous car. You didn't know, did you? *Stupid cunt!*" He said this last slowly and quietly as if it were an afterthought, drawing out the words "stoop-id cu-n-t."

It was frightening. Laramie tried not to panic or let the fear get to her. She didn't want it to show. She remained quiet, watching him as he continued to speak.

"I thought of rising from the back to surprise you with a lick of my tongue on the back of your neck. But I had to nix that idea." He made a tsk, tsk sound with his tongue, then said, "No, that wouldn't do. You see, I wanted to arrive safely without causing an accident.

"You're predictable. I knew you'd head home and wouldn't stop for a nightcap. Not after what I put you through today." He smiled broadly. "I knew where you lived, of course. I know where *all* my employees live. All this time, you had no idea I watched you. You with your self-assuredness and your pretty little ass. You were the only one who turned me down. Of all people, you had the nerve to tell me… *no.*"

"I need to get dressed," she said without emotion.

"No." He paused for effect. "See how it feels? To be denied a basic need. To get dressed, to eat, to drink, to pee, to sleep, to fuck. It's natural, really, but for you—oh no. Miss Tight Ass, Laramie Ellis. The *star* of this show!" Simon rose to emphasize this last pronouncement with outstretched arms. "How dare you!" Simon's demeanor turned on a dime, showing a menace she could only envision in a nightmare.

Laramie remained quiet. She had to think. She didn't know how much time Simon would allow her to lie like that without doing the unthinkable. She could only watch, observe, and listen. Thank God she hadn't eaten; otherwise, she'd throw up despite herself. Simon began to pace the floor. She watched as he softened again.

"You're the epitome of the all-American girl next door. Did you know? The one any man would want to take home to Mama. So enticing. But you're feisty. An enigma. Not easy to understand. You're a wonder." He pursed his lips together, then turned to face her. "I visited your office after you'd gone. Yes, I did. I relieved myself in exquisite ecstasy on your photo. It was glorious. But how dare I do such a thing without thinking! Now everyone will know what kind of pervert I *might* be." He chuckled. "Imagine that? Of course, I had to make it look innocent and blame you, so I trashed the place." He laughed long and loud, almost hysterically. "I threw papers all around and upset all the trinkets on your desk. But I didn't stop there. I went to my office and made a mess there too." He paused then said, "My wife will be so *angry!* She dressed it to the nines—her words, not mine. But then again, it's all your fault, darling Laramie. You did that. Not me."

"My hands are numb." Again, Laramie said this without emotion. Matter-of-fact statements might just bring him back to reality. Listening to his rambling, it was obvious Simon was clearly insane. She was in far more danger than she had first thought. Laramie reasoned that stating the obvious might give her some time to come up with something. But he ignored her, caught up in his own imagination.

"You see, we came here together tonight. You insisted, and I couldn't resist." He smiled at her and continued, "Of course, I complied to calm your horrible temper. When we arrived here, you suggested I tie you up, as you are now, and I obliged. How could I not? Our earlier fight was all but forgotten as we got on with the kind of activity you so thoroughly enjoyed. This kinkiness, hidden inside that brain of yours. But *who knew* it would get out of hand? Certainly *not* me."

"My ankles. They hurt," Laramie said. This time, his attention turned to her.

"This is how it will play out, so listen carefully." He licked his lips, running his tongue over them with relish. "When we're done, or should I say, when I'm done with having my fun, you walk down to the kitchen while I get dressed. I tell you that I must go home to my wife. Your anger causes you to strike out at me with a kitchen knife. I overpower and kill you in self-defense." He paused his pacing to look at her. "That's how it will happen. Do you approve of the plan? Of course, you have to admit to the genius of it." He looked at her for what seemed like forever, and then his face changed to a coldness that almost stopped her heart. "I've talked too much already." Then Simon began to undress.

"How will you explain what you did to my photo?" Laramie asked.

"What?" Simon seemed perplexed and paused in his undressing.

"You heard me. My photo, remember?"

Simon blinked rapidly. Then he heard the floorboards behind him squeak.

<hr>

While gawking at Laramie's car, Charlie hadn't bothered to check the back seat. Why would he? For him, it was natural to think anyone accused of perpetrating a crime wouldn't dare leave so soon after being absolved of wrongdoing. To Charlie's thinking,

Simon would stay, relish his victory, and lick his wounds. But he had underestimated Simon Lathan, who was as guilty as sin. Charlie feared Simon's passion would not be satisfied until he did the unimaginable.

Charlie and James went into full action. After quickly explaining what remained of Simon's office to his brother and his suspicions of what he thought Simon was capable of, he started giving orders.

"Get me Laramie Ellis's address. Then check the traffic reports to see if anyone has seen an accident involving a black Studebaker VI—if they know what that is."

"Already on it," James said.

"Then go recheck the 44th floor. Make sure that asshole's not there. I'll call the police to see if we can get someone to Laramie's."

James barked out Laramie's address, "Twenty-three fifty Quitman Street, Sloan Lake, near Lakewood," then incredulously said, "Son of a bitch, no accidents reported! I'll be damn."

"Got it. Light traffic maybe. Now go!" Charlie dismissed James as he dialed DPD. The dispatch seemed to take forever to answer. When they did, Charlie wasted no time.

"I need to speak to the officer in charge. My name is Charles Simpson—a security guard at the Republic Plaza. We have a possible situation occurring in Sloan Lake."

"Who is this again?" the dispatcher asked.

"Charles. *Simpson!* We had an incident here earlier, and I fear the lady involved is in danger. Let me speak to someone in charge… please!" Charlie insisted.

"Did you say a *possible* situation? What is this?"

"I don't have all night! Get me someone in charge *now!*"

After a few minutes, a gruff voice was heard. "Chief DuPont. What's the nature of your emergency again?"

"My name is Charles Simpson. I'm the chief security guard at Republic Plaza building in downtown Denver—"

"Yes, I know where it is. We sent officers there earlier on a trumped-up charge of sexual assault. What can I do for you?" DuPont said, sounding a little more than annoyed.

"I have a strong reason to suspect it wasn't a trumped-up charge, sir. Recently discovered evidence would suggest otherwise. I fear the woman in question is in serious danger from the perpetrator."

"What gives you that reason—?"

"You need to send someone over to 2350 Quitman Street! She *may* not have long to live—"

"Are you *serious?* You expect me to send officers to help someone who's already tried to stir up trouble on a false—"

"I don't give a shit *what* you think was going on! A woman could end up dead, and you'll have only yourself to blame. As an officer of the law, you have an *obligation* to investigate suspicious felonious activity and false reporting by a crazy son of a bitch who had your officers by the nose this evening. Am I saying too much or *asking* too much?"

"Now, look here! I don't know who think you're talking to—"

"You want to *kiss* my ass! *Sir! Send someone now! 2350 Quitman or I'll do it myself!* And *get over* here to investigate what we've found on the 44th floor!"

Then Charlie Simpson, Chief Security Guard at the Republic Plaza building in downtown Denver, hung up on Chief DuPont, DPD Chief of Police. He then called his brother on the two-way.

⟫◦◦◦⟪

In the state of Colorado, because of the security and exchange offices in the building, they were known as armed security—not unarmed. Charlie undid the safety of his Glock .22 as he ran to his vehicle, and on this night, he was glad his gun was on his hip. He was breaking the rules by leaving his post. He'd radioed his brother James, and they agreed it was the right thing to do. His brother had searched the floor but hadn't found Simon. They surmised it was probably him in the back seat of Laramie's car. It didn't take a rocket scientist to determine what would happen to

Laramie if that were true. Neither did they feel DPD would take them seriously and comply. Charlie thought he shouldn't have said what he did to the police chief at the time, but if he had to do it again, he wouldn't change a word.

The drive to Sloan Lake didn't take long. However, finding the address was a challenge in the dark. In an unfamiliar neighborhood, Charlie was sure he looked suspicious in his company vehicle. Sloan Lake was a beautiful upscale community, tight-knit from all the reports he'd heard. He wondered if the police would be called if Laramie screamed. *Damn it!* He kept chastising himself for not thoroughly checking to ensure she was okay to leave. He'd never be able to live it down or forgive himself if she got hurt.

Charlie didn't dwell on that final thought long. He wanted to stay positive and find her safe and sound. Then he saw her house. The bungalow sat back from the road. Nothing seemed out of the ordinary. He turned the light off as he pulled his car to the curb across the street from her house. *Where's the police? Now what, genius?* He found he couldn't just sit and wait. Urgency got under his skin again. It propelled him to move forward.

However, that wasn't such a good idea. On this weeknight in early June, the neighborhood was still active, with some out walking their dogs or on their front porches. There were even kids skateboarding or hanging outside with friends. To see an unfamiliar Black man in a security vehicle and in uniform caused some to stare and stand back unconsciously.

"Is there a problem, Officer?" one well-meaning neighbor called out.

"No, nothing to be concerned about. Thank you," Charlie responded with a wave.

"Well, what's going on?" another neighbor asked.

But Charlie said nothing in answer. Just lowered his head and walked over as if he was expected to be there. Although it was customary to do so, he didn't want to go to the front door and ring the doorbell. If Simon was inside, that would alert him. So what to do?

He saw Laramie's car in the driveway and pretended to inspect it by shining his flashlight inside. This caused murmuring from some neighbors for a minute, who mostly looked on from the safety of their porches or the street. He suspected some might call the police, which was a good thing. On second thought that was an excellent thing, so why not? He did the obvious. Calling more attention to himself than was necessary, he shined his flashlight across the street to the front porch and faces of the neighbors and bystanders. *That should cause some alarm. Now call the police, nosy neighbors! God bless ya!*

Then he ran to the back of the house to the kitchen entrance, skirting the wrought iron fencing separating Laramie's house from the neighbor next door. Through the windowpane of the back door, he was astonished to see a cat frantically running back and forth as if in a panic. He didn't know much about cats, but what he did know of their behavior told him this was atypical. Something was up, and it wasn't good. He also noticed the lock had been jimmied. Someone had gone in from the outside. Charlie pulled out his gun and stepped inside.

⟫◦◦◦⟪

The voice came from upstairs. Just one. Male. To Charlie, it sounded as if he was giving a speech or something similar. *What's he done with Laramie?* The cat he'd seen earlier sat watching him at the corner of the stairs leading to the second floor.

As Charlie cautiously made his way up the stairs, he said a silent prayer of thanks for the floorboards being solid and not squeaking under his weight. He held his breath and made his way to the top landing.

He had a clear view of the upstairs bedroom, where Laramie lay. Each limb of her body was tied to the bedposts as she listened to Simon speak. As Simon paced back and forth at the foot of the bed, Charlie pressed his body against the wall at the top of the landing. He heard Simon say, "This is how it will play out…" as if outlining the perfect launch of an ad campaign. *Son of a bitch should think twice.* Charlie contemplated his next move. When he heard Laramie ask, "How will you explain what you did to my photo?" He was ready.

Charlie stepped forward just as Laramie spoke again. This time, the floorboards gave him away. Simon turned to look at him, and the registration of surprise on his face was priceless. Laramie screamed. Unarmed, Simon picked up the nearest object and flung it at Charlie. The vase was a near miss as it sailed past his head like a missile just as Charlie ducked and fired his Glock. Unlike the movies, most shots missed the mark. Charlie missed by miles.

Simon ran at Charlie before he could get another shot fired. The impact of their bodies sent the gun flying from Charlie's hand and underneath the bed. Simon landed a few good punches, while Charlie's efforts at right jabs didn't seem to faze Simon.

For a horrifying minute, it became clear to Charlie that Simon's focus was on retrieving the gun. They struggled, with Simon crawling for the weapon and Charlie pulling and grappling at Simon's feet. It would be almost comical if it wasn't so serious. Charlie was able to gain some leverage by yanking him back and away from the bed, but this failed.

Despite Charlie's efforts, Simon was able to grab the gun and allow himself to be pulled from beneath the bed. He rose from the floor in a kneeling position and turned to fire at Charlie. Fortunately, Simon's inexperience in handling the weapon showed, and his shot went wide. In an expert move, Charlie disarmed him, and in a panic, Simon grabbed Charlie by the neck. They were standing now, and with as much strength as Charlie could manage, he pushed Simon backward in an effort to slam him to the floor. But the room was smaller than he realized, and they stumbled. There wasn't much room to run, and too late, Charlie and Simon crashed through the upstairs window, landing on the side of the house below.

The fall was swift and violent. In the momentum, Simon landed on the spikes of the wrought iron fence. Charlie ended up on his right side in the grassy area between the house driveway pavers, just missing the front bumper of Laramie's car. In pain, he knew his shoulder had dislocated and his collarbone was broken. However, Simon was worse. The spike had caught him in the neck and left arm. Simon was dead.

⌗

The sirens were loud as the police cars careened around the corner to Laramie's address. The police found her upstairs still tied to the bed. The violation she felt was acute. It was humiliating and shameful, but she held her head high. Quick action by her neighbors, calling the police and administering to Charlie as best they could after the fall, helped tremendously. An ambulance had also been called, and once it arrived, Laramie and Charlie were taken to the hospital for treatment. Simon was left as he'd fallen for investigation and forensics. Hours later, the coroner took his body away.

The police officers listened raptly to every word Laramie said, and she answered their questions as thoroughly as possible, filling in as many puzzle pieces as necessary. She was assured Internal Affairs would investigate the earlier incident. Somehow, she knew all would be made right on that score. It wasn't until Laramie was allowed to see Charlie, who was sedated and awaiting additional treatment for his broken collarbone, that she cried. She never left his side.

⌗

The memory of the incidents at the office and her home faded, but too much had happened to allow Laramie to stay with the agency, her home, and Denver. Two months later, she resigned after accepting an offer from Ogilvy and Mather in New York as an advertising executive.

After an extensive inquiry, Charlie was eventually awarded for his bravery and courage to do what was necessary when no other choice was found. His exoneration made him something of a hero, which he was reluctant to accept or realize, but Laramie knew better.

Three months after the incident, Laramie waited for Charlie in her Studebaker while he said goodbye to his brother. They were headed east to New York. A road trip they each looked forward to. "You ready?" she asked.

"Mind if I drive?" he asked.

"Sure thing. No problem." She smiled at him.

He was only a few years older than her, shy and handsome. He was a friend and, if luck held out, would be much more than that in her future.

The End

THE DEVIL & EMMA STEPHENS

Emma never considered herself pretty. For her, modeling was easy. A smile to the camera, a Dior turn on the runway, or showcasing the latest fashion trend as it hung from her body was nothing to her. The camera loved her face, body, eyes, and more. Her exotic dark Irish/Welsh look booked her for many modeling gigs. There was no artifice. She was blessed with perfect features and thought nothing of these things. She had "the look," which meant money and fame for her publicist and modeling agency.

However, this was not the life Emma wanted for herself. To be able to sit quietly and watch grass grow or paint dry would be heaven to her. *How do I step away gracefully?* This prospect eluded her as she was pushed and prodded to appear at yet another photo shoot. Emma was growing weary and tired, and it was starting to show.

It wasn't so long ago Emma had lived a life of *mild* poverty—if such a thing existed. She had accepted the Lord Jesus Christ as her savior at a young age. No one fully understood her love of God, not even her mother. Aside from the large cross of Saint David, which her father had given her for safekeeping, the Holy Bible was her constant companion. Emma had become obsessed with angels and considered living a pious life. However, she wasn't a devout Catholic but more of a spiritual Christian in nature. In the religious sense, she never had anything supernatural happen to her. But one occasion came close. While a student at Immaculate Heart Catholic School, the overwhelming fragrant smell of flowers surrounded her. When she asked if anyone else smelled it, no one had. Only her. She later learned this was a sign of Saint Thérèse of Lisieux being near and hearing her prayer, letting her know God was responding. For Emma, it was a sign she should accept Saint Thérèse as her patron saint, and she did.

Each day, she prayed at least ten Our Fathers and Glory Be to heal her sick father and even to Saint Thérèse and Mother Mary to hasten her prayer. It seemed God had ignored her and took him to heaven anyway. Over time, Emma wanted to understand more about why her prayers had failed, why her father had been taken so soon, and what awaited him on the other side of life. *Why didn't Saint Thérèse hear my prayer?* Without concrete answers, she had become listless, and the cross useless. She aimlessly moved through life like an automaton with no direction or desire to pursue much of anything.

One day, on a lark, her mother suggested she try modeling of all things. Emma had no interest in pursuing this at all.

"You've always been such a beautiful child, and now you're growing into a breathtaking young lady. You're tall enough, goodness knows. Why don't you at least give it a try? Take a few pictures and smile for a change. It might be fun. See how it goes? What do you say?"

"I don't know, Mama. It seems silly to me. What good would it do anyway?"

"It'll get you focused on things other than questioning the afterlife. There is so much life to live, and I worry for you."

"Beauty shines from the inside, not the outside, Mama, you always said."

"Such a wise girl. You're right. But maybe, just maybe, you'll get paid for it. Look at it as a job of sorts. It'll give you something to do instead of moping around all day. If you don't like it, we'll find something else, huh?"

At age fifteen, her mother arranged to have photos taken of Emma. Her sultry look and depressed demeanor were like liquid gold to the camera. The local modeling agency shopped her image around on a one-page headshot and information sheet. Photos selected from her contact sheets showcased her talent and photogenic appeal. Before Emma knew it, she was catapulted to runway shows, various fashion magazine shoots, and even covers, becoming the darling of New York's fashion world and ad agencies. However, traveling was exhausting. Emma's mother had tired of it sooner than her daughter. After three years, an unexpected illness took her mother from her life, leaving her completely alone.

At the age of twenty, Emma had become a pro. Secretly, her Bible had been a comfort through the loneliness of living in one hotel or another until her next modeling gig. After a while, she had lost interest in keeping the "good book" nearby. The large cross of Saint David became cumbersome to carry around and was all but forgotten. She enjoyed numerous nights out with other models but never stayed out too late. Eventually, she obtained the reputation of being snooty and not much fun, but Emma didn't care. She couldn't help it if her standards differed from some of her small circle of fashion-forward friends. Besides, the hazards of temptation were around every corner. Being naturally slender, she prided herself on staying healthy and wanted to keep it that way. She avoided the lure of drowning her loneliness in drugs or alcohol, even at some of the swankier parties held by notable designers. She wasn't a prude but was careful of whom she let into her life. Nothing ever lasted long with the guys she met, which was just as well. She remembered her mother's words about waiting for the right person before giving her whole heart.

Still, she waited, wanting more from life other than living one that felt empty and hollow.

The world of modeling was subjective. At twenty-six, Emma still had "it." Looking five years younger than her counterparts, Genesis, her modeling agency, had stopped sending her to go-sees long ago. She was still in high demand and could write her own ticket. But time had exhausted her, and its toll was evident in her demeanor. After all her hard work, she wanted to rest and savor as much of what was left of her life as soon as possible. That included who she was as a person and not a commodity to be objectified by the beauty industry. At thirty, Emma found the courage to leave. Refusing to appear at another fitting, she had announced unceremoniously that it was time to pack it all in and return to a quieter life.

So here she was, back in the state that had made her who she was and a life she wanted to reclaim. Emma had seen enough of the world, including Milan, Paris, London, and New York, but there was no place like home.

⤞◉◉◉⤝

She settled in a modest bungalow in the Washington Park neighborhood of Denver, or Wash Park, as the locals called it. Her home was considered quaint, almost bohemian in decor, decorated in what used to be called shabby chic. It was filled with mementos of her travels and gifts from designers she'd worked with, such as screen prints by Andy Warhol, paintings by Banksy, and some sculptures and ceramic pottery given as gifts from an artist in Milan. Her wardrobe consisted of couture pieces from the Dior, Givenchy, Alexander McQueen, and Celine houses, mixed with L.L. Bean-like everyday wear. She tempered this collection of finery with a homey feel of lived-in furniture and art that comforted anyone who visited, not only herself but also her Lhasa Apso, Sophie.

Emma loved her morning walks in the park with Sophie. That day in early spring was like any other. With her favorite latte in hand, chastising Sophie when she tried to chase after a Canadian goose or an errant squirrel or sitting on a convenient bench to soak up the glorious morning sunshine, a stroll with Sophie was manna to her. The day was cooler than normal, and as a man approached, Emma took a cautious drink of her latte. Nothing seemed unusual about him except the vague impression she might know him.

"Good morning, Emma Stephens?" He seemed unsure of her name.

"Do I know you?" she responded, not surprised she might be recognized. Emma shielded her eyes from the sun as she looked up at him but couldn't make out his features with his back to the sun.

"You should. How's your morning walk so far?" he asked offhandedly. But before she could answer, he spoke again. "Cooler this morning. Good to see you have your drink of choice to keep you warm, not that a coat wouldn't do a better job. I can see you're colder than you think."

How rude! She felt adequately dressed in leggings, a sweatshirt, and a zipped-up goose-down vest. Her shoes were questionable, being slip-on tennies, but otherwise, it was none of his business to judge. *Who is he to criticize me?* So she said the only sensible thing in the form of a reply to his odd comments.

"I beg your pardon?" Emma asked as politely as she could.

"Surely, you don't think you could be any colder than you are now, do you? You could be warmer, you know? How's your career thus far?" His tone of voice was seductive and caring while condescending at the same time.

"What?" Emma asked. She was beyond perplexed by this time.

"Do you still have that special gift left to you by your father? Still reading your Bible?"

At this point, Sophie barked at the stranger. She didn't stop. *Too right.* Emma stood to get a better grip on Sophie's leash and to get the sun out of her eyes. She wanted a better look at the man so she could give him a piece of her mind. He took a few steps backward, the sun was still at his back as if deliberately keeping her from seeing his face and stood closer to an elm tree. Then she heard a familiar voice call to her in alarm because of the barking little Sophie gave the man.

"Is everything all right, Emma?" Karen Cummings asked. They had been friends since childhood and occasionally met at the park to pass the time.

Thankful for the distraction, Emma turned to greet her friend, but when she turned back again, the man was gone.

"Well, I…. Where did he go?" Emma asked, incredulous that he had disappeared.

"Who?" Karen asked.

"The man that was just here. He asked something strange—"

"I didn't see anyone, girl. I just heard a dog barking its head off. When I saw it was you, I headed over." *It's just like Karen to arrive when an incident is over.*

"You didn't see him?" Emma asked, clearly perplexed.

"Uh-uh! I heard Sophie and saw you sitting, then you stood up as if to… well, I don't know what I saw you do. Are you sure you're okay?" Karen asked as she leaned in to examine Emma's face.

"I'm not really sure. That was the damnedest thing!"

"If you say so." Karen shrugged. "Well, he's gone now, so whatever—"

"I know you don't believe me, but listen, he said some bizarre things about how I was dressed, warmth, a gift my father left me, and the Bible. It was weird. You sure you didn't see him?"

"Honey, I saw nothing. You sleeping okay? Getting enough rest—"

"Stop it, all right?" Emma said, sounding more annoyed than she felt. "I know it sounds crazy, especially the Bible… thingy." She waved her hands for emphasis. "Come walk with me while I try to shake this off. I need to get Sophie to the groomer. What time is it anyway?"

"It's almost nine o'clock. What about the Bible?" Karen asked. The reference to a gift was almost forgotten by Emma. "You getting religious on me or something?"

"I put my Catholicism days behind me a long time ago," Emma said with another dismissive wave of her hand. The stranger had given her the jitters, which started to fade as she watched Sophie's shadow bounce up and down on the pavement ahead of her as she walked. "Still, it was strange he'd throw in that reference while asking about the *weather*."

"That wasn't what you just said. He asked about warmth and cold and—"

"Oh, you know what I mean!" Emma said, letting her annoyance get in the way of a friendly conversation.

"Ouch! Testy, testy! Slow down now; it's me, remember?"

"Anyway, as long as I've been back home, I haven't thought of lifting that book again. Life's been good, and so has God."

"So, you served your time to Jesus and the Lord. Now you've moved on, huh?"

"Well, it's not like I'm drawn to it anymore. My life abroad kind of turned a lot of things around. But you know, it's funny. Anytime I'd come near a cathedral or church, there *or* here, for that matter, I felt compelled to enter and pray. Silly, huh?"

"Nah, not really. I understand… I guess." Then, taking a deep breath, she added, "I'm sure glad I came this morning to find you staring at nothing." Karen chuckled, trying to change the mood. She asked Emma something more important. "You still doing that get-together this evening? I'll be there, don't forget. I'm also bringing someone you just might like. I hope you don't mind."

"It's a small gathering really. I suppose it won't hurt if you bring someone. The less I'll have to store if more people are there to eat the food on the menu." Emma then tugged on Sophie's leash. "I need to scoot. Talk to you later?" Emma asked, then, as an afterthought, "And watch out for strange men!" she called after her friend with a tease while she and Sophie waited to cross the street.

"No, that'll be you! You're still taking all the attention from us gals who need a wink or two from good-looking fellas. Bye!" Karen took a skip and started her morning run as Emma looked after her.

Emma smiled, thinking how miraculous their friendship had been. Compared to her tall frame, she would ascribe petite and cute to Karen. Most men seemed attracted to Karen's type of femaleness compared to Emma's, who tended to scare men off. Contrary to popular belief, most of her nights did not involve the opposite sex. She loved men, but nothing ever lasted very long. They never seemed to fall in love with *her*, only the glamour of the world she represented. To have a steady guy in her life right then would be welcome. One could only hope.

⸺◈◈◈⸺

There was a crowd at Emma's home. *Who are all these people?* Emma wasn't very concerned about spills or destroying any works of art; Lord knew she was insured to the hilt. She was more worried about characters of ill repute polluting the air of her home with verbosity and arrogance. This was one of the things Emma found so bothersome and irritating about the fashion industry. She liked salt-of-the-earth individuals full of no-nonsense approaches to life who cut to the chase of the ridiculous. One guess was a girl with a pointy chin, big eyes, and freckles who looked afraid to touch anything, let alone accept the offer of a drink. Emma had no idea who she was, but she looked like the stuff fashion models are made of.

Shamus Wittingham was one of those people she detested the most. Karen didn't seem to understand the loathsomeness of this man. She beamed, smiled, and gushed over his many accomplishments in her efforts to amaze Emma. Karen was trying too hard. Emma was not impressed. After excusing herself from the initial introduction, unperturbed, Emma was immediately cornered by the erstwhile Mr. Shamus.

"You have quite a collection of trinkets, I see. Are these imitations? Surely they're not originals. I've traveled to many countries, stayed at the best homes, and can spot a fake when I see one."

"You think these works of art are fake, do you?" Emma asked.

"*I* wouldn't deign to insult my host by going that far; what do you take me for? Of course, I'm only asking about the origin of procurement."

Like hell you are. "Why is that any of your business?"

"It isn't. I'm trying to converse with a most beautiful hostess whose home I am beginning to admire greatly."

"I… thank you for the compliment, but it might be better to admire without saying anything more," Emma said as she turned away. But Shamus was not so easily dismissed.

"You won't engage in conversation about your travels, work, or art pieces? Isn't that what you display them for—?"

"I display them for my enjoyment, sir," Emma snapped at Shamus with an unwavering gaze. "Pardon *my* rudeness. You're welcome to engage with my guests if you'd like and enjoy the works as I do, but if you'll excuse me." Emma paused before continuing, "I have other guests who need my attention."

She left him gaping at her and wasn't concerned about his thoughts or feelings. That was twice in one day she'd been approached and questioned by rude men. *My karma or the universe itself must be off or something.* She chuckled to herself.

She had the odd sensation of floating on air as music wafted around her and onto the lawn. Her annoyance at Shamus had all but evaporated at the sight of the assembled guests before her in a yard, which was edged with red roses and daffodils in bloom, a nod to her patron saint, Thérèse of Lisieux, and to Saint David of Wales. She descended the few steps to the green grass of her backyard, wearing ballet flat shoes and a cream-colored eyelet sundress that blew nicely behind her as she approached guests.

However, when Emma accidentally bumped the arm of a man she hadn't seen before, she caught her breath. She was instantly attracted and felt embarrassed by the sudden rise in emotion.

"I'm so sorry. Did I make you spill your drink?" Emma asked, unable to take her eyes off him.

"Just a bit, but not much," he responded with a direct gaze that didn't waver. "You so handled *him* well." Emma assumed he was referring to her discussion with Shamus.

"You heard that?"

"I did. You were impressive."

"I swear, *some* people," Emma said, rolling her eyes.

"I'm Devin, by the way. Devin Asher, a friend of Mr. Luce."

"Mr. *Loose, Lucy, or Louse?* Which?"

"L-U-C-E. Luce." Devin laughed at her joke. "It's easy to get his name confused."

"How do you do?" She smiled and offered her hand to shake. "I'm Emma Stephens, the host of this shindig. Who is Mr. Luce?"

"He's a curator of art and *not* a friend of Shamus there. I'm here on his behalf and an acquaintance of your friend Karen."

"Oh, *you're* the one she told me about. I thought it was Shamus." Devin said nothing in response but gazed at her unashamedly.

"You're beautiful. Forgive me for being so forward, but I couldn't help myself," Devin said, caressing her body with his eyes.

"My goodness! "Well, thank you very much," she said, not giving in to the temptation of returning a compliment in kind. He was too good-looking for words. It was as if a light shone from inside and around him. She was inexplicably drawn to him; all she knew was his name.

"I see you found Emma," Karen said, interrupting a conversation just beginning to make Emma blush.

Emma noticed Devin take a step back to allow room for Karen. *You don't see gentlemanly gestures like that every day. I think I'm gonna like this guy a lot.*

"I'm enjoying my conversation quite a bit. We were just discussing the curations Mr. Luce is interested in acquiring," Devin replied.

"Were we?" Emma said, askance.

"I'd like to explain the proposition privately if you don't mind?" Devin asked, turning to Karen.

"By all means, don't let me interrupt," Karen said, seeming not at all embarrassed by Devin's dismissal.

Emma was impressed by Devin's deft ability to take command. She willingly accepted his invitation to privacy while Karen looked on without saying another word.

She left her guests, assembled outside on the lawn, who were well into their drinks and saucers of food taken from the charcuterie board before the main course of salmon in lemon butter sauce, asparagus, and mashed potatoes. Emma had to admit it was a bit much, but her grassroots life couldn't help but be influenced by her European experiences—and it showed. *Maybe I'll be forgiven for trying too hard to make a good impression.* She came to this thought as she smiled and nodded at guests on the way to her private getaway cottage in the back of the house with Devin in tow.

⚛⚛⚛

The backyard cottage-type building was located away from the main house, like an oversized storage shed only with French doors. It was the one thing that compelled Emma to buy the bungalow in the first place. It was quieter here and an escape, holding some of her most special memorabilia. After kicking off her shoes, she settled in the oversized chair with heavily rolled arms. She looked at Devin, who sat on a small love seat across from her. His gaze lingered on her for an uncomfortable amount of time. Emma looked down at her wineglass and wondered how to keep her wits about her if she drank more. Especially if something unexpected happened between her and this handsome man.

"More wine?" Devin asked.

"No, I don't think so," Emma responded while running her index finger along the rim of her glass. "Tell me the reason we need to speak privately again."

"Mr. Luce would like to offer a proposition about acquiring a precious item you possess."

"What, my soul?" Emma chuckled out loud.

She expected Devin to laugh, but his eyes flashed at her instead. *Odd.* However, the moment passed within a nanosecond of it occurring, like a mist that just brushed past her shoulder.

"Do you mind if I shut these?" Devin asked as he rose to close the doors and pull tight the lace curtains covering the glass panes. "You must be cold after your morning walk with your dog. We need to get warm."

How does he know about my walk? Was he watching me? Did he see the strange man too? Emma didn't want to ask for clarification as these questions ran through her mind. If she was being seduced, she didn't want to stand in the way of that. Not one little bit. The last time she had been kissed was a distant memory. The caress of a man was a longing she had ignored until now. Yet, as Emma watched Devin, an uneasiness crept into her consciousness. She liked and loathed the feeling at the same time. Like some taboo, rite, or ritual she was about to engage in but couldn't help herself escape from.

When Devin returned, he bent on one knee in front of her, closer than what was considered decent. When he spoke, it was a whisper tickling her ear.

"As I was saying, you have something, a very *rare* something no one knows you have," Devin said seductively as he leaned close to her face.

"I'm sure you've noticed I have a lot of *somethings.*"

"Yes, but this is different," Devin said, emphasizing the 't' in the word *different.*

They were speaking to each other barely above a whisper at this point. The words were intoxicating and inviting. Emma found herself being swept up as if a wind were rising just inside the shed, whose occupants were only two. Her focus was on his mouth, with lips that looked soft and wet. She wanted to feel them on hers in the worst way.

He kissed her then. The taste of wine on his tongue and his sweet breath were heart-stopping. She returned the kiss deeply and passionately. She let the moment take her without thinking about her guests outside the door. She wanted to immerse herself in feeling everything her body ached for. Emma felt his hands on her thighs as they traveled under her dress and welcomed the feeling when his hands cupped her backside, lifting her toward him where he knelt on the floor. Her legs straddled him as he slid her close, wanting more.

When he caressed and kissed her neck, she allowed him full access. His touch was irresistible, and his kiss was perfect, with lips and tongue searching. She was surrendering to his lustful desire, and she didn't care. He started to undress her. Still, she didn't care.

Then, with one breath, she heard him say, "Yes. Give yourself freely. Yes. We want this. Yes. We want what was bestowed to you. Yes, by all the saints, such as Thérèse." The deep intake of breath at his last *yes* scared her senseless. It was evil. It was not of this world.

"Jesus!" Emma's eyes opened wide as she recoiled and pushed him away with such force that Devin fell back, caught off-balance by her response and action.

"I can give you so much. Don't you know?" Devin asked, moving closer again. "I couldn't wait to show myself to you and offer all on behalf of Mr. Luce."

"I don't know who or *what* you are, but this isn't right." Emma felt caught and sank back into her comfy chair. The fog of desire had not dissipated entirely, so she didn't understand what was happening. *What am I doing?* She was alone with a stranger, a force, who had seduced her with a snap of his fingers. What had she gotten herself into?

"Who are you to argue?" Devin said, almost threatening, but then he softened, trying to be convincing. "You have everything a woman could ask for. You've been able to acquire many things. Won't you agree to give us what we want?"

"I can't give you what isn't mine to give," Emma said, trying to come up with her best argument while still not understanding what he wanted from her. What was it?

"*Au contraire.* Come now. It *is* yours to give," Devin said seductively.

"What the *hell* are you talking about?" Emma spat the words at him.

"*Give it to us!*" Devin demanded. The threat of his words was dark and menacing.

His face became grotesque for a split second, and she recoiled farther into her chair. *No, no, no, this can't be happening! Was it my imagination, or did I see him become something evil? Why is he referring to himself in the third person?* Despite the fog inside her head, she instinctively knew to gather her senses and respond as if her life depended on it.

The music grew so loud it started to hurt her ears, and she knew no one would hear her if she screamed. As the realization and horror of the situation gripped her, Emma instinctively understood who Devin might be, but doubt surrounded her thoughts. In disbelief, she had to ask.

"What is it you think I have? You know *nothing* about me." Emma was trying to buy time to reason it out further.

"We've always known you. We needed the right time to take what you *must* agree to give." Devin's voice had the magic to bring any woman to her knees.

Emma again felt drawn to him, but this time against her will. The feeling was profound and disconcerting. The conflict rose in her mind and body as she fought the unholy desire. She felt dizzy, on fire, and the room seemed to spin. Then she caught sight of her little dog, Sophie, pawing at the door. Although Emma couldn't hear Sophie because of the loud music, she knew her dog was whining. Maybe others would see and come to her rescue.

"Your dog can't help you. It's just you and I, my lovely Emma. You want me, don't you?"

Emma couldn't stop herself from being taken in and have him continue to move his hands on her thighs again. The smell of his body and the heady infusion of sweat and desire were all-consuming. She heard his name repeating in her head, *"Devin, Devin, Devin."*

"You need me to take you, don't you?" Devin asked, almost a breath away from her face.

She was sinking into the turmoil in her soul, which was all Devin Asher. She was succumbing to the lust, the desire to have him, just once. Against sane reasoning, she thought she'd give anything for this one time with him. Despite herself, she couldn't help these unbidden thoughts from taking over her mind, making her numb and giddy with desire. Then she heard him speak again. Whispering seductively as he closed the space between them.

"Curse your friends, Emma. Let them squirm like worms, missing you. Tell them they're scum and you're the whore your mother was. Let them see you naked and flayed. Let them see the evil I put inside you open and burning. You want that, don't you, Emma? Do it! Submit yourself to me. I want you, Emma. I need you, Emma. I want what you have, Emma—your whole body. You'll do anything to give me what I want, won't you, Emma—? I want to corrupt your soul."

Before Emma gave in, let him consume her by saying yes, her mind refocused on his words and not the feeling rising inside her. *Words.* The most important words she knew were from the good book printed millennia ago in many languages and coveted by those of faith. It was that book she clung to when times looked bleak and in her hour of need. The one she had discarded many years ago. The book of God, the Holy Bible.

In a flash of clarity and horror, she realized something terrible was happening. Not the surrender to a handsome man during her dinner party, oh no. But the claiming of her soul by the devil himself! The devil had come for her.

The cross of Saint David on the wall in front of her was obscured by the crucifix of Jesus Christ. She wondered why this was ineffective in protecting her against his evil. Just as in days long ago, she began to pray for protection and strength. Was it because of this weakness, her turning away from God for a life of glamour, that Devin had come for her, seducing her? Forcing her to give up her *free will* and damning her soul to hell?

In all her days of modeling, in all her days of travel, in all her life, she never thought she'd be in a position to call on the Lord Jesus Christ to dispel evil, pure evil, from her presence. Yet here it was. Her faith was being tested—by Lucifer himself. She thought quickly.

"In the name of the Father, His Son Jesus, and the Holy Spirit, get away from me!" she said through gritted teeth. She didn't need to say this loudly; she couldn't while wrapped in the fog of desire. She didn't need to shout, but the effect on Devin was devastating.

He moved away from her as if burned. He was no longer the handsome man of light she'd met earlier and had almost given herself and her soul to. He became monstrous and grotesque, growing, it seemed, too large for the room to contain. He backed away from her, growling and angry. He stood towering above her as she sank deeper into the cushions of her oversized chair.

In that instant, she realized she had power over him, not the other way around. As soon as she uttered those words, the fog in her head cleared. The desire for him was gone, lying like a dead stone in her belly. Emma understood the danger she was in, but she was unafraid. She steadied herself.

"You've watched me all *my life*?" she demanded, rising from her chair, defiant.

"Of course we have," Devin answered, steadily advancing while she circled, trying to keep a distance between them in the confined space. "*We* waited for when you were weakest and your faith lost. Below, we watched you parade in finery and even sprinkled you with the dust of glamour." His tone of contempt was unmistakable. "We opened opportunities that *He* on high would not grant or allow. Do you think all doors opened to you by *His* grace alone or through your beauty? We surrounded you with temptations to persuade you to corrupt your soul. *We* waited for you to succumb to us, but you didn't. We've come to *take* what you will not give freely. Payment is due; you *must* give it to us!"

"You're a *liar!* Modeling is a rewarding profession. I was fortunate through the blessings bestowed on me by the grace of God. You can't get me to think otherwise, as something else is happening here. Well, you can't have what isn't mine to give. Whatever payment you want is not from me but from those *who watch over* me. This is a trick!"

"No trick, but no matter, they who watch over you are no match for us," Devin responded, sounding like the serpent he was, slithering and slathering his tongue when he said the word *us.*

Emma was sickened. She had to get out of this quickly, but how? Then, in a moment of clarity, she knew what to do. She had to get him to say his name. From what she'd read and heard, this might drive him out and away from her. She couldn't be sure but had to try. She could only think of calling on Jesus and all the saints to guide her.

"Who are you? What's your name?" Emma asked. "Beelzebub? Mephistopheles? Belial? Are you Legion? Or is Mr. Luce, *Lucifer*, your master, and Satan himself?"

Devin bent his head low at this question and looked at Emma from under heavy brows. It seemed to Emma his eyes had sunken into his head.

"That's for me to know and you to find out," he taunted in another voice of mischievous singsong with laughter underneath his smirk. "Even if you guess it, we must have what we came for."

From her days in Catholic school, she understood who he might be, but it was a guess at best. All this time, she thought God had forgotten her, and the love of Jesus was lost. But there was strength in her belief; it didn't fail her and would not fail her now. All the trappings of glamour did not diminish who she was spiritually. In this forgotten knowledge, the familiar fragrance of flowers grew from faint to overpowering, giving Emma the courage to carry on. Emma moved closer to the door and the wall where the cross hung.

"I can give you the world," Devin said, pleading. "I can give you pleasure and much *more* than you have now. All the riches in the world could not compare to what you'd have if you just gave us what we wanted. Let us have your gifts!" This time, his seductive words had no effect.

"Come take it then! *Asmodeus!*"

Emma reached for the crucifix and grabbed it just as Devin made an unearthly scream. She turned to face him with the crucifix and the cross of Saint David held together in her cupped hands. As he reached for her with gnarled fingers, the crucifix blazed toward where Devin stood. Emma held on tightly. The gust of wind that swept past her from behind would have sent anyone from their feet to the ground. Still, she stood firm.

"In the name of Jesus Christ, I command all demonic spirits that have gained access to me through curses and rituals be cut off and banished from me and my household, in the mighty name of the Lord Jesus Christ and all the saints that protect me through my Lord God!"

Where the words came from, she had no idea. They just flowed from her mouth and out to Devin. The strong scent of roses engulfed her as the room heaved from beneath her feet. Still, Emma held firm, and with all her strength, she cried out for His help, calling, "Jesus, Jesus, my Lord God, Jesus!" Then she turned her head as a blinding light engulfed them both… and screamed.

<hr>

The light dimmed, and all around her was quiet. Astonished, Emma stood alone in the small room, wondering if what had just happened was a dream. The only evidence of it being real was that the crucifix and cross vibrated slightly in her palms. Regaining her senses, Emma quickly opened the curtains of the French doors to let in more light. She opened the doors to music, which had been loud moments ago. It was now at a normal level. The air that wafted in was fresh and fragrant, smelling of freshly cut grass with the faint lingering smell of roses and daffodils. Still shaken by her encounter, Emma was relieved, yet confused, to see little Sophie lying by Karen's feet.

"Hey girl, you lose something?" Karen asked as Emma came toward her. "Why were you in the shed? I saw you go in, but you weren't there very long. Bored with the company you've invited already?" Karen joked as Sophie pawed at Emma's leg for attention.

"Has Sophie been with you all this time?" Emma asked, trying to gather herself as she lifted Sophie in her arms and hugged her. *Now, this feels normal.* She was more than a little perplexed.

"Yeah, she won't leave my side." Karen shrugged. "I almost tripped over her a few times." She frowned. "What's that in your hand?"

"Oh, something I've had for a while." Emma nervously shifted the crosses from one hand to another. *What's happening?* Sophie wiggled in her arms to be let down, and Emma complied, then asked, "You didn't hear any noise come from the shed just now? Where's Devin?"

"Who?" Karen asked just before taking a sip of red wine from her glass.

"Devin. Your friend," Emma said, trying to keep the urgency out of her voice.

"I don't know what you're talking about or who." Karen stepped back to peer at Emma, then added, "Shamus is still here, though. Do you mean him? That's twice today you've done this to me, asking if I saw some *strange* man. What's going on with you?" Karen asked. Then, with concern, she said, "Let me feel your forehead. Not good for the host to get sick."

"No, no, I'm… fine. Really." Emma brushed Karen's hand away from her forehead. "Never mind. Just… too much wine, I guess."

"Well, come with me." Karen grabbed Emma's arm to lead her back to the house. "I know just the thing to chase that feeling away. Water. Shall we?"

On Emma's way to the kitchen, she passed others in greeting who didn't seem to think she'd neglected them one iota. It was as if just a moment had passed without much concern for her. The encounter with Devin had unnerved her. She felt violated and assaulted, out of sorts. *Something's wrong.*

"Here, drink this," Karen said, thrusting a glass of water at Emma. "You look like you've seen a ghost."

"I think it's worse than that, truth be known. It's not like me to become dizzy like this," Emma said, feigning that she was unsteady and needed to rest. On the contrary, she knew exactly what she was doing. *I need to get my bearings for a minute.* She needed time to process the demeanor of her guests, the change in her surroundings, and the time-lapse of her absence.

"There you are, my dear!" Shamus made a show of missing her. "I've been reviewing your artwork, and I must say the reproductions are impeccable!" Then he leaned in and whispered to her with one hand facing palm out, "Take it from me; you don't need to explain to *anyone* that the paintings and small sculptures are not originals. I, for one, won't tell a *soul.*"

"What are you talking about?" Emma asked.

"Exactly! Keep playing it that way, and you'll fool them all, my dear." He patted her hand like a caring kindergarten teacher. Then, turning his attention away from Emma, he caught sight of another acquaintance and said, "My, my, my fancy seeing you here."

After he left, Karen rolled her eyes and looked at the ceiling in exasperation. "I'm so sorry, Emma. He *can* be a *pill* sometimes. Honestly!"

Emma quickly excused herself to investigate what Shamus had just said to grasp what was occurring. Emma slowly and methodically looked at each piece of her art collection. The colors of her pieces were either muted or overly bright; her clothing was more prêt-à-porter than couture. Imitations, to be sure. Her material possessions were still of good quality and taste but not the kind she thought she'd had before her backyard encounter. Sure, the lived-in look of her furnishings was still apparent, but more so than before. *"What's happened?"* Emma asked herself out loud.

She hadn't sold her soul or given the devil his due, or in this case, what Devin/Asmodeus wanted. The cross of Saint David was still in her hand. What had he said about giving her so much in exchange for what was due him? What payment? Why did Satan want her soul so badly? Why had she been tested? She needed an explanation.

Then Emma considered the cross of Saint David and the crucifix in her hand. She was grateful to have had it handy when invoking the Holy Trinity. However, despite what she experienced in Catholic school, Emma never *felt* blessed by Saint Thérèse or any other saints. But this man, who or whatever he was, thought so.

Along with the crucifix, the cross shone brightly to dispel evil. So much so that it had been hard to hold in her hand when she'd banished Devin. It was special to her father. He'd left strict instructions on how to care for it and protect it from being stolen. Until now, she'd treated the cross as just another object to display.

Along with her Bible, the large cross had always been with her. She thought her locked cottage would be perfect for displaying it and something she could gaze at when meditating. It was unobtrusive and hidden away but still visible. *These puzzle pieces must fit together somehow.*

Amid calls to come out and not hide away all evening, Emma graciously made her way to her study. She dodged guests who wondered when she'd regale them with stories of her modeling days and travels. Emma knew to mingle and not avoid her guests more than necessary, which the demon had asked of her. Somehow, she knew God would understand and forgive this transgression because she had more important things to do at the moment.

The late afternoon light filtered in brilliantly through the panes of glass of her study as she looked out at her guests in the backyard garden. This room was filled with books and lifelong mementos, but most importantly, a notebook left to her by her father. She hadn't bothered to read it until now. Maybe it would supply the answers needed for what had just happened.

Emma scanned the contents and found what she was looking for. Among her father's notes was a certificate of authentication stating the cross was a relic, blessed by the pope and given to her great-grandfather, Emmanuel Stephens, upon his acceptance to the secret Brotherhood of Protectors. *Oh my God! Why didn't I know this?*

With music and conversations streaming in just outside the partially closed door of the study, Emma was fixated on the task at hand. She turned on her laptop to do further research. According to records, the brotherhood had been formed ages ago to protect holy relics from Satan. The selected individuals swore to protect the relics, which would be passed down to their descendants in perpetuity. That would be Emma. Emma's father had also allowed the many saints to protect her by bequeathing the cross to her. And defend her they had, by the grace of God as manifested by the protection of Saint Thérèse and Saint David.

The devil is a liar. That day, he'd lied about many things. Satan covets the soul of man, not material possessions. By seducing her and tempting her to damn her mother, father, family, and friends, Devin/Asmodeus had tested the cross's power to protect her soul from him. By giving her soul freely, evil would have won over good. It was real. It happened. She survived.

⚊⚊⚊◦◦◦⚊⚊⚊

Emma closed her laptop and silently cursed the devil. She reached for the cross of Saint David and scrutinized it. There was nothing extraordinary about it other than its weight in her hand. Could this secret of protection be why she was drawn to the cathedrals, abbeys, and quaint village churches?

By dispelling evil, Emma no longer saw through rose-colored glasses. Yes, she had lived a glamorous life, but that, too, was superficial—an illusion. Emma was vulnerable once she returned to her roots, grounded and unscathed by the temptations glamorous living could offer. Satan had lost and took this opportunity to seduce, violate, and coerce her to give her soul and, indirectly, the cross of Saint David.

She saw everything so clearly now; even her home and surroundings were stripped of the artifice applied to them. How she could have seen things differently than they really were was a mystery. Delusional? Maybe. Emma felt a chill wind around her shoulders and hugged herself, thinking some riddles were better off unsolved.

Rising from her chair, she looked out at her guests through the window of her study and watched as the flowers swayed in the gentle breeze. She sensed her father speaking to her, saying, "Well done, sweetheart."

She found a proper place for the cross of Saint David within the stacks of books lining her library. It would be safest there, next to the Bible of her childhood.

Emma heard the soft pitter-patter of Sophie's paws as she entered the room. She looked like she was asking Emma what was taking her so long. Emma bent down and kissed her, saying, "What d'ya say, girlie? Let's go mingle, huh?"

As Emma left with Sophie bounding by her side, the sounds of her guests greeted her enthusiastically. She didn't see the cross of Saint David glow brightly once again, then dim slightly alongside the crucifix of our Lord Jesus Christ.

The End

HEAVY BREATHING

The Move

———⟡———

Downtown, or Lower Downtown Denver, Colorado, to be exact, was having a resurgence in 1994. It was becoming a trendy place to live, especially with the announcement of a new baseball stadium being built in the area. Businesses jumped on the opportunity to capitalize on the impending revenue a new stadium would bring. Along with refurbished shopping on the 16th Street Mall, several new coffee shops, light-rail stations, and restaurants—loft apartment living was born.

Roseanna Kent also decided to take advantage. Separated from her abusive husband of three years, she wanted a new start. She wanted a chance to spread her creative wings and live the life of a free, unencumbered woman of twenty-five.

She married her husband, Darryl, right after graduating from college. However, much to her dismay, he didn't like her free-spirited style. He had tried to "groom" her, as he said, into the kind of architect's wife he knew she was destined to be. As an artist himself, he had held her back from pursuing her lifelong dream of artistry, be it singing, painting, or drawing. Even the occasional pottery class got in the way of a happy home life. After three years of marriage, he wanted to start a family, but to Rosie's way of thinking that was his way of keeping her bound to him and the kitchen. She wanted children but had a sneaking suspicion he would make a lousy father, just as he did a horrible husband.

She tried hard to please him, but it had never been enough. Unable to argue effectively, she kept quiet, praying his tirades would blow over in time. He never hit her, not once—ever. He didn't have to because God had blessed him with a vicious tongue. Besides, what would the neighbors say if she stepped outside the house with bruises? Many days and nights, comments of "you're so fucking stupid," "at your age, you should know better," and "I can't believe your mouth, you never shut up" accompanied with "shut the fuck up" and "kiss my ass, bitch" echoed in her ears long into the night. Her favorite—"You're such a fucking cunt. You know what that stands for, don't you? Can't. Understand. Normal. Thinking. Yeah, that's you." He especially liked to say this when he wanted a blow job and she wasn't in the mood to oblige.

The night she left was no exception and was all it had taken to make up her mind. The tongue lashings he had given over the years paled compared to the humiliation she imagined he must have felt when arriving home from a business trip to find everything in the house gone. Empty. She had left without him knowing, taken everything, sold what she could, and filed for divorce. The rest was history.

Why it had taken her so long to make that step was something she couldn't answer. But here she was, back in Colorado. A transplant from the Ohio suburbs where she had lived in the lap of luxury with an abusive husband who hid his misdeeds behind a name and position.

Her wealthy family supported her decision to divorce and put her up for a while until she could decide what to do with the rest of her life. The first thing she did was tap into the trust fund left to her by her grandfather. Thank goodness it was substantial and something her ex-husband knew nothing about. The second thing she did was put down roots and purchase a loft apartment in Denver's Lower Downtown district—LoDo, as the locals called it.

<hr>

Rosie loved downtown Denver. The people, the art, the shops, the restaurants, and the nightlife were intoxicating. She had reunited with old friends and, with urging from a few of these friends, decided LoDo was the place to live.

Her best friend and real estate agent, Leslie Strohmer, did her best to showcase what was available. Some were outrageously expensive, and others looked downright dangerous. But the one she'd settled on struck the right balance of potential and possibility. It was the kind of place Rosie could make her own with a bit of imagination and paint. Her creativity could transform the place into a practical, livable space. It had a bohemian vibe with a security gate and private parking. With breathtaking views of the distant Rocky Mountains and the Lower Downtown, Rosie was in heaven.

"Hey! How about I get some help with these boxes?" Her best friend, Connie Harrison, called up to Rosie, who stared at the seventeen-foot-high ceiling the day she moved in.

"Yeah, okay. I'll be right out," Rosie called down to her friend.

The lofts were laid out well in a square configuration. In fact, the complex was called Square Pegs in LoDo. It was an old leather shoe, belt, and saddle factory. In the resurgence of LoDo, it had been purchased and renovated by a conglomerate of real estate developers and investors. They refurbished the exterior with red brick and corrugated steel as a facade. The roof had a flat presentation rather than peaked or curved. The interior held a courtyard showcasing artisan creations of statues, metal sculptures, and ceramic pottery. This was rotated out on a quarterly basis to give resident artists as much exposure as possible.

It only had two floors, but with seventeen-to-twenty-foot-high ceilings, it might as well have been four stories high. The outside set of stairs made for easy access from the ground floor when moving in, but the two flights were a long climb. Rosie's apartment was on the second floor.

"Whew! I'm glad the movers got most of the heavy stuff in already," Connie said, breathing heavily as they brought in a big box containing Rosie's shoes. "I can't get over how big this space is. Will you look at those windows? Wow!"

"I know! I can't wait to decorate this place. Look at this view!"

"You're lucky. You got the best side of this square hole."

"Hey! Watch it now. I like my "hole," even if you can't get over being jealous."

"Jealous! Girl, please. I got enough grass and flowers to keep me busy until the day I die. You, on the other hand, got nothing but concrete and noise."

"Oh, not so much noise. I think I can get used to it."

"Well, you got it cheap, I can tell you that."

"What color do you think I should paint these trusses? They're so exposed; I don't like the black."

"What are you talking about? The black color helps it blend into the even blacker high ceiling. You can barely see them—"

"*I* can. It makes the ceiling seem higher than it is, and the mezzanine, where I sleep, seems cavernous. I'm not sure I like the feeling it gives me."

"Isn't that where you'll set up your painting studio?"

"Yep. I'll get standing shutters to separate the space. One side bedroom, the other side studio." Connie lowered her head and raised her right eyebrow. When she slowly turned to look at her, Rosie rushed on, "It'll be nice… What?"

"Shutters? You've *got* to be kidding." Connie said, vaguely hiding her disapproval.

"Hey, y'all! Who left the door open on the moving van downstairs?" Leslie said. She breezed in without carrying anything, just herself and her perfectly manicured nails and Southern accent. "Hey, woman!" she said, grasping Rosie in a tight hug. "Wow, look at the light in this space. What color you painting the trusses?"

"See, I knew it!" Rosie turned to look at Connie and then to Leslie said, "Constance and I were just talking about envy."

"*We* were talking about shutters." Connie feigned insult and huffed. "Ignore her, Leslie. What? You not helping today?" Connie held her arms open with palms up.

"I just came to give moral support." Leslie harrumphed. "I ain't *about* to break a nail lifting anything. Anyway, Tom and his friends are downstairs bringing up the rear." She turned to Rosie, exaggerating her Southern accent, "Tom is psyched about this move, let me tell 'ya. They'll do the work while we sit and chat. Let's set up a few things here and there, huh?"

Connie and Rosie looked at each other and, with knowing grins, watched as Leslie began placing items where *she* thought they should belong.

⸺◈◈◈⸺

The loft was a vast rectangular space. Near the entry door, facing south, was the designated formal living area. The center mezzanine, not freestanding, jutted out just enough from the back wall to separate the floor space. Three steel columns supported the front of the mezzanine, creating a space for the kitchen area underneath.

Floating stair treads attached to the back wall gave access to the mezzanine. Horizontal round black cables, interspersed with steel upright supports, formed a railing surrounding the mezzanine, which continued down the stairs.

The mezzanine afforded a magnificent view of the distant Rocky Mountains to the west. It was a splendid sight from the enormous windows running from floor to ceiling and directly in front of the kitchen located under the mezzanine overhang. The designated casual living area was on the other side of the kitchen, with a balcony facing north.

After arguing over the best placement for the furniture pieces, they faced another dilemma. The bathroom behind the kitchen was on the right, and the walk-in closet had the same orientation but on the left, very close to the casual sitting space. Rosie couldn't decide whether to use the closet as a pantry or if her grandmother's antique armoire, placed upstairs in the mezzanine bedroom area, would be better. She decided on the latter option.

After bringing up the oversized armoire, Leslie's husband, Tom, and his friends congregated on the mezzanine to look out of the large floor-to-ceiling windows. They leaned on the railing, watched the sunset, drank beer, and ate pizza. Tom took another sip of his beer and called down to Rosie below.

"So, what are you doing with this space up here? Sleeping, painting, or both?" Tom asked.

"Not sure yet. I'm still debating." Rosie sighed with exhaustion in her voice. A bed and armoire had already been placed up there, so having to state the obvious was beyond her.

"I don't know about you, but I could use a glass of wine while the guys drink their beer," Leslie said with a wry smile and a wink.

"I heard that!" Tom called down to his wife.

"I know you did, sweetheart. We'll be outside on the balcony if you need us." Then she blew fake kisses in his direction, saying, "Mwah, mwah."

"Don't forget to put the paper plates in the trash when you're done up there," Rosie said to no one in particular. At the same time, Connie grabbed two wine coolers of strawberry daiquiri out of the fridge. Leslie already had hers in hand.

"Hey, that's not wine," one of Tom's friends called down.

"We know," the girls answered in unison.

"Why don't we get the good stuff, man?" Tom's other friend asked.

"This ain't good stuff?" Tom asked, looking at his beer and then back at the friend.

The day had cooled significantly as the women settled into chairs out on the covered outdoor space of the balcony.

"Ah, this breeze feels good." Leslie sighed as she sank deeper into the Adirondack chair.

"What now, ladybug?" Connie asked Rosie.

"I'm in no rush to do much at the moment. All things in good time," Rosie replied.

"Philosophical. I like it," Leslie said.

"Are your folks coming by today?" Connie asked.

"Not today. They're up at the cabin this weekend," Rosie answered.

"Must be nice," Leslie added.

"To answer your question, Connie, all I know is I'm taking some time to unwind, reassess, and reflect," Rosie said. "Gosh! I don't know where I'd be if it wasn't for my folks, my grandpa, and you guys. Thanks for helping out today."

"You got it!" Leslie said, holding up her bottle for an impromptu toast.

"What are friends for? Toast!" Connie said as they all clinked their bottles together.

They were silent for a while, listening to the rumblings of conversation from the men as it drifted out to them. Their friendship went back a long way. They had known each other since high school and stayed close even through college and their sorority years. Connie and Leslie were among the few who had begged her not to marry Darryl Kent. When she realized they might have been correct in their assessment of him, it was too late to back out of the marriage, especially given the magnitude of her eventful nuptials. Fearing her reasons were selfish, she'd convinced herself she could tough it out like her mother had. Her parents' marriage had worked out just fine, so the odds were favorable.

But her friends didn't let her down when Rosie's life had gone to hell. The horror stories she shared had Leslie threatening to throw a pan of "hot piss on the son of a bitch" if she ever saw him again. She couldn't have asked for better friends; however, Rosie's reverie was broken by a casual question.

"Who lives next door? Anybody?" Connie asked.

"Not that I'm aware," Rosie answered.

"Whoever it is certainly didn't want your corner unit, huh?" Connie added. "Seems to me this one would be snatched up long before the rest. That view from the kitchen and this location. Stunning!"

"Yeah," Leslie said in contemplation. "Come to think of it, I wondered why this was so cheap, considering."

"When you told me about the listing, I snatched it up like that." Rosie snapped her fingers. "No questions asked."

"Nothing to obstruct the view. I imagine it's quieter on this side of the square than the other," Connie said, shifting in her chair. "Security gate to the outside parking area. Private entrance and easy walk-up. Even this balcony is nice. All the comforts of home. What's not to love?"

"Location is everything if you decide to sell." Leslie crossed her legs at the knee and began to swing them, throwing her head back to take a long draw on her bottle of daiquiri. "Kudos to me, huh? I love it!"

"Maybe you have a ghost," Connie said as she yawned and stretched. "How old is this unit anyway? Any murders happen here or anything?"

Rosie's eyebrows knitted into a frown, and then she screwed up her nose. Leslie paused the daiquiri bottle at her lips before taking another sip, letting her mouth hang open as she looked at Connie.

"I don't think so. Why would you think something like that?" Then, Rosie said teasingly to Leslie, "See, I told you she was jealous. Just making up stuff to scare me."

"I am not! Will you stop *saying* that!" With her fingers, Connie flicked some of her drink at Rosie in fun. "You know I love you, crazy girl. I'd never try to scare you, but it is a thought."

"You might have something there." Leslie leaned in to add, "You know, I heard of this family who moved into this house once that was cheap, cheap, *cheap*. No one wanted to live there, but they didn't care. They wanted the house so bad they ignored the stories of strange goings-on." Leslie got more animated when she had their full attention. "But a while after the family moved in, it started."

"What started?" Connie and Rosie asked in unison.

"The noises. The banging. The screams in the night," Leslie continued, using an exaggerated Southern twang. "The husband woke up with scratches on his body in strange places and threatened to kill the whole family! Not only did he change, but the wife and kids did, too! It was creepy and weird. The townsfolk were concerned for the family, but no one did anything to help them." Leslie leaned back in her chair and paused, letting the effect of what she said sink in, trying hard not to laugh.

"Then what happened?" Rosie asked in rapt attention.

"He killed them all! Then he killed himself. It was later discovered that that's *exactly* what happened to the family who lived there before! The exact same! *That's* why the house didn't sell, and no one wanted it. The house was possessed, and the husband's ghost still haunts the place *to this very day*."

"Wait a minute!" Connie said when the realization hit her. "That's the *Amityville Horror* story you're telling us! You!"

"I got you good." Leslie laughed out loud. "Y'all ate it up like butter. Such scaredy-cats." She held her bottle as she pointed her pinkie finger at each of them and snickered, the tip of her tongue protruding through her teeth.

"I can't believe you! Such a jerk!" Rosie laughed. "There are no such things as ghosts, believe me. I think I just got lucky and thank the Lord for giving me a break. After the hell Darryl put me through, someone's looking out for me. So if there is a ghost, *that's* your ghost."

They continued talking, teasing, laughing, and commiserating long after the sun had set, the beer and men had departed, and the wine coolers were gone.

Loft Living

After three months, Rosie's love of her loft had only grown stronger. Sunday was the best day for Rosie. She'd ride her bike to LePeep's breakfast restaurant for brunch and treat herself to an order of eggs Benedict with a short stack of pancakes. This order was her usual from her childhood days. She never finished it all.

Rosie did most things alone. Leslie had her hands full of real estate ventures, and with her marriage to Tom, life was never dull. Connie had a busy teaching schedule and outdoor life with her dog, Misty, and a few male friends to juggle. They didn't live close by, not with Leslie, in the Washington Park neighborhood of Denver and Connie near Boulder. The only time they got together was during a planned event. When they did, she forgot about her living-alone blues. She had her art, which was enough to keep her busy—at least for now.

Her bedroom/studio combination had worked out well. Four six-foot-tall shutters were hinged together to form one set. Two of these sets made one walled partition, which she'd painted off-white. She used these as a room divider, separating her bedroom from her studio. The shutter partition only extended to the end of her bed; otherwise, she couldn't reach either side. In bed, she liked to look through the slats of the shutters to see her drawing studio from the other side. Until the moon settled in the western sky and shone through the floor-to-ceiling windows, the only illumination at night was cast through the transom from an outdoor light fixture.

Rosie liked the industrial look of her loft. Her father had arranged to erect scaffolding so she could paint the underside of the steel warren trusses crisscrossing her ceiling a bluish-teal color. She liked its effect against the black exposed cast-iron I-beams and interior conduit system that ran heat and air-conditioning to her unit. Gigantic black ceiling fans with golden-colored wooden blades hung from the ceiling and looked good against the teal-colored trusses. She had also painted the railing on the mezzanine and stairs the same color as the trusses. The color added richness to the space. It was a nice touch. Her friends were gobsmacked when they saw it.

She already had a showing of landscape paintings in the courtyard. They were well received but not nearly as good as others she'd seen showcased. However, they were moved to the inside gallery and kept there for some time, which was saying something. One side of the square's converted series of old garages, now open stalls, were used as communal creative studios. One stall was used for painting and silk screening, and another for ceramics; sculptures and metalwork were created next to this space. Grinding metal and discussion were always welcome sounds to her ears.

She could lose herself in ceramics, but there was only one room for firing greenware. Most of the kilns were always occupied in the small area used for this work. It was crowded, with only a few throw wheels for wet clay. She'd give anything for a chance to throw just one piece and allow it to dry to leather-hard. Maybe soon. Until then, she'd busy herself with pen and ink drawings. In this case, charcoal was the medium of choice for artistic expression. It was best used for drawing the human form; however, she could never master the skill of depicting the body in all its elegance and grace. This was her one drawback.

At the moment, Rosie couldn't get the strokes right. No matter what she did, the lines on the Strathmore paper didn't accurately reflect what she saw in her mind's eye. The body's anatomy just didn't lend itself to bend the way she'd drawn it. Corrections only created a foreshortening of the torso that wasn't natural. Her art instructor often said, "No line is a bad line." She didn't believe that then and certainly didn't believe it now.

"Oh hell!" she said out loud in the cavernous space.

She'd been at this for a while and needed to stretch and enjoy the view from the mezzanine for a minute. It was getting late, and she was hungry. She put down her drawing pencils, wiped the charcoal dust from her fingers, and then walked down the stairs from the mezzanine to start dinner.

Rosie's shoulders ached from bending over her tabletop drawing easel, and she reached back to rub at the soreness. As she rounded the stairs and ruminated over the drawing, the faucet in the kitchen began to run.

"What the...?" Rosie said as she cautiously made her way to the kitchen sink.

The faucet had turned on by itself. Rosie reached for the knob handles and turned them off. Lately, she had heard weird noises at night and wondered if she was dreaming. She'd hear scratching noises from the other side of her bedroom on the wall behind her bed. She had dismissed it as mice running amok next door. She told herself, *Don't go off the deep end, making up stuff in your head. Check with the management office about the possibility of mice infestation and move on.*

Now this. Rosie turned the faucet on and then off again to see if the washer inside might be loose or if the knobs were not seated properly. But it all seemed fine, not stiff or anything—perfect. She shrugged, thinking this was something else she'd need to look into and, although strange, nothing to be alarmed about.

⟽⊚⊚⟾

Rosie woke with a start. She lay in bed looking up at the vast ceiling, listening. She was never a light sleeper. Deep slumber was her claim to fame. Something woke her, but what? After a few minutes of silence, she heard it again—a scratching sound right where the headboard of her bed met the wall behind it. *What is that? Whoever lives next door surely hears that, right?* Then she heard another sound. That of footfalls. As if someone were walking around downstairs. Alarmed, she thought someone had broken in. She didn't own a gun and had nothing to protect herself. What to do? She lay there, paralyzed with fear. From the sound, it was as if someone were pacing back and forth from the kitchen area through the casual sitting space to the balcony door. The scratching had stopped, so there was no other sound except the footfalls. It wasn't rushed, just a slow, steady pace. She had left an open newspaper strewn on the floor while watching TV the night before and could hear it being stepped on. Just as she thought about getting up and quietly investigating who had invaded her home—the sound stopped. She didn't hear a door open or close. It was quiet all around her. Alarmingly quiet.

Rosie gathered her courage and rose to peer over the banister of the mezzanine to look down to the floor below. She didn't see anything. *What the hell is going on?* She tiptoed around the end of her bedpost and past the shutters separating her bedroom and studio. She gingerly crept down the stairs to the formal living area, still seeing no one. When she got to the kitchen, she grabbed a chef's knife. It was a comfort to feel the heaviness of the knife in her hands. She held it in front of her as she moved gingerly to the back casual sitting area of the loft. She turned on the lamp beside the couch and noted the newspaper on the floor. Even the trinkets on the TV and music console were undisturbed. She walked over to the closed balcony door. Because she was so high up, she saw no need to lock it. *I should start locking this door. Better safe than sorry. Wait! What if he's in the closet?* This thought alarmed her.

Rosie slowly walked to the closet door and quickly opened it. The motion caused her hair to blow back and whip her sleeping shorts closer to her thighs. She flipped up the light switch. Nothing was inside. There was no one to be found. Confounded, she mimicked the sound she'd heard only moments ago by pacing back and forth. She even walked on the newspaper pages to imitate that sound and found her weight creased the papers, as it should. Still, no imprint of a heavy human foot crumpled the paper before hers had. *How can that be? I know I heard it. Was I dreaming?* As she reluctantly turned the lights off and returned to bed, these thoughts plagued her until she fell asleep.

The following morning, all vestiges of panic from the previous night's activity faded in the bright light of day. She loved the mornings when the mountain views showed purple against the sky. Rosie felt silly, thinking someone or something had awakened her in the dead of night. She yawned and rose from the bed, craving a cup of coffee. It was just the thing she needed to get going. After her morning stretches, Rosie pulled her hair into a ponytail. She took the stairs in a jaunty one-two rhythm, still in her pajamas and bare feet. Then she stopped cold. Her chef's knife was tip down, embedded in the hardwood floor.

⸺◦◦◦⸺

Shaken, Rosie called Leslie, who agreed to meet her for brunch. She needed to discuss the night's activity with someone who could provide perspective on what she was experiencing.

"You're just overwrought. That's what it is." Leslie dumped two packets of sweetener into her mocha latte.

"Come on! Tell me you don't really think that."

"I do," Leslie said between slurps of coffee while Rosie played with her maple oat nut scone. Her hazelnut latte was untouched. "Maybe you dropped it on the way to bed, hon."

"But I didn't carry it with me to the stairs," Rosie lamented. "I tell you; it was as if the knife had been thrown down on that spot. I had a time wiggling it free; it was so embedded."

"I don't know what to tell you. I mean… oh Lord." Leslie's eyes opened wide. "It couldn't be Darryl trying to terrorize you? Does he know where you live or anything? He can't get a key, right?"

"Don't be silly! He couldn't care less, believe me."

"I don't know. A man like him… well—"

"It's *not* Darryl." Rosie was emphatic. Leslie leaned back in her chair, looked at her friend, and let the silence build between them. Rosie continued, "I hear scratching behind the walls too. *That* can't be Darryl!"

"I understand." Leslie reached across the table in the crowded Starbucks, took Rosie's hand, and asked, "What are you going to do?"

"I don't know. Maybe it was a fluke and won't happen again. It helps to talk to someone, so thanks for coming." Rosie patted Leslie's hand in thanks.

"Well, if it helps, I know a little shopping always lifts the spirit. So eat up! Let's go to The Market on Larimer for a few minutes. I hear they have some neat kitchen utensils I'm dying to see. Let those heebie-jeebies feelings go?"

"All right. I was so scared, Leslie… I need a diversion." Rosie let out a long sigh.

"Attagirl!"

<hr>

Rosie dreaded going home. The walk to the coffee shop and back had done her some good, but now she stood in trepidation. Rosie thought having a ghost or a bona fide spirit would be intriguing. She had never had one before, and the experience might be thrilling; however, this encounter seemed more menacing and terrifying than odd or scary.

As she walked through the entrance to the courtyard, she had half a mind to go to the management office. After taking a few steps in that direction, she paused and decided against it, thinking about what she could say that wouldn't make her sound looney tunes. At a loss for what to do, she reluctantly walked to the outside set of stairs leading to her loft. Then she had an idea.

At the top of the stairs, instead of going directly to her corner loft apartment, she went to the one next door and knocked. There was no answer. This apartment had a window in the door that ran vertically along its side. She thought it was blacked out, but on second glance, she realized it only looked that way because of the darkness inside. From her vantage point, she could see outside light filtering through the upper windows but not much else. A layer of dust on the wood flooring indicated it hadn't been swept in a while; it had been empty for some time. The apartments were not of a cookie-cutter design. Still, she strained to see up into the mezzanine traversing the bottom floor from wall to wall. It was definitely empty, devoid of furniture or people. She realized asking her neighbor about the scratching noises on the walls was now pointless.

Rosie made a mental note to talk with the management company about her suspicions of mice infesting her apartment. As for it being haunted, she wanted to wait until she had further proof. Either that or maybe Leslie's idea was right. The thought of Darryl terrorizing her, causing havoc to disrupt her new way of life, was chilling.

It Begins

Rosie was having a nightmare. In her dream, she was running from someone out to harm her. She could find no safe haven. Each time she had, the feeling of dread was worse than before. She knew she had to get to a particular location but didn't know where that place was. The menace drew closer, and she woke just when it was about to grab her. In a panic, she lay still, trying to slow her heart beating wildly in her chest. She looked at the clock and noted it was 1:30 a.m. She sat up in bed, wondering what the dream was all about. Rosie cupped her head in her hands and rubbed her eyes with the heels of her palms. She slowly shook her head and sighed.

She had to get the image of the nightmare out of her head and focus on something else, like looking over her latest art project. Usually, studying it helped determine how she should proceed to the next step. Maybe not finishing the project caused more worry than was necessary. Afterward, she could relax and maybe get back to a peaceful sleep. One could only hope. Rosie needed a drink; a glass of cold water was just the thing.

All seemed well downstairs as she drank water and looked at the quarter moon in the sky. Much calmer now, Rosie took the glass with her and walked to her bedroom. Rosie didn't need light to see, what with the moonlight and that which streamed in from outside through the arched transom window above the door. Regardless, she turned on the task light over her drafting table when she stopped to look at her latest drawing project. She hadn't touched it in a few days as it lay under a layer of tracing paper she used to keep the dust off. This grade of Strathmore paper had just enough bite to grab and hold the soft charcoal until she could spray a fixative to seal and protect the drawing from unnecessary smudging. Until then, the tracing paper seemed perfect for the task.

As she lifted the layer of paper protection, she was stunned. This was not her drawing! Rosie stared at a drawing of the scene she had just dreamed of. A girl in a panic seeking safe harbor from something strange, dark, and menacing. The expression of horror was evident as the figure faced the viewer.

"What is this?"

Frantic, Rosie moved the papers aside, looking for the composition she had been working on. *Where the hell is my drawing?* She found it. In her fingers was a smeared mess, as if someone or *something* had tried to erase it with their hands.

Then she heard the footfalls downstairs again. Pacing back and forth and, as before, in the same direction she'd heard a few days ago. She knew no one was down there but couldn't be certain. She hadn't checked as thoroughly as before. Chills went down her spine, and panic set in. She slowly peered over the railing of the mezzanine and saw nothing. To her horror, the sound continued, but she saw no one.

"What do you want?" she cried out. But there was no answer, just the steady pace of walking back and forth. "Who are you?" The pacing stopped.

Then the heavy breathing began. It sounded as if it was coming from the conduits above, in and out. Slow. Deliberate. Deep. Male in sound. The intake of breath was undeniable, the outflow of breath—terrifying. Rosie slowly backed up to the wall of her studio, wanting to feel something solid against her back while she scanned the ceiling for the source of the sound. She could find none. The breathing surrounded her from all directions. It stopped when she screamed.

⟫◦◦◦⟪

It seemed the entire complex was out to watch the police search Rosie's loft. She had called 911 on the upstairs cordless phone, asking for help because an intruder was inside her home. Rosie had been scared shitless. She knew she sounded hysterical. She didn't care.

Two squad cars arrived quickly. The uniformed police officers found her in the courtyard, pointing to her loft apartment. The police presence had a strange, calming effect on her. Just to see another person was the reassurance she needed to ensure she was not alone and going insane. They entered cautiously and searched thoroughly. After a while, they came out to talk to her.

"Ma'am, we didn't find anything or anyone. Except for the vandalism of your work, nothing seems out of place," one of the officers said.

"I see," Rosie said, mildly disappointed.

"Are you sure you heard someone inside?"

"He was breathing and walking around. Just because I didn't see him doesn't mean he wasn't there."

"Well, ma'am, at this point, we can only report this as possible criminal mischief." Then he scrutinized Rosie, frowned, and lowered his voice. "You know, calling 911 when there is no cause is grounds for reporting a false claim. It's a misdemeanor at best. For all we know, you could have smeared the artwork yourself, got angry, and tried to blame it on vandals."

"But I wouldn't—"

"You'd be surprised what some people will try to pull. Now, I'm not saying that's your situation or anything *you* would do. Maybe you called in good faith." The officer held his arms up at his sides. "But I'd think again before calling us out on a false claim. I wouldn't want to cite you for false reporting."

"I understand." Rosie felt embarrassed and silly for going to these extremes. She looked down at the ground and swished her right foot across the front of her left one like a schoolgirl.

"Look, you seem like a nice lady," the other officer said. "I can tell something spooked you. I can't say I believe in ghosts or anything, but next time, try to get a grip on what might be happening before you reach out to us. Until then, I'll need to get your name and phone number. Tell me again what happened so I can file the report. Let's try to end this night before the sun comes up."

"Thank you, Officer. I'll do my best," Rosie replied.

They went inside her loft to take her report. The neighbors dispersed. One of the squad cars left, and all was quiet again. She gave as much information as she could to the officer. After another hour, she was alone.

She didn't sleep that evening, which showed when her parents visited the next day. She cried in their arms in a way she hadn't done since her teenage days of lost boyfriends.

<hr>

Officer Brandon Clemmons didn't like hearing what Roseanna Kent reported. But without evidence, he couldn't pinpoint what might be occurring. After typing his report and getting razed by his fellow officers about responding to "ghostly sightings," he couldn't help but look into the activities of her ex-husband, Mr. Darryl Kent. The funny thing was, he couldn't find much. Not even a complaint of domestic abuse was filed by his then-wife, Roseanna Kent when they lived in Ohio. But he couldn't let it go. He'd been an officer of the law for ten-plus years, and after all that time, he could recognize when an event was legit or not.

His wife, Ada, always said he had good instincts and should trust them more. Rosie's demeanor told him to follow Ada's advice, more so in this case than in any other. There was something about Rosie's vulnerability that touched him. It was in her eyes. He had repeatedly listened to her frantic 911 call, which convinced him *something* had happened. The ex-husband? There had to be a connection of some kind, ghosts notwithstanding.

The next day was his day off. He thought it wouldn't hurt to do more investigating, just a "look-see" to determine if his hunch might be correct. He played with the idea of turning this over to a detective but knew no one would be interested in taking on a case like this. He was on his own.

Brandon's digging around proved fruitful. He hit pay dirt with the loft apartments management company. They reported an anonymous person had rented the loft apartment next to Ms. Roseanna Kent's. A lot of money had been paid to keep the information from being disclosed. Without cause, he couldn't dig any further but found it odd that it had occurred. He then tried to find Mr. Kent but was unsuccessful. It seemed Mr. Kent had sold his home in Ohio, quit his job, and moved to points unknown. *One point just might be Denver, Colorado.* It was a wild guess, but his hunch told him he might be onto something. Next, he drove to the Square Pegs Lofts to peruse the area. It was well situated in Lower Downtown Denver. However, the back, which faced west, afforded a view he found interesting. It looked out on an open field without obstruction. Anyone parked on this side had an unobstructed view into the lofts, including Rosie Kent's.

Driving around to the north side of the gated parking area, where the balconies were located, Brandon could see a screen door left ajar in the loft adjacent to Rosie's corner unit. *How easy would it be to bridge the gap between the two?* He parked discreetly and pulled out his binoculars. Through them, he had a clear view of the balcony. He could see that Ms. Kent had company. Of course, she would after the events of the night before, and who could blame her? He wasn't a voyeur; however, he was looking for movement in the adjacent unit or anything to indicate a tool of access had been used to gain entry to Rosie's apartment. However, the north side was shaded from the sun. Brandon could only see so much, but he was a patient man. So he waited.

After about an hour and a half, it became clear Brandon wouldn't see any more than he had already. The sun had begun its western descent in the sky. As Brandon raised his binoculars one last time, he saw what he was looking for. Yes, it was a good day for hitting pay dirt.

⟨◦⟩

Rosie sat on the floor by the front door and watched her father finish changing the door locks. She occasionally toyed with the diamond tennis bracelet they'd brought as a gift to her. In contrast, her mother sat on the couch that was diagonally situated next to the stairs leading to the mezzanine. While waiting for the water to boil for tea, her mother, Nancy, occasionally inspected the silk flowers behind the couch, wiped at the dust on her fingers, and then smiled sympathetically at her daughter. Rosie forced a smile in return. She was relieved when the whistle from the teakettle sounded, changing the uncomfortable silence between them.

Her father had already installed a new dead bolt and ensured the bolt ran its full length into the wall, not halfway. He had already checked as many of the internal piping systems as possible, including the faucet that turned on by itself as if by magic. As an executive of Martin Marietta's engineering department, he prided himself on ensuring electronics and internal housing conduits worked properly. She should have felt relieved after her father had assured her that his inspections found nothing unusual and her building, ergo her loft apartment, was sound. Instead, she only felt silly, especially after crying about imagined ghosts.

"You know, sweetheart, I heard of this thing where you can call someone to report ghostly activities," Rosie's mother offered while handing her a cup of tea.

"Nancy, can't you see she's been through enough—"

"I know that, Paul! But I can't help but offer up something since I can't check the utility pipes or anything," Rosie's mother said with a huff. "What time do these things typically occur, sweetie? They say these hauntings come at the same time of day or night."

Rosie saw her dad rolling his eyes as her mother insisted on discussing the matter. However, Rosie was glad her mother seemed to take this far more seriously than her father.

"It varies." Rosie stood and motioned her parents to the back living area. "No one particular time. The faucet was at dusk, but the rest was at night. Not much past midnight at the most, I think." Then she groaned. "Oh, I don't *know*. Daddy, are you sure conduits don't make breathing sounds—that it couldn't come from up there?"

"Not in all my years have I known it to happen," her father said, joining them with tools still in hand. "I've told you all I can, and what *you* told me makes no sense." He pointed his Phillips-head screwdriver at the ceiling to make his next point. "Water, sewage, drainage, nothing moving in those exposed pipes up there would produce the sound you described, not even air—or heat in an HVAC system. If it did, it would make a staccato rat, tat, tat noise or a hissing sound."

"Well, from now on, keep track of everything you see and hear as to time and place," her mother said. "You never know when information like that will come in handy. In the meantime, try smudging the air with sage. I hear it eliminates bad spirits." Rosie's mother tried to reassure her, but it only made the situation seem more ridiculous than it was already.

"God, Mom!" Rosie put her head in her hands and continued, "I just wish this wasn't happening. Everything seemed to be just fine, then *wham!*"

"Honey, listen," her father said tenderly. "You've had your share of ups and downs lately, and stress can take a toll. It's good you have your work to keep you busy, but maybe there's something else causing this kind of… manifestation, so to speak." Rosie looked at him in disbelief and opened her mouth to speak, but he noticed and quickly added, "I'm not saying this is all in your head. What I'm saying is the next time it happens, try not to push yourself into thinking the worst."

"But Daddy, it *was* real!"

"I know it seemed that way. I also know you, *and* I know you are a rational person. But just give some thought to what I've said, okay?" He stood up, stretched his back, and motioned to his wife. "Got to get going before it gets dark. I've checked as much as I could. Got that lock changed and a good dead bolt on the door. Except for the sliding door to the balcony, I think you're good."

"Thank you, Daddy." Rosie was resigned to accepting her father's skepticism.

"No need." As they moved to the front door, her father turned and said, "Remember, the security company will be out in a few days to install the system I told you about. You gonna be all right, sweetheart."

"I feel *better* already," Rosie said, trying to sound convincing, but her mother knew differently.

"Uh-huh. I'll call you tomorrow. Goodbye, sweetie," her mother said with a peck on the cheek.

After they had gone, Rosie placed her back to the door and looked around at the vast space of her loft. It was quiet, and all she could think about was what would happen next.

⊸◦◉◦⊷

Another fitful night had Rosie up early the next day. Groggy from lack of sleep, she stumbled down the stairs alongside the wall from the mezzanine. Coming to the kitchen, she felt an unusual breeze. To her surprise, the door to the balcony was open. *I thought I closed this last night.*

Alarmed, she also remembered feeling something tug at her hair, lifting it as if in play while she slept. *Oh my God, was that real!?* She cautiously checked the door and tested the sliding motion, which worked fine. She walked onto the balcony and saw nothing disturbed or unusual. She looked at the balcony next door, which was not far from hers, and noted the door ajar. *Hmm. The gap between us isn't that far apart, is it?* Being careful, she gingerly leaned over and stood on tiptoes to see if she could peer into the adjacent apartment, but that was foolish. *Don't be stupid! You know there's no one living there.* She absentmindedly touched the back of her head, mimicking the sensation of her hair being lifted as in her dream. *Feels the same, but* what *or* who *would do that? Must be my imagination. My dreams are getting weirder every night, and I'm getting forgetful.*

Perplexed, she stood there a minute and let the cool morning breeze wash over her. It was cloudy, and the smell of rain in the air was refreshing, which helped clear her senses and jitters. She returned inside, leaving the door open to allow fresh air to flow. She reminded herself to get a sturdy piece of wood to lay in the track at the bottom of the door. That should deter intruders and give her peace of mind.

The rest of Rosie's day was spent in her studio. She worked long into the afternoon's waning light without a break. She was proud of her progress and loved how the drawing was taking shape. She'd managed to depict the female and male in the subtleness of form. Tenderness was showcased in the hands of the man as he caressed the woman. The female showed vulnerability as she nestled in his arms, safe and secure. It was good.

From her mezzanine studio, Rosie gazed out of the massive windows at the distant mountains. As typical, the morning rain had been brief but welcomed. The afternoon had been full of sunshine, but now the Colorado blue sky was full of different yellow, rose, cerulean, and indigo hues as the sun set behind the mountains. She could only gaze at the sight and say, "Beautiful."

In the distance, she saw a car, alone and idle, sitting in the empty lot in her direct line of sight. *Funny. I've never seen that before.* She couldn't see anyone seated inside. If so, they could see right into her home. *Great! One more thing to keep me on my toes.*

More concerned now than she wanted to be, she remembered to keep things in perspective. *Maybe it's a security guard or something.* It would be a good thing if true, so she dismissed it to consider what to prepare for dinner.

A while later, she noted the car was still in the lot, not showing any sign of life. *Just as well. It's good to know there's security out there keeping watch anyway. If that's who that is. Note to self, find a stick for the balcony door.* With these last few thoughts, the weariness of the previous few days overtook Rosie, and she fell into another night of deep sleep.

⟫⟪

Detective Schmitt looked at Brandon with all the skepticism he could muster.

"You want to do what?" he asked.

"I got a hunch, and I have a motive—"

"For what?"

"This ex-husband of hers lives next door."

"So?"

"That means he might be the one terrorizing this girl. From what I saw the other day, to me, it means he's a creep and vindictive enough to do her harm—"

"He can live wherever he wants. That's no crime—"

"You and I both know how something like this can go down. Why live next door? The real estate agency was sworn to secrecy on that score. Why?"

"He's a *weirdo*. Who knows why—"

"I think… no, I *know* he's up to no good. If you ask me, there's too much cloak-and-dagger after a speedy divorce. She left him without a word and didn't get much, if any, pushback from this guy?" Brandon got up from his chair and started pacing. "Word is he's an architect with loads of money. He has the means and the wherewithal to do who knows what. Quick-tempered temperamental SOB from all accounts. Who knows what their home life was like? I can't shake this feeling, Schmitt."

"There's no record of domestic abuse. No priors. Nothing—"

"Except he up and left without notice to *any*one. Who does that in his profession? What's he hiding? Who's to say he's not after retribution?"

There was a pause in the conversation while Detective Schmitt mulled over this information. He pursed his lips and tapped his thumb on his desk cover. Then he reached for the phone.

"Yeah, tell Chief I need to see him right away. Thanks," the detective said to his secretary.

Brandon looked at Detective Schmitt sternly, eyes tight and steady. Then he said, "Thank you."

"Alls I got to say is you better be right. We'll get a warrant to search his place to see what he's been up to. In the meantime, tell Chief Daniels what you told me, right down to seeing him come out onto that balcony dressed all in black like a fucking ninja."

Confrontations

Rosie hadn't heard anything strange since her last encounter. She usually slept like the dead, but lately, she'd awaken when odd sounds occurred in her apartment. What she was experiencing at the moment was nothing short of bizarre.

Her heart raced as she lay on her left side and looked through the slats of the shutters separating her bedroom from her studio area. The footsteps she'd heard below on previous nights were now pacing back and forth on the other side of the shutters! However, the light filtering in from the transom window and the full moon showed no one was there. Were her eyes deceiving her? She clearly heard someone pacing, but she could *not* see them.

What the hell! I'm awake, right? She slowly moved her right arm to pinch herself to ensure she felt the pain, indicating she was present and in the moment. She listened as the entity paced from the beginning of the set of shutters on the other side of her nightstand to the end of them just past the bottom of her bed's footboard. *Is that a ghost? As sure as I'm lying here, it's pacing just on the other side! Oh my God! Hearing it downstairs is one thing, but this is close! Too close.*

Her father's words echoed in her ears as the movement continued. *Think rationally. Whatever it is, you must prove it's real, not your imagination. Which means you have to confront it with all the convictions you have in the world. It's* not *welcome here!* Although she was terrified, she could not show fear. She had to be brave. She had to stand firm regardless of the consequences.

Okay, on the count of three, run to the end of the bed and face this thing. It won't hurt you, Rosie. It won't bite. Yeah, right! When she heard the footfalls get to the part of the shutters that met the back wall, she pounced. Rosie bounded out of bed and rounded the corner of the shutters at the end of the bedpost. Dread flooded her body instantly over what she might find or what she might be confronting. Her heart pounded tremendously. She felt like it would leap from her chest.

There was nothing. Rosie was stunned. All sound stopped as soon as she stood to face whatever it was. There was no cold spot. There was no mist. There was no disembodied voice saying her name. All she saw was her drafting desk and chair, her wastepaper basket, her drawing equipment, and the empty void of space in the living area below.

"What the hell!" Rosie yelled to the vacant air above. Then the breathing started. The hair on the back of her neck stood on end. The sound was so physical that she should be able to see the person breathing before her. She looked up at the ceiling and the pipes, then turned in a circle, trying to pinpoint the sound surrounding her. It was everywhere and louder than before—in... and out... long, deep draws of breath. If she dwelled on it for long, it would terrify her as before. Giving in to the fright was not an option. She fought the urge to flee. When she realized how unfair it was that she and she alone must fight this intrusion, this entity, this ghost, her adrenaline turned to anger. There was no one to help, only her belief in herself and the Lord above to protect her.

Rosie kept all the lights off, using only the outside illumination of the moon as her guide. She slowly descended the stairs. She didn't call out to it like the last time. Her dread and fear moments ago were replaced by a determination she hadn't felt in years to face whatever or whoever this was.

The breathing continued even as she reached the bottom rung of the stairs. When she reached the center of the front living space, the sound of breathing stopped as suddenly as it had begun. It was darker on this side of the floor space, and Rosie felt exposed. The light through the transom only illuminated so much and cast an eerie glow. In front of her was the kitchen across from the bank of ceiling-high windows spanning the wall. On this side of the building, the light came only from the full moon outside. Rosie felt lucky that she could see at least this far.

The figure moved slightly. It rose from its crouched position and silently slid up the wall on the far side of the bank of windows. Rosie clasped her hands to her mouth to stifle a scream that threatened to escape her throat. The figure was black and shrouded in darkness in the shadow of the windows. It hugged the wall as it slunk toward the casual living area on the other side of the kitchen toward the balcony door. To Rosie's horror, it stopped and looked directly at her. It crouched low, shrieked, and then ran toward her.

Rosie had no time to think. Her courage and anger failed her. More than terrified, she ran up the stairs, but not fast enough. Rosie was tackled by the figure and frightened beyond belief; she thought her heart would stop beating in her chest. The horror turned to shock when she realized it was human. Not a ghost, but a man!

⊰◦◉◦⊱

Brandon had been sitting in his unmarked car for hours. The sun had gone down long ago, and his back ached. He had received permission, reluctant though it was, to stake out this location for any unusual activity. Until they could obtain a warrant from the court to grant a search of Darryl Kent's loft apartment, all they could do was wait and watch.

"You still have some of that coffee?" Officer Evans asked.

Evans was a rookie just out of the police academy and had been assigned to ride along with Brandon on this assignment. To Brandon, it was like babysitting kittens. He talked constantly and was antsy as hell to see some action. This stakeout was no place for rookie cops.

"Naw, man. My cup went dry a long time ago," Brandon answered.

"Shit! How long we gotta sit out here? I need to stretch my legs."

"You'll keep your ass inside the car and like it. You think I enjoy this backache I'm starting to get about now?"

"This is *not* what I signed up for—"

"It's called police work," Brandon said, squinting through his binoculars.

"It's called do-nothing work if you ask me."

"No one's asking," Brandon barely uttered. Then he spotted movement in Rosie's loft.

"You don't like me, do you?"

"Shut up!"

"Say what?"

"Something's happening up there. Here, take these." Brandon handed the binoculars to Evans and started the car's engine. The full moon's illumination was good enough to drive by without turning on the headlights as he drove like a bat out of hell from the empty lot onto the street. "Radio for backup, now!"

"Why? What happened? What'd you see?"

"Just do it, goddamn it!" Brandon yelled at his idiot rookie. "B&E with possible assault occurring."

Officer Evans did as he was told while Brandon tried to focus on what he *thought* he saw through his binoculars. Rosie stood in the gloom of the loft space while a dark figure rushed in her direction. The sight was fleeting because of the speed at which the figure moved. Whatever it was, it didn't look good. Brandon sensed Rosie had only minutes to live.

⟵◦◦◦⟶

Rosie kicked at the man and grappled for the next rung of the open staircase or to find some purchase that would allow her to stand. But he was much too fast, and she found herself being dragged by her ankle back toward him and nearer the kitchen area. He flipped her over onto her back. When he let go to grab at her legs, she pulled them toward her stomach and kicked him in the chest. He went flying onto his back. The move gave her time to get up and make another run for the stairs. Again, she was unsuccessful as she felt him grab her hair from behind. He had a full tuft of it in his hands and, holding tightly, yanked her back and to the floor. She hit the hardwood floor much too hard. All the air escaped from her lungs. He stood over her and straddled her body. He then cocked his head from side to side, seeming to enjoy watching her try to breathe.

She couldn't see his face, and that was not good. She felt her anger rise again, replacing her initial fear. *Who the hell is this? What does he want from me?*

"You want to know, don't you?" he said through the mask, hiding his face.

She said nothing but tried to scoot backward, away from him, with her elbows against the floor.

"All this time, you thought you could escape me." The voice, though muffled, was familiar. Confusion flooded her thoughts as she tried to reason this out.

"What… I don't…," Rosie managed to say.

"But I do. You humiliated me. My reputation is gone, ruined. I want what's mine. What you took from me." Then he knelt with her underneath him and got close to her face. "I need to settle the score." He held a knife in his right hand above her, ready to plunge it into her chest.

Angry, Rosie thought, *If I'm going to die, I want to know who's taking my life.* She struck fast. She snatched at the mask covering his face, scratching him in the process. He yelled and pulled away, but she held tight. The thin vinyl of the mask tore to reveal Darryl Kent in all his horrible glory.

"Bitch!" he said. Then he lowered the knife. Rosie's eyes grew wide, and she screamed.

It wasn't because she realized Darryl was about to kill her. It was because above him was something she had no name for. It was black and enormous. It loomed above them in thin air and pulled Darryl up from behind. It had no discernible shape, but the strength it possessed was breathtaking.

⟫◈◈◈⟪

Brandon heard Rosie scream, which was all he needed to shoot the door lock and rush in. With Officer Evans behind him, they stood in disbelief, seeing a figure dangling above Rosie lying on the floor. The black figure holding Darryl Kent seemed to turn to them. Darryl was clawing the air, legs flailing. The torn black mask revealed a face that was terrified and bleeding.

They watched as the black figure hoisted Darryl higher into the air, close to the blackness of the ceiling above.

"*Shoot it!*" Darryl cried out to the officers below.

Officer Evans took aim, but Brandon carefully reached out with a gesture to lower his weapon, saying, "You might hit a gas line or something." Brandon pointed to the conduits. "Those pipes."

"What is it?" Evans asked in a whisper.

Before Brandon could comment, the figure grew larger, black and menacing. It continued to hold Darryl, who screamed and shrieked. The blackness shook Darryl like a rag doll and, before anyone could think, flung him to the brick wall next to the front door where the officers stood. The sickening sound made by Darryl's head as it hit the wall was something Brandon knew he'd never forget.

The officers watched as the blackness approached Rosie where she lay on the floor. It hovered over her, and what looked like its head bent in her direction. Rosie seemed unafraid and reached out to touch it. It didn't make the sound she'd reported hearing many nights before. It breathed, not deep, and gave a forlorn moaning sigh. Then it lifted and was gone.

⚯

The Galleria in downtown Denver was crowded with patrons. It was Rosie's debut exhibit titled "Portrait Known and Unknown." Many streamed in to view her works on themes of love—lost and found. Mysterious, moody landscapes of the spiritual and ethereal portraits of the surreal. The nature of her work was called poignant and insightful, with the use of a delicate hand, especially in her pottery. She overheard one say, "Tenderness, longing, and strength are always a constant undercurrent in her pieces." Rosie supposed this was true.

She had been through a lot in her twenty-five years of life. One year later, she was here, realizing her dream had come true.

Familiar faces filled the crowd of patrons; one in particular was talking to her parents. *Sergeant* Brandon Clemmons had never left her side during that night of terror. After what he called "babysitting her," he and his wife, Ada, had become like family.

They never talked about that night, not in the conventional way. It was always done with knowing looks or a sly smile, a secret kept between them and Officer Evans, who'd transferred out soon after the incident. Brandon handled all the paperwork surrounding the mysterious death of Darryl Kent.

Apparently, crazed over losing Rosie, Darryl had found and terrorized her. He used a makeshift board to cross to her balcony, jimmied the lock for access, and, dressed in all black, commenced to torment her. Rosie was lucky.

Brandon helped her find another home in Cherry Creek near Leslie in Washington Park. He even scoped out a house with a shed to use as an art studio. Brandon was a good man.

She never understood what made the entity come to her aid. Investigations revealed there had been many deaths at the old leather factory. One was particularly sad about a young man trapped in the machinery. His death was agonizingly slow. Rosie told herself this watchful spirit had saved her that night. The breathing had been its attempt to alert her to danger. This was what she chose to believe. The experience still haunts her dreams. She supposed it always would.

Rosie watches as one portrait draws the most attention. As patrons gather around it, she's not surprised. It depicts a girl looking out in the distance at an ethereal presence, comforted and at peace. It comes through in the expression. It is her masterpiece. It is not for sale.

The End

THE VOICE. THE TOUCH. THE MAN.

I love morning walks. Especially before sunrise. There's something about the quiet that lures me. The cool, crisp morning air wipes away the sleep from my previous night's slumber. My lungs are filled with the newness of the day as I settle into the rhythm of my stride. This is a glorious day with the clearest blue sky in early autumn. It is tranquil and seems magical in the light of early dawn.

This is not a power walk. This is a leisurely stroll in a town new to me. Early mornings allow me to explore the unknown without other tourists getting in the way. I can move at my own pace, gaze at houses dotting the town, and then peer into shop windows that display their wares. A cozy diner or café lures me to visit later, perhaps on the way back to my room at the bed-and-breakfast where I've elected to stay. Maybe visit an out-of-the-way boutique or antique shop later, like this one called Versailles Antiques, to see what might pique my interest.

Versailles is a small town in Pennsylvania. It is phonetically pronounced *"versales,"* not to be confused with the famous city in France pronounced *"versigh."* This town reminds me of my hometown in Kentucky. Its quaintness, name, and location are what drew me to visit. It is tucked away from the hustle and bustle of the city. And only one hour away, I could return in an emergency if necessary.

I come from a family of teachers, so being a university professor was a natural career choice in 1965. Seeing my name, Janice Young, PhD., on my office door took some getting used to, I must admit. However, while the PhD. has grown on me over the years, it has started to mean less and less.

I am a teacher of the humanities and an art historian on sabbatical for a year to discover more about the world of art. This is my first sojourn from my profession. I love this break and am excited to discover new things. The stuffiness in the halls of learning can be taxing over time. Aside from the new batch of students each year, the job has begun to drag on my psyche. I enjoy teaching—of course I do—but lately, the subject matter has grown stale. I feel a need to break away. To recharge my batteries, so to speak, and explore more of the passion that drove me to teach in the first place. After the dean accepted my request, I decided to give myself a weeklong break before starting my travels in Europe. This town of Versailles seemed perfect.

I catch my reflection in one of the shop windows and am satisfied with what I see. I'm still relatively young, although the gray in my hair is starting to bother me more than I want to admit. I still have my figure, long and lean-muscled, with no pudge around the middle *yet*, so elastic waistbands can wait. I've decided middle age is something I need to gradually accept, which I fully intend to do. Growing old gracefully sounds good, and I plan on enjoying every bit of the time left to me.

They call me a bit stuffy, but I don't mind. I have never married. It never seemed the thing to do, or maybe the right man never came along. My work always came first; the students, books, and study seemed more important. At thirty-two, my friends worry about my spinsterhood. They indulge in my "waiting for the right man to come along" philosophy. I know they think it's silly.

I admit I've been flattered by a few male college students. Although catcalls can be annoying, the admiration from the female students when I ignore the wolf whistles is worthy of note. Some think I've been oblivious to the attention, and that's a good thing. Little do they know, I haven't.

One such instance happened recently when I had to walk to the library to search for reference materials. I had heard the calls and was caught by a female student.

"Miss Young, may I ask you a question?"

"Surely," I responded.

"How is it you never seem to notice when the guys whistle when you walk by?" Then she cocked her head and looked at me expectantly. Some would think this an impertinent question, but not me.

"Oh, I notice. I'm not sure if I should be flattered or smack them around the ears for flirting with an old lady."

"You're not *that* old. Are you?" she asked, clearly perplexed.

Instead of responding, I smiled and continued on my way, leaving the student to question why I felt no need to comment further.

Reminiscing about those encounters causes me to smile with amusement as I walk through the town of Versailles. A thicket of trees and a winding dirt path take me to a clearing and a nearby stone bridge. The morning sun causes a glistening effect on the water, making the stones appear whiter than they would normally. The sight from there catches my breath. The soothing sound of water as it gurgles under the bridge creates a magical scene. It is mesmerizing. As I lean over to watch the ripples made on the stream as it moves along, I'm lulled into a daydream of times gone by and imagine the many townspeople who might have passed this way before me.

Turning from the bridge, a nearby church steeple just over a slight rise catches my attention. My curiosity gets the better of me, and the sound of crushed leaves underfoot propels me to walk in that direction to explore further. I'm astonished to see two maple trees stand majestically on either side of a stone entryway, which leads to massive double doors set deep within the walls of a sandstone church. The red leaves on these trees are intense in color. Amazing! Upon closer inspection, the church looks like a medieval abbey. Worn and weathered, it seems older than the town itself. There are no visible buttresses to support the walls, but the spire in the middle crossbeam of the roof indicates there should be. I'm curious about the ceiling's support and wonder if I can or should venture inside to inspect the vaulting. But whom do I ask? As I ponder this question, a strange but comforting silence surrounds me.

There is no sign of life, especially at this hour, so I'm not surprised. However, I'm drawn to a cart on the left of the entryway to the building. Wooden and worn with time, it's full of an assortment of herbs, candles, and seeds for gardening. I gingerly pick through the seed packets and discover a variety of vegetables and garden flowers. *Should planting flowers for next spring be done now or later?* But, not having a green thumb, I can't decide which seed packets to choose, that is, if I plant anything at all.

As soon as I think this and consider inspecting the abbey further, a voice startles me.

"Nasturtiums."

Male and deep in tone—rich in delivery. It is soothing but startling just the same. I look around but see no one. Then he appears: handsome, tall, gray around the temples, with a mischievous smile. If it weren't for the romanticism of the place, I would be able to ignore the allure of his presence. But I can't.

"Nasturtiums," he repeats. "They're a good choice for planting in early spring, after the last frost."

"Ah. I see." I feel the heat rising to my face. *What, I'm a young girl now? What's wrong with you, Janice?*

"They're good for gardens if you do that sort of thing. Edible too. Did you know?"

"No, I didn't know. I don't garden or grow plants of any kind, so…"

Then he smiles one of those smiles I haven't seen in a while. It touches my heart so much that I immediately return the gesture and give a shy, toothy grin. His smile crinkles his eyes, so I know his feelings are genuine.

"This is a beautiful abbey. It seems out of place, but at the same time, it seems a part of the landscape. I wonder if it's open, and if so, may I go inside?"

"Saint Andrews is a splendid place of worship. It's a Catholic church, although it can be considered a chapel because there is no resident priest."

"Oh, I see."

"Yes. It isn't open just yet, early in the day for that."

"Aha." The disappointment shows in my voice.

"If you'd like, come back in a few hours. Long ago, we used to conduct Mass on Saturdays and Sundays, but it's open just for prayers during the week."

"Are you the caretaker, then? Forgive my impertinence, but I'm not sure of the arrangement, being you're here selling these items."

"No apology needed. I look after the place; however, these items are not for sale. You may take what you'd like. Just admire and take what you think you need. Nothing more."

"Take what I *think* I need?"

"I'm sorry if it sounds complicated. It's very simple really. I think you'd like the nasturtiums and… this, perhaps?"

He carefully holds out a beautiful candle that takes my breath away. It isn't one of those ornate cut-and-curl candles with colored swirls and fancy shapes so "in" today. This one reminds me of the church and steeple game I used to play with my niece when she was young. The realism in the flesh-colored carving is striking. It is sculpted of clasped hands, with fingers interlocking across the top. Although the hands are clasped, the index fingers form a steeple of sorts, and the thumbs form what looks like double doors. The fingers across the top give the impression that no "people" would be inside if I opened the doors, as required by the game. *What a shame. A church should always be full of people.* A wick peeks out from the top of the index fingers. *How charming!*

"What an *unusual* carving. This is a masterful work of art, but it can't be free for the taking? If it were for sale, I don't think I could afford to purchase it, let alone attempt to light it. It should be in a museum. Who's the artist?"

"Don't be afraid to enjoy the light it gives. As I said, take what you think you need. It's your choice."

"I couldn't possibly," I say hesitantly, but not quite so.

"It's your choice," he says, not insistent but more in a questioning tone.

"Well, I… I just don't know. I… Can I hold it for a minute?"

"Of course."

With that, he places it in my hand. The feel of his hands on mine is the most wonderful touch. The sensation is indescribable. It is instantly pleasant and all-consuming. It's as if I'm being tickled from inside my body with sparklers traveling from my head to my toes. It isn't sexual by nature, oh no. The feeling is of love. The purest I'd ever known.

"Oh my!" I cry out. Wide-eyed, I look at him, and for an instant, I see a twinkle in his eyes, almost as if the sparkling flashes I feel traveled from my hand back to his, vanishing into his eyes.

"It is nice, isn't it?" he asks.

"Yes, well, okay. I think I'll take it and a few packets of nasturtium seeds as well. I like the idea of growing something. That'll be a change for me, and change is good. Or so they say."

"I think you'll be happy with your choice."

He carefully wraps the candle and places it in a medium-sized brown bag with handles on either side for easy carrying. Then he drops a few packets of seeds in after. He has nice hands, I notice.

What am I feeling? What's happening? I have no idea. All I know is I'm lost in the moment, like a dream. I am clearly aware of my thoughts and actions but unsure if they are mine.

Taking me out of my reverie, I hear him say, "Come back in a few hours. I think you'll be amazed."

"Oh yes. I'll make sure to do that. Thank you for your time and everything else. I'll be off now." I hurry away, unsure where I'm going and not caring at all.

⊷◦◦◦⊶

The sun has taken the morning chill out of the air. *How long has it been? Where has the time gone?* It seems the town has come to life instantly, with bustling sounds now rushing to my ears. Again, I think, how strange.

The yeasty aromas of baked bread, confections, and coffee brewing remind my stomach it's time for breakfast. I walk into a local café called Tasty Beans, where the smell of roasted coffee beans, ham, and eggs makes my mouth water. What a delight! It's not nearly as busy as most neighborhood shops but busy enough for the day. The café offers sit-down and counter service, so I grab a table near a window with open lace curtains, and why not? After ordering two pecan cinnamon rolls, to go, a plate of eggs, a side of toast, and coffee, I think more about the man at the church.

The more I thought about the encounter, the stranger it seemed. He never gave his name, but then again, neither did I. He was well dressed. He looked clean, beard notwithstanding, but even that looked neat and trimmed. His black hair was streaked with gray in just the right places. His look and everything about him caused me to wonder how old he was—my age, perhaps?

Relaxing in the comfort of the shop, I've no idea how the detail of his eye color escaped me, but the memory is so clear. His eyes were intense in color, so profoundly blue they appeared violet. Some Hollywood actors have been known to have this eye color, but only under certain lighting conditions. Could the morning light from the blue sky have caused his eyes to be that color? Aside from stories of God's angels and those with albinism, it seems impossible to have seen someone with violet eyes in real life.

"Take what you think you need." Those words echo through my mind, and I can't shake them. This sabbatical was supposed to be a means to search for more inspiration or refresh my desire to teach. Instead, I wonder if it's a search for fulfillment. Something I've longed for or needed without knowing I needed it. A void to fill or a life to share. Maybe it's time to do just that. Who knows what the future might bring? Maybe here in the small town of Versailles?

As I gaze out the window at the small town, a few young girls enter. College students, by their looks and how they carry themselves. Some look like they've just rolled out of bed. I'm reminded of the women's college just up the street. From my vantage point, it is visible as it sits on a hill in the distance. *It would be nice to visit within the week before leaving.* The girls giggle and talk over one another, as is typical. Instead of sitting, they choose to order at the counter.

While I wait for my order, I carefully take out the 'steeple prayer candle,' which is the name I think appropriate, and unwrap it for further inspection.

"Oh my God!" comes a cry from one of the girls.

The waitress bringing my coffee stops in her tracks. They gape at me and gaze at the candle. *Now, this day is getting more and more strange.*

"Did I do something wrong?" I ask. Then, in quick succession, the questions come.

"Where did you get that?" the girl with the bedhead asks.

"Yeah, how is it you have one of those?" another girl chimes in, walking closer as if to grab it.

"I wanna see," says another who wears thick glasses.

"Back up, ladies. Let her drink her coffee in peace," the waitress warns.

The girls back up in unison, which I find amusing. *What's happening? It's just a candle, for goodness' sake.* Apparently, there's more to this unusual wax carving than meets the eye.

The waitress eyes me suspiciously as she sets the coffee down in front of me. Then she puts the bagged cinnamon rolls to the side, saying, "Here's your coffee. Your order will be out in a jiffy. That'll be five eighty-five please. Can I sit here for a sec?"

"By all means. Please." I motion to the chair opposite me. Ten dollars takes care of the order and tip, but she seems unfazed, intent on me and the candle. "I'd like to know what the fuss is all about."

The girls have backed away; however, they keep turning to gaze in my direction. Each one looks at the candle and me as they place their orders at the counter, nudging each other in whispers.

"We haven't seen that kind of wax carving in this town for quite some time," the waitress says with an edge of wariness, eyes fixated on the carving. "In fact, they sold out after the old priest died. That was a long time ago. He was a master craftsman known for his work in wax carvings. They say there's a special message inside once the wax burns down, but you have to be patient to allow the process to work. You can't rush it," she says, staring at the candle, moving her head from side to side to examine it with her eyes. "Golly! People would give their eye teeth to have one, so how'd you come by this?"

"My name is Janice. And yours?"

"Oh, I'm sorry." She chuckles, a little embarrassed, then with words coming out in a jumble, she continues, "My manners just flew out the window when I saw this on the table, didn't they? I apologize for being so forward. I'm Katherine. Most people call me Kat. I attend the women's college on the hill there, doing this job part-time. Speaking of time, I don't have much of it. I've got to get back to work, but can you tell me? I know we just met, but—"

"I get it. I'm visiting here from the city. I'm a professor at the university there—"

"So you brought it with you!" she said. "Oh. Now that makes all kinds of sense. But why bring it here? Aren't you afraid someone will snatch it up? I mean—it's priceless."

"Is it now? No, I mean, it was given to me by a gentleman at the church… ah, Saint Andrews."

"What man at Saint Andrews?" Kat looks as if I just came in from planet Mars.

"I didn't get his name, which is the darnedest thing. There didn't seem to be a need to exchange names or anything. He just seemed ordinary, dark hair, beard, nice eyes—"

"I need to get back to work." She suddenly stands to leave. "I'm sorry I disturbed you." Then she leans in and says in a softer voice, barely above a whisper, "Take it from me, put *that* back in your bag, and don't let anyone else see it. Saint Andrews has been closed for *years*, and only pranksters go there now. The town's talking about reopening it, but that'll be the day because it's old and crumbling—"

"But there *was* a man there who said to come back later. It would be open then—"

"*Lady!*" This time her voice is stern. "I don't know *who* or *what* you're talking about. The priest died a long time ago, almost forty years now, and he was an old man at that! No one's been *near* that place since." Then she softened, saying, "I'm sorry, and I don't mean to be rude. You seem awfully nice, but whatever you got going on… enjoy your coffee and have a nice day."

I'm speechless. As Kat leaves me, the college girls shuffle out the door with their breakfast rolls in bags, peering at me as if I were a leper. I carefully rewrap the candle and gingerly place it in the bag.

Disturbed by what Kat told me, I eat some of my breakfast and gulp the coffee, the taste for the rolls all but forgotten. What did Kat mean about the priest being dead more than forty years ago and the church being closed for so long? What was the mystery with the candle and the message inside? Who was the man I met that morning? A mysterious encounter I couldn't explain even to myself, let alone casually to a student I'd just met. I think of nothing else. *I need to get back to that church. Maybe get some answers there.*

⊰∘⊱

I feel less alone now with the streets full of tourists and townspeople. I hurry to the church, which seems to take forever. My eagerness to find an answer to all this mystery is overwhelming. The morning's events confound me. *There must be an explanation.*

Until today, I've never considered myself a religious person. Spiritual, maybe, but not fervently religious. I believe in God, His son Jesus, and the Holy Ghost. But praying never came naturally; my Catholic upbringing should've made me devout, but it didn't. However, I've always been drawn to the beauty and majesty of cathedrals. The history, the artistry in design, and the wonder of the master craftsmen have always fascinated me. In fact, during my travels, some of the many places I plan to visit in Europe are these very buildings dotted throughout Europe, in London, France, and Italy: the Cathedral of Notre Dame, Saint Peter's Basilica, Westminster Abby, Saint Paul's, and the Sistine Chapel to name a few, along with other architectural and religious wonders.

Shock and confusion hit me as I rounded the corner of the last building, giving rise to the hill upon which the church stands. The church looks different. Very different. The deterioration of the stones seems worse now. Piles of masonry are strewn around the ground haphazardly, which tells me they lie where they fell. The spire that rose in the middle of the roof is no longer there. The maple trees are bare. Not one red leaf can be found on the branches or surrounding the trunks on the ground. *What's going on? Is this the right church? Did I make a wrong turn somewhere?*

I stand in amazement in front of the building and walk as close as possible. A chain-link fence now surrounds the building, so I can't get far. The bag in my hand feels heavy. I check to see if the candle is still there; it is. *How can this be?* Now I understand Kat's disbelief. How could anyone, let alone me, believe what I said about being given a candle at this church today? *And by a strange man, no less?*

As I turned to leave, I noticed something: a plaque with a photo on the outside wall, just barely visible. It's posted just before the doors to the church leading to the narthex or vestibule inside. It's close enough for me to view a photo of the church in its heyday, standing beautiful and serene. The inscription is a testament to the place and a tribute to the priest that reads:

Herein lie the remnants of Saint
Andrews Church, founded in 1701 &
erected in 1708 in the township of
Versailles, Lancaster County,
Pennsylvania.

May all who come here know it was
beloved & presided over by Msgr.
Henry Cavendish, our last & most
honorable Reverend Father.

May he rest in peace.

Very simply put. I hadn't noticed the plaque before and wondered why; among the many mysterious things of that day, why? I lower my head and turn away, questioning my sanity for the first time.

⟞⊙⊙⊙⟝

While relaxing in my room at midday, an unexpected call arrives. I fully expect it to be from my university. Instead, it's from the women's college inviting me to a late afternoon tea with Mrs. Wellman, Dean of Students. As coincidence would have it, I had planned to visit the school, not as a guest, but as a visitor wandering the campus and taking in the ambiance of the grounds. Hopefully unobserved. I assume the invitation was sent to discuss the students' everyday activities and possible ways to improve them. I have little to offer in that regard, but I welcome the invitation. It might lead to answers about the strange happenings of that morning.

The walk to the women's college is as refreshing as my morning walk. It is a beautiful campus, and just like the church, it sits on a hill. The many students, all young ladies, are typical of most college attendees, coming and going from one building to another with various tasks or classes to attend.

The afternoon sun is still high on the horizon when I arrive. Still, the long shadows cast by the many trees create the illusion of evening coming early. The campus is small, but the Georgian and Greek Revival mixed architecture of the buildings and dormitories, broadly spaced and cloistered on the hill around a central quad, gives it a much larger feel. The tall white Ionic-capped colonnades fronting the red brick of the administration building are impressive, as is Mrs. Cynthia Wellman. Small and petite with delicate features, she greets me with all smiles, seeming more formal than is necessary. We are escorted through an anteroom to her office, where a small lunch has been laid out.

"When I heard you were in town, I had to have you visit our campus," Mrs. Wellman says. "It's Friday, and before the weekend starts, I wanted to make sure we had a chance to meet. I made a few calls to the university in the city. I understand you're a professor of the arts?"

"Yes, that's correct. What a beautiful campus you have here. I must say, I'm impressed."

"Sitting high on the hill, it seems we can see for miles. Especially the old Saint Andrews church. I gather, from one of my students, you had an experience there," she says while pouring us a cup of tea.

"Again, you're correct, Mrs. Wellman."

"Cynthia, please," she says, reaching for a petite sandwich.

"Cynthia. News travels fast, I see."

As I reach for my tea, it's apparent that this visit has nothing to do with student activities. It is about my experience at the church and, I suspect, the candle.

"Well, it's a small town," she says offhandedly. "Nothing to do but talk, and the girls here are the best gossips. It's not unusual to hear the latest news on this campus."

Extraordinary how fast word travels! "Well, then, tell me about Saint Andrews. Who is Monsignor Cavendish?" I ask. *No sense in beating around the bush.*

"I'm told you've been given the gist of the monsignor's special talents. The whole town, as well as the students, know about his work. His carvings are featured in our art classes, which is how your candle was so easily recognized."

There it is! I say to myself as she continues.

"The monsignor was quite the artist, very special to the town and school. It was a somber occasion when he left us at ninety years of age. Now that he's gone, he is believed to present himself in the most amazing ways and disguises. Some say they've talked to him in the guise of an animal or the wind in the trees. Others the embodiment of a person," she says, peering over the rim of her teacup. "So, you see, when I heard about your conversation with one of our students, Katherine, and others came to me as well, I was intrigued. Don't worry; I'm not after the candle but interested in what and who you saw."

"As am I. It's a relief to know you're just curious because I was beginning to think otherwise by the way this was going." I chuckle behind my teacup, then look up at her. "I must say, I was perplexed by the encounter. Still am. The beauty of the candle is exquisite."

"Did you go back?" she asks, leaning closer and dropping her formal demeanor.

"I did, but I found only ruins. The entire area was different than before—just as Kat had said. I couldn't make heads or tails of it."

"Allow me to share something with you. Something you might find interesting."

She rises from her chair and motions me to follow her to an adjacent room full of books. These books contain a history of the college and the town, which I find fascinating. Cynthia Wellman opens a few books for me to review. I listen intently as she briefly explains the college's history.

"Saint Catherine's College at Versailles started as a school for female orphans. Over the years, it has grown from an all-girls Christian college to the college for women's studies it is known as today. Saint Andrews was the church of choice for the students to attend each Sunday. Monsignor Cavendish presided over convocation gatherings and vesper prayers each evening for many years. The church was one of the school's greatest benefactors as far as donations were concerned. From as far away as Italy and Scotland, the constant flow of money to fund the school and support the church never faltered. It remained that way until the death of Monsignor Cavendish. But by then, the school was self-sufficient, and there was no need to rely on the many funds we received. We carry on from endowments, foundations, and donations to fund our school, scholarships, and work-study programs. However, the church was no longer supported and fell into disrepair, neither attended by the students nor the townspeople."

"Was there *any* effort made to rebuild the church?"

"We tried but couldn't raise enough funds to accomplish much. Even selling the monsignor's wax carvings wasn't enough to stem the tide of the church's decay. These days, it's just as well to let the church go to ruin. Demolished and forgotten. There are other churches, to be sure, but Saint Andrews holds a special place in our hearts, named after the cathedral in Scotland. Appreciating art history as you do and the churches' role in showcasing the artistry and craftsmanship of architectural design, I wanted to share this information with you."

"I wish I could help."

"Oh, we all wish we could do *something*. But it's good to know miracles can happen. The candle given to you today is proof that God is still working. What do *you* think?"

"I don't know *what* to think, frankly. I do know something happened to me today. An experience I can't explain, and I'm thankful for it."

I had a lovely visit with Cynthia Wellman. Before leaving, we walk the halls, admiring the photos of administrators and benefactors who contributed to the school's success. I stop to gaze at one picture and am stunned. Staring at me is the man from the church. It was he who gave me the candle.

"Who is this?" I ask. It's hard to keep the tremor out of my voice. I have already guessed the answer, and it terrifies me.

"That's Monsignor Cavendish as a young man."

I say nothing in response but continue to study the image of the man, this person who made me feel more special than I had in years. The love that touched my heart most profoundly was something I will never forget. The spark and connection I had with him will always be with me. He gave me a gift I could never repay and one I will treasure always. As I said before, I'm not a religious person. I also do not believe in ghosts or spirits of any kind. But this day. In this town. I believe.

<hr>

My visit to France is glorious. Here, I start to feel the mental bonds of confinement fall away from me. The sights, the vibrant sounds, and the smells of the Old World invigorate my sense of being. I spent hours at the Louvre Museum, then went on to the majestic Cathedral of Notre Dame. This marvel of engineering does not disappoint. Rediscovering the history of fine art and architecture all over again is the shot in the arm I needed. It was a special treat to be allowed to visit the South Tower to view the great bell, Emmanuel. But my visit to Versailles, Pennsylvania, is never far from my mind.

I spent three weeks in Versailles, and I've never forgotten that fate-filled day in early autumn. After my time with Cynthia Wellman, I called the university and spoke to a few contacts about Saint Andrews. I gave them the history of the college and its relationship to the church. Amazingly, this prompted some to make their own calls to invest in preserving the church site and the grounds as a historic landmark.

During my travels, I've often spoken to Cynthia, who updates me on the progress being made at the church. Kat has volunteered to work with the landscapers and tends to the gardens as much as possible. She takes special care to check on the flower beds where the nasturtiums bloom. I passed on the gift of seeds to her. I hear she is developing a budding romance with one of the contractors. When I return home, Versailles will be my first stop.

⚯

After moving through France, Italy is a delight. I'm in my hotel room in Florence, Italy, overlooking the River Arno. It is springtime in this beautiful city, full of history and art. I haven't felt this free in quite some time, and I enjoy letting my hair down and loving every minute. I've fallen in love with Italian cuisine, and prosciutto ham's mild saltiness is one of my favorites. Aside from mortadella and soppressata, Italian meats are delicious; the cheeses aren't bad either. I must watch my waistline, but I allow myself to indulge, at least for now.

The region of Tuscany, full of gently rolling hills and cypress trees, is even more magical and romantic than I had imagined. Like France, with its gentle breezes wafting the fragrance of jasmine through the air, I'm transformed. I will visit the Duomo in Milan, Vatican City, and Saint Peter's Basilica in Rome tomorrow. England and Scotland after that, and then back to America… and Versailles.

Saint Peter's Basilica in Vatican City is awe-inspiring. The reverence I feel brings unexpected tears to my eyes. Unlike the Cathedral of Notre Dame, there is a closeness to God, which humbles me. As I run my hands over the surface of the rough stones or feel the contours of the colonnade of columns and smooth marble surfaces that support the interior, I'm struck by profound knowledge and understanding. In all my years of study and lecture, I never let the person behind the creation touch my heart.

Observing and commenting on beauty, art history, language, and culture is one thing. It's another to understand the reasons behind the artistry. I never took the time to understand the *artist*, the drive of the man himself, other than the ego. The innate gift of artisan craftsmanship, urged on by the passionate desire to create, had to be an otherworldly experience for them. A need to be closer to God. This reverence and drive are what I have been missing. I can't help but wonder if all the other great artisans of their time, before or since, have had this experience. Aside from Raffaello (Raphael) Sanzio da Urbino, whose original design for Saint Peter's was replaced by Michelangelo's, I want to know. The spiritual pull is overwhelming. In that beautiful, majestic cathedral, I bend my knee to pray. I pray for the longest time.

As I leave the basilica, a calmness envelops me. Also, there is an expectation of something, of what—I don't know. At the Vatican Museum, I'm greeted by a guide. A transplant from America. Amazingly, this man reminds me of someone I met once near a church on a hill in Versailles. I'm drawn to him. The smile and hair are similar. The touch is familiar, but the feeling is so much more.

His name is Henry Campagna, or Cap, as he likes to be called. It quickly becomes a running joke between us to call him Harry Cap. He seems to like my dry sense of humor. He's a freelance architect visiting his Italian relatives and works as a seasonal guide whenever he's in Rome. It doesn't bother me that we spend lots of time together. I *want* to spend time with him. I look forward to our outings of long walks through the Italian countryside and sampling other delicious foods I know nothing about. His eyes crinkle at the corners when he laughs. He's funny. I often think *I'm giggling like a girl again, and I love it.* He fills a void, a darkness that is now light. I think I'll allow him to steal my heart. On second thought, I'll gladly give it to him. I feel this is meant to be.

The candle reminds me of the wonders I've yet to experience. I watch it now as it glows. Oh, I had to light it at least just once. If nothing else, I wanted to see if the rumor about a special message inside was true. After carefully photographing it from every angle, I struck a match and lit the wick. I have been careful to let it burn at its own rate. I've tracked its changes with photos of every burning process, and each time it burns, it gives another gift of beauty, then another, and another.

Over these many months, I've watched the wick burn down the fingers that make up the steeple. Amazingly, the burn rate allows the melted wax to coat only the roof of the carving. It never drips along the front of the candle to obscure the thumbs. Now that has ended and, they are in jeopardy. I watch the wick slowly burn the thumbs away—or doors—as if they are slowly opening. An engineered work of art and pure genius.

Today, the wick is burning through the thumbs. Almost done. Lounging on the balcony of my room, I'm lulled by water rippling in the wash of a passing gondola. An unusually cool breeze blows against my skin and hair, hanging loosely around my shoulders. Then the air warms again. I am content. After a few minutes, I hear a crackling sound from the candle. Alarmed, I go to the candle and see a glimmer inside. *What in the world?* The candle goes out, and inside—a small golden band is seen.

With trembling hands, I carefully extract it, surprised at the softness of the metal. It is pure, I think. I examine it closely and see an ornate engraving with an inscription that reads:

I AM YOUR CONSTANT COMPANION

I'm thunderstruck. *His eyes were so profoundly blue, like the color violet.* Of course. God's angels are known to have this eye color. My journey has led me to this moment. A moment of rediscovery, fulfillment, mystery, reverence, and love. He was always with me. He sent His angel to guide me the whole time. Now I understand.

The End

ABOUT THE AUTHOR

Donna Lawrence writes in the genre of women's fiction set in historical periods, even touching on coming-of-age in small-town America. *Miss Virginia and the Sweet Sisters* is her debut novel. She is also the author of a published work of poetry titled *Loooking In from Outside: Poetry & Prose.*

She is a poet with works published in a compilation. Two of her poems, "The Rain" and "The Heir," are featured on the 9/11 Memorial Museum website.

Her current novel, *Pen Pals: A Novella and Other Stories*, is a work of Literary Fiction that stands alone but also includes associated short stories. This compilation marks her first foray into publishing an anthology of fiction.

Donna Lawrence was born and raised in Kentucky but has been a longtime resident of Colorado. Both states hold special meaning, and the many experiences she's had are ones she draws on in her writing. She posts monthly on her personal blog.

Works by Donna Lawrence:

Miss Virginia and the Sweet Sisters: A Novel. Genre—Women's Fiction, Historical Fiction, Coming-of-Age.

Looking In from Outside: Poetry & Prose. A collection of poetry and prose. Genre—Poetry.

Coming soon: *Light from an Unburned Candle: A Novel.* Genre—Women's Fiction, Historical Fiction, and Coming-of-Age.

Contact

Crescent Hill Press
PO Box 200754
Denver, Colorado 80220

Email: donna@donnamarielawrence.com
Website: www.donnamarielawrence.com